THE CRYSTAL SKY

JENNA NELSON

To unemployment, for the time you gave me to finish.

Pause you who read this,

and think for a moment,

of the long chain of iron or gold,

of thorns or flowers,

that would never have bound you,

but for the formation of the first link on one memorable day.

~ Charles Dickens

CHAPTER ONE

The Sanctuary of Caelum nestles in the southern-most tip of Winterhaven, in a curvature of the land known as the Gilded Horn. Though the seaport city is small, the landscape is dramatic, with a deep fjord rising at its back and impressive waterfalls and caves carved within. Ruled by the Nereids, the Sanctuary of Caelum is home to the Veneficum—a council of Winterhaven's sagest—owing to its peaceful and idyllic setting, and more importantly, its secrecy.

A massive gateway provides entrance from the Dendrite Sea to the inlet where ships and barges pass through by special invitation only. To the naked eye, the gates are invisible, although rumors abound of wintry moonlight ghosting their outlines. Most sail around the Gilded Horn never knowing of the city beyond. To those entrusted to pass, the gateway offers a shortcut saving near to a month's time, but the price is a king's sum, which is why the hidden land is so wealthy. To the commoner, the Sanctuary of Caelum is nothing more than myth, a fantastical place that lives on only in legend. Until I'd awoken five days ago, my time at the Sanctuary was spent in a deep and dreamless sleep in recovery from a deep wound to my shoulder. A wound made not by an ordinary blade but by the twisted metal of a Soul Splitter, which effectively removes one's soul upon stabbing. Before that horrifying moment, an Infernal had raked a claw through my back as I tried to escape its clutches. And courtesy of the Sylph Eirene, I'd suffered temporary paralysis from the waist down. In time I regained my ability to walk again, but my legs are still weak, not what they once were.

As I put on my deerskin boots and tighten my robe, I practically laugh out loud at the absurdity of this list and almost yearn for the boredom of London. Oh, to be back at Cimmerian's Curio Emporium restocking Dr. Mountebank's Reducing Pastilles for a slimmer figure! They were a best-seller and never threatened my very existence, mediocre though it was.

To be honest, I miss almost nothing when it comes to my life back in London—the Other World. But where my past is concerned, too many questions remain unanswered: who am I? Who were my parents? Was I born in Winterhaven, the land inside the snow globe? And if I am from this wicked place, how did I end up in London with my so-called Aunt Henrietta? These are the missing pieces of my life's puzzle. During my last foray to the Other World, Henrietta, contemptible and unhelpful as ever, made it quite clear she would never disclose the truth, so I'm left to my own devices to figure things out.

The natural hot springs at the Sanctuary hold healing powers, and the largest of all exists inside of a cave not far from the fortress where I've been convalescing. Each day Lark has been my escort, but I'd awoken earlier than usual this morning, unable to sleep. Since the little girl had been deep in a dream, I decided to leave her be and come on my own.

My lungs burn from the mind-numbing cold by the time I enter the cathedral-like space. Frozen walls bleed indigo in the predawn light, and the rotten egg scent that is sulfur calls out in greeting. My bath sheet bears the same intricate water symbol gracing the bed covers, blankets, and everything else at the Sanctuary, even the cutlery. I hang the lit lantern on one of many ice spikes in the wall, and my robe and slippers find the one adjacent.

The gauzy smock is enough to cover me yet thin enough for the water to adequately soak through and heal my injuries. If only Henrietta could see me now...I would pay good money. With my inky hair free from my chignon and so much of me exposed, she would be bonded to her fainting couch for weeks if she bore witness to my unladylike appearance.

My uneven gait is a blatant slander of my comportment classes as I climb down the steep, rocky embankment. *'You are a graceful swan, Miss Renfrew, not a flapping chicken with a broken wing,'* my instructor Miss Cornbaum would scold. I always wanted to remind her that swans were hideous, vicious creatures, but I only smiled and offered my best ladylike flourish.

I check my pocket for two bamboo shoots, tools to knead my muscles. Steam shivers high into the frigid air, the stalagmites coated in frost, a mouthful of daggered teeth bearing down. At the water's edge, a shelf of sand slopes to an eventual drop-off. From there the cove seems bottomless. My skin turns to gooseflesh as I wade deeper, the warm water rising past my kneecaps, past my belly and breasts, until I find my usual spot atop an elongated boulder resting right below the surface. So flat is the top, it's reminiscent of a chaise lounge.

A sigh of contentment passes through me as I flop indecorously onto propped elbows, the warmth a curative salve. The scar from the Soul Splitter aches, throbs at times. I suppose it will never go away, a forever reminder of that fateful day when Queen Belisama Agni perished in Mount Serius.

The clicking gears of the Aeriscloque rub against the silence as I tug the smock up my thighs and knead my legs with the bamboo. Something about the queen's demise still niggles at me, an itch

4

that can't be mollified no matter how hard I scratch. And do trust I have scratched, to the point of rubbing my skin raw. According to Guernsey, I was brought to Winterhaven to kill Queen Belisama because I can weave Fire, Earth, Water, and Air into all kinds of objects, weapons included. Although I'd helped to solve the riddle of the Emerald Tablet—an intricate symbol that holds one of many secrets to eternal life—it all feels flimsy in hindsight and had nothing to do with my Elemental abilities. Granted, I'd created the tidal wave in Mount Serius, but that didn't kill her. The spellbound waters from the Fountain of Youth had.

Throat-clearing from somewhere deep within the cave. *Blast.* Immediately I sit up, knees drawn to chin, and tuck the bamboo away. Never did I expect someone here, certainly not at this ungodly hour. Due to the impropriety of the sheer smock, I should leave now and return later with Lark as my lookout. But getting out will expose me for one and all.

Now there is whistling. *Annoying and infringing whistling.* There must be a second entrance to the cave around the bend. Silently I slip into the water and swim into the shadows to wait things out. A cluster of rocks jut from the water, so I paddle behind them and hang on. Across the way, a lantern's flame exposes a man standing on the ledge. A man I know all too well: the attractive yet oft-infuriating Shán Einfarí. Unaware of my presence, he casts off his cloak and shirt, and his trousers drop to the ground.

My pulse quickens. All at once, the water is a woolen blanket, warm and overbearing. Shán's stature is captivating. Henrietta used to opine, *'The devil goes away when he finds the door shut against him.'* This door is decidedly ajar, and I plan not to close it. Of course, I may plunge to the tenth circle of Hell, but come what may. I can't look away, even knowing how wrong it is. I've seen the male form many times in the paintings and marbled statues of my history books and up close in the South Kensington Museum in the Other World. Never in the flesh.

When the Infernal had wounded Shán, I'd nursed him back to health. I'd seen his chest and stomach along with his legs and toes when I bathed him. At Isceald Castle, I'd caught a scandalous glimpse of his bare backside. Now he's standing here in all his glory. Despite the low light, the whites of my knuckles practically glow.

Into the water he goes, circling around the cove, never quite coming out this far. Minutes pass, many of them, and when it becomes clear he'll remain for a time, I swim back to my place around the bend. The cave is plenty big. As long as I remain quiet, Shán will never know of my presence.

Kneading my muscles is the perfect tonic, but my sighs are kept inward for fear of being overheard... *Who am I fooling? My mind is not on recuperation, not in the slightest.* With only a modicum of guilt, I revel in the thrill of having just seen Shán naked, the image burned into my brain. My mind and heart war with one another when it comes to Shán for too many reasons to count. At the moment, neither my mind nor my heart are dictating, only my body, and it leaves me wanting.

The splashing from yonder ceases; Shán is done with his swim. I breathe a bit easier knowing I'm alone again, and I flex my feet to stretch them. Bubbles surface in the darkened waters mere yards away. Lark had warned of precarious things lurking in the cave's depths. I'd dismissed the warning, knowing the little girl's penchant for the dramatic. Still, I grasp the bamboo shoots, one in each hand, ready to strike just in case.

Shán's head breaks the surface. "Why, Sondrine Renfrew," he says coyly. "Fancy meeting you here."

Again, my knees go up, this time to cover my breasts. "Go away, Shán. I'm—"

"Naked?" He offers a self-satisfied smirk. "We're a pair then, aren't we?"

One bamboo shoot goes well over his head but in his direction as warning. "I'm not naked. I'm in a bathing gown, I'll have you know. Now leave me be. I'm trying to cure my ailments. This is inappropriate, and you know it."

"And watching me undress wasn't?"

My mouth opens and closes like a beached mackerel. I grope for an explanation but find none, because the only true explanation makes me look like the depraved voyeur that I am.

"Did you enjoy what you saw?" he continues.

"Well...I heard someone," I say, trying hard to form a coherent sentence and doing a bad job of it. "When I realized it was you, I swam away. I saw nothing other than your chest, which I've seen

7

countless times. Really it's quite unremarkable."

Shán is a Voyant; he can read people's minds. He claims he rarely uses his magic, not that it matters. From the quirk at the corner of his mouth, he knows I'm lying.

"Good to know I'm unremarkable," he quips. "And no need to worry. These waters run darker than a moonless night. Couldn't see anything even if I wanted to."

Do you want to? The tone of his voice indicates he isn't much interested. "What are you doing here in the first place?" I ask.

He floats on his back, his lower torso dangling just below the surface. "A quick soak before target practice," he says, his voice bouncing off the massive walls. "My archery skills are lacking these days. Ready for the meeting with the Veneficum?"

The itch returns. "Why must I meet with the Veneficum if the queen is dead?"

"Because King Varius Andronicus is still alive. Maps must be drawn, strategies devised and put forth. One mustn't enter a war without an extensive plan. The objective is to kill the king. And remain alive while doing so," he adds in a sardonic tone.

Ah, the noted humorist. "The thing is," I hedge, "I'm unneeded now, since the queen is dead; wouldn't you agree? The king must have an infantry five thousand strong. Between you and the Veneficum, surely an infantry of your own can be amassed to match his."

He raises his head to look me in the eye. "Ten thousand, more like. You having second thoughts, then? About helping to overthrow the king?"

Second thoughts? Ha! I'm having third and fourth and tenth thoughts—too many to count, really. "Answers about my past are here, so I must remain in Winterhaven. The war is not mine to fight, not any longer."

"This is everyone's war. War is the price of freedom. For any of us to be free, the king must die."

He's not wrong. After what the king did to me, I want him dead as much as the rest. Still, I shake my head at the stoicism in his voice. "Doesn't it feel strange to say such things? King Andronicus is your father, your own flesh and blood."

Shán's gaze reverts to the cave's ceiling, his arms paddling the waters to keep him afloat. "My father wants me dead. There is nothing between us. Neither honor nor duty. Not a whit of affection on either side. Only true blood binds us. The thick of his stained against my sword would be the greatest of rewards."

"You said yourself Winterhaven was thriving under his rule."

Shán swallows a mouthful of water, swishes back and forth, and spits in a high arc. "Compared to when Belisama was queen, yes. But a land is nothing without amity. The people of Winterhaven live in fear of the king. You'll find goodwill among the upper classes, to be sure. Anyone else would be pleased to see his head spiked to the Mourning Tree."

The macabre sight of severed heads in the Mourning Garden is something I wish I could forever erase from my mind. "If your father has an infantry ten thousand strong, more than those in the upper class respect him."

"People were tricked and lied to, promised riches or power or whatever else was needed to persuade them. Very few came forward of their own accord."

I watch as he swims in a wide circle. "You could be a great ruler, Shán. As heir to the throne—"

"How are you feeling?" he asks. "Are the hot springs helping? Legs back in working order?"

Shán's ability to change the subject is often maddening and never maneuvered with great finesse. I know not to press him, because as always, it will prove pointless. "Better, I suppose. My shoulder is giving me the most pain at present."

Shán rights himself. Even in the obscure light, his face is readable, a distressed look shadowing his features. He swims toward me, and panic rises within. There is nothing I can do, nowhere to go. He grabs hold of the rock and starts pulling himself up. Immediately I push him back into the cove. "I told you to stay away." My face turns to avoid the splash.

Shán shakes the water from his hair. "Right now, you resemble nothing more than a floating head. Everything below your neck is invisible, I promise."

It's true, I'm sure, for he looks the same. "You're naked; I am nearly so. Do the people of Winterhaven have no morals?"

"I just wanted to see your scar," he mutters. "Nothing improper."

"If you're so interested, you can see it when we're dressed," I say in my best dismissive tone.

He swims to the front of the rock, hoists himself up, and before I can look away, my mouth drops open in surprise. "You're—"

"Dressed," he says in a smug tone. His drawers, cinched at the waist, drop just below the knee.

Confused, I shake my head. "But I saw—"

"Saw what?" Shán says, badly repressing his laughter. "You claim to have seen only my chest."

My belly burns with fire. From getting caught in a lie or just plain embarrassment, I'm not quite sure. The depraved voyeur has been outed.

He settles next to me, and my whole body stiffens. "At ease, my lady," he jokes. "All in good fun. With a war looming large, I'm doing my best to find a little levity given the dire situation. Can't blame a man for trying."

No, I can't, and so I smile. It's nice to see Shán so playful instead of brooding—his usual default emotion.

"Truly I was unaware you were here," he says. "Only when I saw someone swimming away did I suspect it was you. Then I dressed myself."

I'm thankful for the darkness, glad it hides the flush in my cheeks.

"May I?" he asks, his hand hovering above my shoulder. "I don't expect we'll be alone for some time. After we meet with the Veneficum—if you choose to do so—we will likely go our separate ways."

"For good?"

He shrugs. "For a good while, let's say."

This is something I hadn't realized. Whatever the Veneficum's plan might entail, I'd assumed Shán would be at my side for the entirety of things. When I nod my consent, he gently eases down the smock's strap to expose my shoulder. His thumb traces the scar. "This is of my doing," he whispers with regret.

Goosebumps rise across my skin. In London, an unattended single woman is never allowed in the presence of a man. For this I would be hung, drawn, and quartered. Well, socially anyway.

Midnight blue glints within the strands of Shán's hair, his broad shoulders capturing the dripping water. Droplets move around the raised skin on his chest—the wound made by the Infernal, the one I'd personally stitched up. My fingers trace the droplets in a hesitant path. "It appears we have matching scars," I say softly.

Pine and the earthy scent that is Shán breeches the sulfur of the springs, and every part of me yearns for him. My hand settles against his chest, my fingertips aware of his heightened heartbeat, perfectly in cadence with mine. I lean in, mouth parted. More than anything, I want to taste him again.

"Soak your wounds." He tugs the strap back over my shoulder. "This may be the last opportunity for quite some time."

My mouth clamps shut, and my hand falls away. The rejection stings worse than a dousing of ice water. "Go away," I snap. "Now."

The lines between his eyes sharpen, evidence of confusion by my hostile tone.

"This is an invasion of privacy of the worst sort," I continue. "You think you can enter my space, touch me with your filthy hands, and expect me to go along with it? Never mistake me for one of your whores, Shán." I focus on my knees and hug them tight. Humiliation does terrible things. An apology on my part is warranted but will never happen. My wounded pride will win this battle.

"I'll give you some privacy, then." He dives in, and I watch as he swims around the bend and out of sight.

I recline on the rock, wishing the hot springs would cure my bruised ego. From the very beginning, Shán had tantalized me in a way no other man had. Not that I'd had many suitors. One to be exact. Hubert Teasly—the loathsome dentist-to-be—my betrothed by way of Henrietta's cunning machinations. Were I still in the Other World, we'd be married by now. He'd be attending dentistry school, and I'd be quizzing him on tooth decay, the proper ways to floss, and whether brick dust was effective for brushing.

I'd rather have my teeth drilled. The scent of Shán lingers on my skin, and my eyes close as I sigh with frustration. Shán is a man of the world, a warrior who has fought many a battle even at his young age. He's of royal descent, a prince who divorced himself of the title long ago. Now a steward of the Veneficum, he wants to bring peace to the realm and restore alliances between the great cities of Winterhaven. Much to my dismay, he's also a bit of a lothario, something I've had the misfortune of witnessing on more

13

than one occasion.

A light tickle against my right foot prompts my eyes open. "Shán, I told you to leave me be." Another tickle, this time my left foot. Bringing both knees to my chin, I smile, unable to resist his playfulness. I'm glad my barb wasn't taken to heart. Quite mature of him, so I must follow suit and set aside my pride. "I'm sorry, Shán. I shouldn't have lashed out at you."

I wait for him to pop up, to accept my apology with a pleasing smile. The water remains unbroken. Unless he's part fish, he's been under too long. "This isn't funny, Shán—"

Something dark and shiny seethes beneath the water. A tremor shakes the cove's bottom, then rings murmur outward along the surface. Nervously I eye the rocky embankment behind me and then the ledge high above where my robe and boots await. *Not too far.* However, I will have to swim to get there.

The cove has grown quiet, but it's time to leave. Whatever might be lurking below, I'm in no mood to make new friends. My heart practically gallops when I lower myself into the water, my feet grazing the rocky bottom. Other than my trembling hands, all remains still, so I back my way to shore, the water growing shallower with each careful step.

Almost there. Breathe, for mercy's sake! Plenty of things live underwater. No need to panic.

Large bubbles rise across the surface.

Time to panic. I turn toward the embankment and start running through the water, then up the slippery slope, the rocks

14

like glass underfoot. A massive wave rolls up and catches me in its path, takes me down hard against the boulders. Shaking the starbursts from my eyes, I glimpse a shadow above, growing in length and in girth. Terror pools inside me, drowns every breath as I chance a look over my shoulder.

Rising out of the cove's depths is a creature so fearsome and so behemoth it puts the Infernal to shame. Dorsal scales of sable green run the length of a limbless body, with parasitic snakes writhing betwixt and between. Ivory eyes glinting with malice stare through the darkness.

The serpent hisses wrathfully. Sharpened fangs the size of small children bear down on me. With nowhere else to go, I scramble into a crevice between the boulders, large enough to fit inside but too small for an ample bite.

My breathing is shallow and quick as the forked tongue sniffs and searches. The creature's body, thicker than four oaks, slithers amongst the crags. Lamplight dances as the shadowy image stalks me. Fangs clamp down on a neighboring rock, the sound like clashing iron, and I bite my lip until it bleeds. Over and again the serpent does this, each time moving closer.

Though I cower to make myself smaller, the sheltering boulder is uprooted, fully exposing me for the taking. "Stay away from me!" I scream. I dive for another crevice and claw at the sand to dig myself farther in, but my legs are flopping bait and the serpent's tail coils around them. "Stop!" I cry out, trying to break free of the tightening grip.

The serpent slithers into the cove, its tail waving me about like a rag doll through the air. My body crashes against the stalactites, knocks a slew of them into the water. The pain is horrendous, and the wrong angle will impale and kill me instantly.

"Let her go!" The echo of Shán's voice reverberates through the cave. He scrambles down the rocks toward the water and shoots an arrow at the serpent's head. A snarling hiss bursts forth, and the serpent glides around to face Shán. Another arrow flies past the forked tongue and down the serpent's throat, causing it to scream in pain.

Nausea goads me as I'm plunged into the water and out again, completely at the mercy of the creature. For a brief moment, I attempt to form a whirlpool. But I'm weakening mind and body, the serpent's grip too tight. The tail swings me high into the air, dangerously close to the stalactites' sharpened tips. I reach for a small one, and it breaks free in my hand. The icy surface proves hard to grasp, so I dig my fingernails in hard. With quick, jerky movements, I stab at the scaly tail until bloodied chunks fall to the water below.

"Over here," Shán yells in an effort to distract. The creature attempts to strike more than once, and each time, Shán lets loose an arrow to the head. Though they daze the creature, Shán's supply is running short. The battle will end soon, and not in his favor. Nor in mine.

Using all my remaining strength, a final stab at the tail sets me free, and I fall into the bloodied cove with a splash. Adrenaline propels me through the water as I swim in furious strokes toward Shán. When I'm close enough, he takes my hand and yanks me to my feet.

The serpent rears its battered head. Jaw unhinged, the monster hurtles straight for us. In a moment of desperation, I flick my wrist at an icy stalactite moored on the embankment. It flies through the air and miraculously impales the serpent's left eye. Shán leaps forward and drives the stake in farther.

A bone-chilling screech that won't end. Writhing in pain, the serpent falls backward and takes Shán with it. Waves pound the rocks on all sides straight up to the cove's ceiling, and I flail in the sudden current. The serpent and Shán are a rolling log, over and under, over and under. Amid a flurry of bubbles, they disappear below the surface.

All goes eerily still. Only the light patter of water that slides off the stalactites and rains into the cove breaks through the quiet. I tread water, turn in every direction for some sign of life.

"Shán?" My whispered voice trembles, same as the rest of me. "Where are you, Shán?" This time I yell the despairing words, but they echo off the empty walls and fall into nowhere.

An explosion of water launches me backward. Out comes the roaring serpent with Shán clinging to the impaled spike. With an insidious hiss, the creature shoots straight for me. Not a moment to think. To move. To scream. The pink gullet closes in on me.

A trident of shining metal blasts through the back of the serpent's throat. The decapitated head drops into the water, and the massive scaled body follows with a thunderous crash. The sudden tide flings me halfway up the embankment. Anchored by the sharp rocks beneath me, I watch the bloodied waters churn until eventually they find their calm. *I wish I could find mine.*

Something shimmers in the depths of the cove. A woman walks along the water's surface dressed in glistening swaths of aqua. Her skin is black, and seashells and seaweed entwine her long dark curls. I'm certain my head is concussed and I'm seeing things.

Shán staggers up the rocks, his body cut and bleeding but in one piece. He helps me stand, beckons me down to the shallow water where there is sand underfoot.

"Ione," he says to the woman in a low, grateful tone.

"Who?" I croak.

"Mage of the Nereids, ruler of the Sanctuary of Caelum," he expounds, his head bowed in respect.

Try as I might to follow Shán's respectable lead, I stumble, the pain and nausea relentless and overbearing. Ione must sense this, because she holds up a hand. "No need for formalities, especially when one escaped death's grip only moments ago." She pries the trident from a boulder and sloshes the steely prongs through the water to rid them of the serpent's flesh.

"Your aim is admirable," Shán says to the mage. "Two hands closer and the trident would not have spared me."

Ione's gaze falls on me, accusing and intransigent. "How did Ykuza find you? Did you summon the serpent with your Elemental magic?"

18

How could I call on something when I didn't know it existed in the first place? "The creature came of its own volition," I promise in the weakest of voices.

Eyes brighter than a cerulean sea shine against Ione's black skin. "Someone called it," she says in an ominous manner. "Ykuza dwells near Mount Serius in the depths of the Dendrite Sea, where even the deepest waters stay temperate due to the excess lava flow. While the waters are clement here too, this is not the sea serpent's natural habitat. Never once has Ykuza surfaced in these parts."

My body shakes, and I whisper through chattering teeth, "Mount Serius imploded recently. I'm unsure how much remains, if anything. Perhaps the waters were disrupted and pushed Ykuza to live elsewhere."

"A plausible theory," Ione concedes. "The increased lava flow could have chased the monster from its home. However, Mount Serius and the Sanctuary of Caelum are at opposite ends of the realm. Surfacing here is nonsensical." She looks us over head to foot. "The answer will come soon enough. For now, I shall take my leave. You both are alive and mostly unharmed."

"Because of you," I say, the gratitude thick in my voice despite the quaking.

Ione offers a sage nod. "Next time your fates may choose differently."

She removes a metal adornment from the trident's handle and hands it to me. The shape is a conch shell with an aquamarine sphere tucked deep inside the flared opening. A toggle juts from the spiraled top.

"What is this?" I ask.

"A Petard—a weapon, among other things. Long ago, I fashioned the housing—the literal shell. Remove the pin and throw the shell in the direction of any adversary. The thunderpowder within will ignite, and in turn the enemy will be decimated. Keep it somewhere safe."

Though small in size, the Petard sits heavy in my palm. I wonder how easily the pin can be removed. With my luck, it will come undone and render me into a thousand incompetent bits.

With the trident in hand, Ione dives into the water. Off in the distance, a flash of a fish tail breaks the surface before disappearing from sight. My head shakes in bewilderment.

"Tell neither Snap nor Lark of our battle," Shán warns. "The children need not know. I will apprise Guernsey when I see him." He takes my hand, and together we climb up the embankment.

As I wrap the robe around me, I realize the cotton smock, now stained dark pink, has left nothing to the imagination. I hardly care. Nothing much matters right now. Once again, I've eluded death, and not by my own doing. This doesn't bode well for the future of Winterhaven.

Before we start for the Sanctuary, I look down on the serpent, already rotting in the warm waters.

This is an omen, a bad one. If someone summoned the serpent, they are nearby, watching. They want me dead. Since I survived, this can only mean one thing: they will try yet again.

CHAPTER TWO

By the time I'd reached my chamber, the adrenaline from the battle had worn off, and I'd fallen onto my bed, intent on gathering my wits about me. Now, almost six hours later, I wake to the reek of sulfur and blood hardened against my skin. As for my wits, they've scuttled away, never to be seen again as far as they're concerned.

Lark draws the bathwater in silence. The stench has made her dubious of my claims of having just woken. Asking her to let me bathe in solitude only adds to the little girl's suspicions.

From my knapsack, I take out the lavender bar of soap from Cimmerian's Curio Emporium. My knapsack is near and dear to me because it holds everything of importance. For one, tinctures and medicinal herbs and other therapeutic remedies I took from the emporium. Well, 'stole' is the better, more technical term. I'd restocked at my Aunt Henrietta's expense. 'Thief' was a nickname she'd given me. When it comes to my aunt, that's practically a term of endearment.

Also tucked away is *Secretum Secretorum*, otherwise known as *Secret of Secrets*, a cryptic book that holds answers to the many secrets of the universe. For one, the Emerald Tablet, a symbol that reveals the secret to eternal life. Zhang the Elder had loaned the book to me on the condition I would one day return it. The Petard gets stuffed deep in the knapsack, wrapped in the scarves and tucked below the shirts and grey cap from home.

The warm water and lavender soap wash away the rancid scents. Deep red welts sear my skin where Ykuza squeezed tight. It looks like I've been struck with a kind of deadly pox. Nothing my clothes won't hide. But the sea serpent's indelible mark on my mind is another story. Naively I'd thought the demonic Infernal were the worst of Winterhaven. Never will I forget the stench, their horrific screeching burned into my memory. Now I've got Ykuza to add to my ever-growing list of nightmares.

I dress in private, only coming out once I'm completely clothed. Lark wrinkles her nose in disgust.

"Sondrine, you are meeting with the Veneficum. Other than the king, they are the most important people in Winterhaven. You can't go before them in plain trousers and a blouse or they will think it a mockery. A gown or at least new robes would be far more appropriate for the occasion. Please trust me when I tell you these things."

Warmed by her forthrightness, I offer a smile to the little girl. "My trousers suit me better than any gown or robe, and they are far more comfortable. You should try them. Playing with Snap and Hoarus would be easier than in a dress, I can promise."

"At least let me braid your hair," she says grudgingly. "Should you look inappropriate, they will think you flippant."

My hair is a revolting, twisted mess. Cutting it short would offer the best solution, but as the past indicates, the curls would grow right back, so I succumb to the little girl's request. She chatters on about the Veneficum, and when the final pin is pushed into place, I take the evergreen cloak and throw it around my shoulders.

Lark shakes her head with growing disapproval. "Why do you wear the cloak of a dead woman?"

"A very good question," I say, grinning. "For one, it keeps me warm. Also, strange as it sounds, I rather fancy the thing. Someday I would very much like to discover who this woman was. If I survive my next quest, that is my wish."

"Survive?" Lark's face goes pale as the wall behind her. "Sondrine, are you going to die?"

I'm about to assure her no such thing will happen when I decide against it; lying would be a disservice. Tired of everyone's lies concerning me, I do not wish to do the same to her or anyone else. I kneel before Lark. "Indeed I may well die in this battle against the king. Don't be frightened. You will be safe here. And should I die, you can live on knowing my death was for the good of Winterhaven."

A series of light knocks at the wooden door interrupts my bloviated speech. Snap, Lark's more mature triplet brother, enters with a folded garment in hand.

Lark squeals in delight. "Did you finish?"

"Nearly," Snap replies. He shakes out the garment for me to see.

"A vest?" I ask. "Did you make this yourself?"

"Maille," he says. "Protective armor for you to wear under your garments."

The fabric feels fragile to the touch, the grey silken rings linked like mesh. "This will protect me? How?"

Lark giggles into her hands. "Magic, Sondrine."

Snap pulls the maille over his shirt and hands me the sword at his hip. "Go on. Try to maim me."

If I stab Snap, the blade will go straight through his tiny body. He'll be dead in seconds. "Do know I trust you, Snap," I say with apprehension. "However, I cannot—"

"The maille will work," he assures me. "A small swipe at my shoulder will suffice."

Guernsey appears in the doorway dressed in his sapphire robe, the metal sceptre firm in his clawed hand. Lark was right. If the sorcerer is any indication, I'm downright slovenly.

"Perfect timing," Snap says to Guernsey. "I've been working on a special sort of maille. Since Sondrine won't stab me, will you do the honors instead?" He indicates the sword in my hand.

Guernsey too looks dubious, and Snap's smile fades. "Lark?" he begs, but Lark shakes her head.

Annoyed with us all, the little boy takes the sword and plunges the blade straight through his stomach. Lark screams, I gasp, and Guernsey's eyebrows stitch in concern. Snap staggers about the chamber, his eyes whiter than the hair on his head. He drops to his knees then onto his side. "What...have I...done? Help me."

"You can't die!" Lark hurries over and drops to her knees.

Before Lark can start crying, Snap pulls out the sword, untainted. He jumps to his feet and takes a decorous bow. "Told you the maille would work."

Lark claps enthusiastically, and I join in.

"Quite impressive, young Snap," Guernsey says with the usual scratch in his voice.

"This one here is for Sondrine. It needs to be a bit longer. Everyone should wear the maille. Even you, Guernsey."

The old sorcerer scratches his beakish nose. "There is many a thing that might kill me in this war. A sword is not likely one of them. Now then, the Veneficum await our presence in the Citadel. We must make haste."

I take my knapsack and slip the straps over my shoulders. If I've learned anything since my arrival in Winterhaven, it's to never leave my belongings in any one place. Danger lurks around every corner. Best to stay vigilant and prepared, because Winterhaven is as safe as an arsenic bath.

Lark wishes me luck, and Snap promises me the maille by tomorrow as Guernsey leads me through the corridor and out into the afternoon air. The Citadel must be reachable only by horseback, because I've seen nothing rising from the land the few times I've been out and about.

We head down a long slope, the smell of salt heavy on the wind's uptake. Below us the inlet spreads forth, and not until we reach the water's edge do we stop. Guernsey approaches a beached rowboat, the wood half rotted away.

"We're leaving the Sanctuary of Caelum?" I ask with some hesitation. *In this paltry thing, no less? Another battle with Ykuza would prove safer.*

"The Citadel is yonder." Guernsey points somewhere toward the horizon. "We will stay well within the inlet, and thus the waters should remain calm."

Should. On a scale of one to ten, this offers a negative twelve in terms of comfort. Ykuza *should* have been in the depths of the sea far below Mount Serius, nowhere near to here. I've had my fill of sea monsters to last the rest of my days. The absurdity of that statement makes me want to cry.

Though Guernsey is half my size, I take his clawed hand and step inside the boat. He pushes off and leaps inside, telling me to row while he steers the rudder. Chivalry is not only dead, it's buried and blessed.

Chunks of ice rake the boat's sides from time to time, a brutal reminder that should we capsize, we would quickly perish in the frigid waters. My optimism these days is an ever-shrinking violet. In the distance, evergreens crowd a small strip of land, and a chevron of gulls wheel above. My eyes strain through the misty air, but no fortress can be seen.

The sun is falling, the air less temperate by the time the boat noses shore. My arms throb, and my fingers ache with cold. So much for a grand entrance.

No one is here to greet us. A beach of powdered sand sullies my

27

boots as we cross it, and once we breach the taller grasses, a mosaic of black tile embedded in the ground stretches before us. Circular in shape, it spans the length of six men laid out head to foot. Guernsey walks around the ornate piece to the far side and fits his sceptre in the crux of a V-shaped sculpture.

Sixty full ticks of the Aeriscloque pass, but nothing transpires. "Is there...something we're waiting for?" I ask dumbly.

Guernsey nods in his usual cryptic manner without saying a word.

The sun's rays fan through the trees. As the light glides further down, it pierces the crystal orb within the sceptre's tip, and the snowflake alights like fire. Light streams from every dendrite and hits a series of tiles, turning their black color to vibrant blues and greens. An intricate pattern forms: the water symbol belonging to the Sanctuary of Caelum.

Slowly the tiles spiral away, the ground below a gaping maw. I shuffle over to the edge. What lies at my feet is nothing I could have imagined. An inverted tower of white stone, edged with a staircase winding far into the earth. The Citadel is beneath the land, safe from enemies of any kind.

Guernsey pulls the sceptre free, and together we descend the staircase, the heavy mosaic resealing itself. The moment I'd descended Isceald Castle's hidden staircase does not go unremembered, the hearth closing above as I escaped the king's violent advances.

Strangely, sunlight from below dances across the masonry,

enough to reach through the darkness and guide us along. The air grows more temperate the deeper we wind into the earth, and though the scent of sea salt remains thick, something more floral fingers through. Massive rounded windows ride up the walls, the source of the dappling sunlight.

Guernsey continues down the stairs, for this is no novelty to him, but my curiosity brings me to a standstill. The glass is frigid to the touch. Marine life scaled in the most dramatic colors darts through the icy waters. Not only is the Citadel below land, it is below the Dendrite Sea.

When Guernsey is no longer within sight, I hurry down the staircase to catch up. At the bottom, we move through a series of tunnels until we find ourselves in an enormous room built of stone and walled glass, a virtual aquarium on all sides. Guernsey gestures to a lone high-backed chair before the long table where the Veneficum are seated. This I do not like one bit, but I take my place without voicing an opinion. Perhaps this is where all guests sit; I'm unconvinced.

Ione is seated at the table's center, all flowing hair and seashells and fabric, the trident angled against her chair. The same trident that saved my life mere hours ago. Adjacent to the vacant spot on her right is a giant of a man who takes up three seats on his own. His head is bent beneath the vaulted ceiling, his hands the size of boulders. In fact, he appears to be made of rock and ice—shiny black and blue—as though some sort of living ice cliff.

29

Backed against the wall, hidden among the shadows, Shán offers the slightest nod in greeting. There is no smile, no warmth behind the blue of his eyes.

"Per usual," Ione says with contempt, "we await Lord Kian. At this particular meeting, I hold no confidence he will grace us with his presence, for this matter is of no interest to him or his kind."

"He will be here," Guernsey counters. "I personally sought him out at the Keep of Wintersgaard, and he gave me his word."

Ione scoffs. "Lord Kian's word is as unreliable as the weather at present. Why he is part of this council I often wonder, for his intentions never align with ours."

"Lord Kian wants Winterhaven to endure, trust in that," Guernsey says. "Let us commence, for time is of the essence, and time is something we have little of at this juncture. Zhang the Elder will not be present, although he sends his best. Carrig of the Regolith, of the commonwealth Titan Dome, is here," he notes with a quill set to parchment, and the behemoth rock man nods once. "Ione, Mage of the Nereids, territory of the Sanctuary of Caelum. And myself, of course." He gestures the shadows. "I have requested Shán Einfarí's attendance. Although not an official member of the Veneficum, he serves us unfailingly and has played a key role in bringing Sondrine Renfrew to Winterhaven. Here she sits before us."

Ta da! Once again, I'm a rare insect pinned under glass for everyone's observation. "Thank you one and all for the invite. I'm honored to be here. The thing is, I'm unsure about my role—"

"She needs training," Ione says. "By what little I've seen, I am unimpressed, and I have no confidence in this girl. She is filled with fear and doubt. Moreover, she is an Elementalist and did nothing with her gifts when Ykuza surfaced. Having an alternate plan may be prudent."

How blatant. And rude.

"The stalactite was coated in ice, and therefore I was able to impale Ykuza's eye. You missed that part, I'm sure." My churlishness is not understated. And yet I can say nothing more, because it was she who killed Ykuza, not I.

Carrig thinks long and hard before he speaks. "She can hone her skills near Titan Dome," he says in a booming voice. "The Cloister is secluded, and the Solitary could take her in, train her for the pending war."

Train me? To kill the king? I'm confused why this might be necessary but decide to await further explanations, in no mood to come off as the village idiot.

Guernsey nods in agreement. "The Solitary can teach what is needed, and indeed the secluded area makes it viable. Moreover, they are well-versed in alchemical lore. My concern, of course, is time. Were it on our side, Sondrine could build an army all her own. Already there are reports of fires in the west. The war has begun."

It's then that a man enters, dressed in a cotton tunic with pants tucked into suede boots. His face is a marbled carving, angular and hard. Pearlescent hair shimmers to the small of his

31

back in a flowing veil of grace. He kisses Ione's hand in greeting, offers a slight bow of his head to everyone else, and takes his place next to Guernsey.

Guernsey says, "Lord Kian of the Keep of Wintersgaard, ruler of the Mór, thank you for coming. We were discussing Sondrine, how she might train for this war. Do you have any thoughts on the matter? Your input would be of great value."

"What you choose to do or not, I will approve, if only for the sake of saving Winterhaven," he says. "By saving, I mean the land itself, not the Duine who reside here. Were it my decision alone, the Duine would perish so the Sylphs could rule the land once more as we did thousands of years ago."

He's a Sylph? I thought they were tiny beings, like Eirene and Murgh and all the others at the Sacred Grove of Willeaux. Lord Kian looks near-human and stands tall as Shán, although the tips of his ears form a slight point. "Duine?" I ask, seeking clarification.

"Humans," Shán answers from the shadows.

By the way Lord Kian's mouth curls into a sneer, he is sickened by the very word.

Guernsey looks unfazed. "The plan is to win the war and bring peace to Winterhaven, where we can all live in harmony without any one person to rule the land."

"Then pray, why is King Andronicus ruler of Winterhaven?" Lord Kian spits. "The man is a plague upon this soil. His hateful rhetoric and vile atrocities run deep to the root."

"He rules only the Duine," Ione hisses. "King Andronicus would never dare set foot at the Sanctuary of Caelum. On more than one occasion, it has been made clear that he is not and never will be welcome in these parts."

Carrig nods in agreement. "Those in my clan could stand in for his army of thousands, though he would never inquire of our fellowship, for he knows it would be futile. We live amongst ourselves and swear fealty to no one."

"You are leader of the Regolith," Ione parries.

Carrig's eyes narrow between the icy rock. Again he's contemplative, taking many moments to answer. "We rule as one. Were there sufficient room here at the Citadel, other Regolith would join us. All decisions are made as a collective. I am here only to retrieve and relay information, to be the voice of my clan. My power is no higher than the others.'"

Guernsey holds up a hand to bring down the dissenting voices. "For now, Sondrine will head to the Cloister, then on to Titan Dome. Send word once her skills are improved, Carrig, and we shall put our plan into motion."

"Excuse me," I say, rising from the chair. "You speak as though I'm not present. Since you believe me to be so vital, I should have a say in how this war will play out. I'm not some pawn to be used on a whim to settle old scores for past grievances. Furthermore, the king is weak—you said so yourself, Guernsey. Why in the world would I need to practice my Elemental capabilities? Yes, they could use some honing, but sending me off to the remotest regions is nonsensical when I could stay here or elsewhere nearby."

33

"Soon enough the king will taste defeat," Ione says. "Nothing would bring me greater pleasure than to do to him what he so readily does to others. His head impaled on the Mourning Tree would be the greatest of victories. And the greatest of ironies." She runs a finger along the sharp trident. "But the rising threat at the moment is the queen."

I offer a quizzical stare, surprised by the peculiar statement. "The Sanctuary is remote, I do understand. Yet I'm astounded you have not been apprised of the news. The queen perished in Mount Serius weeks ago." Ione says nothing, and I take her silence to mean disbelief. "Tell her," I say to Guernsey, but he only looks at me with unerring eyes.

"Shán?" I say, a little more desperate. "Tell Ione how you fed Queen Belisama the fountain's waters, how drinking from the ivory chalice killed her."

The room has grown quiet, and if I'm unmistaken, the sentiment directed toward me is one of disturbing pity. "For mercy's sake," I say with more bravado. "Would someone please tell Ione the queen is dead? The fact she does not know this is upsetting at best. I was brought to believe the Veneficum was a collective of Winterhaven's greatest, most powerful minds."

Shán steps from the shadows. "The queen is alive, Sondrine. There have been whisperings, growing suspicions. Now the rumors have been confirmed."

Guernsey adds, "Eirene said through the iron bars of her cage, '*The queen lives on and will destroy you in due course.*' You do remember this, do you not?"

"Of course I remember," I say hotly. *Having your death
promised is like an onslaught of angry boils—not easily forgotten.
Or ignored.*

"I speak of the former part of her declaration, '*The queen lives
on,*" Guernsey says evenly, unaffected by my tempestuous tone.
"For Eirene to utter such a thing would be nonsensical lest it were
true."

"It was an empty threat," I say, dumbstruck by his naiveté.
"Eirene was angry about being captured, about not killing me, and
most of all, about failing to keep the queen alive. Queen Belisama
Agni's death was Eirene's biggest failure. How you cannot see
what is so blatantly obvious is beyond me." The strength of my
voice bounces against the walls.

"You were to be told about the queen earlier today," Shán says.
"But you slept much of the day away, and we were unable to
inform you until now. Make no mistake, we kept nothing from you.
It was agreed upon by all you would be told at this council."

Affirming nods all around. I want to ask how they know she's
alive, demand proof to confirm such an outlandish declaration. But
I stop myself. I've known something was not right, and my own
defensiveness only highlights this. The sight of Ione's trident
serves as a particularly poignant answer. *Ykuza.* The sea serpent
did not come of its own volition; it was sent forth by the queen
herself. Everyone here must know that.

My chair catches me as I fall into it. "How did she survive? Her

35

very skin melted away in a cascade of liquid flesh. And Mount Serius imploded. I saw the whole thing with my own eyes."

"Many theories exist," Guernsey says. "The Soul Splitter was deemed a possibility. However, the soul must return to its rightful body, and hers was destroyed when she was locked inside the snowflake obsidian. Indeed the queen perished in Mount Serius, make no mistake. The more likely answer is Samsara."

I shrug, for the term is unfamiliar.

"After you die," Ione states, "you begin life anew in another body."

"Spiritism," I mutter. "The belief exists in the Other World, although it's mostly met with skepticism because there is little empiric evidence."

"The Realm of Halcyon is where everyone aspires to upon death," Guernsey says. "However, attaining transcendence—where mind, body, and spirit intersect in equal parts—is not easily achieved. Those who fail return again to begin another life. If the life previous was one of kindness and compassion, they are granted rebirth in human form. If violence, hatred, murder, or any combination thereof was practiced, they will return to this life as animal or vermin."

"The queen may be a common housefly?" I ask. No one laughs. Embarrassed by my poor judgment, for this is quite the serious matter, I take a deep interest in my thumbnail.

Carrig shifts in his seat, and small bits of rock roll off him onto the table. "One caveat exists."

"Like for like," Ione imparts. "If a human or like-bodied creature is already vile, and if they are accepting, the soul can transfer."

"Then the queen could be in human form, after all?" I ask.

Guernsey scratches his jaw. "The queen is quite whole, I surmise. Perhaps not in the same manner as she once was but strong enough to annihilate this land and rise up to rule it. Where she might be at this juncture is anyone's guess. Even under great duress and imprisonment, Eirene never revealed the queen's whereabouts. Rumors abound."

"Eirene can be coerced, can she not?" I ask.

A grievous exchange between Guernsey and Lord Kian. "Eirene escaped. She never returned to the Sacred Grove of Willeaux," the old sorcerer says.

"Apropos of rumors," Ione says in a callback to Guernsey's previous statement, "Belisama is creating an army, a lethal one. Her Infernal can now breathe fire, unlike their predecessors, and a new race, called Tartarean, have been molded from lava and dark magic. The Infernal can succumb to water, same as before, although the Tartarean are immune. Only blades forged from molten metal can kill them."

This is too much to comprehend. My mind whirls with confusion. "If the Solitary can train me and they are well-versed in Elementalism, then obviously they have the skills needed to kill the queen. Her new army too."

"It is you who must destroy the queen, and no other," Ione

intones.

My arms cross in defiance. "An army of Elementalists could destroy the queen more easily than I alone. Winterhaven is full of them, each with varying degrees of skill. And if this theory of Samsara is no theory at all and actually exists, then she will continue to come back for all eternity regardless of whether she is killed now." A series of shaking heads, so I look to Guernsey. "You promised I would understand and all answers would come in due course. The time is now."

The room falls silent, and I realize my tone, my demeanor, is out of line for the Veneficum, especially for their leader. In London this would be social ruin. But if I'm going to lead this war and kill the queen once and for all, I better bloody well know why.

A concessionary nod from Guernsey. "Eternal death, where one can never again return in any form, is only possible when flesh and blood commits the bloodletting."

The shock of his words hit me with such force I grasp the chair's back to steady me. "At best you jest, Guernsey. At worst you are mistaken, grossly so. My mother died in childbirth. Aunt Henrietta told me this herself."

"Your aunt is a liar," Shán says. "You know this to be true. Her lies are one of many reasons you stand before us today."

Fair point. When last I saw Aunt Henrietta, I'd asked who my parents were, and she'd stuck to her story. My mother could have died in childbirth. But the queen is an Elementalist, a coincidence I cannot deny. Too stunned to speak, I look to each council member

38

to renounce Guernsey's claim. Only steely gazes befall me, a confirmation of the horrible truth.

CHAPTER THREE

My eyes blur, and I stumble through near-darkness, the sunlight no longer my guide. Up the winding staircase I go, not knowing how I'll get out and not caring as long as I get away from the Veneficum, away from every person in this whole sordid world. At the stairs' end, I bang my palms against the mosaic tile with unabashed fury. "Let me out of here," I scream.

To my surprise, the mosaic peels open, and I rush out of the inverted Citadel and back to the beach, where I fall to my knees in the sand. My hands clutch my stomach as if this will somehow keep me from vomiting my disgust. The cool, salty air appeases me, but it also beckons the tears to break free.

This can't be true. This must be some sort of cruel joke, a way to get me on their side....

The sound of snapping flames taps me from behind. Without needing to look, I know the torchbearer is Shán. He says nothing, which, of course, says everything.

"Stay away from me," I spit, my voice shaking with anger as I shoulder away the tears. "You're a liar, same as the rest. The queen cannot be my mother, do you understand? My mother was a good person who died while giving me life. I will prove it. I will prove you and the others wrong." Shán's continued silence encourages my defensiveness. "What I need is time. Time to figure things out, to find some sort of proof of who I truly am." On unsteady feet, I stand and wipe the sand from my trousers.

"If finding proof will help you to realize the truth, then do so." He moves around to face me and stakes the torch into the sand. "But time is running thin. Have faith when I say that is true. I trust Guernsey with my life. If he says something is fact, then it is. You can't deny the queen is an Elementalist—"

"So is your father! There are many in Winterhaven; Lark told me as much."

"True. Yet only you can wield all the elements, no one else, my father the perfect example. Snow and ice, he can maneuver quite well. Along with the dark spell, those elements were used to imprison the queen inside the snowflake obsidian. Were fire or air needed or anything else, we would not be having this conversation." He looks at me, unwavering. "Your Elemental gifts matter, make no mistake. Likewise, your bloodline. You and only you can kill Queen Belisama Agni."

I stare out at the icy sea, a mirror of the early evening sky. "If she is my mother, there is no way I can kill her. It would be too wrong, somehow."

"She tried to kill you," he reminds me.

"Why didn't she say something in Mount Serius? Did she not know who I was? This seems an impossibility. If she doesn't know,

41

I can appeal to her, convince her this war is of no use."

"How do you suggest we find her? Only Eirene knows of her whereabouts, and she has escaped."

"Guernsey said there were fires in the west. Her reign of terror has begun. Someone must know where she's hiding. I can use myself as bait, offer my blood to help give her strength—"

"No," he says in an admonishing tone. "You underestimate the queen. If she learns of your blood ties, she will kill you all the swifter, for you are a clear threat."

His words cut deep, but I have no delusions. In the near-future, the queen and I will be neither sharing a pot of tea nor forming a mother-daughter bond like no other. However, if she learns who I am, she might feel something akin to love. Would she truly kill me knowing I'm her own flesh and blood?

"Spies are everywhere in Winterhaven," Shán says in breach of my thoughts. "Since Eirene escaped, she is likely conferring with the queen. She is but one of many spies, were I to guess."

The thought of Eirene saddens me. She was so kind and sweet, and there was nothing in my mind's eye to suggest a betrayal. As the youngest of the Sylphs, she was easily seduced by the queen's promises of grandeur and power.

"Guernsey lied," I say coldly. "He said I was brought to Winterhaven because of my Elemental gifts. Oh, they may help. Nonetheless, I am here for no reason other than being the queen's daughter."

Infuriated by the willful deception, I head to the rowboat and lean into the bow to unharness it from the sand. Shán follows, claps a hand on the boat's frame to stop me. "Let go," I say, and I mean it. "This is my journey, not yours, not anyone else's."

"What is your plan?"

"To return to Isceald and look for proof of my birth, proof that Belisama is my mother."

Shán scoffs. "Should you set foot anywhere near to there, you will be killed on command. You drugged the king, do you forget? There is a price for your head throughout the realm." He draws in a breath to calm his heated voice. "If you want to fight this war, Sondrine, you must learn how to be a warrior, and that requires instruction, not an impetuous nature."

"I'm not impetuous," I hurl back. "I'll return to the Sanctuary and devise a plan."

"What sort of plan? You know nothing of this land."

Touché. I don't even own a map of Winterhaven. And my sense of direction is dismal. Getting lost on the streets of London had been a weekly occurrence. Often I'd found myself at the shoemaker's rather than the baker's. "Where is the nearest city to here?"

Shán points over my shoulder. "Due north. Drumoak is close enough, right up the coast, but—"

"Come with me. Be my guide."

"On the morrow, I'm off to gather my fleet. Securing only land for this war would be foolish." He takes me by the hand, gently pulls me away from the boat. "Go to the Cloister. Learn from the

Solitary. They have libraries far vaster than those found in Isceald. There you'll have the same chance if not better to prove your birthright, and meanwhile, you can hone your Elemental skills."

Those deep blue eyes have a magic all their own, and I lose myself for a moment as I memorize them. "Will you be in danger where you're going?"

"We are all in grave danger. The Infernal and Tartarean are obvious enemies, but there are many who tread these lands with silent footsteps. To trust anyone beyond this immediate circle would prove a fatal mistake."

I offer a solemn nod. "You're right, I suppose." *I'm sure he is. But this sits as well as a drunkard at a teetotaler convention.* "I'll leave come morning, I presume?"

"At first light." Shán's hand falls away as do the lines of concern between his eyes. "The winds earlier were heady. My boat is yonder on the other side of the isle. Wait here and I'll fetch Guernsey to bring you back. We'll sup tonight at the Sanctuary, get you packed, and send you on your way."

'Send you on your way.' Like a menial package sent through the post. I'm a means to an end. *'Believe what we tell you.' 'Hone your skills.' 'Kill the queen so we can win this war.'* This is essentially what Shán is saying. Why not pat me on the head like a well-trained puppy? It feels no different.

My anger resurfaces, and when Shán is halfway up the beach, I take the flaming torch from the sand and twist it into the hook at the bow. Then I push the boat off, jump inside, and start rowing as fast as I can. Shán spins at the sound of splashing water and runs toward me.

"What are you doing?" he yells from shore. "Tell me you're headed back to the Sanctuary."

The icy waters are a lethal barrier, and he cannot jump in, not without freezing to death. Knowing I'm at a safe distance, I ease my rowing. "I could tell you as much, but it would be a lie. I'm not going to train for this war before I know who I am. The Solitary's library may or may not tell me anything pertinent. I need answers, and I need them now."

"It's a sodding start! The Dendrite Sea is deadly, do you understand? You'll meet your death before you ever reach new shores."

There is so much fury in Shán's words, I can hardly stand it. Guernsey hurries to his side, and I watch as Shán points and yells, his words but an echo, no longer discernible. With his level of magic, Guernsey could easily pull me back to shore. For whatever reason, he does nothing, only watching as the waves pull me away, a burning light in a literal sea of darkness.

***

The cloak and hood provide ample warmth, but my fingers are numb with cold. There's no point in rowing for the moment, so I ease the oars back into the boat and pull some flames from the torch, rolling them between my palms. My fingertips tingle with blood flow soon enough, and I fish out my gloves from the knapsack and pull them on.

Far off in the distance, the Sanctuary's lights flicker. Right then, something occurs to me. Shán might use his boat to search for me on his way back. Or Hoarus may be flown over the inlet. Much as I appreciate the torch, it is a beacon of light pointing straight toward me, so I fling it overboard. A deflating hiss, then nothing but the sound of lapping water.

***

Nighttime folds around the inlet, the full moon caught in a living net of stars. Too bad I know almost nothing of celestial navigation, although Polaris—the North Star—shines down the same as in the Other World. I tap on the Aeriscloque around my neck, and the tiny hinged doors flutter open at my touch. The divided face of black and bronze that displays the positions of the sun, moon, and stars shows Polaris burning bright. I can use the Aeriscloque to follow that direction, travel along the coast to Drumoak.

My Elemental skills are wretched when it comes to Water, but perhaps I can conjure a small current to help me along once the gates open to the sea. When that might happen is anyone's guess. From what little I've been told, ships sail through weekly, sometimes daily, depending on the season and the tides. When the last one had come through, I have no idea. If too much time passes before one appears, I will have to rethink my exit strategy. The inlet is vast, but come sunup, the search for my boat will begin.

I feel horrible not giving a proper goodbye to Lark and Snap.

But I'll return to the Sanctuary regardless of what I discover about my filiation. If I am the queen's daughter, then I must head to the Cloister and train among the Solitary. If I'm not, I'll need to figure out what my place in this war is, if any.

Ice chunks scrape the boat's side, a harrowing reminder of my hasty decision to go it alone. Starting my journey on land rather than by sea would have been smarter. Shán wasn't wrong about my impetuous nature, much as I hate to admit it. My heart aches thinking of him, how angry he was as I drifted away. Were the roles reversed, it would've felt like an outright betrayal. He was leaving in the morning, and my not-so-stealthy escape was not how I pictured us parting ways.

And yet it is I who feels betrayed. By Shán, by Guernsey, by the deceit of so many. I pull the cloak tighter around me, lean back against the stern, and watch the stars fall through the sky. The gentle rocking waters are a balm to my tangible fears, but they do nothing to temper my ire.

***

A deep, resonating sound breaks through the stillness and startles me so much I nearly capsize the boat as I scramble upright and peer through the misty void. *Is Ykuza rising from the dead?*

Though the gates are normally invisible, the pre-dawn moonlight catches their outline, the tops of them lost to a layer of fog. They are massive—perhaps not quite as tall as the newly erected Big Ben in the Other World, but close. Slowly they open, and I grab both oars and begin to row. The wider the gates open, the faster the Dendrite Sea rushes in and pushes me back. No matter how hard I concentrate, the churning water rocks my boat, jostles it about through newly formed waves.

My rowing becomes more fervent as the waves grow higher and more treacherous, dousing me and filling the rowboat's bottom. Up and down the waters toss me, each freezing wave a painful blow. *I'll never survive the turbulent sea in this worthless thing. Once I'm in the open waters, I'll surely capsize.* I may capsize now—I can't catch my breath, let alone row fast enough to break free of the current.

And then it cuts through the fog bank: a wooden bow, reaching masts, brilliant vermillion sails swollen by the wind. The ship is moving straight toward me. Halfway up the side is a lifeboat, harnessed into place by a set of pulleys and ropes. One of the ropes hangs free, likely loosened by the barrage of waves, the knotted bottom dragging the water's surface. If I can get to it and climb up, I can stowaway inside the lifeboat.

Ankle-deep water straddles my boots as I row faster, trying not to capsize or lose my positioning. When the gates begin to close, the sea calms inside the inlet and offers a brief reprieve. Soon enough the bow noses past, then a walled mountain of wood, terrifyingly close. Seizing the rope seems an impossibility. Even if my Elemental skills get me close enough, climbing it with aching arms and frozen fingers is unlikely. And if at any point I lose my grip, the ship's rudder will pull me under to a bloody, watery grave. Still, I must try, so I dig the oars into the water.

The ship throws off a turbulent wake, and the faster I row, the faster the water surges, pushing my boat back and dumping over me in a freezing tide. Try as I might to concentrate, my Elemental skills prove too weak, and the rope swims past, much too far from reach. I'm soaking head to heel, quickly freezing to death. Dejected and exhausted, I glance over my shoulder to the remote lights of the Sanctuary burning through the morning fog. I don't want to go back there, but the ship, though slower inside the inlet, is still outpacing me. Admitting defeat feels colder and steelier than the ice water against my cheek. I'll have to return to land and form a new plan—

A thick, heavy net drops over me. I flail, thinking I've been spotted and captured by the crew. But a whole series of nets spider out to the waters below. They must be fishing before heading out of the inlet.

Now I'm moving faster—the net is dragging my rowboat along. Hope rises within at the second chance. But too soon the Sanctuary's horn sounds, and the unrestrained arms of the sea rush through the opening gates on the other side of the inlet. My boat starts to spin, caught in the heavy net and the ship's potent wake. In fear of capsizing, I clutch the net with sopping hands, and the oars slip away into the water.

"Help!" I yell into the wind, clawing at the net and pulling myself closer to the dangling rope. The waves pelt me from all sides, the water knee-deep, the stern of my boat gone under. *I'm sinking.* "Come on, you blasted thing," I swear as mouthfuls of

49

saltwater drown my pleas. Clinging to the net with one hand, I reach with my other as the rope bounces tauntingly against the ship's side. "Just…a little…closer." With a flick of my wrist, the wind breezes up enough to vault the rope closer. My fingers snag it, and I yank hard, but the rope topples over me and rolls away into the sea.

"No!" I scream in frustration. The rope was never fully secured. I pray to whatever god is listening that the net is, because with a rallying cry, I grasp it with both hands, step onto the sinking bow and leap, my body clashing against the icy waves.

***

They say right before you die, your life flashes before you in a series of vignettes, all the little important moments in your life. Memories from childhood, years at a time, to the very instant you leave the earth. They say there's a beautiful and blinding light, a sheltering light filled with warmth and love and a sense of utter peace.

Nothing appears before me except the ship's substantial side, and my body heartily slams into it. Searing pain shoots through every rib and knocks half the breath from my lungs. Beneath the thick veil of sea spray, the rowboat goes down in a twisted, defeated heap. The ship is picking up speed, the wind whipping and unmerciful. My feet are tangled, yet the net secures me in a way the rope never could have.

Trying to catch my breath, I start for the lifeboat one frozen step at a time. I'm tempted to climb past it, over the ship's rails and onto the deck, but I'm unsure how long the net will sustain my weight. Moreover, a crew of men might be waiting, likely to cast me back overboard. Or worse.

A tarpaulin covers the small boat. By the time I loosen it and flop inside, I'm covered in frost, drenched and tired, my heart beating too fast for comfort. Thankfully it's plenty dry inside. Had I the means of creating a small, contained fire, all might be well for the moment.

At any rate, the wind is blocked, but I'm shivering violently. I can barely ease the sopping knapsack from my shoulders. To my surprise, the lining has kept the clothing mostly dry. The grey cap goes over my head, my pinned, frozen curls crunching as they're pushed under and away. Everything else is cast off, and the cloak is slung over the side in hopes the salty breeze will beat it dry. Like the moment I first fell into Winterhaven, I wrap every spare piece of clothing around me. The epitome of fashion, I am not. But for now, nothing matters. I only want to survive another day.

***

Survive I do. Sunlight shines down against the tarpaulin, the lifeboat warm and cozy save for the wood bottom elbowing my back. I'm unsure how long I've slept—perhaps a day, maybe more. My cloak has dried out, same for my trousers and boots, so I shed the extra clothing and pull them back on.

Crisp sails above cut along the bluest of skies when I poke my head outside. The headwinds are strong, and a hand goes to my cap to keep it from blowing away. I take out my canteen and swallow several sips of water to ease my parched throat. *Not much left.* Provided we're not at sea long, I can remain here until we pull into port. The crew will be none the wiser.

I can't help but smile smugly. Though the risk was high, the reward feels greater, sweeter. Raising the canteen to the wind, I toast my endeavors. "To freedom, to the truth. To victory!"

A cranking sound interrupts my grand delusions of stowaway life. The lifeboat is rising toward the deck, and like a trapped rat, I'm going along with it.

CHAPTER FOUR

With the knapsack at my back and the emerald cloak tucked inside, I crouch beneath the planked wood seats in hopes this is some sort of routine check of the ropes and pulleys. With any luck, they'll never gander a look inside. They'll lower the boat back to its original spot, my presence undiscovered, and all will be well.

The tarpaulin is pulled back with a violent snap.

So much for luck.

"For cunny's sake," a male voice hisses. "Another damned stowaway."

A filthy hand yanks me by the collar, and I stumble onto the deck. A wire of a man bears down on me. Where there should be hair, there is only black ink across his scalp—a coiled serpent with daggered fangs. "Look at 'im," he scoffs. "Scrawny as the rats in the galley."

Him. He thinks I'm a boy. My eyes make a quick sweep from under the cap's rim. At least ten unsavory deckhands stand before me, but a ship this size undoubtedly houses dozens more below.

"You must be starving, eh?" he says. "A bit of food to help ya feel better?"

Something tells me he's not being the good-natured host, about to show me a cozy cabin with a plate full of fresh scallops and a nice ale to wash it all down.

Another crew member indicates the inked man. "Answer our good man Naedder," he goads. "You got no manners?"

Warily I nod, for I know if I defy these men in any way, this conversation will end quickly and not for the good. "Thank you," I say in my lowest voice. "I am quite famished."

"The lad is famished. Did you hear that, mates?" Sneering laughter all around. "Glad to help. Eat this." Naedder's fist connects with my jaw.

Down I go, blood spilling over my teeth and splattering across the wooden planks. More laughter and cheering as I'm kicked in the back, then in the stomach. If I yell or cry out, they'll know I'm no boy, so I lay there and hold my ribs, the pain so severe I feel it in the roots of my teeth and the depths of my spine.

Naedder crouches next to me and runs the flat of a blade across my cheek. "Once our respectable Captain Seybourne gives me his say so, I'm going to cut your bony fingers off one by one. Then your shriveled nuts. I'll save your sugar stick for last." Cruel, soundless laughter dances in his narrowed eyes.

"Lock him in the hold." The stern command comes from behind, from an older man who joins up with the group. "I'll confer with the captain before you make a stew of this lad."

Naedder stands and salutes him along with the rest of the crew. "Aye, Chief Mate," he says, the words drawn out as though he's spitting on each one.

Two men haul me across the expansive deck, my boots dragging against the boards. Near the hull, a grated hatch is opened, and I'm shoved down a ladder I barely use. Somehow I land on my feet but stumble, the iron bars of a cell helping me to stay upright. The air chokes with waste. One man kicks me in the face as he lowers himself in, and this time my ankles give way. The other drags me inside the cell.

"Thick sard," the shorter of the two swears. He yanks off my knapsack and holds up my wrists to shackle them. "Bony thing, aren't ya? Good thing these are heavy or you might blow away." He tightens the screws, and I groan in pain. Once more he turns them for his own amusement. The thickness of my boots makes the fetters secure easily around my ankles.

Each man kicks me once more before they leave, the taller of the two locking the cell door. "Chum for the sharks," he says. "Nothin' tickles my dangly bits more than watchin' stowaways walk the plank."

My eyes widen, but I say nothing as they leave. Neither of these men are the captain, and he's the one I must appeal to.

The hay is old and soiled. No one is here, which tells me the last stowaway is not above enjoying a savory fish stew with the captain. My ribs are screaming, and I know they're fractured, perhaps broken, because every breath is a metal spike in my side.

Despite the heavy shackles, I manage to pull out my canteen. I'm lucky they didn't take my knapsack. A stowaway doesn't carry anything of value, I suppose. Try as I might to drink, my lip is swollen and cut, and the water dribbles out the side. Flies buzz about, determined to inspect my eyes and nostrils, so I wrap a scarf over my head to block them.

Day turns to night thrice over according to the porthole drilled into the wall. Whenever sunlight stems through, it's so unbearably hot one would never think we were crossing the Dendrite Sea. At night the air is frigid and brutal. The only comfort is the gentle rocking of the ship. If a storm comes to pass, I'll be cursing this notion.

The hatch creaks open on day four. Through the blurred haze of swollen lids, I watch Naedder climb down the ladder. He crouches, slides a bowl through the small space between the bars and the floor. My head feels like a boulder when I lift it. *Smells like fish.* The flies briefly leave me to walk across my breakfast.

Sweat shines the ink on Naedder's scalp, his shirt soaked down the front and under the arms. Though stifling in the hold, on deck it most certainly is not. He stares with cold eyes, the smirk on his face so full of sadism it reminds me of King Andronicus. For a brief moment, I wonder if the food has been poisoned. But something tells me Naedder is a man who derives more pleasure from cutting people into tiny, torturous pieces than offering a swift, uneventful death.

Despite the insect picnic, I need to eat. No utensils are offered, so I set the bowl to my lips and let the rancid mash of watery sardines and legumes slide down my throat. The less movement I

56

make, the happier my ribs will be.

I bite down on something chewy. The low light reveals the mash is moving. I fling the bowl at the bars and vomit, hoping every last maggot comes out of me. If my ribs were mending in any fashion, they're now beyond repair.

Naedder's laugh ebbs with cruelty. "Didn't agree with ya, lad? Upset tummy? No worries. Soon things will be coming out the other end." He indicates the bucket in my cell. "You and the chamber pot will be getting cozy right quick."

"Where are we going?" I croak, too weak to speak in full voice.

"*We* are headed to Taliin. You, lad, are chum. Stowaways don't get a free ride." He reaches for the bowl but stumbles a little when he stands. "Captain would've been down here already. Not feeling so well as of late. Count your blessings. You've lived longer than most."

"Water," I mouth to him.

Naedder takes out his knife, presses his face into the bars. "Pleasure. One cup of water straight away. But it will cost ya." He shoulders away dripping sweat from his brow. "One pinky." Immediately he waves off his own demand. "Nah, you pick. Any one of your fingers will do just fine. I'm not choosy."

My middle finger is offered. What do I care at this point? He thinks I'm a boy, and any boy would do the same. Might as well take advantage and act the part.

He sniggers. "Be right back with your water, then."

Once he's gone, I stagger to my feet and press my face to the porthole to breathe in the fresh, cool air. No land in sight from what I can tell. And no weapon to help me. I could concentrate, try to ease water into the ship and sink it, but the metal bars of the cell are solid, and I'd drown along with the crew. A storm could bring us closer to land, but I don't know how close we might be to shore. Besides, the sky is bereft of clouds.

I slump along the wall and bury my face in my arms. "Guernsey," I whisper. "Can you hear me? Or Shán, if you can read my mind. I'm an idiot, locked in a ship's cell in the middle of the Dendrite Sea."

My aching head shakes. I'm still angry with Guernsey, and Shán would think this served me right. Even if he could hear me, the sea is vast, filled with hundreds, perhaps thousands of ships. In my crazed attempt to get aboard, I never noticed the name, assuredly painted alongside the hull. I could ask Naedder. Perhaps for a finger or a toe, he would tell me. This is what it's come to. Offering up body parts for the chance of survival.

***

Beeswax has helped to calm and cure my split lip, but my tongue is swollen, so parched am I. A full day has passed since Naedder promised me water, and two days since my canteen ran dry. I thought he would be back right away, anxious to start torturing me. If he doesn't return soon, I'm going to die of thirst.

Boots hit the rungs of the ladder. Knowing my finger is about to be sawed off causes my heart to pound. But I need water, and I need information.

58

Someone emerges from the shadows with a bucket in hand. The face is podgy. And where I expect ink and a bald head, there is hair. Lots of it. Golden brown and shaggy and with a bit of a curl at the ends. It's a boy, a few years younger than I. He says nothing, just scoops a cup through the bucket and thrusts his hand through the bars. On hands and knees, I shuffle over and take it gladly. The water looks and smells fresh. I know not to drink quickly, but even the first little bit makes me choke and cough.

It tastes so good I want to cry and almost do. The boy watches in silence, and when I hand off the cup, he passes it through the water once more and gives it back. Something glints in his other hand.

"You here for payment?" I whisper.

He nods silently.

"Where is Naedder?" I ask.

"Not up to dick. Can't get out of bed. Sent me in his place."

The boy looks more scared than I do. My voice low, I ask, "Have you ever cut one off before? Fingers are tricky. It's important to know where the veins are; otherwise I might bleed out."

He chews his lip as the shag of hair shakes back and forth.

I use his uncertainty to my advantage. "You don't have to, you know. If Naedder is sick, he'll never find out."

"He told me to bring it to him as evidence."

I sip more water while trying to stall. "You don't quite fit in with the rest of the crew. What's your story?"

"I fit in just fine," he spits.

59

My hand goes up in resignation. "Didn't mean to offend. You're young is all."

His shoulders relax. "Thought you were calling me fat. I mean, I know I am, but I don't need a filthy stowaway telling me such things. Bad enough the crew teases me."

"You're not fat," I say honestly. "Little bit of youthful padding. A couple more years, and it will practically melt away. You'll be fending off the girls soon enough."

He smiles a little. "Ya think so?"

I nod, because I do. His eyes are kind, and his smile tells me he'll have the girls lining up by the time he's my age. "What's your name?"

His smile fades, and he squints, suspect. "You're not a flattercap, are ya? Trying to get on my good side?"

"Making conversation, nothing more."

His eyes go to my chained limbs. He must deem me safe, because he unlocks the cell and steps inside.

"Before you get to things," I say, "can you tell me the name of this ship?"

"Why?" He draws out the word.

I shrug, as if I don't care. "Reminds me of the HMS Hăimă, a ship I was aboard awhile back. Thought this might be the same."

"Bart," he says.

"Bart is the name of the ship?"

"No, my name—Bart Dewar. I'm on the ship because my da told me I was a coward."

A tiny bit of hope rears its head. *He's opening up to me, a good sign.* "Any reason in particular?"

He sets the bucket on the ground. "Some lads were manhandling my sister near the town square in Birr, where I'm from. They were bigger than me, had weapons too. I tried to save her but was knocked out sure quick. Fortunately, my da was nearby and saved her. This is my punishment. He said I had to 'nut up' before I could take over the farm."

"Sorry," I murmur.

His face turns ruddy, and he looks down at the knife. "We should get on with things. Naedder is waiting, and patience isn't his strong suit."

I don't have the strength to fight him, and besides, there's nowhere to go, especially imprisoned in chains. He takes the chamber pot and kicks it over so we have a flat surface. With the lack of food, I've barely used it.

Bart kneels, and I offer up my middle finger. "No disrespect to you," I mutter in my lowest tone.

"Naedder told me. Made me laugh. I'd've done the same." He nods in earnest as though there's a kinship between us.

I shrug. "What does it matter? I'm chum. The sharks won't care."

"You've got a point."

So much for kinship. "Before we begin, may I have one more cup of water? I have laudanum with me. It will help to numb the pain, but the taste is very bitter when taken alone."

61

"Fine by me."

I rifle through the knapsack, the bottle buried near the bottom. He gives me the water, and I chase the liquid from the dropper with one long swallow.

My stomach is going to hate me. It will cramp and expel whatever is in there, which at least isn't much. "More time would be helpful," I say, eyeing the blade. "The medicine takes a few minutes to take effect."

Everything begins to soften. The opiate tugs at my eyelids, and my heartbeat slackens as it surrenders to the potent sedative. Groggily I set my hand on the bucket. "Cutting off fingers is a messy prospect. The blood tends to spurt." With clumsy hands, I take one of the scarves in preparation of stanching the blood flow.

Bart shakes his head. "Though you'll probably lose every digit in the coming days, Naedder told me he wanted your right earlobe as punishment, for, you know." He points to my middle finger. "He can't really take a joke—gets offended right quick."

I want to beg him for mercy, but there's no point. Euphoria and the numbness that is laudanum has staked its claim. I sink into an anesthetized heap and lay my face against the bucket's bottom, rotted with waste.

"Might want to remove your cap," he says. "The blood will soak through, likely."

"My cap is a good thing," I say with a soft tongue. If Bart discovers my gender, I'm as good as dead. His hand tremors above me, the blade tossing the sunlight about. "Set the blade on my lobe," I whisper. "Then press hard, like you're slicing off a bit of cheese. Be swift."

"All right, then. Thanks for that."

My screams send the flies into a tizzy. The pain is rooted to the periphery of my awareness, but it's there, scathing and present. Bart stands over me looking terrified, my right earlobe dangling from the knife's tip. He throws the scarf at me. "Use that to stop the blood," he trembles. "Might help."

In seconds he's gone from the hold, and the laudanum's seductive fingers pull me into a sinking and painless sleep.

***

My consciousness is a rolling tide, same as the waves underneath. A violent winter storm starts late into the night. In bits and pieces, I'm aware of little things: hordes of flies; squares of gauze; rumbling thunder; Bart visiting the cell more than once. When he'd first returned, I thought he was claiming my other earlobe or my promised middle finger. Not so. It was water he'd brought, enough so that every time I awoke a fresh cup awaited me. Though I can't be sure of much, I do believe he came of his own volition.

The laudanum has worn off, and I'm in agony when I wake to Bart's hot breath against my cheek. "How did ya get your ear bandaged?" he asks.

Bleary-eyed, I sit up and touch the side of my head. "I keep some with me. Must have done it in the middle of the night."

"Been two days, actually. You're lucky Naedder is so sick or I would've been back for whatever he wanted next." He chews the inside of his cheek. "Sorry to say, but each digit taken will earn my da's approval and respect." From the way his face screws up, he knows how wrong and horrible the words sound. "Your ear looks infected. Pus oozin' out the edges. Not surprised. The blade has a bit of rust and was never sterilized."

My ear pulses with a beastly pain. Porphyry is what I need. Mistake number one: I'd wasted it on King Andronicus to heal the wound from the ice dragon's bite. Mistake number two: I hadn't restocked when I'd gone back to Cimmerian's Curio Emporium. The calendula in my bag will have to do. I soak a piece of my scarf with the liquid and dab blindly at my ear.

"Probably have to remove the bandage," he notes. "Your cap's in the way. Let me help."

Before I can stop him, the cap is off and a few unpinned curls tumble out in limp, greasy waves. "Please," I beg. "You can't tell them. They'll kill me right now."

"No, they won't," he says quietly. "Not yet anyway. We've been at sea for months…" His voice trails off, but the insinuation is there in his tone, in his pained expression. "Anyway if I wanted to give ya up, I would've by now."

Thunder rumbles as I stare at Bart. "You knew?"

He jabs at my cheek with a stubby finger. "You've been down here near to a week in sum. You're older than I, and even a few hairs poke about my chin after a day's time or two."

"Blast. I never even thought about facial hair." My shoulders sag from the weight of the reality. *I'm doomed.*

The hatch flies open. Penetrating light reveals a pair of heavy boots descending the rungs. I shove my hair under the cap as Bart jumps to his feet. He salutes a man of substantial girth and height, bedecked with shining medals across his coat. In his wake is the chief mate.

"Bloody wintry hell. What are you doing down here?" the decorated man demands of Bart. His baritone resonates in the small space. Hair and beard are wirier than a scrub brush, and though his skin is black, it carries an ashen tone beneath a sheen of sweat.

Bart keeps his pose, chin up, but a terror hides behind his honor. "Naedder told me to fetch a finger, Captain Seybourne." He flashes the knife as proof.

"You his toffer?" the captain asks, and the chief mate sniggers.

"Sir, no sir," Bart stutters.

Captain Seybourne removes a glove, swats at the flies. "Nutter, that one. Worse than most. I heard about the damned earlobe." He looks me up and down. "Scrawny bloke," he remarks. "Not much meat for the sharks, and yet they'll be plenty glad. How you climbed aboard my ship makes me question the diligence of my crew." His stare never wavers from mine, but the accusing words wipe the conceit from the chief mate's face. "No matter," he continues. "When we offer up a body, the gods grant us safe passage. You've done us a favor, and we thank you for it."

"Please, Captain," I grovel in my lowest tone. "I'm not looking

65

to ride for free. I can work as payment."

He staggers ever so slightly but grasps one of the iron bars to maintain his composure. "What are you suggesting?"

Judging by his tone, he's placating me—he has no desire to bargain. "Anything. I can clean. Wash dishes. Scrub the deck. Your crew can have a break while I take over."

The ship creaks and rocks beneath us, and a jag of lightning briefly alights the cell. A hand goes to the captain's gut, and the accompanying groan tells me he may lose its contents any moment now. From which end, I don't want to know.

"Bring him on deck," he wheezes and starts up the ladder. There's much heaving, then liquid spattering from his mouth. The chief mate jumps out of the way. "Make it fast," he says over his shoulder. "My chamber pot is calling."

I'm dragged up the wood ladder, the rungs dripping with the captain's sick. Still shackled hand and heel, I stumble onto the rain-soaked deck. After a week inside the infested cell, the fresh air is a glorious drug, and I breathe in deeply and savor it. They shove me down the length of the ship, my metal chains clanking mournfully. We stop before a long plank, an arrow to my death.

"Last words?" Captain Seybourne asks. He can barely speak let alone stand, and not because the ship is rocking back and forth in the turbulent waves.

The crew before me is three times larger than when I was first found. Toothless and dirty, skin scarred and scabbed, they make the men at Sold & Gilvers look like the upper crust.

66

"I beg you, Captain," I say, the sleet stinging my cheeks. "Spare my life, and I shall repay you one hundred-fold down the line."

The men share greedy smiles. They must relish listening to this part, to the pleading for one's life. Captain Seybourne answers with a wave of his hand, a go-ahead to Bart, who looks genuinely sorry as he shoves me onto the plank. Below, the sharks keep pace. There are no rails, and with the rough seas, it won't take much to lose my balance and fall overboard.

"Do you know Guernsey?" I shout out. Name-dropping can be a winning proposition, Henrietta used to tell me. A name can be a key to a previously locked door. "He's part of the Veneficum, the leader. He's my friend and can vouch for me. If you will spare my life, he'll give you gold, whatever you desire."

Staggering forward, using the ship's rail for support, the captain says, "Guernsey and I are well-acquainted."

"Thank goodness." I inch back toward the ship.

Captain Seybourne draws his sword and sets the sharpened tip to my heart. "The sorcerer is a sworn enemy, no friend of mine. I work for King Varius Andronicus and swear fealty only to him."

Wrong name, wrong key.

He waves the blade in careless circles. "Get moving or I'll spear you myself and cast—" More vomit goes over the side and into the water below.

"I'm a healer," I blurt, squatting and clinging to the plank, the ship banking in the waves. "You and your crew have dysentery or scurvy or both, and I can cure you." I've no clue what they've got or if I can help them in any way, but this is my last hope.

The captain's breathing is labored and shallow. "Push the lad over," he says to his crew. "Bloody freezing out here. I need to get back to my ch—" He collapses in a heap, and his men rush around him.

"Your captain is going to die," I state, perilously teetering as the sea roars below. Chained wrists and feet are ridiculously unhelpful when trying to maintain balance. "He might be the first but certainly not the last. Anyone can see the lot of you are sick. My meal was crawling with maggots."

A man with olive skin and long, shiny white braids steps forward, a grease-smeared apron at his waist. "I'm the ship's steward. Found rats in the grains. Now with the storm, the flame's runnin' dry. Can't use the stove or the ship might catch fire."

The captain is clearly the sickest, but a quick read of the crew's faces tells me many are drawn and peaked. Naedder is not even here to watch my gruesome demise, a sure sign he's dying.

"Raise your hand if you're experiencing cramps and are fevered?" I ask. With some hesitation, the men look to one another. More than half the hands go up. "Dysentery is extremely contagious. For those who don't yet have it, you will soon enough. Fetch my knapsack down in the hold. You'll see—it's filled with medicinal herbs. Give me a chance, and I can help you. All of you."

The chief mate leaps onto the plank, sure-footed. "Captain Seybourne gave you an order, boy. Be done with it or I'll push you over myself." He brandishes his sword, causes my heart to leap into my throat.

"The lad speaks the truth." It's Bart talking. "I saw his knapsack. The thing is filled with loads of medicine. He told me how to cut off his earlobe. And he took some kind of medicine to ease the pain."

"Laudanum," I proffer to the blade. Laudanum may not exist in Winterhaven, but I pray it sounds impressive.

The chief mate growls, "Your ear's got pus pissing out of it. If you're a healer, we've got no chance."

Some of the men nod in agreement. It's the sick ones who don't, who look at me with hopeful eyes.

I scream as a rogue wave pounds over me and sweeps me off my feet.

"Man overboard!" a crew member yells.

Not yet. Legs dangling in the air, I hug the plank with every bit of strength within me. There is screaming below, mixed with the wind and the waves. The crew rushes the rails, and I follow their line of sight to the white caps stained with the chief mate's blood.

"What's a few more days?" I beg. I do my best to not sound hysterical; I'm a failure in every way. "You can toss me overboard if there's no improvement. Your captain is dying, as are half of you."

The steward appears at the rail with my knapsack in hand. "Bart speaks the truth," he says. "Same for the lad. Went below to the hold. Not sure what all this stuff is, but there's a mess of medicine inside."

The captain snarls something to his men. Even through the crashing waves, I'm convinced he's ordered my death. I don't want to die like this. I'd rather go of my own volition and with my dignity intact.

My eyes see nothing now, only the red behind my lids. I release my hold—

on the plank, on the world—and let fate take its course, come what may.

CHAPTER FIVE

Fate comes in the form of Bart and the ship's steward. They have me by the wrist chains and under the arms. I'm thrust onto the deck and fall to my knees right where the captain lies.

"Get to helping us," Bart says in his most commanding tone. "By order of Captain Seybourne."

"Thank you, Captain," I say in a shivering whisper, and I stumble to my feet.

His eyes are rolling marbles. "Don't thank me," he groans. "Save me."

In my lowest, gruffest tone, I say to the depraved group before me, "Get Captain Seybourne to his quarters straight away. Those who are unwell, return to your beds. I'll tend to you once I finish with the captain." I turn to the steward. "Bring me to the galley."

Bart frees me of my shackles, my wrists hued in deep blues and purples. Certain my curls have been exposed, I feel around my nape and forehead. The icy water has hidden my identity by freezing the cap in place. Although these men need me, if they discover I'm decidedly not male, they might well refuse my help.

"Show me the largest pot you have," I say once we're in the

71

galley. "We'll need several to boil water."

"With what?" the steward says. "We've got no fire, remember? Besides, the wood and kindling are soaked through. Galley flooded when the storm started."

I unhook the lantern from the wall. "We'll have to take our chances."

"You don't get it. Flint and stone are not enough. The stove needs sustained fire so the bricks can warm all the way through and keep everything hot."

"You must trust me. Enough heat can burn wet wood and kindling. Now please, fill up your largest pots with water." Slowly I pull the fire from the lantern and entwine the flames.

Mouth dropped open, the steward stares. "Well, roll me in pig fat and call me the king," he mutters. "You're a healer *and* an Elementalist."

"Tell no one," I say, and he makes a cross over his heart.

As he loads the stove, the fire becomes an intense ball of sparking flame. Carefully I maneuver it between brick and wood until the kindling catches. There is ticking and popping from the metal above as it soaks the heat, and soon burning air roils out. "For now, I can keep the fire going. Worst case, if you need more dry wood, this ship is made of oak. A few missing chunks here and there won't be missed. Better to have a honeycombed ship rather than the pervasive sickness here, agreed?"

His deep brown eyes go wide, then a nod speaks of his approval.

72

From my knapsack, I take out every last vial of cardamom pods, fennel seeds, scurvygrass, and psyllium husk powder and dump them into the boiling water. The anethole-like scent suffuses the galley. Most of my herbs will be needed to get the crew back in working order. For those with mild symptoms, the medicine should work quick enough. As for the captain and a few others, it may take weeks before they mend. That and some luck. Hopefully it will set them on the path to recovery, and once we reach port, medics there can continue any additional treatment. Of course, if my experiment fails, everyone will perish, myself included. A ghost ship, adrift at sea. Not a comforting thought.

When the herbs have sufficiently steeped, Bart escorts me to the captain's quarters, my fingers warmed by the mug's steaming concoction. The cabin's air is cold and stale. Captain Seybourne lies between soiled sheets, his clothes waterlogged with sweat.

"We need warmth," I say to Bart. "Light a torch in the galley and bring it here in a flame brazier. Fire on a wooden ship is a dangerous prospect during a storm, but we have no choice." As he makes for his leave, I grab him by the arm and point to the overflowing chamber pot. "If you would, throw the contents overboard and bring the pot back clean. Your da will be proud of you for helping me save the crew. This won't be an easy task. Bravery comes in all forms."

"Right, I'm a lion," he says with affable sarcasm, but he does as I ask.

"Captain," I prompt. "You need to sit up a little."

73

The captain's eyes roll to white and back. "Can't move, can't lift my head. Feels worse than mal de mer."

"Yes, I've got something expressly for that. But right now, you must drink this tea. The herbs will kill the parasites in your gut. Once they do so and you can keep things down, I'll give you something to rid the nausea."

Grunting in pain, he pushes himself against the pillows. The tea is cool enough when I set the mug to his mouth, his lips lined with spittle and peeling from dehydration. He sips a little at a time. When the mug is empty, Bart returns. The room warms considerably thanks to the small fire.

"Help me get the captain out of these clothes," I say to Bart. "They'll need to be washed—everything will. All clothes and bed sheets aboard the ship. Everything must be sanitized. You'll need to designate an area close to the galley for boiling water but not close enough to re-infect anyone or anything."

By the time Captain Seybourne is stripped and washed, and fresh linens are laid out on his bed, more than an hour's time has passed. Two portholes are open, and lit patchouli helps to cleanse the air. I leave Bart to tend to his needs.

The scent of grilled fish and smoked mussels leads me back to the galley, and the steward looks pleased with his vat of soup when I walk through the swinging doors. I inform him of my plan for a quarantined area, and he shows me one of the cargo holds down the passageway, mostly empty and far enough from the galley to eliminate worry about contamination. He then instructs a

74

crew member to gather all linens and any sick deckhands into the spare space. Two men carry the pots of boiling medicine to the cargo hold and set them on a series of empty wooden crates.

The men crowd in, and the steward belts out, "Drop your bedding in the corner then line up along the wall and"—he leans toward me—"What's your name, lad?"

"Saunders," I mutter into my shoulder under the pretense of wiping sweat from my cheek.

"Saunders'll give you some medicine. Drink up, mates. Then strip yourselves and add your clothes to the bedding pile. If you don't have a clean uniform, make do with the blankets until we can get your clothes back to you." The steward points to the smallest bucket of water. "Wash your dropsy arses there. If you lot are up for eating, a hot meal will be served in an hour's time."

Most shake their heads. Food is the last thing they want.

Chin tucked, mustering my deepest voice, I say to the men, "Tomorrow you'll drink one cup of the medicine in the morning and another before bed. If you can keep anything down, sip water throughout the day."

One by one they take the medicine, and after serving nearly two dozen deckhands, I find myself in a roomful of naked men bathing themselves. There's nothing stimulating about it. The sickness has beckoned their ribs forward, and even the darkest men look pallid and drawn.

According to the Aeriscloque, it's three o'clock in the morning by the time every man is clothed and asleep. The steward, who I've learned conveniently answers to 'Stew' and rewards himself often with generous cups of mead, leaves me to find his bed and a dream. I'm about to rest my head to catch my own bit of sleep when Bart staggers in. "Naedder," he says. "He needs help straight away."

How could I have forgotten about that filth? Part of me wants to let him die. My earlobe, for one. But I say nothing as Bart leads me to the chief mate's quarters. Apparently Naedder had crawled in here once he'd heard of his shipmate's untimely demise.

Naedder is in bed shivering and sweating. The cabin is smaller than the captain's but reeks of the same sick. I've got a tin cup filled with the medicinal liquid in hand. "Sit up," I say coldly.

"Piss off, bint," he spits. "Don't need your help, little twat."

Bart looks at me wide-eyed. The same surprise hits me square in the chest, but I don't let it show, on my face or in my voice. "You knew all along?" I ask.

"Think I'm stupid?"

"No. Just surprised you didn't tell the others. That you didn't—
"

"Have you myself, ankles to ears?"

I don't nod. I'm not sure if that's what I was going to say or not.

"My mum was jumped by six blokes. Which got 'er me. I see what it did to 'er, all messed in the head, pissed on mead day and night. As a vow, I promised to never commit such savagery."

"You just cut people into little pieces instead?" I say.

My sarcasm begets a sickly laugh. "Every man has his limits.

Mine ends at fingers and toes. And the occasional earlobe here and there."

I want to vomit my disgust over his inked scalp. "If you don't drink this, you're going to die. You still might," I add bluntly. "This isn't a cure-all."

"I'm fine with dying. Shoulda never lived this long anyway. Got more than one life in me. Shed my skin, and I'm off to a new one."

Fevers bring about strange words. But I wonder what Naedder is, if any kind of magic lies within him.

Naedder looks at my bandaged ear, then over at Bart. "Never brought me the other earlobe, prissy little sard. Did your nutsacks never drop?"

Bart takes the cup from my hand and throws the liquid in Naedder's face. Then he storms off without saying a word.

"Go cry to mummy," Naedder yells after him, clutching his stomach in pain.

I follow in Bart's footsteps and return a short time later with another cup of the medicine. Naedder's eyes are closed, but he's still breathing, albeit in quick, shallow fits.

Strangely, a molted snakeskin lies near his feet. *Where did this come from?*

"Brought you more medicine," I say to Naedder. No answer other than the soft hiss of breath, so I set the cup down for him and leave. Whether he chooses to drink it or not doesn't concern me. I've done my part.

CHAPTER SIX

Naedder's body goes over the ship's rails two days later. No one says a prayer or a good word. Caps pressed to chests is all he gets. I have respect for the dead, but I also have respect for my own well-being. No chance is my cap leaving my head for anyone's funeral or it may result in my own.

One day after that, two ravens are sent to the nearest city of Kihanis for additional herbs. I don't have nearly enough to get us through to Taliin, our designated port, and the townsfolk will never let us dock with so much sickness aboard.

Days turn to weeks. I've become indispensable to Captain Seybourne and the crew. Judging by the popping uniform buttons, the loosening of belts, and the cheeks kissed with sun, the medicinal concoction is working.

Captain Seybourne is at his desk writing when I enter with his nightly medicine. "Good evening, Captain," I say. "Each day you're making marked improvement."

He nods to the mug in my hand. "The herbal remedy certainly has broken my hourly relationship with the chamber pot. At most we see one another twice a day now."

I offer a small smile. Since the moment we met, he's been

nothing but gruff. I'm not much into discussing bodily functions, but it's good to know he's on the mend and can make light of the situation.

"What will you do once you're in Taliin?" he asks in his baritone, his eyes remaining on the page.

I'm no longer being considered for shark chum. The relief is greater than I imagined it would be; my shoulders somehow feel lighter. "Libraries," I return, not wanting to give much away.

His quill continues to scratch along the parchment. "Libraries. Interesting. I've yet to find a stowaway who boarded my ship, bound for a new city for the sake of reading."

He's being droll, but I'm not sure what to make of his comment. "My birthright, my ancestry," I explain. "I'm not sure if I'll find answers in Taliin. I'm on a quest of sorts to find out who I am."

"Braving even the calm waters at the Sanctuary of Caelum tells me much. You were desperate to leave. Makes me wonder why you were at the Sanctuary in the first place. The territory is a highly secretive spot, and you made mention of Guernsey. Something tells me you're not who you say you are."

Now his eyes catch mine, and I don't like what he's intimating.

"Saunders." He says the name carefully. "A boy on a quest in search of his parents? I think not." He shakes open a scroll. My face stares back at me, my name written in script beneath. *REWARD* in bold letters along top and *DEAD OR ALIVE* below. "The resemblance is there in the eyes and the mouth," he remarks, "although your grey cap is throwing me."

79

The mug in my hand shakes so much the medicine trickles over the sides. I've gotten too comfortable, let down my guard on one occasion too many. "My good captain," I manage in my lowest voice. "She's a girl, some rogue twat—"

I can barely get the last word out, and he breaks into hard laughter. "The most wanted lady in all of Winterhaven is a stowaway aboard my ship. What are the odds, Sondrine Renfrew?"

My name is a punch to the gut. "How did you figure it out?"

"I was given this poster long ago, well aware of who you were. Then Stew mentioned you were an Elementalist. He meant no harm, do know. Too much mead makes for a careless tongue. The pieces added up right quick. None have seen you piss off the ship's side, and though they are small, your bee stings far surpass anyone else's around these parts."

"You've been biding your time," I say through gritted teeth, my arms folded over my not-so-ample chest. "You'll get me to Taliin and hand me over to the king for a lifetime's worth of gold."

He takes the mug, drinks the medicine down in one swallow. "Long ago I swore fealty to King Andronicus. He's my employer. This ship carries vital and expensive cargo—grains, raw metals, weapons, and textiles—to different ports throughout Winterhaven. The gold lining my pockets comes direct from his hand." He indicates a small cage filled with writhing snakes. "These vipers alone mean a month's wage. Their venom is used for arrow tips. So lethal is the venom that one drop can fell a grown man. This sort of poison is in high demand, what with the pending war."

The molted snakeskin comes to mind, and I wonder if a viper had escaped.

"Understood," I say, returning to the subject at hand. Namely my death. My head is as good as gone. The Mourning Garden will be my final resting place, after all. Frankly I'd prefer being shark chum, given the choice.

"We find port tomorrow," he continues. "When the anchor lowers and the ropes get tossed to the sea, I suggest you go with them. If you're seen leaving this ship, my death is fated, same as yours. I'll send a raven to ensure a bundle of blankets awaits beneath the docks. That's as much as I can do. If you survive the waters, of course. Not many sharks close to shore, but the sea has greedy hands to pull you away from this life and into the next."

"You—you're letting me go? You said you swore fealty to the king."

He pours powder over the ink then blows it away. Holding up the parchment, he says, "This is my sworn statement. You were a prisoner aboard my ship. You killed the guard and escaped into the shark-infested waters of the Dendrite Sea, never to be seen again."

"Why must you tell the king at all? When we reach port, I could leave the ship and none would be the wiser."

"I've thirty-seven crew members. Remember what I said about mead? Too many loose lips. I can't afford it if I'm to stay in business. There are rumors, and there are facts. Along with two witness signatures, this states my claim as fact. Come morning I will inform my crew of your unsavory misdeed. I can easily make

81

up the name of the man you murdered to ensure your escape. These men work hard, but their brawn got them their jobs, not their brains."

Slowly I nod. "Now I'm wanted by the king *and* I'm a murderer."

"Indeed. This information will go wide. Once people learn you've murdered a man, they'll want you dead for the reward and for the public good. Though you saved my life, it's imperative I never lay eyes on you again. This one time you've been pardoned, Miss Renfrew. There won't be a second."

***

We sail into Taliin before dawn, the water reflecting the sleeping sky. Lit lanterns from dozens of anchored ships glow and blink through the dark like heedful eyes watching over the mercurial sea.

Land is not far, but I can't take that for granted. Freezing water is a dangerous weapon, wielding death quickly and without remorse. The moment the ship lays anchor, I shimmy down the ropes and into the bitter swells. I gasp from the cold shock to my system, which repays me with a mouthful of fishy, salted water. Coughing and gagging, I begin my swim to shore.

Several layers of clothing cocoon me, most of them stolen from the laundry piles. The cold is unforgiving, and the extra shirts and trousers prove an unforeseen weight as I brave the icy waves. Long strands of seaweed claw at my boots and gloved hands, eager to drag me under.

Soon my arms are numb, mortared posts, so I roll onto my back and stare though frosted lashes at the fading stars as I will the waves to pull me along. Though I beg my legs to fight through the freezing water, each kick seems a losing prospect. Even the gulls above sound somber and pitying. Slowed heartbeats echo against my ears, and my crystal breath trips over chattering teeth like ghosts escaping into the ether.

My mind turns to Guernsey and to Shán. Though my anger has lessened over time, I need proof, something more than a rote proclamation stating who I am. That I never was Sondrine Renfrew. That I was and have always been Sondrine Agni, daughter of Queen Belisama Agni, the most vengeful woman in Winterhaven, whose sole purpose lies in destroying us all.

My abhorrent lack of control regarding Water is evident, not only from my time in the inlet but from my foray into Mount Serius. The fountain's waters had been meant to merely douse the queen, not to turn tsunamic, nearly drowning Shan and me in the process. But I'll sink soon if I don't try harder, so I concentrate intensely on the waves at my back. The tide surges all at once and pushes me toward shore. Tossed about, over and under, I'm delivered unkindly onto a pebbled beach. Not what I was aiming for, but I'm safe. On frozen hands and knees, I crawl under the docks, where the promised blankets await.

***

All my energy must have been spent getting me ashore, for I awaken to bright sunlight edging through the slatted, sheltering planks. Beneath me the earth rises and falls, an illusion the captain warned me about that feels all too real.

"You made it." Bart lumbers toward me through the sand. "Wasn't easy smuggling this knapsack off the ship, mind. If the captain knew, I'd be good as dead."

Last night I'd told Bart of Captain Seybourne's plan and sworn him to secrecy. My fingers are tacky with salt as I take the knapsack and pull him into a quick hug. "Everything would have been soaked through and ruined had you not done this for me, Bart. You took a great risk, and I appreciate the courage it took."

He flaps a hand. "I'm a lion, remember?" My gratitude pushes a smile into those paunchy cheeks. "You best change into some dry clothes," he notes. "Your lips are blue, and the sun doesn't shine long this time of year." His boots shovel sand back and forth. "Most wouldn't've lasted more than a minute in the Dendrite Sea before succumbing to the cold. To be honest, I didn't expect to find you here."

My ability to withstand extreme temperatures had been confirmed in the fiery depths of Mount Serius, but the Dendrite Sea was a looming question, and I seem to have found an answer. Had I stayed in the icy waters much longer, it's anyone's guess if I would have survived or not.

Bart turns his back to give me some privacy. I was hoping he might go to the docks above, but I can't worry about decorum at this point—that was tossed to the wayside ages ago. I peel away the layers of damp clothing and change into my trousers, a new blouse, and my evergreen cloak. The newfound warmth sends a welcome shiver through my body. Bart offers a pair of his boots until mine dry out, and though they're too big in the toe and much too wide, a few scarves stuffed into each one makes them workable.

Now we're two blokes strolling the open market. And what a sight to behold it is. Taliin does not disappoint with its grandiose displays of fresh-netted fish, of eels and crab and giant sea snails. Adjacent stalls hold sacks of wheat and barley, sugar and rye, overflowing and stacked. Goats and pigs and bleating sheep are led through the crowds, their heady scents a threat to the simmering mint and garlic that coat the wintry air.

Colorful toy flags throw punches into a perfect sky, and musicians with their stringed instruments vie for attention from passersby, the wind carrying the vibrant songs up past the sun and away. This is only the market itself. The town is yonder, pegged into the hills.

Captain Seybourne had furnished a pouch of gold coin as payment for my services. I offer some to Bart for risking his life by helping me, but he declines, so I treat us both to liberal skewers of beef with fire-burnt tomatoes and juicy, sweet onions. Under a generous oak, we settle in and watch the market undulate around us while we savor every bite.

"Will you stowaway on another ship?" Bart asks between mouthfuls.

"My days of hiding on ships are all but used up for the moment.

My adventure will continue on solid ground, thank you very much."

He eyes me. "What's your story? Shouldn't you be married about now, having kids and whatnot? Why are you pretending to be a boy? And what is your real name anyway? Between the sick on the ship and the daily chores, I never got the chance to ask all my questions."

The oak's trunk at my back, I peer up through the thick, rabid branches. "I'm afraid I can't give you answers other than I'm looking to find more about my birthright."

Bart stops mid-bite. "What's the big secret? Ya famous or something?"

I nearly choke on a sweet onion. "Me? Famous? Not even close. Birthright was the wrong term. I'm just an orphan who wants to find out who her mum and dad were." Bart looks more interested in his food than my story; I hope I've thwarted his curiosity. To be certain, I add, "By the way, women don't need to get married if they don't want to. It's not some kind of unwritten law."

Bart tugs a sleeve across his mouth. "Where I come from, it is. Girls don't make it much past fifteen years before they're sportin' bellies big as balloons."

"There's a whole world out there for me to see. I've no desire to be tied down by some ornery man and half a dozen wanting mouths."

"No boy you fancy? Or maybe it's quim you like?" He shrugs. "Makes no difference to me."

Shán comes to mind. He was leaving to gather his fleet when last we spoke. He could be here in port for all I know. I look out to the sea of heads, as if the midnight sheen might stand out amongst the others.

"No one," I say solemnly, using the wood skewer to pick tomato seeds from my teeth.

Bart belches. "Sorry." He covers his mouth.

"You wouldn't apologize if you were here with your shipmates. I'm not a girl, remember?"

"Sorry," he says again, and I shake my head in exasperation.

A juggler strides past, gives us a personal show. We clap, and I toss him a coin. "Bart," I ask when the juggler moves on. "What sort of magical capabilities do you have?"

"Me?" He laughs. "Most who wield true magic are of sovereign blood. 'Course, some are heathens who choose to use it for the Dark. A lesser sort of magic, such as making coin disappear and the like, is common amongst the carnival folk, but I possess no such things."

My conversation with Lark returns, how she'd said everyone in Winterhaven could wield magic. Growing up in Isceald Castle surrounded by royalty, I suppose she thought it was so. Why Snap can perform magic is anyone's guess. The more glaring and unfortunate part of the conversation means this is yet another checked box regarding who I truly am. "Yes," I lie. "I thought perhaps you were of honorable descent."

Bart sits up a little straighter. "Good to know I give off such a

87

stately air. My village of Birr is mostly farms and peasants." He eyes me. "Been wondering about you, though. You're an Elementalist. That sort of magic is true as it gets. Perhaps your parents were of royal blood."

"Heathens more likely." When I check the Aeriscloque, Bart strains to see, so I tuck the timepiece back inside my collar before he gets the chance. "Isn't it time you head back to the ship? If I'm going to find a place for the night, I best be on my way."

"Thought I'd stay in town with you. I've been with those blokes for months now. Got a bit over two days here. If you don't mind the company, 'course."

The reward poster and Captain Seybourne's proclamation swim up before me. "I'm a wanted woman, even if I am in disguise. Should someone see you in my company and figure out who I am, you're a dead man."

Bart waves off my concern. "Unlikely. If someone discovers you, I'll play the witless card. With your disguise, I don't think you'll need to worry much. It's a chance I'm willing to take."

He's sweet, much like dear Lark. The thought of the little girl brings a sting to my heart. I wonder how she and Snap are faring back at the Sanctuary. How I hope she's not worrying too much about my whereabouts.

"Why not, Bart?" I say, standing and stretching my arms. "Taliin holds promise, I think. Perhaps for us both."

***

After three failed attempts to find a room, I say to the fourth

88

innkeeper, "Why are there no vacancies? Are things always so busy in Taliin this time of year?"

Bart sets a hand to his nose and speaks from the side of his mouth. "You stink of raw fish and seaweed. A wash might be of use in helping to secure a chamber."

I do smell like Billingsgate, a seafood market along the River Thames back in London. Until I can get a room, I'm destined to reek like shellfish stew.

The spindly man holds up a piece of worn parchment. A macabre picture shows women with three eyes and men with horned heads. Flames shoot from a child's mouth, and a bevy of jars hold faces inside. *ICHOR SAMHAIN* is written in fancy lettering up top.

"Word spread faster than witchfire the carnival was coming to town, and my inn's been full ever since. These are depressed times with war on the verge. People will cling to anything for a bit of levity, even something as macabre as this. Every town north and south of here is booked as well."

Bart swipes the piece of parchment from the innkeeper. "They only pass through every five years or so, when blood veils the moon. We can't miss it."

"I need a library, not a contortionist," I say crossly. "Does a library even exist in these parts? If not, I'm happy to go elsewhere."

"She's an orphan looking for documents concerning her parents," Bart adds apologetically.

"The Great Tower of Annals is what you need," the innkeeper states. "We boast one of the largest in these parts. All public record is kept there."

The news perks me up. "Good to hear. But it means I must stay in Taliin, and there's no place to sleep."

So crowded is the town, there's nowhere to sit and formulate a plan, either, so we head for the outskirts, where we happen upon a tavern named the Barmy Goat. Not what one might expect from a pub, the place feels homey with its divans, round settees, and plush rugs softening the floor boards. Oil-burning chandeliers blaze above, the walls smoldering in tawny shadow.

The place is busy enough, but a divan opens up right near the hearth, and we happily settle onto the plush cushions. I order a mug of blackthorn brew, and though Bart protests, I tell the barmaid to give him a ginger dandy. The innkeeper gave us a map of the town. As I begin to study it, two young girls about my age sidle over dressed in corseted gowns. One girl has a river of silver down her back. The other is leaner, taller, her topaz eyes a contrast to her crop of obsidian and gold.

"Good evening, gents," says the latter. "I'm Adina, and this here is Leeyla. Looking for some company tonight? We're feeling quite lonely."

I look at the girls and then to the others scattered throughout. Some sit on men's laps, others stand along the staircase on display. The seductive smell of winterspice hits me over the head with the obvious. "Move along," I scowl.

Doe-eyed, Bart pipes up, "S'all right. I'm in a companionable sort of mood. We need a place to stay. You local? Got any suggestions?"

Adina takes this as invitation and plops into his lap. Leeyla edges herself between Bart and me. Given the sour look on her face, I'm certain it's because of my briny stench and not my snappish attitude.

Adina fondles Bart's shaggy strands. "Young and eager, just what I like." She giggles and inches a finger across his chest.

"Get lost," I mutter.

"What're you being so rude for?" Bart chides. "She's just looking to chat."

"With your private bits…and your purse," I add.

Bart ignores me. "Where are you from?"

More giggling from Adina, and I truly want to ask her what's so bloody funny. I refrain.

Adina slips her fingers between the buttons of his shirt. "From Birr originally—"

"Same here! Small world."

"You don't say?" she says with a feigned look of excitement. Bart appears elated by their common birthplace, and Adina takes advantage. "Taliin is sold out because of the Ichor Samhain. Leeyla and me, we've got a room here. We can share if you like."

Leeyla twists silver strands around her fingers.

"How much for the night?" he asks eagerly.

"They charge by the hour," I say, my exasperation unbidden.

91

"Oh." By the way Bart draws out the word, he finally understands. "Don't suppose we could use your room, nothing more? We could pay you."

Adina fiddles with a curious pendant around her neck, a bronze hammered skull with eyes of jade. Her painted nails click against the pendant. "We each charge ten florins per hour. For say six hours, that's sixty florins twice over. We're in a generous mood. We'll cut you and your friend a deal and give you the room for one hundred flat."

If my eyes could roll any farther, they would be out the front door.

"You're asking a king's sum," Bart exclaims, swallowing hard.

She nuzzles his neck. "Why don't we go upstairs for a little while. Test the waters. You're a virgin, I bet. I could teach you some things."

Bart's face is a rising tide of red. "Don't have much to spend. Can only afford half the hour at those rates."

Adina takes this as confirmation and pulls Bart from the divan.

I slap her hand from his. "Absolutely not."

"You're not my mother," he retorts.

Leeyla stares at me in my trousers and cap. Bart just blew my cover without realizing. Adina giggles obliviously, but Leeyla looks as if she's making a mental note. The barmaid sets down our drinks, and I pay her, glad for the interruption.

Bart leans in close so Adina can't hear. "My da will be pleased. When I tell him of my tales, including bedding a woman, he'll be proud of me."

"Bart, no." I shake my head downheartedly. "Don't you want to wait, to be with someone you love?"

"That's *girl* talk," he says with a wink and a needling laugh.

Adina continues to stand there and smile. "No woman wants to be bedded by a lame lover," she assures him. "By the time you leave my room, you'll be a man of many talents. By the time you bed your true love, she'll stay with you forever."

"By the time you leave, you'll be broke," I spit. Bart looks unfazed, too caught up in Adina's charms. "Fine, go on. She'll make you plenty happy until your purse is empty. Then she'll be on to the next. My guess is Adina works on the half hour. She'll use twenty-seven of those minutes to stroke your ego, two minutes to stroke your private bits, and one minute to convince you of another half hour."

My tongue has become plenty lewd since falling into Winterhaven. Listening to the men speak on the dim, cobbled corners of London gave me plenty of ideas as to the goings-on in the local brothels. But never would I have spoken of such things aloud. Social suicide at best.

Bart doesn't listen. At least not to me, and not with his ears. I watch as Adina coaxes him upstairs. "Wait for me," Bart says over his shoulder.

Knowing she stands no chance with me, Leeyla saunters away and onto her next victim. I take the blackthorn brew and drink away my disgust. The alcohol burns my throat, same as always.

93

My attention returns to the map. We still need a place to stay, and Bart is right—I smell like a heathen, which will win us no favors should we find a vacancy. "Place to wash up?" I cough to the passing barmaid, and she points me out back.

Night has fallen over Taliin, a steely sky bright with stars. The alleyways are reflective of those in London, the smell of sewage elbowing its way along the narrow passage. A large barrel of rainwater sits in the gutter, and I take out the lavender soap and scrub the sea's remnants from my face and hands.

Bawdy sounds clatter down from the overhead windows. Screams of delight, recurring gasps of validation, and desperate pleas to the gods above. *Who knew brothels inspired religion?* I snicker at my own joke.

Wood wheels scrape over cobblestone. A man stumbles past pushing a hand-held cart with stinking laundry piled so high it's a wonder he didn't knock me over.

"You for sale?" he asks. "I like me some pretty boys." His tongue is soft, and the glass in his eyes reflects one drink too many.

"Bugger off," I snarl, wiping my face with my sleeve.

He shrugs, parks the cart, and staggers through the brothel's back door. I'm surprised he left the cart unattended, because thieves steal everything, even dirty laundry. Then again, alcohol works wonders on common sense.

The ground jolts once, so sudden and sharp the rainwater sloshes in the barrel. Fear awakens inside of me. I look up and down the alleyway for something worse to happen. The rats continue their scavenging; the obscenities above are still forthcoming. With a relieved smile, I shake away the paranoia and return to my washing.

A tap on my shoulder, and I sigh with exasperation. "I said bug—" My cap is swiped from my head, and before I know what's happening, my own likeness is staring back at me: the *REWARD* poster, caught in Leeyla's hand.

"Knew something was up with you," she says. "And not the maypole in your pants. Or lack thereof."

I study her, try to stay calm. "A trollop *and* a jokester. Your parents must be so proud."

"My parents are dead. And I need money fast." She sets a hand to her stomach. "No one knows yet. A second mouth to feed costs money I don't have. That's where you come in."

The soap goes into the knapsack, and I pull the straps tight. "Let me guess. You're blackmailing me. Pay up or you'll go to the king."

Her eyes shine against the silver strands. "Smart one you are, Sondrine Renfrew."

"And how do I know you won't go to the king anyway to turn me in and procure a second payment?"

"I've no desire to meet the king. Ever. Cross my heart."

"You need a heart to cross." I believe Leeyla as far as I can throw her, but I have no choice except to buy her off. "I can give you enough gold to get by for a fortnight. Stretch things to a month, if you're frugal."

"Not enough," she threatens. "You'll need to match the king's reward. Fifty-thousand dinari. Or near enough to it. I'll give you two days or I'll go straight to the king."

"Two days? I only just arrived in Taliin. Regardless, the amount he's offering—whatever fifty-thousand dinari amounts to—I'm certain I can't raise that sort of money, not even in a month's time."

She shrugs with indifference. "Guess I'll be rich. And you'll be...dead." Tucking the poster under her arm, she strolls to the back entrance of the brothel. "You know where to find me. Two days."

Leeyla disappears inside, and I curse Bart under my breath along with my own bad luck. "Of all the places in Taliin, we happen upon the one brothel with the thieving harlot—"

A line of fire tears open the evening sky. A second jolt rocks my feet, then a third and a fourth, and the barrel crashes against the cobblestone, sending water in every direction. High-pitched screeching from above squeezes my soul dry, and the rooftops go up in flame.

"Fire!" someone yells from the window above.

No. Infernal.

I race back into the tavern. Chandeliers swing perilously, a storm of burning oil raining down. There's screaming and panic, including my own. I climb up the staircase and clutch the railing as the earth rocks beneath me. Fire and smoke plunge through the thatched roof and consume the brothel as half-naked women and men push past.

"Bart!" I scream blindly, rushing between rooms. My weakened gait is a disservice, and my fear only worsens things. Rogue flames eat away at the wood beams, the smoke so thick it coats my tongue and slides down my throat. "Bart, where are you?"

"In here!" Bart's cry comes from the last chamber at the end of the hallway. Beneath the bed, he chokes for remaining air.

"Stay there," I shout, and I run back to the stairway landing to assess the easiest way out. Through the chaos and smolder below, a momentary flash of Leeyla's silver hair. Her panicked eyes connect with mine moments before a giant chandelier crashes to the ground and takes her with it. From the twisted angle of her body, I know she's dead.

Terror propels me back to Bart's room, to the open window adjacent the bed. People pour through the alleyway screaming for their lives. Everything in every direction is on fire. I can make it out of here, but Bart won't survive.

"We'll have to jump," I say. With a flick of my wrist, I momentarily smite smoke and flame from the room, but the hallway is an inferno. I yank Bart to his feet and push him toward the windowsill.

"Are you mad?" he bellows through the din. His hands stopper against the wood frame. "We'll break every bone in our bodies."

"Do you prefer broken bones to charred ones? Aim for that." I point to the cart below, piled high with dirty laundry. Bart climbs

97

onto the sill, and when he hesitates, I shove him out and quickly follow, jumping and crossing my fingers.

The cart collapses beneath our weight. I'm bruised, Bart is dazed, but the laundry has cushioned our fall. People trample over us, flee every which way, their faces marred with terror. Smoke whirls so dense it hides the Infernal above, but their piercing cries signal how close they are.

Bart coughs madly as I tug him down one cobbled street after another. A stone dwelling offers a staircase, a means of escape and hope. We climb the steps, all the way to the top, perhaps six stories or more. Panting and out of breath, we stop on the landing and look off in the distance. Three Infernal soar through the night vomiting fire and death in every direction. My heart is wrung out by the sight, by the sheer size of their charred, skeletal bodies. By their webbed wings fanning a firestorm across the city.

Ione was right. Their predecessors pale in comparison to these Infernal.

The earlier sky was cloudless with no rain in sight. How I wish I could make it rain to kill the Infernal and temper the fires. Thundershowers are an oddity in Winterhaven and Queen Belisama would know I was here, but doing so would save countless lives.

Fear and disbelief consume me as I stare out at Taliin, alight in murdering flame. *What am I thinking? The queen already knows.*

***

When the sun rises, so do we. Aching and stiff from the

cramped utility closet, Bart and I step onto the landing to stretch our legs. For hours we'd sat huddled, listening to the Infernal, wondering if we'd be burned alive. Stone repels fire better than wood, and by the look of the timbered shops beaten into submissive heaps, the stone structure surely saved us.

A blood-red sun shines down, the chilled air pregnant with smoke and ash. The Infernal made their mark, but they appear to be gone for the moment. We scrub layers of soot from our faces with water out of an alleyway barrel then begin our trek back through town.

A stink rises from the rubble, rancid yet different from that of the Infernal. "Bart," I gasp when we turn a corner. Charred bodies litter the road—people trying to escape the Infernal, caught in their flaming wakes.

"Don't look," he says. "Keep walking."

The first standing inn has a vacancy. Speaking in a whisper, clearly shaken by the events of last night, the innkeeper states that most who came for the Ichor Samhain have left town. Or are dead.

After we secure two rooms, I say to Bart, "Seems prudent to wait things out, but sitting here all day is pointless. Do you want to come with me? I'm going to the Great Tower of Annals to look through their records. Hopefully it didn't burn down and is open for business."

"Should check on my shipmates. With those Infernal, I'm wondering if the ship caught fire. I'll see you back here at sundown."

The mood of Taliin is somber and quiet. Townsfolk remove the dead; panhandlers line the street with their empty coffers. I'm paranoid any one of them could be a spy. Someone told the queen I was here; everyone is a suspect. I look for Eirene's golden trail of dust but see nothing of the sort.

Off in the distance, an impressive tower of sandstone points to the sky. The shape reminds me of a many-tiered wedding cake, with its wide base and gradual tapered stories. And yet according to the map, I've reached my destination. A smallish structure built of brick and mortar stands before me. The Great Tower of Annals is an exaggeration of monumental proportion. Disheartening, for it can't hold many records given the size.

An ill-placed window in the middle of the door slides open when I knock. A pair of spectacled eyes peer up at me.

"Good day," I say. "Are you open for business?"

"Depends what your business is." The tone is low and raspy. "Solicitors of any sort are unwelcome."

"I'm an orphan trying to find my parents. I thought there might be some information here about who they were."

He hesitates. "Today is not the best day. What did you say your name was?"

"I didn't."

"Your parents' names?"

Under no circumstance am I disclosing such information. "Kind sir," I say with a forced smile. "I'm unsure of anything having to do with my heritage, which is the sole reason I'm here."

"Are they from Taliin?"

"How am I supposed to know?" I say with growing frustration.

The window slides shut. One minute ticks past, then five, then a quarter of an hour. I stamp my feet from the cold, wishing I'd curbed my frustration. *'You catch more flies with honey than with vinegar.'* Henrietta had always proffered this advice but never exercised it herself. She was far more sour than sweet.

I can't afford to make more enemies, so I lower my hand to knock again and apologize. As if the man had just read my very mind, the door creaks open, wide enough for a chicken bone of a finger to poke out and signal me inside.

***

Timeworn parchment and the coppery scent of fresh ink settle around me, the darkness broken by a lone lantern propped against the wall. The man's bald head barely breaches the desktop before him, and his nose looks victim to one too many brawls.

Drawers and cabinets of every size climb the walls, floor to low ceiling. While there's room enough to turn around, were I to sneeze, we might be in serious danger. I suppose the good news is I'll find what I need or not quite quickly.

The air is warm, so I place the cloak inside my knapsack. My cap remains. A laughable disguise, but it's all I've got. The man ignores me, and I shrug from the uncomfortable silence. "Shall I start in the corner and go from there?"

"This is my office," he scolds with a voiceful of gravel, as if I should have known. "You must go through the door then take the lift from there." He motions somewhere behind me with an aggravated wave of his stumpy hand.

There is no door other than the one I just walked through. *This is Winterhaven. A door could be anything.* I open a few cabinets, tap others in a pattern, pull on a few books.

"The door," he says with annoyed emphasis and points near my feet.

My first thought is the floor; a trapdoor makes sense. A brass knob attached to a tiny green door along the baseboard ensnares the lantern's flame and calls attention to it.

"You must be joking," I say. "Not even a field mouse could squirm through that thing."

Lantern in hand, he pushes past and bends over, opening the door and pushing up on the tiny frame until it expands to his height. "Be quick about it. I don't have all day."

Though nothing should surprise by now, these moments still astonish me. I duck through, and he follows, the door returning to its regular size when he lets go.

We're standing in a booth of cushioned walls: the lift he spoke of. "Are we going below ground?" I ask.

No answer, only a gesture to one of two standing seats across from another, one at his level, one at mine. With much trepidation, I follow his lead and back myself in, holding onto the extended arms. A flip of a switch and we're hurtling sideways so fast my screams bring a smirk to the man's hoary face. By the time we come full stop, my knuckles are bone-white, and my stomach gives thanks for the lack of food. I stumble out and take deep breaths to calm myself and gather my bearings.

"Historical records are from here up," he says. "Birth certificates included."

Tiered, open stories soar in circles so high my chin tilts to the ceiling. Small windows circumvent the uppermost level, and the domed, glass ceiling accommodates a blue sky striated by black smoke. Below us, countless levels stretch into darkness.

"How in the world will I find records for my date of birth? There must be thousands of files."

The man shrugs a thick shoulder. "None of my concern." He indicates a bell on a small table. "Ring this once you've finished, and I shall retrieve you."

Retrieve? Do I look like a dog awaiting its supper? Before I can protest, he's back in the lift and out of sight. How do I know he won't forget about me and lock up for the night? Or longer? Bart knows I'm here. Finding me is another story.

There are books and ledgers, catalogues and scrolls, even tablets made from wax. The smell of papyrus is delectable, and if I lived in Taliin, I'd be here every day getting lost in the beauty of the written word. My fingers dance across the weathered spines as I walk along the floorboards. A book from the 9th century is clothbound in black. It creaks when I open the cover, and dust wisps out from the pages. *Death certificates.* I shudder as I push the book back into place.

The leather spine of another, tooled and gelded, reads *Weather Almanac of Taliin*. The book is huge, not easy to hold. Curious, I open to a random page. A cold sun along with a nest of snowflakes bursts forth on April 18, 1129. Dried leaves swirl out on October 31, 1281, the chilly wind smelling of cinnamon and orange spice. Toward the back, The Great Storm on December 8, 1594. Before I can think to close the almanac, raging water pours out in droves.

"Stop!" I cry out. The muddy riverbed whirls out madly, drenching me and flooding the library floor. So strong are the gusts, I can barely hold onto the book let alone close it. Desperate to dam the waters, I throw the book on the ground and drop onto the cover. The water fights back, too strong for my paltry muscles.

Before I can yell for help, a voice says, "Stand back."

Startled, I look up to see an incorporeal figure before me—a young girl about Bart's age, outfitted in fur and armor. A metal band crowns her short, wavy tresses, and there's a slight depression over her heart fanned in scarlet. I scramble to my feet as she impales the flopping book with a metal pike. Then, with impressive strength, she manages to get the book closed for good. She shakes the pike loose and shoves the book back into the shelf. "The almanac hasn't been opened in over fifty years. Unlucky for you—it's in the wrong spot. Should be on the fourth tier with the other almanacs. Regardless, the same thing happens every time. Once some nobleman paged through to the Catastrophic Cyclone on March 21, 1413. Took weeks to clean up and restore order. Gœbel was furious. This might be worse. Took you a long while to get the book closed."

She says this in earnest, but the shame of being seen as weak and helpless gets the better of me, especially by such a strong young girl. "Where I come from, books spark imagination, not an outright battle," I snap. The girl raises an eyebrow but says nothing. I relent, set aside my wounded pride. "Ghosts don't exist, either, although I appreciate the help. I only wish you'd come sooner."

She takes my cap lying victim on the floor, squeezes out the water, and hands it off. "Specter, if you please. People are frightened of me, so I try to approach them in the quietest way possible. Long ago, a gentleman's heart stopped when I merely said hello. Died right on the twelfth tier: land conveyances." She shrugs. "I'm Illya, Virago Warrior. What brings you to the Great Tower of Annals? I've been here three hundred and twelve years. I might be able to help."

Virago Warrior? Though tempted to ask, I stick to the task at hand. "Birth certificates. For a friend of mine. From 1857."

I squat to clean up remnants of the storm. There are no windows at this level, no lantern flames to warm the space, so with my own breath, I blow across the standing water. Although dismal with Air, I manage a few small wind eddies that bounce off the bookshelves and the banisters until the boards dry from soaking wet to damp. For good measure, I bend a few rents of sunlight onto the floor to aid in the process.

"You're an Elementalist," Illya says with an impressed nod.

105

She points above. "1857 is recent. Those birth certificates are near the top, forty-seventh and forty-eighth tier. If he—or she—was born in Taliin, the records ought to be there. If not, it's anyone's guess. Some of the archives from other cities are here in duplicate, many are not."

My stomach drops a little. There must be hundreds of cities across Winterhaven, each with their respective hall of records. Visiting them could take years, time I don't have. "I'm unsure of her birthplace. I'd hoped there would be one general place that held all birth certificates for Winterhaven."

"What is her name? I can help you look."

In no way can I risk telling my real name. "Another reason I came here was to research someone," I deflect. "Do you know if the tower holds any books about Queen Belisama Agni?"

Illya spins the pike thoughtfully. "Funny you mention her. Months ago, rumors abounded about how the queen perished in Mount Serius. Yet last night I saw Infernal through the windows above. Why Taliin was attacked of all places makes me wonder. Have you heard anything?"

When I say I've heard nothing, which in theory is truth, because I only saw things—horrible things—she tells me biographies are two tiers down.

In my flood-addled boots, I follow the winding staircase and take as many books as I can carry then settle onto one of the chaise-lounges. Numerous stories touch on her early life, when she lived in Gaulle with her sister Gilleanne and her mother Áine, then-ruler of Winterhaven. When the land was called Summerhaven, a vista of slavery and madness and death. More recent stories speak of her rise to power before King Andronicus defeated her and imprisoned her in the snowflake obsidian.

Illya stays close, practices moves with her pike as the shadows drift from one side of the tower to the other. "Nothing mentions her romantic life," I say after skimming the ninth or tenth book. "Was she married? If so, to whom? Did she have any children? Where did they live?"

Illya walks over, the scarlet indentation looking on too close for comfort. "I know very little concerning the queen. She was born five hundred years ago, before even I. When Gœbel claimed she died in recent months, I knew it could not be true, for she is Immortal. The Infernal in Taliin are proof enough."

I'm about to tell her the queen is, in fact, not Immortal, but I stop myself. My firsthand knowledge of this will rouse suspicion. "The book here says she was born in Gaulle. Have you heard of it?"

Illya stabs at an invisible opponent. "Though I can't be certain, I believe Gaulle is near Mount Serius. Quite far from here. Maps are seven tiers down."

New shadows rise over the walls. The tower has taken on a warm glow, with candles lit throughout. When Illya did this I can't be sure; perhaps self-lighting candles are a magic all their own. I look up to the glass ceiling, where the sky has sunken into folds of indigo. "I'll have to come back tomorrow. Fatigue is stinging my eyes, and the low light will only make things worse."

"Might I make a suggestion? Why don't you use your Sablier to find the needed answers?" She points to my neck.

The Aeriscloque must have dropped out of my collar when combatting the storm. "This is a timepiece of sorts. Pray, what is a Sablier?"

Illya leans against the railing. "A device, clock-like. They come in all shapes and sizes and are used to visit the past or future, whichever you choose."

Time travel. I marvel at the thought.

Illya's head tilts to one side. "Perhaps more could be found concerning the queen if you had some sort of date."

The prospect of time traveling to my date of birth or thereabouts is an excitement reflective of my heart, now stepped up a few beats. "Where can I find a Sablier?"

"They are rare. More so than the existing Hereats, which are few."

I wince, for I added to that figure. When Aspara's shop went up in flames, so too did the Hereat.

She *tsks.* "Sabliers are forbidden in the commoner's hands; I wondered how you came to have one. Barring some sort of private collection, you might find one amongst the Underground."

"Which is where?"

"Not where. Who. Nefarious folk. Cons, performers of dark magic, even murderers." She inadvertently touches the indentation on her chest, and the sight chills me. "Forgive me, I shouldn't have mentioned the Sablier. Best to stick to books. Much easier.

Certainly more lawful."

I wish Illya a good night and ring the bell to leave. The moment I set the bell down, the door opens with Gœbel standing there, seemingly impossible given the twists and turns of the tunnel. By candlelight he looks far more sinister than before, and I'm thankful when he returns me in one piece through the front door and onto the moonlit street.

***

One would think the events of last night would keep people shuttered away in fear, but the Barmy Goat is three deep at the bar, and the singed settees and divans are such that if one empties, a brawl will break out for the coveted spot. A fiddler's upbeat tune contributes to the charged atmosphere, and the drifting pipe smoke offers an air of mystery to the flock of corseted women displayed along the banister. Perhaps people find solace in each other under such dire circumstances. *'Misery loves company,'* Henrietta used to say whenever she looked on at the luckless pickpockets huddling for warmth on the street corners. I suppose there's some truth to it, even if the aforementioned company is bought and paid for.

Adina flirts with a young lad who looks eager to be swindled. Bart is slumped on one of the sought-after divans, sulking into a pewter mug. Now I understand why he came back here. I shoulder through the crowd and flop down next to him.

"The innkeeper told me where to find you. A wonder this place is still standing and doing business, as though last night never happened." The thatched roof has been repaired remarkably fast, but the fire's remnants stamp the floors and ceiling with its smoky footprint. No response from Bart, so I carry on. "Good day at the ship? Is it still afloat and in one piece?"

Bart looks sidelong at Adina. The barmaid comes by, trades his empty mug for a full one, filled not with a ginger dandy but instead blackthorn brew. I order one as well.

"Seems Adina is inconsolable, grieving the loss of her good friend Leeyla," I say. The Infernal had inadvertently freed me from the threat of blackmail. But freedom's price was Leeyla's death, along with her unborn child. None of it makes me feel good. Bart doesn't bat an eye at my sarcasm, so I say pointedly, "You can't get depressed over someone who only wanted you for your money."

"Should've stayed on the ship," he mutters into his mug. "You're doing me no favors, Sondrine Renfrew."

I stare at Bart, my name a lethal blow. He ignores me, lobs his gaze between Adina and his blackthorn brew. The barmaid breaks up the moment by handing off my drink. Calmly I pay her, and when Bart and I are alone again, I say, "Adina told you, didn't she? You know of the plan, then, of Leeyla blackmailing me?"

"Before the fire broke out last night, Leeyla came up to our room, interrupted us. She and Adina spoke briefly. She didn't stay long."

The puzzle pieces ease together. *Leeyla wasn't pregnant. This was a joint con.*

Bart goes on, "Since Leeyla is dead, Adina offered to cut me in."

110

My finger traces the mug's edge. "Really? You're a team now?"

"Why are you wanted by the king?" he asks in a low voice.

I could make a run for it. But in seconds, the entire brothel would know my name and attempt to hunt me down like a wayward sheep, courtesy of Adina's greedy mouth. Bart looks undecided as to what he might do or say, so I try to sway him to my side. "There are fires in the west. A great war is coming. Queen Belisama Agni wants to rule Winterhaven once more, and she will destroy the land by burning it down until it is so, unless I can defeat her."

Bart's arms cross in defiance. "Doesn't answer my question."

A few gulps of blackthorn brew offer some courage. As usual, the alcohol burns my throat, makes me cough and my eyes tear. Bart stares me down; there's no point in stalling. "I grew up in London, one of the largest cities in the Other World. Not so unwittingly, I was brought to Winterhaven on behalf of King Andronicus' orders. I was to marry him and defeat the queen with my Elemental abilities. None of this was asked of me. It was demanded, all against my will. I escaped Isceald Castle, and he's been looking for me ever since."

"Lots of Elementalists exist in Winterhaven," he says in a disbelieving tone. "The dominus in a neighboring town where I grew up had a son. The boy could turn water into all sorts of things. What makes you so special?"

"Fire is what I do best, although I'm well-versed in all of the elements. My capabilities are only the half of it." I draw in a breath. "The queen must be killed by her own flesh and blood." Another few swigs to carry away the bitterness of the words.

Bart's mouth forms a stunned O; a few curse words dribble out. "You're Queen Belisama's daughter?"

I'm thankful for the racket drowning out his not-so-discreet proclamation.

"Explains the Infernal," he says, nodding. "And why you're trying to find your birthright."

The burn of alcohol beckons more tears. Or perhaps it's my misery. "I've been told as much by more than one person, but I don't know if the assertion has any factual basis. I'm desperate to verify the truth, because if it proves false then I cannot kill the queen no matter how much I want to. If she is my mother then I must aid in her demise." The bottom of my mug stares back at me. "Look, Bart, I don't want any trouble. But I honestly cannot pay you or Adina—"

Bart holds up a quieting hand. "I don't want your money. Nothing happened with Adina and me last night. Had to pay her up front, and we were just getting on to things when fire burst through the roof." He leans in close. "Before you got here tonight, I asked for a rescheduling of sorts. She told me I would have to pay her more—there were no makeups or refunds to be had."

The conversation has taken a lurid turn. *This is what lads do—they talk about salacious things over a pint or two.*

"I'm mad I got cheated. My da would shake his head at my foolhardiness." He sighs into his mug. "Anyhow, that's when she

112

offered to cut me in. Guess she thinks I have a better chance of getting the money than she does." He looks me up and down. "What happened to you? Looks like ya brawled with a mud puddle. And lost."

I tell Bart about the Great Tower of Annals, about Illya, and mostly about the Sablier. "Finding one would save time, years even," I finish. "My questions could be answered in an instant."

Bart casts a doubtful eye. "Those things are against the law."

"Illya told me. Is there anyone who might know of such things? Where one might be? She mentioned the Underground. Any thoughts?"

Bart pulls the piece of parchment from his coat pocket, the one about the Ichor Samhain. "I'll bet someone here knows. Carnival folk are strange creatures. Heathens, some of them. Let's head over there on the morrow. Wanted to go anyway, and maybe someone will know about a Sablier or where to find one."

"What about Adina? I'm supposed to have the money to her by then."

Bart finishes his drink and belches. "I'll play along for now. Before we head out tonight, I'll tell her you begged for another day. To keep her suspicions at bay, I'll say I conceded to a half day, no more." His voice lowers, barely audible over the clamor. "The cargo has been removed from the ship. They're restocking now and on the morrow. Then overmorrow, we set sail at first light. By the time we three are set to meet, I'll be long gone. I suggest the same of you."

"What if I don't find answers about my birthright by then? I can't just leave. I'm going to need more time."

Bart stands, and with a covert toss of his head, he gestures Adina to meet him out back. "She's well connected in Taliin, for obvious reasons," he says. "If you don't leave when I do, half the town will come looking for you. Your birthright will be the least of your problems."

Adina catches my eye as she follows Bart through the brothel and out the back door. My distress is real, and given the sneer on her face, she's plenty content to bear witness to it.

CHAPTER SEVEN

Come morning, Bart and I hurry through the cold, empty streets in silence. After meeting back at the inn last night, Bart had said Adina conceded to the extra half day, although she was plenty suspicious. Then he left to sleep off his many mugs of blackthorn brew while I lay awake, trying to map out my next move. If my needed answers don't come today, I'll have to hope someone at the Ichor Samhain knows the whereabouts of a Sablier.

My lost battle with the *Weather Almanac of Taliin* proved a costly misstep. Gœbel demands half my gold before he'll let us in, stating I've ruined the entire twenty-sixth tier. An exaggeration, surely, but if we want to gain entrance, I must pay.

Bart and I take the vexing lift deep into the Great Tower of Annals. When we stumble out, Bart whistles in appreciation at the splendor of the morning sun emptying ribbons of gold through the domed window. Gœbel reminds me about the bell, and the moment he's carried away, Illya shows up. She does a once over of Bart.

"You brought a friend," she says. "Is this your beloved?"

At the same time, Bart and I say, "No."

Bart helps me page through the hundreds of files containing

birth certificates. Now that he knows the queen might be my mother, he's as eager as I am to find the answer. Two heads are better than one, or three as it were, because we tell Illya the truth, knowing our secret is safe with her. Bart confirms the queen grew up in Gaulle. He even finds a few books about the king, possibly offering a clue about the queen.

As the day marches on, while paging through *Luminaries of Winterhaven: Past and Present,* I stumble upon a brief section about Guernsey. My heart smiles. The picture staring back is from his youth. His shock of white hair is black as night, and the lines that now grace his face are erased by rakish youth.

Son of Nylan and Everan Satori, Guernsey Satori was born at the beginning of the Secondary Age. His early life was spent as an apprentice to his father, a horologist, but his extraordinary gifts quickly came to light. They were many: Shifter, Elementalist, Voyant, Foresight, and a great wisdom like no other. He studied with the Solitary at the prestigious Cloister, and there he met many of his contemporaries. Together they formed the Veneficum, a council of some of Winterhaven's sagest.

How I wish I had time to read more, but my questions continue to go unanswered. And it seems I'm on my own, because Bart seems utterly charmed by Illya and her warrior ways. The way she cajoles him, the feeling is mutual. Their latest conversation causes my ears to prick.

"What happened to you?" Bart asks. "How did you die?"

Illya frowns. She turns her attention to her pike.

"Didn't mean to offend," he says with apology.

The words, soft and sincere, coax Illya to look him in the eye. "My death is not something I speak of often, if ever. Last time was over a century ago."

"No need to on my account," Bart says. "Curious was all."

Illya stalls for a moment. "Have you ever heard of Madrigh Sgot?" Bart shakes his head. "He was a brilliant but deranged medic, widowed with a young daughter. No one knew at the time, but he would randomly kill people so he could conduct experiments on their organs. Destitute men and women, mostly as they would never be missed. However, when his daughter contracted a pox and bacteria affected the ventricles of her heart, his murdering ways became a personal quest to find her a new heart. Anyone could fall victim, and no one was safe.

"Some friends of mine formed an all-female group called the Virago Warriors. We fought crime in Taliin, quite well I must say. And when the murders began, we made it our mission to find the killer. Mother warned me not to walk along the shores of the Taliin River at night..."

Bart puts a hand on her shoulder, but it goes right through. "Sorry. What a horrible way to die."

"The only good to come of it was that my heart did save his daughter—gave her nearly ten years. And I was his last victim. The Virago Warriors found him soon after my death. In time he was convicted and executed. His daughter died along with him, for her heart could not withstand the tragedy. Quite the irony, wouldn't you say?"

A long, pulling silence before Bart says, "Leave with us tonight."

Her eyes widen at the proposition. "Never could I leave this place. Took me ages to get in. Gœbel was not at all happy, and if I may be so bold, I believe he was scared of me for a time. He spent years trying to vanquish me. But I prevailed, and for the most part, he's given up. He doesn't seem to mind me the way he used to."

Bart gestures behind her. "Can't you just, you know, walk through walls?"

"People think so. But the tower's stones are coated in salt, a ward for specters. I've inadvertently created my own prison."

Bart trails her as she drifts to the tier above. I can see them across the way. "You can follow us when we leave through the tunnel and out the front door."

"And then what? You said you're setting sail at first light. I have no living family, no one I know in Taliin. I'd be left alone in the world." She points to the window above. "Besides, this affords the best view of the city. I like to see the crime, even if I can do nothing about it."

"Must be lonely, though," Bart claims.

"You're never alone when you're surrounded by words. And every once in a while, people like you visit. Perhaps you'll come back some day?" They stand as close as two can.

Poor Bart. Such a sweet boy. I truly hope he finds his way back home and proves his self-worth to his father. I let the book fall shut in my lap and look at the patchwork of files, all filled with birth certificates, none of them mine. Candlelight once again breathes shadows along the tower's walls. The day came and went along with any opportunity to find more about the queen or myself.

"We should be on our way," I say gently, hating to interrupt their tender moment. "It's getting late, and the carnival starts at midnight."

Illya marches across the open space to where I sit. Bart must go around. "You're going to the Ichor Samhain?" she exclaims. "The reason they show up unannounced and leave the same way is so they will not be held accountable for the deaths. People die there, and their souls dwell forever underground."

"People die at a carnival?" I ask. "How?"

Illya taps her chest. "A heart can only take so much fear. Whatever the carnival reveals can be too much for the weak."

I look warily at the thousands of books and files. If the answer to my birthright lies within these curved walls, it will forever remain a mystery. Come sunup, Taliin will be part of my past. My only hope is the Sablier. However, if what Illya states is true, I may not survive long enough to find it.

***

At the farthest reaches of Taliin, the catacombs sit beneath the city's cemetery. Wind sweeps through with a pitying moan, rattles the wrought-iron gate that barricades me and the rest of the impatient crowd from entering the graveyard. I'd headed back to

119

the inn on my own so Bart and Illya could say their goodbyes. That was hours ago. With midnight fast approaching, I'd given up waiting and had come on my own.

Through the thin cloud cover, the lunar eclipse is near-complete, the moon a slivered bit of light losing ground to the thieving shadow. I pull the evergreen cloak tighter. The Aeriscloque reads nine minutes to midnight. On the bronze and black dial, Polaris shines bright, and the moon is eclipsed, same as above. The larger thunderbolt forecasts a light snow, and I'm grateful the fires didn't upend the chilly weather. Something tells me the cold is short-lived.

Bart's shoulder tap makes me jump. "You should have stayed with Illya," I whisper. "No sense in us both risking our lives."

Hands in his pockets, Bart shrugs off the notion. "The Ichor Samhain trumpets death as a scare tactic for fun. Puffery, nothing more." The words betray the frightened look behind his eyes.

We watch as crimson light is cast over the full moon. Off in the distance, a tolling bell shivers twelve times through the night. A hooded figure approaches, torch in hand, the flame doing battle with the taunting wind. Bart and I trade uncertain looks as the skeleton key turns in the lock and the gate creaks open to usher the crowd inside. We follow in silence betwixt the gravestones, careful not to waken the dead.

We're led into an enormous mausoleum and down a narrow staircase that goes on a little too long for my comfort. At the bottom, a series of rickety, connected carts stretch out on a set of wooden tracks. If anything spells death, these do.

"Get in," the hooded figure croaks to the crowd. "Hold tight. We come back for no one."

Every part of me shakes as I climb in with the rest. There are terrified children, and I want to question every single one of their parents' sanity.

"If anything happens to me," Bart murmurs, "I'm going to the Great Tower of Annals to be with Illya."

He winks as if it's a joke, but I can tell he means it. Such a sweet thing to say, and I almost forget how my own death may be moments away. There are no bars to secure us, only ropes to hang on to when the carts jerk forward to a start.

For a while we inch along, the dirt tunnel low and bleak with nothing more than a lone torch here and there to light the way. Only when a small boy says from behind, "Mama look, dead people," do I peer more closely at the walls. *Skulls.* Thousands of them stacked on top of each other. Their morbid smiles are reminiscent of the dead woman from Isceald Castle, the emerald cloak a forever reminder.

Now we're moving faster. Down and around we go, deep into the earth. The tighter I hold the rope, the more it burns my flesh. The slope is steepening; the wind is damning. Tears burn my eyes. A young girl's scream punches the air then unravels away. Whether it was her fear or she was lost to the tracks, I don't want to know.

Without any warning, the brakes shriek to a sudden halt, and

121

my neck snaps so hard it's a wonder my head didn't fly right off.

"Get out," the man snarls. No one needs to be asked twice.

A labyrinth of tunnels rolls out before us. Small grottos carved into the walls glimmer in different colors, light pulsing from each one of them. An odd sense of exhilaration dances around the portentous mood, and the unexpected scent of spun sugar and roasted chestnuts helps to ease my fright.

Bart and I approach the ticket booth manned by a pair of detached, skinless hands, and we buy twenty tickets apiece. To avoid the crowds, we decide to head all the way down the farthest tunnel and work our way back. Over my shoulder, I watch the empty carts trail away. There was no mention of how we would get back above ground...or when.

For the next hour, we walk in and out of the various grottos filled with acts from the bizarre to the morbid to the arcane. There's a room where blood rains down from the ceiling, and the sandy floor sponges it away as though feeding upon itself. The sign says not to touch, but no one is standing guard. This reminds me of the bloodletting fountain back at Isceald Castle.

Jars of every size fill another grotto, dirt floor to low ceiling. Inside of each one is a face. Faces of children, adults, even dogs and cats and birds. The sign above says: *Moment Before Death*. I lean closer to study the jars. Eyes bloated with terror. Mouths contorted into screams. One man has tears crawling down his withered face.

Bearing witness to this unsettles us, sends us back to the

tunnel where skeletal clowns wander past hissing warnings of plague and death against our ears. When I discreetly ask one about the Sablier, I'm offered a bracelet of teeth. By another, a dead long-stemmed rose.

People saunter out of one grotto, cheerfully chatting with one another. In desperate need of some levity, we go in. Dozens of weeping candles light the space. A woman dressed all in black beckons us forth with long, curled fingernails, and Bart and I take a seat at her table. I gasp inwardly when she looks at me. Two irises inhabit each of her eyes. Blue and yellow on the right, green and purple on the left.

"Welcome," she says in a low voice. "I'm Jeyna, seer of the Ichor Samhain. Who wants their misfortune told first?"

Bart laughs at the joke, but I'm unconvinced she meant it as such. "I'll go," Bart volunteers. "Tell me if my da gives me the farm."

The seer shuffles an ornate deck of cards until he says when, then she lays out three cards before him. I recognize tarot cards well, a staple in traveling carnivals in the Other World. We sold them at Cimmerian's Curio Emporium, always a top-seller. These are similar, although unsurprisingly not quite the same. An angel with a trumpet; a heart pierced by a sword; a cup sitting on a cloud.

"Your future is foreboding," Jeyna says without emotion. She taps the first card. "Judgment. There will be judgment upon your return." She squints as if searching for clarity. "To your home, it

123

appears."

Bart nods eagerly. "My family's farm in Birr."

"Your victories, which are many—one especially significant—will not have proven enough." The second card is indicated. "Lone Sword. The heart, yours, pierced by your father's disgust. He will forever label you a fool, an incompetent one."

Bart sits in a brief silence while he digests her words. "All those months on the ship, everything I've done, has been for naught," he mutters.

"Tell my earlobe that," I say to lighten the mood.

Bart slumps in his chair, his smile turned into an inconsolable frown. "Whatever I do in the future will mean nothing to my da."

"There must be some good too," I say, glaring at the seer, willing her to break Bart free of his despair.

Jeyna nods with some reluctance as if stating anything positive is not allowed. "The Aced Chalice. Great and everlasting love. Love born from tremendous pain. But life is pain, is it not?"

Bart leans forward, interested once again. "Love? Great and everlasting? Are you certain?"

"The cards never lie." She offers the cards to take.

Bart stands and tucks them away, looking pleased with himself. "Get your fortune told, *Saunders*." He winks at me. "I'll be back in a short while. I'm going to find us something to eat."

Jeyna shuffles the deck. I want to ask how the three cards will be replenished, but magic is the answer, I already know. "Do you always dress like a boy?" she asks.

Her question surprises me, makes me wonder if she can see through my disguise or she sees things others cannot. "None of your business," I mutter.

Her lips, painted black, purse. She says nothing more as she sets the three cards before me: A woman surrounded by a wreath with stars above and four figures in each corner; a queen on a throne, armed with a steely sword; a skeleton with two long scythes crossed against each other. This last card I recognize. I swallow hard and tell myself this is all foolery. Death in regular tarot means good things, but this is Winterhaven, not the Other World. What it represents, I'm afraid to find out.

She begins, "World of Winterhaven. The woman on this card is a seeker of truth. As you can see, the wreath is wrapped in heavenly skies, and the figures in each of the four corners are representative of the elements: fish/Water, bull/Earth, dragon/Fire, eagle/Air. This card is important. There is a strong vibrational pull. The answer to your question lies here."

I sit up a little straighter. "Which question, specifically?"

"Your most important one."

Vague. To keep from sighing forcefully at the ridiculousness of it all, I point to the next card. "What about this one?"

"Queen of Swords. This represents relationships. The woman is stern, without emotion. Punishing. Perhaps the queen represents your mother?"

My mouth goes so dry I could spit tumbleweeds. *The queen on the card is representative of someone in my life; it's not literal.*

125

Likely the woman is Aunt Henrietta. She fits all those descriptions, although insipid is more befitting.

"Last but not least?" I say, moving on. "What does the Death card have in store for me?"

"You're familiar with Taerou," she notes. "Then you know the Death card is feared by most. It can be ambiguous, unquestionably. Your demise is imminent, this is possible. Or an old life gone and a new one born. Does this resonate?"

All too well. "Anything else?" I say with a forced smile.

A candle gutters out, the lingering smoke serpentine. "War, pain. Loss. Your future is bleak, I'm sorry to say." The slight smile on her face betrays her apology.

"Thank you. That was uplifting." She hands off the cards, and I hurry back to the tunnel to find Bart looking spry. The possibility of love does that, I suppose.

"Roasted chestnut?" He offers a paper cone filled with them. I shake my head. "Bad news from the seer?"

I tuck the cards into my knapsack. "Who believes such nonsense? We need to look for the Sablier."

One grotto, far larger than the rest: *Hall of Mirrors.*

Bart says, "Nature calls. Go on in. I'll meet up with you in a few minutes."

A maze of contiguous mirrors wends through the space. My reflection in one is so squat I'm a gnome. In another I am giant. Farther down the line, where there appears to be a corner, there is none. Retracing my footsteps finds not the exit but an illusion of eternal corridors stretching to the fore and behind. I'm completely turned around. I hear Bart laughing from somewhere on the other side, probably at a mirror showing him with two heads.

"Sondrine."

The sound of Lark's sweet voice makes me go right about face. She waves with her usual exuberance from one of the mirrors. Warily I say, "You're not real."

"Of course I am, Sondrine." She jumps up and down with excitement. "How I miss you so. Snap does too. When will you be back?"

"How can you see me?" I ask.

"Magic, naturally. Where are you?" She strains to see, on tiptoe.

Still suspicious, I approach the mirror and kneel so we're eye level with each other. "Guernsey told me there was no Hereat at the Sanctuary of Caelum. Is this some sort of magical looking glass?"

Lark nods. "I'll show you once you come back. You will come back, won't you?" The sincerity painted in her voice, in her large, amber eyes, is convincing.

Bart is still chuckling somewhere in the distance. "I'm at the Ichor Samhain. A carnival of sorts."

"A carnival? How I wish I was there! Perhaps I can meet you?"

"Not this time. The carnival is not for children." I squint to see behind her. "Are Shán and Guernsey with you?"

"Both are gone." She giggles into her tiny hands. "Shán misses

127

JENNA NELSON

you, to be sure." A ring encircles her thumb, the stone blood-red and glinting.

My heart spirals into my gut. "Bart," I call out, maintaining my smile to hide the fear behind.

She presses a finger to her soft, pink lips and leans in close. "You know."

A sob burbles out of me. "You've killed Lark. Who are you?"

Cruel laughter. "Lark is too valuable to kill. Her blood is mine, same as that of any ally of yours. My spies are everywhere, and any time your loved ones bleed, their blood becomes mine. You can never again be sure of who's who."

She removes the ring from her finger, and those soft amber eyes harden to emerald. Pink, cherubic cheeks sharpen and cut through alabaster skin. Queen Belisama Agni's cruel face stares back at me. "For me to live, you must die, Sondrine."

I try not to scream. I try to see myself in her face. "Please, I beg you, this war need not play out."

"King Andronicus must pay," she hisses. "He wronged me in so many ways. He robbed me of my body when he locked me inside the snowflake obsidian. But a body can be replaced." She laughs to herself as if she knows something I do not. "The greatest love of my life cannot be replaced, however. The king killed Arún, my one true love. Because of the king, my sister too is dead. I vowed revenge, and I will never let up until King Andronicus is dead and I am ruler of Winterhaven."

"We all want the king dead. We can work together. Please, it

128

does not have to be this way. Thousands will perish. If I can convince the Veneficum of an alliance, would you agree to it?"

Her eyes ring with hate. "The Veneficum want me dead. Why do you think they brought you to Winterhaven? They must die along with you."

Before I can get to my feet, a bony hand reaches through the glass and clasps my wrist. Her other hand holds a dagger, and through the glass, the blade plunges toward my chest.

Something heavy hits my side, breaks me free, and rolls me out of the way.

"You all right?" It's Bart. He bolts to his feet and helps me to mine.

The queen moves to the next mirror in line and throws the dagger.

"Get down," I yell. The blade sails past and shatters the mirror behind us.

Bart grabs my hand. "This way, toward the entrance."

Heads tucked, we run through the maze as another dagger comes at us then another, dozens of blades slicing the air from every mirror and in every direction.

I'm completely turned around, but I trust in Bart to lead the way. We run and duck, and I can see the entrance ahead, awaiting us. Bart pushes me across the threshold to shield me, but a dagger hits my back and down I go, my face smearing the ground and piling dirt into my mouth.

Panting, trying to catch my breath, I wait for the inevitable

129

pain. Nothing comes. I pull myself to my knees, spit the dirt from my mouth, and shake the pack free of my shoulders. The hilt of the knife is buried in the thick, woven face. I open the mouth of the knapsack and find *Secretum Secretorum* inside, the blade sunken deep into the cover. I almost cry with relief. *Books really do save lives.*

It's then I notice boots. Many, and of different shapes and colors and sizes. I look up to the crowd and then over to where they're pointing. At what. At whom. At Bart on the ground, three daggers deep in his back.

Everything moves in a blur. Each blade removed is a dam unleashed, the blood escaping in furious rivers. Carefully I roll Bart onto his back, the light fading from his eyes.

"You're fine," I whisper, holding back my sob. "I'll get you stitched up in no time."

When the Infernal had wounded Shán, he nearly died. These wounds are far worse and threefold. "Help me," I yell to the surrounding crowd, but no one moves, and my plea loses its voice along the tunneled walls.

Bart's lips quiver, his voice a tiny feather. "You'll kill the queen, Sondrine. And I helped. I saved you, right? I'm a lion, right?" His breath cracks as blood fills his lungs. "Tell my da I saved your life, that I helped save Winterhaven. He'll be proud of me, finally."

"You know I will." I'm nodding because he's right; he did save my life, and now I can't save his. Someone kneels beside me, and it takes a moment to see who through blurred eyes. "You lied," I say to Jeyna as the tears break free. "All the things you said to him, that he would find everlasting love, that his father would forever label him a fool. You made it sound like he would see Bart again, and he would tell him to his face."

"His ashes will be sent on," she says in a grave tone. "We will see to it. But a dead son spells defeat, not victory."

"He saved my life," I say with blistering venom. "I'll find his father and tell him the truth. Someday I will." How I wish this were true, but I don't know if I'll survive another day.

The seer says nothing. She points down the farthest tunnel. "The Sablier awaits."

Her statement takes me by surprise, how she knew, but I shake my head. "The Sablier no longer matters. I must tend to Bart." Aimlessly I dig through the knapsack for needle, for thread, for anything that might bring him back to life.

"You're in shock. There is nothing more you can do now."

"Don't say there is nothing," I whimper. Her hand tamps down on mine, and her head shakes intently. I know she's right, but the ache is all-consuming. Never again will a smile push at Bart's paunchy cheeks.

"His face will go to the jar, his body to the pyre. He is our possession now, not yours." She says this in a solemn voice. Not maligned or vengeful, more matter of fact.

"Please make an exception," I beg. "I can't bear to think of Bart's face traveling around forever with this carnival."

She smiles, a kind one, and it's unexpected. "You mean no disrespect, and I will take it as such. The body is nothing more than a shell. His soul is already free of this place." Again she points down the tunnel.

Leaving Bart's body to strangers is gutting. I walk away trusting she will do as she says, my hands, my trousers, my cloak, stained with the remnants of Bart's life.

CHAPTER EIGHT

Something intangible lures me through the tunnel, past the other grottos, so far down no one is in sight. Numb with grief, I stumble into a frigid space. All is black and white and grey. A metallic melody like one found in a music box creeps through the strands of wandering fog. Ahead, the outline of something grand appears, and as I move closer, the entirety materializes: a tented carousel with wooden horses moving up and down. The circular platform groans and turns.

"Hello? Is anyone here?" My shuddered breath comes out in frenzied clouds.

Someone emerges from the mist. A pinstripe suit and top hat outfit a thin, overly tall frame. The face is a grey smudge with no distinguishable features.

"I'm always here. Watching. Waiting." The downy voice belongs to a man. No sign of breath marks the air when he speaks.

"Stay away from me," I cry in realization. "You're Memento Mori. This is the Scissure of Lost Souls."

"The Scissure of Lost Souls is paradise compared to this place if you stay long enough." He breathes in deep and long. "Fear. Desperation. They smell one and the same."

"What do you want?" Along with the rest of me, my voice trembles.

"Not what I want. What *you* want; it's why you're here. You need to see your past, need to know who you are."

I squint through the fog to better see him. "How could you have possibly known such a thing?"

For every step he moves forward, I take three back. "I know everything, *Sondrine.*" He stretches my name between unseen teeth as proof. "Step on. The Sablier will reveal all." His hand sweeps to the side in a flourish.

My breath is ragged but determined. "At what price? My soul?"

Low, acrid laughter. "Your soul is already mine. When I choose to claim it is anyone's guess but my own."

His words cause my scalp to prickle. If he's Death incarnate, his point is well-taken. If he's something else, I'm making the biggest mistake of my life as I walk past him and hoist myself onto the nearest horse, sitting sidesaddle.

The eerie music continues, but the carousel slogs to a halt. I look around for the man to tell him the needed date, but he's nowhere to be found. A jerking movement then the carousel starts again, only this time it moves in reverse. Slow at first, then gaining momentum. A brass ring above beckons through the mist. No way can I reach it from this ladylike position. Since I'm no longer in London and no longer acting as a lady, I throw one leg over the saddle so I'm astride. Faster and around I go. Standing in the stirrups, holding on to the moving pole, I stretch to the balls of my feet and pull the ring.

My horse is galloping across a bright, snowy field, a bowl of blue staring down. Gone are the carousel and the eerie space, and if I had to guess, Taliin too is long gone. Nothing looks familiar, but the horse seems to know the way. Steam flares from its nostrils, the kicked snow like daylight against the night of its coat.

Only once have I ridden a horse. Daintily it trotted me sidesaddle around a well-manicured pen. Darcy Hightower and I along with a few other girls from our dormitory had sneaked out of school to visit St. Giles' Fair in Oxford. Of course, we were unattended, a thrill in itself. Not to mention the gentlemanly fair-goers who doffed their felted hats to us or the carnival workers who served up crafty glances beneath their long tresses.

Shán crops into my mind, for a carnival worker is exactly what I thought of when we met in the Petrified Forest. Dark curls streaked in midnight blue grazing his shoulders, eyes bent with fearsome ideas. Before I'm lost to the memory, the horse slows to a stop at the edge of a thicket of trees. A path points to a modest manor framed in stone and wood with chimney smoke losing ground to the rallying wind.

I tie off the horse, unsure of what to do next. A full-figured young woman hurries out the front door and heads down the path straight for me. Her head is half-hidden by the cloak's hood, but her brows are stitched in distress. There is nothing around, no place to hide. *What should I do? Where can I go?*

"Hello," I blurt. "I'm lost, I think—"

She doesn't so much look up, let alone stop. *Is it Queen Belisama?* She would be younger, her cheeks and hips ampler than now.

"Excuse me," I say again.

This time she stops. Snow on the path impedes her way. With a slight flick of her wrist, a strong gust sweeps in and clears it away, blowing off her hood in the process. *She's an Elementalist. Air is her gift.* Her blue eyes look straight through mine, and when she whisks past with no acknowledgement of my presence, I realize she can't see me. A cascade of dark curls shows more rose than fire against the evergreen cloak around her shoulders. I shake off the coincidence, for the cloak appears similar to mine, although perhaps a bit more vibrant. Evergreen is a common color among textiles. I'm sure a thousand cloaks were made just like this one.

Off she goes through the trees, a basket of wicker in hand. *Do I follow?* As if in answer, some unforeseen force pushes me toward the manor. I walk up the path to a terraced garden and peer inside the nearest window, conveniently cracked open.

A handsome man with chestnut hair and curls hinting of amethyst paces about the living area. On the low table are the markings of afternoon tea: a plate of pastries, a decorative teapot, cups and saucers. I gasp when I spy the ivory chalice with the symbol of the Emerald Tablet. The man speaks in a raised voice to someone in an armchair, a striking woman with long tresses of auburn and emerald eyes that swore to see my death.

My heart skips a beat for another reason. Cradled in Queen

Belisama's arms is a baby. A baby with a crown of black fuzz, the tips whispering of fuchsia. On tiptoe, I strain to better see myself and to hear the conversation.

The baby fusses.

"There, there, my precious, Sondrine," the queen coos. "Hungry, are you?" She unbuttons her blouse and offers her breast.

My blood turns to ice as I watch the baby nurse happily.

The man looks on with a wavering eye. "Your sister and you have had many an argument over the years, but this one is too great to accept as true. Why was I kept in the dark? How was this an irrelevant detail? And how can you both be over five hundred years of age?"

Belisama lightly pats the baby's back. "We were afraid to tell you, and until now, it was unnecessary. Since the water must be drunk every one hundred years to continue the cycle, we are due. I will drink again in the coming weeks and so must you."

"Did you not hear what I said before Gilleanne stormed out? I will do no such thing. I have no desire to be Immortal. Gilleanne too said she's done. This is insanity, you do realize?"

Belisama giggles, pure and joyful, almost child-like. Nothing like the wicked laugh she delivered in the Hall of Mirrors. "Gilleanne is foolhardy, Arún. You know this. But you and I, we are smarter. It must be done."

Arún. My father. The love of Belisama's life. I remember when Zhang the Elder had told me the story about Arún and the queen. *Little did I know they were my parents.*

137

Arún's face hardens. Belisama must sense his anger because her smile fades. "Finish your tea and relax," she gently urges. "I understand your distress. I'll start with dinner. The butcher is only an hour from here, and Gilleanne will be back soon with the fresh mutton. We can speak more of this later."

With some reluctance, Arún swallows the last of his tea while staring at the ivory chalice. After a few minutes pass and several deeps breaths are taken, he appears happier, calmer. He pinches some dirt from the small potted plant on the table and rubs it between his fingers. A white lily blooms.

He's an Elementalist too. Earth and Water are his gifts. Fire from my mother, Air from my aunt.

Belisama sets the table. Arún takes the baby from her hip and places her into a nearby cradle. When he returns to the queen's side, he tucks the lily behind her ear.

"We can accomplish a lot in an hour," he says, a callback to their conversation. "A man has needs, and those needs have not been met as of late." Her blouse is still half-unbuttoned, and he finishes the task.

"A fine husband you are," she teases. "Being with child and afterbirth bring about great fatigue, in case you haven't noticed." Her tone is dismissive, but there's a resonance of love behind it.

He smiles and kisses each of her breasts. "I'll do all the work. How does that sound?"

She lifts off his shirt in answer, and I watch him lead her into the room adjacent.

My fingers tremble against the windowsill. *There it is. My mother and father. And me. But how did I get to the Other World?*

The air around me shimmers with a penetrating heat, and now I'm in a noisy town square populated by merchants and townsfolk alike. Church bells toil above the coterie of fresh-picked carrots, tanned cowhides, and cloves from the local spicerer. I follow a herder of goats to a water trough where I leave the horse, then the intangible force prompts me up a long flight of stone steps and into the church.

Every pew is crowded by men, women, and children alike. Since no one can see me, I follow the middle aisle through the nave, noting how every person is dressed, their clothing fit for royalty.

My father and moth—Queen Belisama Agni—stand at the chancel before a marbled font. To his left is Gilleanne, the queen's sister. A vicar dunks me in the water. *My Rite of Purification.*

An audible gasp trips over my lips when I slide into the lone empty spot in the middle of the front pew. On the aisle seat is King Andronicus, his mouth twisted into a sallow frown. I'd forgotten that he and Arún were half-brothers. A dark-haired boy, perhaps six or seven years of age, fiddling with a slingshot, sits between the king and a pretty, fair-haired woman to my right. Undoubtedly she is the king's companion, and I wonder who she might be. Her chatelaine bag is stitched with the initials NE.

The rest of the pew leftwards holds the king's behemoth Sentinels, their uniform armory and subdued expressions just as I remember. As I watch the ceremony unfold, the Sentinel to my other side covertly tucks a small scroll into the pretty woman's hand. I'm invisible to them both, but I squirm because this is happening across my very lap. She rebukes his actions with a punitive glare, although her coy smile tips off the mutual attraction. Her eyes dart to the king to make sure he isn't watching, and she unfurls the paper.

Nalina, love, meet me tonight in the belfry of Isceald Castle, at half past eight.

The guardsman is quite pleasing to the eye, his dark chestnut hair with the same sapphiric cast as the king's. There is a familiarity I cannot place.

"And who offers this child today to partake in the responsibility of practicing the faith?" the vicar asks, his voice thrown back to us by the ornate stained-glass windows.

Queen Belisama says, "I do."

"Aye," my father says, and Gilleanne nods in agreement.

Once more the air vibrates with an unrelenting heat. Twilight bends through the windows of Arún and Belisama's manor, and firelight chases the walls. I'm inside this time. Arún is before the hearth drinking mead from a mug, and King Andronicus stands opposite. An unspoken tension weights the air.

"To what do I owe this visit, brother?" Arún asks.

"We must end this hostility between us for everyone involved."

Arún raises an eyebrow, suspicious. "An offer of parley?"

The king waves his glove through the air. "Not a white flag, but

140

this will have to do."

Arún sips his mead. "It was you who started this war between us, not I."

"Our mother pitted us against one another. I blame her."

"She loved me more than you, I will attest. And I will never condone her actions. But it was you who made me the enemy. Do know, your hatred for me was never reciprocated on my part." He turns his back to the king and stokes the fire with a poker.

"I did hate you because of Mother's affections," the king admits. "Now I hate you because you stole the woman I love."

Shocked by his brother's words, Arún turns, just as the fire brazier smashes against his head. My screams go unnoticed. Arún staggers. Blood runs down his face. He collapses onto the wood floor and the king smashes his head twice more.

The king looks indifferent as he drags Arún's limp body outside to a small shed. I follow along, my body quaking with fear. King Andronicus removes a copper ring from beneath his cloak and dips the diamond in the pool of blood next to Arún's head. "Sleep well, brother."

"The Dead Ringer," I whisper.

The king's outward appearance is now that of Arún, and he returns to the manor. As he cleans up the wood floor, Belisama walks through the door with a basket filled with food. "Gilleanne will be along shortly. She's tending to the…Is that…blood?"

King Andronicus shrewdly smiles. "Some spilled mead is all."

Belisama shakes her head and laughs. "Look where my mind

141

goes. I'll get you another."

When she returns, he trades her the bloodied rags for the mead and takes several sips. The queen watches, and after a long moment, she says, "You've been avoiding me." She kisses him, her hand traveling down the front of his shirt to his trousers.

"What are you doing?" he murmurs.

Belisama takes a sharp step back. Eyes narrowed, she wipes her mouth with disgust. "Who are you?"

He rubs his temple. "Who does it look like? Arún, of course."

Belisama looks at the bloodied rags in her hand. Hesitantly she brings them to her nose and sniffs. "Arún!" she yells. She runs through the manor shouting for him.

"You've gone mad," the king says, trailing her.

I follow her outside where she finds Arún in the shed. She screams into her hands. "Be still, my love. I'll fetch a medic."

She turns to leave, but the king is in the doorway, blocking her way. "You're going nowhere," he says.

Belisama's emerald eyes are wide. She spies the Dead Ringer on his hand. "Varius. What have you done?"

"What have *you* done?" He holds up a small bottle. "What is this?"

Belisama moves to take it, but he jerks his hand back out of her reach. "You'll never get away with this," she trembles. "Leave at once."

"I'm going nowhere."

Angry tears pool in her eyes. "You will pay for this. With the
142

gods above as my witness, I will kill you if it's the last thing I do."

The heat pulls me away, and now the horse gallops uphill, my fingers bound to the reins. Isceald Castle rears before me, a malignancy against the blue skin of the sky.

"Why are we stopping here?" I murmur when the horse halts before the drawbridge. "I don't care if I am invisible. Never again will I set foot in that horrid place."

A boy stumbles across the drawbridge, a knapsack slung across his shoulders, his head tucked to avoid the prying eyes of the stalwart guards. *The same boy from the church.* On horseback, I follow him down the hill and into the depths of the forest. All day he walks through the snow, until the sun dries up and only the stars light the sky. He collects an armful of kindling, looks left to right, and disappears inside a small cave.

I slip off the horse and peer through the cave's opening. Skillfully he builds a small fire. There is wailing, loud and fervid, and my mouth drops open when he pulls a fully-swaddled baby from the knapsack and sets it onto the earthen ground. He unsheathes a dagger from his boot with a trembling hand. Tears chase the boy's cheeks as he presses the blade to the baby's neck.

"This won't hurt but a moment," he promises in a whisper. "Please, stop your crying now. You won't feel a thing."

"Stop!" I run over to the boy and knock the knife away. Try, anyway. My hand goes straight through his. I stare at the baby's face, shriveled and ruddy, untouched by time. Blue eyes swollen with tears stare back. The signature fuchsia-tipped curls are

143

telling. *Did he kidnap me? How did I come into his possession?*

The boy shoves the dagger into its scabbard. "I've a better idea," he says, discomfited by his actions. "Freezing to death is painless and peaceful, like going to sleep."

He gathers me up and sets me in the snow just outside the cave's entrance. I want to scream at him, but there's no point, for I survive somehow. Unable to watch the infant's demise, he returns to the cave and paces about, awaiting a death that will never come. Firelight traces his youthful face and then his dark strands, the telltale midnight blue beckoned forth.

"Shán?" I exclaim aloud.

He looks right at me. No, at someone behind me, a man who said his name at exactly the same moment.

"What brings you to the Petrified Forest, young Shán?" The deep scratch braided into his voice tells me who he is even before he pushes past.

"Guernsey," trembles Shán, his eyes gripped with panic. "My father tasked me with something important to fulfill my honor. I promised to carry out his wishes."

With the baby nestled in his arms, Guernsey settles on a log before the fire and rubs my tiny hands to warm them. "You must kill this child if I'm not mistaken."

Shán stares at the old sorcerer through the flames. "How did you know?"

"I know many things. And among those things I know, you are no murderer."

144

"She's a danger to Winterhaven," Shán says with youthful defiance. "She must die for the realm to be free."

Guernsey looks over to where I stand, and I can almost swear he sees me. "Nonsense," he says. "She is a source of contention, a thorn in your father's side, for he loves Sondrine's mother. She chose his brother over him, and now he's going to destroy them both by destroying their child."

Shán shakes his head in confusion. And why should he understand? He's a boy of six, seven years at best.

"In the end the reason doesn't matter, Guernsey. I have to obey my father. He asked me to kill her, and so I must. Or he will kill me."

Guernsey offers a slow nod. "I'm afraid you speak the truth when it comes to the latter. As to the former, there is an alternative."

Shán lowers himself onto the ground. A deep and abiding terror befalls his young face, but he looks on with anxious eyes.

"We shall give her away," Guernsey decides. "Your father will be none the wiser."

"You don't understand. He asked for evidence. I must bury her in the forest and bring back her heart as proof."

My legs nearly buckle. The king is a murderer, this I know. Asking his son to kill me and cut out my heart…It's too much.

Except for the baby fussing and the flames of the fire sparking, an impregnable silence stills the cave walls. "Get some sleep," Guernsey says in a dark tone. "We leave at first light."

Shán stands, arms over his chest. "No, Guernsey, I will not run away."

"We're not running, boy," he says, his voice charged with fire. "We're walking. With purpose. Everything will be solved on the morrow."

The penetrating heat finds me back in the saddle, trailing Guernsey and Shán through the early morning light. So strange to watch my tiny head bounce against Shán's back in the knapsack.

They walk all morning, through one town after another. Finally, they stop before an expansive stone dwelling with a thatched roof, home to several chimneys. *Valetudinaria* is carved on the front façade. Shán follows Guernsey up the stairs, and I tie off the horse and do the same.

Camphor and other medicinal ointments chase the corridors inside. Guernsey requests to speak with the head nurse, and after a time, he and Shán are shown into an office where they are instructed to wait. With the baby tucked into the crook of his arm, Guernsey takes out the Aeriscloque from his pocket. He slips it over her neck and tucks it away beneath the swaddled blanket.

The Aeriscloque came from Guernsey. His father was a horologist, this I just learned. Why would he give the timepiece to me?

A full hour passes before a woman walks in.

"Apologies for your waiting time," she says, closing the door behind her. "We are understaffed at the moment."

Guernsey stands, so too does Shán. She nods to them both. "I'm

146

Nurse Renfrew. How might I be of assistance?"

"Aunt Henrietta," I say in a stupefied whisper. She's younger, the frown lines less pronounced. No sign of kindness lives behind her dark eyes, a sign one would expect not only from a less jaded woman but from someone in such a prestigious position. She looks the same miserable person she's always been.

"You are a busy woman, Nurse Renfrew," Guernsey says in greeting. "We do understand. Please, call me Sir Corvus. This here is Lir."

False names. Clever.

Guernsey and Shán resume their seats once she's situated behind a small desk. "Is the infant sick?" she asks. "Or is it the boy? No mother, I see. Either way, you will need to sign papers first before admittance."

"The children are both in good health, I can assure you," Guernsey says.

Aunt Henrietta raises an unruly eyebrow. "It's you who is ill, then?"

"My age has worn me thin, though for the moment I'm here to stay. Illness of any sort is not what brings us here on this day. Nurse Renfrew, I have a most interesting proposition, one I should like you to consider. Were I to offer you gold in exchange for relieving your duties as head nurse, enough so you would never again need to work a day in your life, would you accept?"

At first Henrietta shifts in her chair, made uncomfortable by the pronouncement. Then she grins, humoring him. "No more

147

weeping, pus-filled wounds or emptying of day-old chamber pots? Most certainly." She clasps her hands. "Sir…"

"Corvus."

She nods formally. "I am a very busy woman dealing with an infirmary filled beyond capacity with the ailing and the dying. As you well know, a plague has spread through the various cities and towns near to here. While I appreciate the humor given the calamitous state of affairs, I must return to my duties, so please do tell me how I can help you."

"Indeed the plague is dire. But I do not jest. If you leave your post as head nurse on the morrow, I shall offer a lifetime of gold. Enough to never again be obliged to tend to the sick. Your days would be carefree, filled with whatever passions lie within. Something tells me this is not your life's calling."

"To the contrary," she protests, although thinly.

"Next time say it with more verve, Henrietta," I murmur.

Guernsey scratches his beakish nose. "Everyone ceases to work at some juncture. Already at your young age you have put in a lifetime of dedication. Now is the chance to sit back and enjoy the fruits of your labor. A woman of your position is not paid what she so richly deserves."

"You speak the truth," she admits.

Henrietta is breaking; I know the look all too well. Money does this to her. A wolf licking its chops when it spies wounded prey.

She goes on, "Although the offer is appreciated, I must refuse. People here rely on me—"

The door opens, and a young woman pokes her head inside. "Pardon the interruption, Nurse Renfrew, but it's urgent. Lady Phelan fell and hit her head—she's seizing."

Henrietta hurries out of the room without so much as a goodbye.

Shán looks inconsolable and slumps in his chair. "My father is expecting me. He gave me two days to complete the task. Should I fail, he warned me to never again return to Isceald Castle. Is there someone else who might help us?"

Guernsey appears unfazed by Henrietta's decision. "Money is a great seducer, a siren with a song. It is the uncommon person who can resist her charms. Something tells me Nurse Renfrew is as common as they come."

Three quarters of an hour passes before Henrietta returns. The faintest smell of vomit follows her in, and the white of her apron is tainted in blood.

"You're still here?" She sounds relieved, not annoyed as I would normally expect.

"On the off-chance you might reconsider," Guernsey says.

She settles back into her chair. "Riches beyond my wildest dreams?"

I almost laugh. *You hardly missed a beat, dear aunt.*

"I've always wanted my own apothecary," she confides in a low tone.

"Done."

She taps a finger in nervous habit, and her eyes squint,

149

suspicious. "Now for the fine print. What must be done to be in receipt of the gold?"

"This infant—Sondrine is her name—is in need of a guardian. Before you are quick to refuse, might I add, in addition to the monthly sum paid to you, she will come of age soon enough. She will marry, the dowry adding to your riches. Sondrine may well carry you deep into the folds of an affluent society, possibly one of nobility."

Henrietta looks at Guernsey with hungry eyes. Those eyes turn cold when she looks at the fussing baby. "She might be ugly, thus an old maid. Then what? I'll be stuck with her for the rest of my days."

My eyes roll. The capacity for empathy skipped Henrietta.

"I know of her parents, both decidedly striking. Furthermore, her lineage carries Elementalism on both sides. Her talents will call forth many a gentleman suitor."

Now I laugh aloud. One sole caller: Hubert Teasly, the lurid dentist-to-be.

Henrietta flicks non-existent lint from her sleeve. "Something tells me there's more to this story than you're letting on."

"Two additional things, yes. You must raise the child in the Other World and never again return to Winterhaven."

Henrietta springs to her feet. "Preposterous. Why would I ever leave Winterhaven? This is my home, where I've lived my entire life."

He eyes her barren ring finger. "I see," he says. "You have a husband here."

Guernsey is good; he's playing her. Same as the sharpers and magsmen in London.

Henrietta smooths her hair but says nothing, answer enough.

"The Other World could offer you many things," he continues. "A new beginning. Perhaps a gentleman caller of your own."

Henrietta's cheeks brighten, but she doesn't protest. "You mentioned two things." She sits again; a good sign.

Guernsey hands off the baby to Shán and leans in close, his clawed fingers laced together. "The child has been ordered to her death by King Andronicus. At this juncture, I cannot share in the why and wherefore of this decision, only that it is so."

Her shocked expression draws a hopeful look from Shán, who sits up a little straighter. "You mentioned Elementalism on both sides," she whispers. "That kind of magic is usually found in sovereign blood. This is the reason I must head to the Other World?"

"In part. The king has demanded her heart as proof of the murder."

A hand flies to her mouth. She looks genuinely horrified, and it gives me a small measure of satisfaction how even this is too much for my stone-hearted aunt.

Guernsey's eyes bore into hers, unyielding. "There are children who have perished in the recent hours or days from the plague and are awaiting proper burial at the dead house, yes?"

"Some," she manages after a short silence. "The youngest is

151

perhaps two years of age. There have been no infants of late."

Guernsey pauses a moment, thinking. "To the commoner, would the difference in heart size be discernable?"

Henrietta pulls a book of medicine off the adjacent shelf. Her lips move while she leafs through and reads a passage to herself. "Unlikely from what I can gather. Though the king may call on a medic for expertise."

"Oh, he will do so. The king is no man's fool. However, if I must wager on the matter, he will demand confirmation that the heart is human and not of an animal, nothing more."

Shán's face pales to the color of the wall behind him. Poor boy. He will have to suffer through this all. When the king will discover his son's betrayal makes me wonder. Something tells me not now, but he will, of course, for he ordered my return to Winterhaven, brought here by Shán himself.

Guernsey pulls out a pouch filled with gold coins and sets it before her. Henrietta appears mesmerized by the sight. "I will need the heart now," he states. "The fresher the better, so I can send Lir on his way. At first light, once you have gathered your needed belongings, I will personally escort you and the infant safely to the Other World." He stands; Shán follows suit. "Do know I will periodically check on you to be sure you are keeping up with our agreement. If so, your financial account will be filled monthly. While it may not be riches beyond your wildest dreams, you will never again want for money."

I try to think of ever seeing Guernsey before the disastrous

152

night at the Teasly mansion but nothing comes to mind.

"What you're asking is unlawful," Henrietta declares. "If the king or anyone in his high court discovers my misdeeds, I will find myself without a head. I need time to think this through. These are monumental decisions, ones that carry dire consequences should my actions be discovered."

"Decisions rewarded in gold," Guernsey reiterates. He nudges the pouch of coins closer. "You will be safe from harm in the Other World, you have my word. An hour's time is all I can offer. Should you decline, we must be on our way, for time is of the essence. There are many who would not hesitate at the opportunity."

The air shimmers with heat, and I'm back to the present, inside the cemetery of Taliin. No more horse, no more Ichor Samhain. *No more Bart.* Empty paper cones litter the ground, half-buried in snow that sifts through the clouds. I'm alone now, with only the unwanted company of a question finally answered: I am the daughter of Queen Belisama Agni.

An awakening sky bruises the headstones with blues and purples as I leave the graveyard with a heavy heart. I look behind to cast a final glance to Taliin. Smoke from yesterday's fires sighs from the rubble and screens the Great Tower of Annals in the distance. I squint. Through one small window at the very top of the tower, two shadows fissure the candlelight. Whether my eyes betray me or it's just wishful thinking, I can't be sure. But still I raise my hand: hello and goodbye. Hope beyond hope, I pray that Bart is with Illya, his great and everlasting love.

CHAPTER NINE

For the kind of riches at stake, people will ride horseback through every town, city, and village until they capture me and bring me to the king, dead or alive. I need to get far away from here, back to the Sanctuary of Caelum, and then on to the Cloister. My own two feet won't get me quickly out of Taliin. But I have no horse, no kind of transport.

The innkeeper's map shows how the River Mourne divides Taliin, north and south. If I follow along the riverbank, perhaps someone will come by and offer passage. I'm through with large ships, but a sturdy rowboat will suffice. To better disguise myself, I rub dirt and mud on my face. People pay no mind to vagrants. How I wish I could cut my hair to better disguise myself, but since it grows right back it will prove a pointless feat.

Down one embankment, up another, and into the forest I go. Fallen branches and pine needles crunch beneath my boots and break the calm. Not long after, water sprinting over stone echoes through the snowfall. The sound is an easy compass, and soon the aromas of peaty moss and churning mud join in and lead me straight to the source.

A canopy of trees cast long branches over the river, the winter sun splintered into moving webs along the surface. My cloak and

154

boots provide sufficient warmth, but after walking for a time, my stomach complains, empty and wanting.

Reedmace grows in abundance along the muddy riverbed. The plant is edible; it grows along the River Thames, and many of the working poor use it for sustenance. Everything from the roots to the leaves to the spike on top can make for a working meal.

After collecting a solid bunch, I pull out the dagger that almost killed me and study the intricate, silver-laced hilt, my palm where hers was there last. The metal burns cold against my fingers. Though it sickens me to use the dagger, I cut and slice each of the reedmace into pieces and set them in a tin filled with the icy river water. A fire will give me away. With a little concentration and some time, some bored bubbles pop along top. The broth goes down easy and warms me from within. The spikes I eat like cobbed corn, the seeds crunching in bursts between my teeth.

My breath feathers in the wind after a long, satisfied sigh. Sitting on the riverbed, knees drawn to chin, I watch the river pass by. This is the first moment I've had to think about the scenes in the Sablier. About who I am and therefore what I must do. Not everything makes sense, but the most important thing does. The thought of Queen Belisama Agni as my mother makes the broth in my stomach threaten to repeat on me.

For every single one of my eighteen years, I believed that my mother had died in childbirth, that I was the cause of her death. And also the cause of my father's, since he took his own life when she died, his heartache too great to bear. These were the lies fed to me by my aunt, the ones I have shouldered with tremendous guilt and remorse. Since my arrival in Winterhaven, it came to light this may not be the case. But to see the truth with my own eyes, to understand it in a way I could have never imagined without actually witnessing it for myself, only deepens the wound, makes it bleed harder.

The grief creeps in, soundless but emboldened. My head nods with the realization of what's to come. My spine hurts; so does my head, and my heart feels like it's been dragged from my chest as my sobs go into my knees, the sound drowned by the passing river.

Knowing I am not the cause of my parents' death should find me elated. And yet learning that my father is dead because of the king's inane jealousies and that my mother is a murderer, the vilest person in all of Winterhaven, brings about a different sort of heartbreak.

Shadows shift in the falling light, and the air grows cooler. When the tears slow to a stop, my resolve is what remains. I vowed to fight this war and kill the queen long before I knew the true reason why. Now I must get to the Cloister and train for the imminent battle.

Horses hooves pound against the snow. Quickly I stuff everything into my knapsack and dart into a thicket of bushes, the only thing around to hide me. Rapid breaths bounce off the branches as I peer at the dozen men on horseback upstream and on the bank opposite. Are they passersby? Or townsfolk looking for me?

The answer arrives when Adina does, her horse galloping into view. Every swear I know swirls in my brain and trips over my tongue. There is conversation and the pointing of fingers, no doubt assessing my whereabouts. She begins to cross the river, and the others follow. The water is deep in parts and perilous, judging by the horses' slow movements and the riders' prompting assurances. Stirrups and boots go underwater. Halfway across, four men dismount to urge their horses forward. The embankment behind me is steep. If I make for my escape, they'll spot me easily, but staying here means awaiting capture. With no other option, I close my eyes and will the water to rise and send them back to the riverbank.

Whinnying and the shouting of voices startle me. My eyes open to find the river upstream crashing over the rocks, flooding the banks as it heads toward me. Two men and their horses are swept away. I too will join them unless I flee now. Halfway up the embankment, an arrow misses the intended mark, instead hitting a tree trunk to my left. Then another to my right. Slipping and sliding in the mud underfoot, I try to climb in a zigzag to avoid the onslaught, but the earth is too slippery to gain footing, and I slide backward to the flooded riverbank, where the motley riders await.

Adina drops to the ground, her fur pelt and conservative fare dripping with water. Her smile reeks of victory. "Not a bright one, are you? Cooking is a recipe for capture. We didn't know if the scent was from you or some vagabonds making a meal. You gave us a clue we couldn't help but follow."

157

Silently I chide myself, especially since I was so careful to avoid making a fire. *Who knew boiled reedmace would spell my demise?*

"Thought you could renege on the money?" she says, hands on her hips.

I look at the men above, their clothes soaking wet, their horses' coats frosting over. "What money?" I ask, playing dumb.

"The money promised to Leeyla."

My hands grip the knapsack's straps. "Nothing was promised. Leeyla threatened me. When she died, the threat died with her."

Adina's head shakes. "Leeyla and I were in on things together. Now, some friends." She gestures the men. "Bart said he told you. He promised you would meet me at noon today to pay me off."

"Bart told me nothing of the sort. Besides, he's dead."

Adina's brows go up briefly, but she signals the men down. "You're lying."

"About Bart telling me? Or that he's dead? Both are true. And I don't have the money. I told Leeyla the same."

She laughs. "Oh, we know. Trust me, I prepared for you not to show. The king's Sentinels are meeting us back in town. We bring you to them, we get our gold. Simple enough."

"I am not going back to Taliin."

Adina smiles. "We knew you'd say that too."

She nods to one of the men behind me. Before I can run, an arm nooses my neck, a sedating handkerchief buries my nose, and the river sighs and reels away.

***

I'm laid out on a divan at the Barmy Goat, an ample pillow beneath my head, when I come around. Eager, hungry eyes stare down on me, the stuck pig at their feast. This is not the tavern's usual throng. Gone are the music and the corseted women. From the look of things, this show is for an exclusive crowd only.

Adina is next to me, dabbing at my brow with a cool cloth. "We promised them you'd be unharmed," she says.

"Mostly," one of the men crows, followed by snorts from the crowd.

If I'm not mistaken, he's the same man who drugged me. I sit up and spit in Adina's face. She slaps mine in return. More snorts, but what do I care? I'm going back to Isceald Castle, back to the lecherous arms of a deranged king. I choose the Mourning Garden over his bed this day and every day thereafter.

"They've arrived," announces a young man at the front window.

The tavern buzzes with excited whispers, and when the door opens, two Sentinels march in outfitted in armor and helmets, their swords at the ready. Seems a bit much given the circumstances.

"We are here under direct order of King Andronicus," the leaner of the two states. "Present the fugitive, and you shall receive your reward."

Adina stands, waves them over. "This way, kind sirs." She yanks me to my feet and then shoves me down into an unwilling curtsey.

The Sentinels move forward with caution in each step. Judging

159

by the low murmurs and shrugging shoulders, the mob is as confused as I by their careful entry. Adina too looks unsure of the combative stances.

Chin up, she says in a friendly manner, "One Sondrine Renfrew for the taking. We offer you to her unharmed. First and foremost, we serve our king, but do know we appreciate the gold."

I scoff at the absurdity of her statement. Were it not for the gold, I'd be a free woman.

The lead Sentinel removes his helmet. Firelight teases the strands of midnight blue, accentuates the scruff on his jaw. The relief of seeing Shán makes me weak-kneed. But his eyes are layered ice, hard and impenetrable. With a rough hand, he turns me around by the shoulders once, twice.

"As I suspected," he growls. "An imposter."

This is some kind of ploy. He's pretending, and I must play along.

"Good sir, this is Sondrine Renfrew, the woman wanted by King Andronicus." Adina holds up the poster for comparison. "We've spoken. She's admitted as much."

"You were tricked. Sondrine Renfrew is dead," he declares. A communal gasp, and even I wonder where he's going with this story. "She was lost to the icy waters of the Dendrite Sea more than thirty days past."

Clever, Shán. He's going to convince them I'm dead and then take me away as their prisoner.

Shán sets the sword at my shoulder. The tip pierces my skin, and I cry out in pain. *Ease up! This is taking things too far.*

"What are you?" he hisses. "A Skinwalker? Or perhaps the Dead Ringer was used?" His lips twitch with rancor, and the words come out thick and controlled. "I should kill you right now." He twists the blade.

"Shán," I scream in pain. "I'm Sondrine, I swear to you." *This is no act. He truly believes I'm dead, that someone is impersonating me.* My head spins, trying to conjure up shared memories. "You brought me to Winterhaven for the king. After the Infernal attacked, we stayed in a cave where I nursed you back to health."

His grip on the sword is solid, unwavering. One more word from my mouth will see me without a head, so I decide to appeal to his Voyant capabilities. *You kissed me at Sold & Gilvers as the rain poured down in droves. Never have I forgotten that moment.*

The wrinkles at the corners of his eyes grimace with something. Recognition? Belief? No, an emotional connection; he must know it's me. He sets the blade on my shoulder, eases it along as he moves closer until his mouth is nearly on mine.

"Oh, Belisama," he seethes. "Do you play me for a fool? My Sentinel and I intercepted the raven sent to my father. Your plan to lure him here under the guise that Sondrine Renfrew was alive so you could kill him and move one step closer to the throne was uninspired. Do you truly believe I or my father would fall for such a ruse?"

I look sidelong at the blade devastatingly close to my neck. "I'm not the queen," I breathe in a terrified whisper.

161

"This I now know. You work for her, one of her many thieving spies. We've caught a dozen or more of your kind, and none have lived to see the light of day." He takes a sharp step back and sheathes his sword. Surveying the crowd, he asks, "Is the Magister of Taliin present?"

The man who drugged me tips his hat in response. "Aye."

"Throw her in prison," Shán commands. "Impersonating another goes against the laws of the land." He tosses a meager pouch of gold onto the table and looks Adina in the eye. "For your time. You were a meager pawn in this game, no fault of your own." Shán signals the Sentinel, and they make for their leave, the crowd stepping back to create a path.

"A ship cut through the Sanctuary of Caelum," I shout in desperation. "I managed to climb aboard but was taken prisoner. A plague had broken out, and over the passing weeks I cured the captain and the crew. This is how I came to be in Taliin. Please, you must listen to me, Shán."

Shán stops at the door, slow to turn my way. "*Sir* Shán. And must I listen? Who are you to command anything of me, filthy traitor?"

"Ask anything," I beg. "Test me."

I look up at the oil-lit chandelier to assess what I might create with the flames to prove who I am, to prove I'm the Elementalist he knows.

Shán walks toward me in hard, deliberate strides. "Skinwalkers assume the memories and the talents of those taken, same as the Dead Ringer. Nothing you say or do will convince me you are Sondrine Renfrew."

"Give her a chance," Adina chimes in quickly.

Ah, greed. No surprise there. My success will lead to hers. The given gold assuredly pales compared to the king's reward.

The Sentinel moves to Shán's side, and they look at one another briefly. Whatever advice the guard is silently extolling, Shán seems piqued, given the way his mouth tightens in a line. Resigned, he says, "Do enlighten us, Sondrine." He spits my name. "Divulge the name of this so-called ship."

The first question hits me in my gut. All eyes are on me, awaiting an answer I can't give. "You see, although I asked, I...I never actually learned of the name."

"The captain's name, then?" Shán says more firmly.

I breathe a sigh of relief, for this question is not only answerable but verifiable. Captain Seybourne sent off a sworn statement to the king as proof. But my stomach sours with the realization I've just committed a major gaffe. I told Shán and everyone else at the Barmy Goat how I cured the captain and the crew. Yet Captain Seybourne's written account stated I was a prisoner who murdered a man and then escaped. Two very different stories. If I reveal the captain's name, he will be labeled a traitor and killed. "He told me to address him only as 'Captain.' Really, I mostly tended to the crew because the captain recovered quick enough."

A bitter smirk. "A name. Any name. After all, you cured an

163

entire ship's worth of men. Passage from the Sanctuary of Caelum
to Taliin is near to a month's time. There must have been thirty or
more deckhands working the ship. One name so I can verify this
story of yours."

"Well," I stammer. "A steward aboard the ship helped me nurse
the crew to health. 'Stew' was his name." The tavern erupts in
sanctimonious laughter, and I feel my doom creeping in. "There
was a man named Naedder," I offer loudly, more desperate.

Shán's eyebrow goes up, and his mouth opens to acquire more
information.

"But he's dead," I say before he can ask. The words are choking,
for they paint me a liar.

Shán's anger is palpable. His hand grips the sword's hilt;
another blunder will find me sliced in two, breast to gut.

"Bart," I blurt. "Bart Dewar."

The magister steps forward. "Dewar is a common surname. Is
the bloke here in Taliin?"

Bart is dead, of course, but I don't dare say the words or my
fate will be sealed. Then I remember. Adina met Bart, intimately
and more than once.

"Tell him you know Bart," I plead, spinning around to face her.
Along with the pouch of gold, Adina is gone. I look back at Shán
and the Sentinel with pleading eyes. "Find Adina, verify my story.
She knows Bart, I promise you."

"She knows he was aboard your ship?" He takes the
uncertainty behind my eyes as answer. "Lock her in the irons,"

Shán says to the magister. "The queen is nearby. This is nothing more than a trap to stall for time until she gets here."

"I'm Sondrine Renfrew," I yell as the magister ties rope around my wrists. "Do you hear me, Shán?"

He doesn't. He and the Sentinel are already long gone.

***

The jail cell sits below ground and reeks near as bad as the one on the ship. A small barred window providing a modicum of fresh air sits at street level. I kick over the chamber pot, toe it below the window, and use it to stand on. My face pressed to the cold iron, I beg for help, but no one pays me any mind. This goes on for hours on end, but my pleas yield only a barrage of rotted food and insults from the passersby. Sometime between a maggot-infested tomato splitting on the bars and a drunken man relieving himself of water into my cell—narrowly missing me thanks to bad aim—my voice leaves me altogether.

Repulsed and exhausted, I step off the pot and examine the iron-barred door. Another cell facing mine houses a stick of a man. His lascivious looks and lewd remarks drive me to the corner. I study the stone walls and the earthen floor. Earth is my least favorite element and my weakest, but I must concentrate if I want to break free of this place.

Throughout the night, I mentally attempt to dig my way out. My Elemental efforts produce miserable results. Fissures cobweb the walls and cleft the ground, all so insignificant not even a roach could use them for a hasty escape.

165

Early morning light ushers in a burly guard.

"Cleanse yourself." He shoves a tray through the space between the bars and the ground. "Change into the provided clothing. I'll be back in one hour to escort you out." His words whistle through gums orphaned of teeth.

Within the tray is a small cloth, a larger rolled towel, a bowl of water, a thin robe of blue cotton, and a pair of woven corded sandals. Though I don't want to part with my clothes, for now I must do as he asks to get above ground.

By the time the guard returns, I've washed myself as well as I can, given the circumstances. He tuts when he sees the knapsack at my back. "Won't be needing that where we're going."

"I'm not leaving without my belongings." My voice is barely there. He shrugs a shoulder, lets himself into the cell. The coil of rope in his hands makes me back away. "Please, do not tie me up. I promise you I won't run off."

"Hands and ankles. Got no say in the matter."

"I'll get you gold," I plead. "Set me free right now, and I promise to make you a wealthy man."

His eyes look tired, as though he's heard this speech a thousand times. "Don't like forcing anything, but I'll call in another guard to hold you down if I have to."

The man in the other cell cackles, yells something about watching and enjoying himself, so I hold up my hands in resignation. "Where are we going?"

"You'll see soon enough."

Wrists bound at my back, ankles tied to one another, I shuffle through the streets as the magister and the guards prod me along like a wayward sheep. Toiling church bells and the dull roar of a mob lead us into the crowded town square, half-covered in ash and rubble from the Infernals' atrocities. We cut a path where people paw at me, denigrate me with curse words, their hundreds of eyes fixed upon me.

"Death to you, filthy witch!"

"Devil monger!"

"Burn in wintry hell, Skinwalker!"

With the insults come food. Radishes and potatoes feel like stones when they pelt my head and spine, and a small cabbage nearly knocks me over when it hits my left knee. My heart pounds against the rising taunts as I'm led up steps to a small platform centered with a large pillar of wood. Splayed from every angle are columns of stacked timber like a pyre—

"No!" I gasp, and I try to flee, but the guards have me by my shoulders. Brutishly they cut off my knapsack and then bind me to the pillar.

At the edge of the jeering crowd are Shán and the Sentinel, both on horseback. I try to scream Shán's name, to plead for my life. My voice is a whisper lost to the raucous chants of, "Burn the evil, smite the darkness!"

The magister climbs the stone steps of an official-looking building to my left, all columns and ornate stonework. At the top, he raises a hand to quiet the riotous crowd. Pulling a piece of

167

parchment from his breast pocket, he reads, "Under the laws decreed by King Andronicus, sovereign of Winterhaven and champion for all, the great city of Taliin does not tolerate Skinwalkers who impersonate another unlawfully. Furthermore, Queen Belisama Agni is a sworn enemy not only to the citizens of Taliin but to the citizens of the realm. The king, though merciful, seeks justice. Let this be a lesson to all. Should the queen be conferred with in any manner, the sentence shall be harsh and violent, your death the same as this one here. Say 'aye' if you understand this decree."

"Aye!" roars across the square with fists pounding the air.

The magister signals for the torch. I try to break free, my heart racing in terror, but the ropes make it impossible to move. Flames crack and bray as the guards circle the base of the pyre. The kindling catches quickly. Smoke drifts around me, seeps into my lungs and nostrils and suffocates my silent screams.

The bloodthirsty crowd cheers on my death. The higher the flames go, twisting and turning and finding new life, the louder the chanting grows. A barren sky shines down, boundless and blue. Across the way, a flag limps in the breeze—languid but present—a last hope for escape. My mind reels, the heat so scalding I can barely think as I try to concentrate on a gale so strong and so punishing it will wipe dirt clean from the cobblestones.

Full of fury, the gale gusts in, howling and piercing and potent. Instead of smiting the flames, it fans them higher, longer, sending them through the crowd like quicksilver. The unlucky scream in pain while the rest flee for cover. Not Shán, nor his Sentinel. They wait and watch. Through the shimmering heat and the swirling smoke, Shán's potent gaze is the last thing I see before the wood pillar burns away and dumps me deep into the pyre.

The fire is a pride of roaring lions, so thunderous it hurts my ears. I scoot my wrists under me until they're out front. Then I gather myself up and shoulder my way into the blazing wood. Once, twice, thrice. The logs are thick, weighty and confining. I madly claw at the ashen wood until my nails break and bleed, and then I claw some more.

"Help me!" I scream in a voiceless plea. "Don't let me die!"

Unlike in Mount Serius, the heat is scorching, fierce. My skin is slick with sweat, and I cough from the excessive smoke. I may be an Elementalist, but I'm not Immortal; even I can only tolerate so much.

How else can I smite the flames? The more desperately I look for an answer, the more light-headed and disoriented I become. I stumble and fall to my knees. The pyre is engulfed on all sides. There is no escape, no other hope. Head bent, I surrender to the blaze, to the smoke beating me, choking me. Slaughtering me.

PART II

It is not in the stars
To hold our destiny
But in ourselves
~ William Shakespeare

CHAPTER TEN

A raven's cry echoes across the void; wind despairs against bones of the dead. The sounds bore a hole through my consciousness and awaken me. Yet I am stone, the pyre's remains a weighted shell that harbors my body. Eyelids push against ash caught in my lashes; lungs gasp for newfound air. A blanket of dying embers slides from my skin as I stagger to my feet and blink at the sky. Day has surrendered to night. Falling snow and rising ash marry in the chilly breeze and sweep over my naked body. Only the Aeriscloque remains.

The town square is eerily silent and empty. Empty save for Shán and the Sentinel on horseback. Silently Shán slips off his horse and walks toward me with tenacious steps. A profound sorrow lives behind his eyes as his cloak goes around my shoulders, and he draws in a deep, shuddering breath.

"Take me to safety," I say, my voice whittled to dust.

At full speed, we ride out of Taliin, the Sentinel close in the lead. My arms stay tight around Shán's waist, my face burrowed deep into his back. Time becomes liquid; only sounds and scents are markers. Rushing water to my left, a rallying cry of wolves on my right, the ebb and flow of wet snow falling all around.

And smoke. Perhaps the heady scent comes from my body or perhaps from the fires set by the queen burning down Winterhaven town by town, brick by brick.

The sky is twilit when the horses ease up before slowing to a stop. My head lifts to a woodland hewn of frost and ice. Shán dismounts, and the Sentinel follows, his silver strands sent tumbling when he removes his helmet. He's no Sentinel at all. He's Lord Kian, the Sylph from the Veneficum, leader of the Mór.

Shán guides me down from the saddle, and I stumble into him, our mouths a whisper from a stolen kiss. More than a month ago, I would have yearned for this moment, dreamt of it. Now everything feels different in so many ways, and a kiss is the last thing I want.

Our inadvertent embrace gets lost to the sight of a woman advancing through the icy forest. A sweeping tide of bluish robes embrace her willowy body, and a twisted silver headpiece crowns her short, pearlescent hair. She embraces Lord Kian, long and loving, her eyes hooded in concern.

"Lady Aniyu," Shán says when they break apart, his head bowed in greeting.

She responds in kind and turns her gaze on me. "Welcome to our home, the Keep of Wintersgaard. Your journey has been long and unkind. We offer a warm meal and a soft bed, a reprieve before your passage to the Cloister." She regards my bare feet. Not until now did I notice, and from the surprised look on Shán's face, neither did he. Moreover, I'm naked beneath the cloak.

"As of yet, the cold has left me unaffected," I say hoarsely. "If the Keep is not far, walking is of no concern."

"This here is the lower forest," Lady Aniyu states in an ethereal voice. "To ensure your safety, I shall bring you to the Keep myself."

Voluminous white wings bloom from her back. If I had any voice at all, I would gasp at the incredible sight.

Lord Kian gathers up the reins. "We shall be along shortly. The horses need tending to."

Lady Aniyu takes my hand in hers, and together we drift deep into the silent, snowy world of Wintersgaard. Her wings beat soft and steady, enough to keep us aloft. Beyond the treetops, beyond a world of low-lying clouds, lives a highland, home to a castle forged of frosted ice, haunting in the gloaming. Kissed by moonlight, the spired towers and flying buttresses drip with behemoth icicles as though a waterfall poured over each one and froze it into place.

We land in the bailey before curved double-doors, and they open to us knowingly. The air inside the Keep is temperate, a surprise given the wintry architecture. Lady Aniyu leads me down a massive corridor, the vaulted ceilings carved in a lacework of design. Two paces in the lead, she seems to glide rather than walk, as if still aloft. But her magnificent wings have receded beneath

173

her robes.

A marbled tub of steaming water awaits in the bathing chamber, same for a hot cup of tea. Lady Aniyu indicates a clean robe and matching slippers. "Soak yourself for as long as you like. The tea is suffused with medicinal herbs and honey to help soothe your throat. When you finish, you will find us dining in the Great Hall, should you care to join us."

"Thank you for your kindness," I say, my voice raw and unsteady. With that I'm left alone. My reflection in the oblong mirror is startling. I'm a witch aged a hundred years. My hair is drab and grey; same for my skin. Even the underside of Shán's cloak creates a cloud of dust when it falls in folds to the ground. Ash licked from my lips tastes gritty and burnt, the splash of scarlet a contrast to my sickly pallor.

A quick tap on the Aeriscloque and the doors flutter open to the three clock faces, all of them unscathed: the hour reads five minutes past eight o'clock; moon shows as gibbous, the constellations shining—Polaris especially; predicted weather is cold and clear. How the timepiece withstood the blaze is a mystery, a magic all its own. My knapsack is gone. So too, then, are the Petard and *Secretum Secretorum*, which I vowed to keep safe. Zhang the Elder may never forgive me.

Provided pearls of soap smell near as good as the lavender bar and work wonders against the layers of ash, the water clouding when I submerge myself beneath the suds. Fuchsia curls bloom from my inky hair, and my sloughed skin looks pink and clean

174

once more. I search my body for burns or signs of trauma, but there are none; it remains pristine.

Though my body is untainted, my mind is another story. Each ordeal reopens old wounds. I'm unsure how much more I can take of the killings, of the near-deaths. Of the fact I'm the daughter of a malevolent queen. If I don't end up dead, I may well end up in a padded cell.

And yet it is so. With a hard swallow, I banish the lump in my throat. My former self would be crying right now. Unattractively so, complete with swollen eyes and a red, bulbous nose. But she is no longer. I have accepted my fate to kill the queen and save Winterhaven or at least die trying.

I savor the tea, the medicinal herbs and honey a balm to my sore throat. The last swallow is tepid, same for the tub water, so I step out and dress myself in the provided clothes. The fortress seems empty of servants, devoid of people altogether, so I follow the scent of cooked meat down one corridor and into the next until the Great Hall unfurls before me.

Lady Aniyu and Lord Kian sit together at the head of a long table, with Shán diagonally to Lady Aniyu's right. The men stand when I enter, resuming their places once Lord Kian tucks me into a sizable chair directly opposite Shán. Not ideal, because if I look up at all, his eyes will greet mine every time. So I don't. I stare at my prepared plate of food and pick at the meaty game hen, herbed potatoes, and glazed beets as if they're the most interesting things I've ever encountered.

The mood feels somber and uneasy. Even the fire in the hearth sounds rough and unwelcoming. I've not forgotten the sting of Lord Kian's words, how the Sylphs despise the Duine. Shán must be a rare exception and me a paltry concession.

For some time, there is only the scraping of forks to accompany the silence—the kind of silence born from discomfort rather than ease. When Lady Aniyu asks if wine would please me, I'm careful to look solely at her. "Thank you; yes, it would."

Back to my fascinating beets. The tea helped, made my voice stronger. The wine also helps, gives me courage, especially when Shán pushes his plate aside; the questions are forthcoming. It should be me asking questions, and oh, how I will, but there's a time and a place, neither of which are now.

"Since you left the Sanctuary of Caelum," he starts. "Have you found any information of interest concerning your lineage?" There's an unexpected kindness in his voice.

One swallow of wine then a second. "Many things. The first night we spent in Taliin should have been carefree. I was told about the Great Tower of Annals and figured I would try to find information concerning Belisama. But somehow, she discovered I was in Taliin. The Infernal burned down half the city in an attempt to kill me. Although we managed to escape, the queen's second attempt found me at the Ichor Samhain inside the Hall of Mirrors."

"We?" Shán inquires. "Someone was with you?"

"Yes. Bart, a young man I met on the ship. I made mention of him in the Barmy Goat." Shán shifts in his chair but says nothing, so I continue with my story. "The queen used the Dead Ringer to appear as Lark in one of the many mirrors. When I got within striking distance, the hall became a chaos of flying daggers. Thanks to Bart and his quick thinking, I was shepherded to safety."

I decide to spare the details of Bart's death. The wound is too fresh. "Of note," I add, "I found a Sablier at the Ichor Samhain. Are you familiar?" Shán nods once as do Lady Aniyu and Lord Kian. "When I stepped on—"

"I?" Shán says. "What happened to *Bart?* Who is this young man, and what kind of night did you two spend exactly?" The kind quality in his voice has turned accusatory.

I shake my head in confusion. "What are you going on about?"

"At the beginning of your story, you said 'the first night *we* spent in Taliin.'"

The temerity in his tone makes me scoff. "It wasn't like that."

"What was it like? Shall I presume the bloom is off the rose?"

Affronted by his insinuation, I throw down my napkin in disgust. "How dare you? Who I'm with and what I do is no one's affair but my own. Bart befriended me, and I'll be forever thankful. He helped me find answers; he helped me find the Sablier. And if you really want to know who Bart was, he was a kind and loyal soul who saved my life, and now he's dead because of it."

My voice, so loud, throws echoes off the high ceiling. I look at Lady Aniyu and Lord Kian to apologize for my outburst, but their

177

chairs sit empty.

"The Sablier," Shán presses coldly. "What did it show you?"

How you tried to kill me. That's what I want to say. "Queen Belisama is my mother." The words taste so bitter my tongue recoils as though tasting poison.

Shán leans back in his chair, his jaw working in anger. "Just as I'd said. Just as Guernsey and the rest of the Veneficum had said. And yet you didn't listen. Instead of believing us, you recklessly ran off with no thought to your actions and how they might affect others."

"What you call reckless, I call mindful," I say in a reproving tone. "Am I to believe whatever you tell me? Certainly if the topic is inconsequential. Something this monumental? Never. There are things in this world, truths we must discover for ourselves. Finding out who I am was one of those things. I needed proof, and I found it."

"Fine. You found out for yourself. Feel better? Your actions cost us a significant loss of time. Also a life, possibly others? Perhaps you and your mother are more alike than you would care to admit."

My anger rises out of me, drives me to my feet. "And you like your father: sadistic and horrible. Perhaps you'll have my head as punishment. Stick it in the Mourning Garden for all eternity?"

Now Shán is standing, his mouth dropped open in scorn.

"Oh yes," I add with malicious intent. "Murder runs through your veins, same as the king's. The Sablier was telling. Had Guernsey not rescued me, you would have left me to die in the

178

snow, cut out my heart, and brought it to your father as proof of my murder. And in Taliin, you watched me burn. Happily, for all I know. If either of us is like our parents, Shán, it is you." With both hands, I grab the table's edge to steady me. "Get out of my sight. If I never lay eyes on you again, I'll be the better for it."

My words cut deep, so much so his eyes burn with a hatred so strong I'd be dead thrice over if they could kill.

"Done." He kicks his chair back and leaves the room, throwing the doors open with such force they bounce against the adjacent walls and slam shut behind him.

I flinch from the thunderous reverberation. My anger is a storm inside of me, so wrathful and tangible I'm trembling head to heel. I can't believe Shán's malice. I can't believe my own. Shán may be right. The cruelty that lives and breathes within my mother's blood may well live within my own.

The doors reopen, this time soft and hesitant. Though I half expect to see Shán, it's Lady Aniyu who walks through them.

"My deepest apologies," I say, my head bowed in respect. "I didn't mean to chase you away when you've been nothing but gracious and welcoming. The conversation took a heated turn, and it was ill-mannered at best." *Congratulations, Sondrine. Job well done. If the Mór hate the Duine as much as I know they do, my behavior has sealed the sentiment forever.*

Lady Aniyu walks toward me, slips her arm through mine. "You're exhausted, understandably so. Let me show you to your quarters. A good night's rest works wonders on the soul." Her smile is kind and sincere, and together we leave the Great Hall behind.

My chamber is cozy. The walls are forged of ice, opaque and frigid, immune to the hearth's docile fire. Double-doors lead to a balcony, and a canopied bed swathed in white silk awaits me. To my surprise, my knapsack sits on top of the coverlet, and I rush over and peer inside. Though smoke hemorrhages from every crevice, all is intact: the Petard, my emerald cloak, and *Secretum Secretorum*.

"How can this be?" I ask. "I thought the knapsack was destroyed."

"Lord Kian demanded your bag from the magister as proof of your death for the king." She pauses. "That and your ashes. Certainly, Lord Kian had no such intent, but the magister took him on his word and complied."

Lady Aniyu pulls the coverlet back, a telling gesture to sleep now and save questions for later. I kick off my slippers and crawl beneath the sheets. She sits next to me, her hand over mine. "You're shaking," she notes. "Are you chilled? I can add wood to the fire if needed."

"I'm plenty warm, thank you." I pause for a moment then query her about something that's been niggling at me. "I'm unsure why I survived the fire in Taliin. My Elemental gifts seemed not enough—the smoke and heat eventually caused me to lose consciousness. Yet, here I sit. I'm not...Immortal, am I?" I can't believe I'm asking such an outlandish question. *My padded cell awaits.*

"Few are Immortal in this realm. Your gifts do seem to offer an advantage when the situation involves the elements. Yet the tip of a blade would likely draw blood and all life, I'm afraid."

Embarrassed, I nod. "Is there anything else you might need, Sondrine?"

"More insight." *Loads more.* "After you and Lord Kian left the Great Hall, Shán and I exchanged words—harsh ones. He said something so horrible I still can't believe it. How could he be so cruel?"

Her head tilts, her eyes round and assessing. "You're very young, Sondrine."

What does my age have to do with Shán's actions? "I'm eighteen, nearly an adult in the Other World."

She smiles, unaffected by my defensive claim. "Age is but a number. I speak of youth because it is often sightless regarding reality and understanding. Perhaps a better word is *inexperienced.* Whatever Shán said tonight was born of hurt, born of great pain. You must know this, do you not?"

Silence is my answer, so she continues. "When Shán left the Sanctuary of Caelum to gather part of his fleet, he passed this way briefly. He presumed you dead. For days he had searched for you, and never once did he sleep. Not until your boat washed ashore in nothing but pieces did he stop. I've known Shán since he was a little boy. He has always been reserved; unsurprising given King Andronicus raised him. Never have I seen Shán so distraught as

181

when he came here last. He was devastated by your death."

Her words come as a shock to me. "I never meant to cause him such pain. Had I known, I would have sent a raven to let him know I was safe."

Lady Aniyu shakes her head as she tugs the covers. "Get some rest. Come daybreak, we can speak again should you wish."

"It wasn't only Shán," I confide. "I lashed out at him, said something just as terrible as he'd said to me. Worse. How he was exactly like his father. I told him to leave, how I never wanted to see him again, and he conceded to my wishes." Difficult as it is, I keep my voice even. "You speak the truth. I am inexperienced in these kinds of affairs." Unable to look her in the eye, I stare at the bedcovers. "In men," I add quietly. "How am I supposed to understand their feelings when I can't even sort through my own?"

"Heed my words. Same as youth, the heart can be blind, unseeing the things right before it. To grow, you must open your eyes. You must *see*." She goes to the door. "Find comfort in your dreams, Sondrine."

She leaves me to sleep, and I do try. My body aches with exhaustion, but my mind reels. I need to look for Shán, to at least extend an olive branch. Lady Aniyu is right. I should have seen things for what they were, at least questioned them. It makes me wonder if we forever stay our childish selves and only put on certain airs or if we mature and leave all the foolishness behind. *The former, likely.*

The Keep of Wintersgaard is a city unto itself. Moonlight

shifts, drops in different shapes across the floors and high ceilings, the windows splashed with its silvery dust. Once again, I pass the Great Hall, and then the larder and buttery. Dozens of bed chambers and solars occupy the upper levels, and at the far end of the castle is some sort of sanctuary with windows of stained glass. The lowest level of the Keep is frigid, a vaulted undercroft storing weaponry of all sorts.

I hurry back up the stairs and along the corridors while trying to decide what I might say to Shán should I find him. One wrong word or wayward emotion will send him running. He reminds me of a cautious stag chancing a drink from a stream. One stray movement that reads like danger and he's gone.

The Aeriscloque reads half past midnight by the time I return to my chamber, unsuccessful in my search. Chilled to the core, I warm my hands by the fire. Most likely Shán complied with my wishes and now he's long gone. *Brava. First Lord Kian and Lady Aniyu, now Shán. I've mastered the uncanny ability to send people running.*

From the corner of my eye, a shadow dances outside of the window. I move closer and draw back the drapery for a better look. Perched on the balcony is the white raven, eyes bluer than a shallow sea. I'm strangely happy to see it.

I pull on my boots and the emerald cloak then flee down three levels before I find my way outside. The raven takes flight, wills me to follow across the walled bailey. Two stone staircases and one archway later, we're inside the frosted woodland.

183

The sky is luminescent, a majestic aurora of violet, the snow foaming up in a purple tide. Undaunted by the perils that befall any forest, I trail the raven through the night. Flashes of white flying and landing, flying and landing, always allowing me to catch up before it continues on.

Will the raven offer another key? Lead me to a place like the Nowhere in Particular? Soon enough my answers come in the form of a stone bridge rolling itself into a crag. Across the raven goes and through the jagged opening. Unfailingly I follow.

The frosted walls are lit with sconces as though some smaller variation of the Keep. Statues carved in ice rise up on either side, standing sentry to what must be a sacred space, perhaps even a mausoleum. My heart beats faster, less from fear and more from anticipation of where I'm being led to, and to what.

The tunnel empties into a small cavern, and the raven disappears inside. What I see stops me short of entering, to stare at the wonder and the beauty. And the magic. Somehow it's snowing inside the cavern. Light, swirling flakes, not dissimilar from the gentle shaking of the snow globe.

In the middle of the space is an orb of latticed ice suspended in midair. A purplish light emanates from the orb and breathes life into an inscription on the ceiling. The raven is perched on a small outcrop in the wall. Head cocked to one side, the bird watches as I step across the threshold to read the words aloud.

"*Through the stars I come. With me, I bring the treasure. Within me, I bring the Aether. The final gift to Winterhaven.*'" I

184

look down to the protected source of light, an amethyst gemstone shaped like a half-moon.

"What is this?" I whisper to the raven.

"A piece of the Cintamani Jewel."

The answer comes not from the raven but from behind. From a voice I know as well as my own. Shán moves around to stand crossways from me on the other side of the orb.

I watch him through the purple light and the falling snow. "Cintamani Jewel?" I whisper.

"An ancient relic comprised of gemstones, each representative of an element. Rumors abound of how the jewel offers eternal light, forever smiting the darkness. Some offer a contrarian view. They say the stones will bring a mortal plague, an eternal damnation to the world. No one truly knows, for the stones have never been reunited. The one consistent theory holds that the Cintamani Jewel is all-powerful and will offer immortality to the bearer. This here is purple Kyanite, the authentic gemstone of Air, which is why the Mór have possession."

Intrigued, I ask, "Where are the other jewels?"

"They could be anywhere. Or nowhere at all. Much lore surrounds the Cintamani Jewel, including the question of its very existence. Perhaps the answer lies in *Secretum Secretorum*."

"The jewel must be important, because the raven led me here," I half mutter to myself. *The faithful raven, always finding me, always leading me to the right place. Snowy feathers, the same as those of the taloned raven in the Scissure of Lost Souls, the same*

185

white as the shock of hair. And those aquamarine eyes....

Guernsey? I turn to the outcrop to ask him myself, but the raven is nowhere to be found. I sigh, for I'm probably deluded.

"What do you think this means?" I ask, my attention returned to the inscribed ceiling. Shán studies the words a long while. "As with anything in Winterhaven, the inscription may carry more than one meaning. Lord Kian and Lady Aniyu know the answer. Whether they will tell us is a question of another kind. The stone is protected by the orb. Only an answer to the inscription or Lord Kian's own hands can remove the kyanite."

He pulls a stray root from the ground and attempts to penetrate the orb. A spark crackles, so loud and powerful the root ignites with flame. Shán drops it to the ground and shovels snow with his boot to extinguish the blaze.

We stand in a complicated silence. There is so much to speak about, so many questions. So much regret. I wonder where to start, what the right thing is to say.

"I thought you were dead," Shán says.

Right to the point; I'm grateful. "Lady Aniyu told me. Shán, had I known—"

"I was in the seaport of Lagos recruiting men and women for the Veneficum's army and securing the rest of my fleet. A raven had been sent to the king for ransom of your capture."

I nod knowingly. "The raven sent by Adina."

"We intercepted the scroll. In my mind's eye, there was no possible way you could be alive. I'd grieved your death. Accepted it.

186

We believed it to be a trap set by Belisama herself. A trap to lure my father to Taliin so she could kill him there, vulnerable without his army."

"Why come to Taliin at all if you thought it was a ruse?"

"The perfect opportunity had presented itself. Pretend to be there under my father's orders and then maim the queen right there."

"Maim?"

Shán's exhale commingles with the snow. "With you dead, we knew Belisama could not be killed. But we could injure the queen, incapacitate her until we devised a more permanent solution akin to the snowflake obsidian."

I blow air into my hands to warm them. "If you thought I was the queen, why didn't you kill me in the brothel?"

"We were prepared to do so. Were it Belisama herself, we knew she would attempt to take my life. A dagger to my heart. Or any other weapon she may have procured. When none of these things transpired, I believed you to be a minion of the queen. But I couldn't piece everything together—why a Skinwalker was there and not the queen herself. When you asked me to test you, I complied only because Lord Kian spoke to my Voyant capabilities. He thought it might indeed be you. Soon enough, when you proved unable to answer my questions, we decided it was a tactic to stall until the queen arrived. Our army was still north of us in Lagos. Biding what little time we had, we headed to the docks to find reinforcements for our battle. A handful of men agreed, persuaded mostly by gold rather than valor."

Shán moves around to my side, pulls off his gloves, and offers them to me. Though too large, they are warm, and I'm grateful for the gesture.

"What reason did you have to watch me burn?" This has been the foremost question on my mind. To have to ask is painful and distressing, but I keep my anger tempered until I hear his explanation.

"With our newfound army, we camped beneath the stars, lying in wait. Since the Infernal had been in Taliin the day previous, we figured it was only a matter of time before Belisama materialized in whatever form she was currently in. Admittedly, when she didn't show, we were perplexed as to why. Still we went to the execution as bait, believing the queen would find us and make an entrance. She could kill me and half the city of Taliin all at once. Perhaps even Lord Kian had she a weapon forged of iron, a Killing's Heil for all Sylphs, as you know. Why would she pass up such an opportunity?

"Lord Kian and I waited with our men at our backs. When neither Belisama nor the Infernal showed, and when the gale swept through out of nowhere, I then questioned who you were. By then the pyre was fully ablaze. It sickened me to watch you burn, angered me, but I had no choice except to wait things out. If you were a Skinwalker, you would die in the pyre. If it was truly you, then you would survive."

His statement puzzles me beyond compare. "How could you

188

have known when I did not? I was certain my death was imminent."

The corner of his mouth eases into the faintest of smiles. "To be sure, I did not know explicitly. From everything you'd divulged concerning your past, and from everything I had personally borne witness to, especially in the depths of Mount Serius, I could only hope you would survive."

Hope. I look up at him through tired eyes, the snowflakes falling against his dark lashes.

"You're exhausted," he notes. "You need to rest. We both do. I'll escort you back to the castle and then—"

"Leave?" I draw in a resolved breath. "Before the raven led me here, I went looking for you in the castle. Shán, never should I have said those things. Never should I have told you to go."

"Fatigue got the better of us both," he murmurs. "Perhaps we should leave things at that. I'll remain in the forest here to usher in a good night's sleep before heading north."

"The forest? Why?"

"When I visit the Keep, I stay elsewhere."

I pull my cloak tighter, understanding the insinuation. If the women of Wintersgaard look anything like Lady Aniyu, someone must be awaiting Shán's company.

He shakes his head. "I'll be alone tonight."

"You were reading my mind?"

"I was reading the sour expression on your face." He laughs quietly, and it makes me do the same.

189

I move closer, aware of the pine and firesmoke so reminiscent of him. "Shán, I don't want to leave you, not tonight." In a bold move, I slip my hand into his.

His eyebrows arch in surprise by my forthright declaration. He pauses, long enough to cause concern that he will spurn my wishes. But his fingers tighten around mine, and he leads me back outside.

We walk for a long while in an impregnable quiet under the icy leaves and snow-laden branches. I'm curious as to where we're going but decide not to ask questions.

Shán stops abruptly and stares at the stars. "You're nothing like your mother," he says in a quiet tone. The pronouncement comes out of nowhere, so much so it startles me. "My words were harsh and undeserved," he continues. "They stemmed from resentment. While I was mourning your death, you were with another."

"I was with no one, not in such a manner," I state emphatically.

He smiles, rueful. "Makes no difference, don't you see? Matters of the heart tainted my delusions. The reveal was ugly, not what truly mattered. You are alive, and forever I am grateful."

Any answer feels wrong, so I squeeze his hand in gratitude. We continue through the forest until a tree made of ice rises in the woodland, the grooved trunk startlingly similar to the one I created at Cimmerian's Curio Emporium all those months ago.

"This is where I stay when I visit Wintersgaard. After growing up in the largesse of Isceald Castle, I prefer more intimate spaces."

THE CRYSTAL SKY

At the top of a winding staircase lives a snow-covered treehouse, similar in appearance to a squat turret nestled among the tree's highest branches. Crafted of birch and ice, the house is a most curious combination. The climb is short but steep enough to make my already tired legs ache further.

Inside the treehouse, our breath darts out in diaphanous clouds. Occupying two walls are an oak-framed bed and a cold woodstove with an armchair at its side. Opposite to those, cupboards hover above a flat work space. Animal hide rugs are scattered across the timbered floor, while a rounded ceiling of ice fans over us, so transparent the stars shine through with conviction.

Shán eases the knapsack from my shoulders and unties my cloak. I'm still in my given robes, perfectly comfortable for sleeping. I kick off my boots and crawl into bed, beneath the furs and feathered blankets, my head burrowed into the soft pillows.

Creaking hinges of the woodstove's door; flint striking steel; kindling catching fire. The rustle of footsteps and a sweet, whispered goodnight against my ear. These are the sounds I hear before I hear no more; when the silence rises, the dreaming kind, the kind that folds around me and carries me away.

CHAPTER ELEVEN

The sweet perfume of apple and cinnamon rouses me come daybreak. My eyes flutter open to a violet sky, unchanged although perhaps a little lighter in hue. Unlike last night, the air in the treehouse is warm thanks to a robust fire in the woodstove.

I look around for Shán. A blanket is draped across the empty armchair; a pillow lies forgotten on the ground.

Did he leave without saying goodbye? A spike of panic prompts me to sit up. On a small bedside table is a full cup of tea along with a scribbled note: *Back soon.* Relieved, I lie against the pillows and sip the tea, the same aromas that awoke me now dancing across my tongue.

Sleep has worked wonders, and for the first time in ages, I feel anchored. From the moment I stowed away on the ship, my life has been a maelstrom of events, one thing after the other with no time in between to breathe.

My mind wanders back to last night, to what Shán said before we climbed into the treehouse. '*I'd grieved your death*' and '*matters of the heart.*' And, of course, what Lady Aniyu imparted, how she had never seen Shán so distraught.

Shán cares for me. How could I fail to see? Unless...it's what I want to see and not what is so.

Footstep against the stairs. Shán appears in the doorway, his hair wet, the strands tipped with frost. "Went for a quick swim and caught this on my way back." He holds up a dead goose. "Not much to eat in here—I'm heading back out soon to pick some winter fruit and possibly some morels and river kelp if I'm lucky. But I was getting worried and wanted to check on you first."

"Worried? Why?"

"It's well past noon."

I check the Aeriscloque around my neck. "Why didn't you wake me?"

"No point. You needed to sleep."

I hold up my cup as a thank you gesture. "What now? Am I to go to the Cloister today?"

Shán sets the goose on a hook. "You must be escorted up the mountain. Lady Aniyu and Lord Kian have sent word, so in a few days' time, depending on how soon your guides can get here."

I swallow the last bit of tea and set the cup on the windowsill. "The sooner the better, I suppose. No point in waiting."

Shán hesitates. "Time is of the essence, admittedly. I'm glad you're ready, and of your own volition."

I'm as ready as a cat is for a swim. "In the interim, may I join you on your scavenge?"

Armed with burlap sacks, we leave the treehouse behind and trudge through fresh-fallen snow. Shán explains the different

193

kinds of berries. Those that I ate while following him to Isceald Castle are called thorned snowberries, and they are as good as I remember. The familiar jammy taste fills my mouth, sour at the start and sweet on the finish.

"What do you make of the Cintamani Jewel?" I ask as I lick pulp from my lips. "Do you think it could help in my quest?"

"You would need to find all four gemstones, and time is running thin. The other stones may well not exist. One would never know from here, but the war has begun. Winterhaven is burning, and thousands are already dead. Our armies, including the king's infantry, are making little progress, largely because the queen's exact whereabouts remain unknown."

Had I believed Shán and the Veneficum from the start, so many lives could have been saved. Seeing the truth with my own eyes set me free, but the choice to do so will forever be a burden of remorse and guilt. My lone triumph spelled defeat for so many. Downtrodden, I continue to walk along collecting berries from the various bushes.

The Cintamani Jewel must be important; vital even. "Any chance there's a Hereat in Wintersgaard? We could summon Zhang the Elder. He might know of the Cintamani Jewel and all of its inner workings."

"Using a Hereat is not an option. Too dangerous given the uncertain climate. Last time we ended up in Mount Serius because of the queen. We must be far more careful this time around."

Point taken, although something tells me Zhang the Elder

would know about the jewel in some manner.

"Were you with the queen? Intimately, I mean. Were you in love with her?" My questions stumble out, honest yet blunt. But I need to know, and Shán must understand this, because the look on his face is neither anger nor indifference but understanding.

"Had I been with the queen, know me well enough I would never have kissed you at Sold & Gilvers. A man has his boundaries. The time spent with the queen was strictly platonic. Remember, she was locked inside the snowflake obsidian."

"Why did you go to her in the first place?"

Shán plucks a cluster of morels and tosses them into the burlap sack. "No one needs to tell you what a vicious and cruel person my father is. From even my earliest memories, he was always foreboding. My mother was there to protect me, then one day she was not. Eight weeks shy of my seventh birthday, I went wandering through the castle looking for her. Minutes became hours, and when day turned to night, I retired to my chamber, waiting for her to tell me my usual bedtime story along with a prayer to the gods above. Never once had she failed to be there. Come morning, when I awoke alone, I asked one of the Sentinels of her whereabouts. 'She had to leave quite unexpectedly,' he'd told me. I'll never forget the look on his face, the betrayal of the lie behind his eyes. Soon thereafter I found her head on the Mourning Tree. Why my father killed her, I may never know. But I never forgave him."

My heart hurts. Never once had I thought my inquiries would

195

unearth such horrible memories. I want to tell Shán to stop, that it doesn't really matter, but judging by the look of resignation on his face, he seems to want to share the story.

"Over the years, the dislike between my father and I grew, and soon enough I was at an age of defiance. I wanted to hurt him the same way he'd hurt me. Befriending the queen seemed the utmost betrayal. She was the enemy, my father's greatest.

"The first time I entered Mount Serius, I had no idea what I was embarking upon. A woman trapped in snowflake obsidian. I wondered if she could even speak or if she was frozen within the crystals, devoid of all life. She was very much alive and in desperate need of company. In the beginning, I only came by when it suited my fancy. Our conversations were short, uncomfortable. In time they grew more intense and much longer. Belisama was smart, clever, like no woman I'd ever met. I found her intriguing, so much so I soon found myself in Mount Serius daily. The betrayal of my father felt seductive, and I did develop an affection for her. In all honesty, had she not been trapped, I cannot know what might have transpired between us."

The aftertaste of the berries has gone sour in my mouth. Now I regret my line of questioning. "I understand."

"I don't think you do. I'm grateful she was untouchable. Years passed before I realized she was baiting me. Slowly, carefully. If she lured me to her side, made me feel sorry for her, I could break the spell. She knew I hated my father so, and she used my hatred to her advantage as leverage. If anyone could find out what the spell was, the dark magic used, it was I. Did Belisama love me? She claimed it was so. As for me, I know what love for a woman is. Whatever I felt toward the queen, the admiration and the respect I had for her, never was it love."

The relief of hearing this is more than I could have anticipated. My gut has been home to this concern, a knot that unravels with the newfound knowledge. I'm curious to ask how Shán knows what love for a woman is, but I decide not to ask. In the end, it's none of my business. "How did you come to see the queen for who she was and what she was doing?"

"Guernsey. He helped me to gain clarity." Shán twists a small golden apple off a tree and bites through the skin. When he nods in appreciation, he hands off the apple and takes another for himself. Months ago, I would have bitten the side opposite. Now I bite partially where his mouth was, to get an inadvertent taste of him. Whether it's Shán or the apple or both, the flavor is sweeter than honey, and I let the taste linger against my tongue.

"Why do you think the queen brought Eirene into the fold?" I ask.

"The queen did not trust me, not wholly. She'd asked me to search my father's library, through his journals or anywhere else he might have hidden the spell. The longer I stalled, the more her suspicions grew. Eirene was a secondary plan. The perfect, unsuspected spy. She could get in and out of the castle easily. My father is a pragmatist, wise to never leave a trail. Whoever created the dark magic behind the spell is likely living in the Mourning

Garden. His or her head anyway." He shrugs. "Mount Serius erupted, and the queen was freed, the spell ultimately unneeded."

A stag wanders into view. Antlered spikes resemble the branches of a barren, majestic tree, and the fur coat is whiter than the snow underfoot. Slow and careful, Shán unsheathes the dagger from his boot, the sharpened blade glinting in the light. I'm about to shout '*No!*' to scare off the stag and save it from an untimely death when Shán quarters the golden apple and holds the pieces in his palm.

Large, assessing brown eyes. Then cautious steps as the stag approaches and nibbles at the apple.

"Kashmir, old friend," Shán says, scratching behind his ears.

I watch in wonder at the sight, at the kinship between the two, and I revel in the beauty.

***

Back at the treehouse, I ask Shán to loan me some garments while mine air out. Everything I own reeks of smoke. He only concedes because the given robes are far too thin in fabric and provide little warmth.

"What do you think?" I ask once I've changed. The linen chemise is so large I'm drowning in it, and the trousers are held at the waist so they won't fall to my ankles. The picture of fashion I am not.

Shán looks up from plucking goose feathers. His eyes flick to my breasts, unbound beneath the linen fabric, and they signal the lingering chill. "Ridiculous," he mutters as his eyes fall away.

"There's an extra belt in the chest at the foot of the bed."

I find the belt and pull it on tight as it will allow. Then I help him prepare our meal, slicing the morels as I retell my adventures since I left the Sanctuary of Caelum.

"I'm scared for Lark," I say when I get to the part about the Ichor Samhain and the Hall of Mirrors. "Before the queen tried to kill me, she said Lark was too valuable to kill."

Shán slows his plucking. "As long as Lark stays at the Sanctuary of Caelum, she should be safe."

"Should?" I'm starting to hate that word.

He looks at me, steadfast. "No one is safe anymore. Ykuza tried to kill us at the Sanctuary of Caelum, one of the safest places in all of Winterhaven next to here. There is nothing we can do but move forward and try to find the queen and—"

"Kill her."

The thought is unnerving, and Shán must sense this, because he pours us each a cup of mead. When we finish cooking, leaving the stew to simmer on the woodstove, Shán cleans up and lights the lanterns, and I take to the armchair with *Secretum Secretorum* in search of the Cintamani Jewel.

For once luck is on my side. The Cintamani Jewel is part of the extensive table of contents, and I flip to the assigned page. The chapter is short, the lettering tiny, and I angle the book to best capture the firelight.

Lore states the Cintamani Jewel began as a star descended from the Realm of Halcyon, representing Aether* to contain the

199

power of Above. As the jewel fell to Winterhaven, it gathered Fire, Water, Air, and Earth to form the power of Below. The shape was most curious, a five-tiered stele: The cubed base, Earth; Water, sphere; Fire, pyramid; Air, crescent. Aether, gem-shaped, crowned them all. When the Cintamani Jewel crashed to Winterhaven, the stele broke into five gemstones, each representative of an element. In isolation from one another, the gemstones lie dormant in their power. Together they are all-powerful, offering eternal life to the bearer while forever destroying evil.

*Aether, also known as Quintessence. Dissent amongst scholars exists as to whether Aether is comprised of starlight or dark energy.

"Shán," I say, studying a picture of the stele. "Do you know anything about Aether? The inscription above the kyanite mentioned it. When I learned I was an Elementalist, I studied the different elements only knowing there were four. Guernsey mentioned Quintessence when he spoke of the Emerald Tablet. From what I recall, this fifth element relates to the stars. Does Aether carry another meaning in Winterhaven?"

I look up for his answer. Instead, I find a wooden spoon filled with stew cupped by Shán's hand. "Taste."

The book falls to my lap, and I take a bite. "Not bad."

"Not bad?" He sets a hand to his heart. "You do know how to break a man's spirit." Back at his workspace, he chops several sprigs of parsley. "If my memory serves correctly, Aether is the heavens, all things celestial. Some say the soul is comprised of

200

Aether."

"Wherever in the world would I find the stone, regardless of its incarnation?"

Shán pours the stew into bowls. "Keep reading. Perhaps the book will tell you."

We dine on the floor, akin to an indoor picnic. We have seconds and Shán has thirds, and when I'm fully sated, I recline against the bedframe. I show him the dagger thrown by Belisama and the Taerou cards from Jeyna. Shán knows of Taerou. He shrugs off the Queen of Swords and the Death card but studies the one called *World of Winterhaven.*

"What did the seer say about this one?" He flicks the corner with his finger.

"The woman is a seeker of truth. The fish, bull, dragon, and eagle each represent an element. Nothing was mentioned about the wreath wrapped in heavenly skies..." Shán and I share a knowing glance. *Heavenly skies. Aether, the fifth element.* "She said this card was important; there was a strong vibrational pull. She finished with 'The answer to your question lies here.'"

"Which question?"

"I asked the same but got no answer. In the Other World, Taerou is used for divination purposes, mostly as a lark, although some take the foretellings serious enough."

Shán hands off the card. "I don't know the intricacies of Taerou pertaining to Winterhaven. Do you believe her?"

My throat tightens. "She read Bart's cards and foretold his

201

death. One of the cards made no sense, not to me anyway, but the others came to fruition." Bart's face crops up before me: his smile, his paunchy cheeks. How good and kind he was to me. How his future will never play out and how his father will never know of his son as an unheralded hero. How I hope he's with Illya in the Great Tower of Annals for all of eternity. To think of his face in a jar forever traveling with the Ichor Samhain is something I can't bear, the horribleness all too great.

Shán leans in, thumbs away an unexpected tear. "You cared deeply for him."

"Like a sister for a brother." I shake my head in sadness. "At least I was with him at the end. I made him a promise I hope to fulfill someday." The words barely find life. "He's dead because of me. All of these people...They are dead or dying because of me."

Shán edges close and sits beside me against the bedframe. "Make no mistake. People are dying because of Queen Belisama Agni, not you."

My head rests against his shoulder. "I'm scared to die, Shán. Trust me when I say I've accepted my fate. But I'm not a warrior, not like you. I'm a fraud."

He looks at me with a gentleness in his eyes. "Show me a man or woman unafraid of war, of dying, and I will show you a liar. You are no fraud. You care; you *love*. Fiercely and without apology, and that makes you the truest of them all."

My hand slides around his neck to bring him closer, to taste him again. And Shán responds in kind, his mouth touching mine.

Slow and hesitant at first, with each kiss hungrier than the last. I invite his hand under my shirt, and he accepts the invitation. My fingers stumble along his shirt buttons to feel his chest, to kiss it the way he's now kissing mine.

Our hands and mouths become defiant, reckless, wanting for more. Shirts and belts and trousers come off in a tangle amidst spilled wine cups and empty plates, the bed somehow too far away. Between heated breaths and sated sighs, Shán yanks the feathered coverlet off the bed and spreads it haphazardly on the floor, lifting me onto it.

Blindly I reach for my knapsack and dig inside until my fingers discover the heart-shaped phial.

"What's in there?" Shán asks when I take it out, his chest rising and falling in a rapid cadence.

"Silvium, a medicinal herb from the Other World. A protectant."

The lines across his forehead deepen once he understands. "Are you certain? We don't have to, you know."

"We shouldn't," I admit.

"Your intended?"

I laugh, especially at the image of Hubert Teasly wolfing down bacon-wrapped scallops. At the time, he disgusted me. Now I find the whole thing droll. "No, I'm thinking of your father and mine. They're brothers, which makes us cousins. While familial interrelations aren't frowned upon in the Other World, what of Winterhaven?"

203

"Half-brothers," he corrects. "Which makes us half-cousins."

"Your grandmother is the same as mine. We do share a blood line."

"Had we known one another as children, attended feasts and other family celebrations while growing up and coming of age, perhaps this wouldn't be happening." He sits up, takes the phial from me, and runs a hand through his hair in frustration. "And it shouldn't. Not because we share blood ties. Because I can't do this to you."

"You're not doing anything *to* me. I want this."

With those dark eyes of his, he looks at me, unflinching. "It wouldn't be fair, to either of us. I will do everything within my power to win this war and see you again, but we both know it might not be so. Likely it won't be."

"The very reason I want to be with you." I pluck the phial from his fingers, uncork the stopper, and swallow the liquid to reiterate my claim. "The chance of surviving this war is miniscule at best for either of us. I'm prepared to meet my fate. But not now, not tonight. I don't want to leave this earth without being with you, wholly and without apology." My lips brush his, and he complies by deepening the kiss.

I breathe in the snow and the smoke on his skin, allow my eyes and fingers to wander the length of his body, to feast on his imperfections—the birthmark splashing his right hip, the second toe longer than the first—that feel every bit perfect to me.

"This scar," I say, tracing the raised skin along his back. "What is it from?"

"My father's sword. A tale for later. For now, let's stick to happier things." Shán kisses each of my fingertips softly, then the inside of my wrists, the feeling like warm summer rain. "How long does the protectant take to work?" He gently tugs my lower lip with his teeth.

I'd made note of the correct dosage and how it stayed in the system for up to two days, but I'd passed over the rest. "I'm unsure. I didn't think to look."

Panic colors the forced impassiveness in my voice, and Shán must recognize it, because he tells me to relax, tells me he knows how to pass the time. Down my body he edges, dropping kisses along my breasts and stomach, and though my whole body trembles at his touch, I'm perplexed by what's happening, my inexperience besting me.

Shán rests between my legs, and there the kisses linger, soft but incessant, urging and unyielding, the perfect give and take. Dizzying heat eddies through my body. A whirlpool in a river circling faster, gaining momentum while pulling me to its center. Silently I beg for mercy. But I don't want him to stop, pray for him not to, and when I can take no more, when there's no air left to breathe and nothing more to hang onto, I surrender to the moment and fall endlessly away.

***

Every part of me is numb and tingling as though I've sat on my foot too long and it has awakened as I shift. "I won't ask how you learned to kiss a woman in such a manner," I tease when Shán is again at my side.

"Smart woman you are." He says the words into my ear, his warm breath sending an excited shiver through my body.

Woman. My heart smiles, the way the word resonates. "You once mentioned 'enjoying the ways of a woman.' Until now, I never fully understood what you meant." I duck my head into the crook of his arm, embarrassed by my naiveté.

"Enjoying you in such a manner is only the beginning. There is so much more." He lifts my chin, traces my lips with his finger. "Are you sure you want this?" he says softly.

Twice I kiss his fingertip. "I'm scared—I've heard it hurts. And yet I've never been surer or more wanting of anything in my life."

"I don't want you to be scared. I certainly don't want to hurt you. Tell me to stop, and I will."

When I nod, more than once for assurance, he eases himself over me. I'm a shadow beneath him. A shadow consumed by fear. Fear of the unknown, and he must sense that fear, feel it in the way my stomach and legs quiver, because he asks if he should stop. And my hands, at the small of his back, answer by pulling him toward me, into me. At once it is pain, cutting and deep, a pain that soon submits to yearning, to wanting of more. But my narcissistic desires smolder beneath his whispered words of longing, of needing, fed into the length of my neck. More insistent are they, more demanding, the words spill forth, mirroring the way our bodies move: together, away, and toward.

And neither is it *I* nor *he*. But *we*. Climbing, reaching, soaring. Weightless. Boundless. Until we plummet back to earth, a lightning strike crashing down. And while we lie in breathless stupor, no longer am I shadow; I am light. Radiating light. Unrepentant for losing myself in another. Only I'm not lost. I'm present. Here. Found.

***

Through the clear, icy ceiling, I watch as snow falls from a violet sky, as if Shán and I are caught in our own little snow globe. How I wish we could stay like this forever. *Safe.* From everything out there waiting to take us away from this world.

Careful not to waken him, I ease from his arms and reach for one of the furs to wrap around me. The window lures me over, and I wipe fog from the glass and watch as the forest captures the falling snow. I'm besotted by the beauty.

My thoughts turn to Queen Belisama Agni. By way of the Infernal, this forest will turn to meltwater, and the beauty that once was will be no more.

The warmth of Shán's hands against my shoulders comforts me, the window revealing his reflection. "Can't sleep?" he asks.

"You once said death is never far away. Always watching, waiting. There is so much truth in those words. The notion that death is so close I can feel its cold iron jaw at my back is what haunts me."

"Though your fears are not unfounded, it's imperative you come to this war knowing you will defeat the queen and live to see

207

another day."

I turn to face him and lean against the window's ledge for support. "And what of your father?"

"The Veneficum have formed their own infantry, and he is well aware. We share a common goal in killing the queen, and thus he has agreed to the alliance. Once she is dead, our interests will deviate, unknown to him. He believes her death will secure his sovereignty. But the king must die for Winterhaven to be free of tyranny."

"And who will rule in his stead? If you survive, will you take the throne as rightful heir?"

He scoffs. "Never. Likely I will not live to see the day when Winterhaven is free. I can only help to make it so."

His sentiment is a blade to my gut. "Someone must rule. Should it not be you, then who?"

Shán stares at me, resolute, and I laugh derisively from the insinuation. "In your words, never."

"You are of royal descent. An Agni no less. My mother was a commoner from what I know."

"So was my father—your uncle." I run a finger down the soft pelt around me. "It matters not. I have no desire to rule Winterhaven. Never will I assume the throne even if I survive. There ought to be some sort of doctrine, of who will rule Winterhaven should the king die."

"Ought to, aye. My father will not agree to another, not even in script."

"But surely he must. He is not Immortal and will die eventually. If not in war then sometime thereafter. Who is his successor if not you?"

The air is losing its warmth, and Shán leaves me to tend the woodstove. "I have a strong suspicion about something," he says, opening the stove's door and poking the embers. "Lark and Snap may be my paternal half-brother and half-sister."

The idea of his claim jars me. "The twins were sired by your father?"

"Triplets originally. Something tells me it is fact, although there's no confirmation to be had. Do you not find it strange, children living within the walls of Isceald Castle?"

Slowly I nod. "Never once did it occur to me until now. But he killed Vinca, and he believes he did the same to Lark."

Shán jostles small logs into the woodstove and closes the door with a turn of the handle. "He left Snap, an heir. Same as me."

"The only way to know what is true is to find a Sablier. No?"

"Perhaps. Snap knows of my suspicions; I shared them before I left the Sanctuary. He must find out his true paternity, preferably before the king is dead."

"Let me," I say when Shán collects the dishes from the floor. He waves me off, so I settle onto the bed and continue my thought. "Your father shows no mercy for anyone. If he can kill his own flesh and blood then no one is safe."

Firelight spills across Shán's naked body as he sets the dishes in the wash basin. *The depraved voyeur returns.* I revel in the stolen moment, watch as light and shadow play against the small of his back and yonder in both directions. "What of your scar?" I ask.

Shán reflexively touches his back. "My father and I have had various feuds over the years. One of the worst being my visit to Belisama inside Mount Serius. The single worst? When I told him you were alive."

Horrified, I pull my feet up and under me. "The last thing I saw in the Sablier was Aunt Henrietta agreeing to give you a deceased child's heart. I wondered how everything played out."

"After my father inspected the heart, he called in his personal medic for a full examination to make sure it was not of a wolf or bear or any other animal. When the medic confirmed the heart was indeed human, my father congratulated me on a job well done. Never again did he question me. Never once did he ask how I had killed you. He swore me to secrecy that day, to never make mention of the misdeed for as long as I lived. When I agreed, he gave me a poached pear tart specially prepared by the castle's head cook."

I shake my head with disgust. "Quite the novel way to show your approval for such a macabre act. To a child, no less."

"Over the years, my father grew jealous of me."

"Jealous of what? He was and still is the most powerful man in Winterhaven."

Shán dries the cups one at a time. "I'm a reminder. Of his youth, of what he once was. Remember, he was in love with the queen. She rejected him, so he bedded many women until finally one bore him a son. I was the product of a woman he never loved. When he discovered I was visiting Belisama in Mount Serius, I thought he might kill me in the moment. Instead he took one of my lovers to his own bed. What he did to her, I don't want to know. But her head was in the Mourning Garden come daybreak."

I gasp, not only from the vile story, but from the realization of something that hits me only now. "Since the day at the Citadel when you and the Veneficum revealed Belisama was my mother, I've been thinking of myself as an Agni. But my father was your uncle. I'm an Andronicus like you."

"In name only, not in blood. Your father was the product of Queen Meriel and a commoner. Who he was none of us know, although the truth is out there somewhere. When she was forced to marry Carreis Andronicus, Arún took his name. I changed my surname and suggest you do the same. For whatever it might be worth, though they grew up together, your father was nothing like mine. He was good and kind and honest. I hope it helps to know this."

I nod, because it does. "Where did Einfarí come from?"

"Nalina Einfarí. My mother's maiden name."

This warms my heart. "I'll stick with Renfrew for now. It's what I've always known. Down the line I may make the change if there is something more befitting." Pensively I chew my lip. "Zhang the Elder told me about my father, how he was born out of love. Queen Meriel never loved Carreis, and therefore she never loved Varius. Consequently she directed all of her love to Arún. Amazing how a parent's love can affect who you are and what you ultimately become." From the brief but pained expression on Shán's face, I recognize the inadvertent slight. "I'm sorry. I didn't mean to bring all of this to light."

"I survived with only a few scars." He offers an assured smile. "My father banished me from Isceald Castle when I told him of my kinship with Belisama. Years later when Guernsey foresaw the future, though he knew it might not come to pass, I was forced to disclose the true nature of your death. To say my father was furious is a gross understatement. He beckoned me back to Isceald Castle under the false pretense of forgiveness. Though wary, I complied. He challenged me to a duel the moment I set foot on the castle's stone floors. We both suffered wounds, hence the scar."

"This was recent, then."

"You made the poultice at Cimmerian's Curio Emporium. Of course, the scar was only an excuse. Guernsey told me the snow globe must be delivered at once."

I nod along, fascinated as the puzzle pieces fall together.

"My father is as good a swordsman as I. We may have killed one another were it not for Guernsey. Without question he saved me. He admitted the truth to my father, how your survival was of his doing because he'd seen the future. How if I had killed you, you could not return to be his bride and save Winterhaven from the queen's peril. Sick man he is, my father took pleasure in knowing the daughter of the woman who scorned him would soon enough be in his bed and together you would conquer the queen. Suddenly I was a hero for not killing you."

I know the rest; I lived it. I toss off the pelt and slip under the sheets. Shán slides in next to me, and I prop myself on an elbow, tracing my fingers along the muscle in his chest, watching his skin turn to gooseflesh. "You'll be leaving soon?"

"My fleet is still in Lagos. We are gathering more ships at three other ports. From the last, we will sail the Dendrite Sea to the final battlefield."

"Which is where?"

"You will discuss the particulars with Guernsey. Honestly I do not know. None of us will until we figure out where the queen is hiding, although we suspect northeast of here."

"What if the queen doesn't agree to do battle? What if she appears out of nowhere like she has in the past?"

"Always a possibility, I'm afraid." Shán takes my hand, kisses my fingers. "I'll be leaving overmorrow, first light."

I fall against the pillows and stare at the falling snow. "This is it, then. My last moment of peace and happiness."

Shán props himself up and touches the Aeriscloque between my breasts. "What is the time?"

I take the timepiece in my palm, the doors fluttering open in response to my touch. "Almost an hour past midnight. Why?"

"There are many moments left."

This brings a smile to my face, parts the clouds that have settled in. I push Shán back to the pillows and climb astride.

213

"Miss Renfrew," he feigns demurely. "Where is your moral compass?"

I laugh aloud. "Cracked. Gone, never to return again. It's your lucky day, good sir." Gently, my fingernails ride down his chest until the gooseflesh returns. "I'm in charge now."

"Oh?" He folds his arms behind his head as a complicit grin rises across his lips. "Whatever you say, love."

I stare into those impossibly blue eyes and see Shán. Truly see him. And in the remaining hours, we are lovers and friends, allies and confidantes, exploring one another body and mind; eating, sleeping, laughing, living in a dream I wish would never end.

CHAPTER TWELVE

Delivered farewells are somber and stoic as we stand before Lady Aniyu and Lord Kian in the lower forest of Wintersgaard. When the morning had still been buried in deep violet, Shán and I had said our goodbyes amidst tangled limbs, strained voices, and dry eyes, the lattermost done at Shán's behest, to which I'd reluctantly complied. I joked by stating that never again would he dictate anything of me.

Now I watch as he rides off through the mist and the trees. A shadow, a whisper, now gone forever. All that remains are his scent on my skin and the memories in my heart.

The walls of the Keep rise at my back, and the coldness seeps in, the reality of war looming, despite the idyllic setting.

"Are you prepared to traverse the mountain to the Cloister?" Lady Aniyu asks in a hushed tone.

Her query further highlights what awaits. I need more time to understand the Cintamani Jewel. But the answers may never arrive, and stalling means more lives lost. I must move forward, train to hone my Elemental skills, and hope those skills will render the queen dead. "I am. When shall I expect to depart?"

"On the morrow. Should there be any delay, I will keep you informed." She awaits my concession, which comes in the form of a reluctant nod. "You have no need for your chamber in the Keep, I presume?"

Lady Aniyu *knows.* No, she *sees.* Where there should be embarrassment on my part, there is only peace of mind. "If it's all the same, I'd prefer to remain in the forest."

Her head bows in eloquence. "As you wish. Should you need sustenance of any kind or company to stave off loneliness, we are happy to comply."

Lord Kian does not look at all happy to comply or otherwise. Without Shán here, he is anxious for me to go—I'm a human stain on the Keep of Wintersgaard.

The treehouse is empty and lifeless inside, and yet I'm content to be here more than anywhere else in the world at this moment. At least the memories can momentarily sustain me. With the woodstove's fire burning strong and the lanterns lit to keep darkness at bay, I settle into the armchair and page through *Secretum Secretorum.*

Far as I can tell, there is not a whole lot about the five-tiered stele, although the book is vast. I reach for my knapsack. Buried between scarves and gloves and phials, the queen's dagger stares back at me. Small rubies comprise the hilt, none large enough to warrant the size of the needed gemstones.

Does Belisama know of the Cintamani Jewel? Something tells me yes. She is in a weakened state. To win this war and claim the throne, she will need more than the Infernal or Tartarean. And with the chalice and fountain forever buried in the heart of Mount

Serius, the jewel may well be her only hope.

An aquamarine glint catches my eye. The Petard, the bestowed weapon from Ione. I'd forgotten about it until now, and I wince, wondering if it could have been used at the Ichor Samhain to kill the queen and in turn save Bart's life. Wintersgaard is safe, according to Shán. And yet the Sanctuary of Caelum had also been deemed safe. *Look how that turned out.* Should the Infernal strike or the queen herself, best to have this at the ready, so I tuck the Petard into my pocket.

After a time, when the light of day is strong and my eyes burn from strain, I set the book aside and leave the treehouse to stretch my legs. I revisit the cluster of bushes where the golden apples hang like festive ornaments. Quartering one of them, I glance around for Kashmir in case he wanders into view.

If only I could summon Zhang the Elder or Guernsey. I'm almost certain the Keep of Wintersgaard has a Hereat or something equally mystical within its confines.

"What am I thinking?" I mutter aloud. "Lady Aniyu and Lord Kian must know about the Cintamani Jewel. After all, the Kyanite is here. They must know of its history, of how the jewel came to be." The apple pieces get tossed to the snowdrifts, and I fetch *Secretum Secretorum* and the Taerou cards from the treehouse before heading to the Keep.

Lady Aniyu and Lord Kian are supping in the Great Hall when I find them. I bow my head in greeting. "Forgive me, I didn't mean to interrupt. Should I come back at a later hour?"

Lady Aniyu beckons me forth with slender fingers. Lord Kian's jaw works in anger. Out of courtesy and certainly not respect, he stands to help me into my chair.

"I'll leave you two be," he states, his plate piled with food.

"Lord Kian," I say before he reaches the high-arched doors. "Your feelings regarding us humans are quite clear. Winterhaven was yours first, and you want to reclaim the realm as your own, I do understand. Is it not possible to live together in harmony? Though Duine and Mór are different from one another on the surface, surely we must share some commonalities. If not in mind then in matters of the heart?"

Lord Kian offers no response. He walks through the doorway, leaving Lady Aniyu and me behind.

"Lord Kian means no disrespect," she says against the angry echo of closing doors.

I laugh blithely as she gestures the wine decanter, and I give myself a healthy pour. "He does so, but I don't understand why. Not fully. Murgh, one of the Sylphs at the Sacred Grove of Willeaux, offered a brief explanation as to why there is enmity where the Duine are concerned, but I suspect there is more to the story."

With a cloth napkin, Lady Aniyu dabs at the corners of her mouth before retiring it to her lap. "For thousands of years, the Sylphs lived in peace. We are two kinds of one race, both born from the Faie. The Chisana are the smaller, more colorful Sylphs who mostly reside in the Sacred Grove of Willeaux. As for those like

218

myself and Lord Kian, we are Mór. The Keep is our refuge. As soon as Duine came to Winterhaven, they brought the threat of war and made good on their promise when we would not surrender our land. King Kartanesi was their ruler. He wanted us dead so he could decree Winterhaven as his own.

"Thus the First War was born. Though we are Immortal, weapons forged of iron—a Killing's Heil for all Sylphs—were used to capture and kill us. We had soldiers of our own, substantial in number. Seasons came and went with enough bloodshed to fill a thousand rivers. When the dead on both sides outnumbered those left standing, a truce was finally called to end the slaughter. A treaty was written and ratified, territories were drawn. Our intentions were made clear. Never again would we help Duine in any manner. And should they go to war with one another, we would watch with heedful eyes, but never would such things concern us. Our greatest hope would be a massacre, one of such magnitude that all Duine would be eradicated, thus allowing the Sylphs to reclaim Winterhaven once and for all."

A shiver rushes through me from the macabre sentiment and the cold manner in which it was spoken. The low creeping hum of the Chisana comes to mind. So too the time when Murgh had removed an enemy's beating heart and had savagely eaten it with verve. Recalling Eirene's silver-needled teeth only keeps the shiver alive. I look at Lady Aniyu and wonder if her smile might reflect the same should anger compel her. I take a much-needed sip of wine and change the subject. "You befriended Shán. Why?"

219

"We met Shán as a child. Innocent and wanting of friendship. Who does not embrace such a thing?"

The king, for one.

She continues, "Shán has always been good to the Sylphs, Chisana and Mór alike. Honest and kind. Trustworthy when most were not and never have been, not since the beginning of Winterhaven."

I'm glad to know the Sylphs think so highly of him, an honor not bestowed on many. "Beginning of Winterhaven?" I ask. "Do you know how this land came to be?"

Lady Aniyu smiles decorously. "A long but wonderful story for another time. At present, you came to query something else of me."

I take out *Secretum Secretorum*, open to the bookmarked chapter, and set the book before her. "The Cintamani Jewel. You must know of it, yes? If I can find all five stones, will the jewel help me defeat the queen?"

She studies the picture. "The stones together are all-powerful. Finding all five could prove near-impossible. The Cintamani Jewel is not a novelty, for the one who comes into possession will be invincible, to death most of all. Thus, we have protected the Kyanite with a potent magic. In the wrong hands, the jewel could lead to the demise of Winterhaven, and us along with it. Our existence has been threatened on more than one occasion. The Rock of Morbid Bay is but one example. There are many, many others."

220

"Rock of Morbid Bay?"

Lady Aniyu stiffens in her seat. "Shán did not speak of this?" When I shake my head, she goes on. "Before the First War was formally declared, King Kartanesi appointed the best ironsmiths in the land and sent them to a small island where they built a domed prison forged of iron. The intent was to capture us all and bring us there to die. For too many years, we were hunted. One by one, the Sylphs began to disappear. To this day, hundreds remain imprisoned, while thousands more are dead."

"They're still there?" I ask in surprise. "Who is watching over this prison if King Kartanesi is long since dead?"

Lady Aniyu shrugs a willowy shoulder. "No one, we guess."

I indicate Lord Kian's plate of food. "How could they still be alive? You need food to live. If they are imprisoned, how would they get any sustenance?"

"We dine on bread and wine for the joy of it, but food is unneeded to ensure our survival. We are Immortal regardless. Iron is our downfall, makes us weak. In potent doses, it can kill."

Her eyes fill with tears, and my voice softens. "In all this time, why has no one freed them?"

"So powerful is the iron, no Sylph can get near the Rock of Morbid Bay. Do trust many have tried, Lord Kian included. From all accounts, the surrounding waters too are perilous, hence the name. With the exception of Shán, no Duine has ever offered their help. The animosity we bear for each other is no secret. If the Sylphs rise, the Duine will fall."

221

"The Veneficum could help, could they not? Guernsey and Carrig. Certainly Ione could navigate even the most treacherous waters."

She draws in a breath. "Lord Kian would never ask for their aid in such a matter. As for the Sylphs and the Duine, I concur with your earlier sentiment. We can live in harmony. Know I am mostly alone in my thinking."

My hand goes to hers. "Shán will help you. As will I if I survive this war. If we both do," I add, for it feels like an empty promise.

Lady Aniyu clasps my hand gratefully. "There are other worlds to which we can flee. We may leave Winterhaven once and for all instead of engaging in yet another blood-stained battle."

"Other worlds? Something tells me you're not referring to the one where I was raised."

Her eyes shine in the firelight. "Winterhaven is but one world. There are other snow globes with other worlds."

My head feels like it might shatter from this knowledge. "If at this moment you cannot discuss how Winterhaven came to be, can you share more about the Cintamani Jewel?"

Lady Aniyu stands, offers her arm. "Come with me."

We walk through the Keep, up a long, marbled stairway leading outside to one of three watchtowers that overlook the snowy forest. The wind up here is more potent, and I pull my cloak tighter to fight off the chill. "Where are the rest of the Mór? The ones who live here?"

"Some live with us in the Keep; others reside in the woodland of the upper forest. With you here, they have been in hiding, I'm afraid."

They really do hate Duine, me in particular. A leper might be more welcome.

Lady Aniyu averts her gaze to the violet-hued sky. "The Cintamani Jewel rained down from the heavens as one large celestial stone, born of the stars. As the jewel fell through the sky to Winterhaven, it cracked into five gemstones. The stone that fell to Winterhaven first embodied the base. Air consumed another, carried it away. One gemstone caught fire and lit up the sky, akin to a passing comet. When it finally grazed the land, the stone scorched much of Winterhaven. The fourth descended straight into the sea. And the last stone remained aloft, forever part of the heavens."

I nod, for this story mostly mirrors what *Secretum Secretorum* offered.

She continues, "It was Lord Kian who discovered the Air stone—the purple Kyanite—many thousands of years ago while flying through this very forest when the Keep was not yet built. They say each stone attracts its intended keeper. However, to this day it remains unclear if all stones have been found, let alone claimed. We have kept the Kyanite here, protected and safe from harm, from the very beginning."

This part of the story fascinates me, a strange fairytale unto itself. "What of the engraved inscription on the ceiling? '*Through the stars I come. With me, I bring the treasure. Within me, I bring the Aether. The final gift to Winterhaven.'"*

Lady Aniyu offers a measured look. "Only you know the answer, Sondrine. The inscription changes depending on the reader. If I visited the Kyanite now, alone, the words would read very differently from what you just stated."

I nod. This is similar to Cimmerian's Curio Emporium, how the smells of the shop differ from person to person and day to day. "Shán saw the inscription. Why didn't the words read differently for him?"

"It chooses. You were the intended reader."

As with everything in Winterhaven, the magic is complicated and beyond my realm of understanding. I remove the Taerou cards from my pocket and show her *World of Winterhaven*, the one with the heavenly body. She nods with a knowing sense, but before I can question her further, a sharp cry echoes through the forest and surges above the treetops.

"Lord Kian," Lady Aniyu cries in a frightened whisper. In a flurry of light and feathers, her wings expand, and she grasps my hand. Up and away we rise, high above the Keep. The forest is expansive and dense, and the falling snow hinders our vision as we fly over the woodland.

A circle of red blots the wintry white below. The speed of our descent is that of an eagle to spied prey, and we find Lord Kian on bended knee, his head bowed in mourning. The blood belongs not to him. A river of red pulses from Kashmir's snowy fur, the light behind his large brown eyes forever extinguished. "What happened?" I ask through my fingers.

Lord Kian shakes with anger. "You did this."

Lady Aniyu helps him to his feet, her eyes cast downward, abashed by his tone.

"You must believe me," I say. "I did no such thing, nor would I ever. I've been in Lady Aniyu's company all this time. Ask her yourself."

I look to Lady Aniyu for confirmation, but her head shakes at the misunderstanding. "He means your presence in Wintersgaard. Something vile has entered our sacred space because of you."

Her words strike fear in my heart, and I realize right then that the treehouse is straight above. "The queen," I whisper. "Or the Infernal. But they are hard to miss. If it's me she wanted, why kill Kashmir?"

"To lure you here," Lord Kian snaps as though this is obvious to everyone but me.

No. She's had ample time to show herself. I look for prints in the snow. The queen is not in human form, this much I know. But where there should be prints, there are only wide swaths of flattened snow. "She wasn't luring me here," I say with sudden alarm. "She was keeping me away. All of us."

"Keeping us from what?" Lady Aniyu asks.

"The Kyanite, I'm almost certain. We need to see if she's taken the stone."

Lady Aniyu and Lord Kian try to extend their wings, but after several attempts, they are unable. "Ferrum," Lady Aniyu says.

There is a fright in her ethereal voice I've not yet heard. She points to a pair of yellow eyes bleeding through the low light. Eyes of a hulking wolf, the blue-grey coat akin to armor, spiked and impenetrable.

Lord Kian draws a sword carved in crystal; Lady Aniyu unsheathes a dagger. The trees are laden with icicles, but I sense my Elemental powers will prove useless the same way sword and blade will.

The wolf growls with malicious intent as it leaps onto a boulder to stare down on us. A second wolf slinks in, then a third and a fourth, and then too many to count thereafter, all gathering around the boulder's base.

Lord Kian addresses the wolf above. "Nashoba, the Ferrum are unwelcome here. You and your pack are in violation of the laws of Wintersgaard. Leave at once or I will have no choice but to cut your throat and sup on your innards." Normally sure-footed, he stumbles slightly in the snow.

"The Kyanite," Nashoba snarls through sharp bared teeth. "Give the stone here, and we shall do as you command. If not, *your* innards and those belonging to Lady Aniyu will make for a fine meal. You are in no position to make such threats." In unison the wolves howl as if in agreement. Or perhaps in forewarning.

If the situation were less dire, I would be in awe, for a talking wolf is a novelty. "What do you need the Kyanite for?" I ask through the eerie symphony.

Nashoba jumps down from his perch and sniffs the air. "The

226

stone is near."

"The queen," I say in answer to my own question. "Are you working for her?"

"Alliances," he grunts. "Save for a common goal and our own welfare, the Ferrum work for no one."

The wolf pads closer, his haunches bursting with muscle. One false move and I'm an hors d'oeuvre before the main course of Lord Kian and Lady Aniyu. I try to stand my ground, to show I'm unafraid. And yet I glance sidelong at my hosts, hopeful they are priming for flight and taking me along with them.

The unexpected sight makes me look twice. Both Lord Kian and Lady Aniyu lie crumpled in the snow gasping for air, their weapons wrapped in slackened fingers.

"What are you?" I cry to Nashoba, slowly backing away. Only there's nowhere to go. The rest of the pack has us fully surrounded.

"We spell death for every Sylph, our coats made of iron and will." With his powerful jaw, Nashoba easily takes Lord Kian's sword and casts it aside. He does the same with Lady Aniyu's blade. "We're Prussian Blue, the most potent form of all iron.

"The Kyanite," he says again to Lord Kian, this time with more force. "Or I will take Lady Aniyu's fingers one by one. Then each arm and each leg. My pack will finish her off before I start on you."

Lord Kian's face twists in anger. "Never." He looks to Lady Aniyu, who concedes with a weak yet resolved nod.

The wolf sneers. "Such dignity you possess. But the Lady's screams, the white of snow spoiled with her blood, tells me

227

otherwise." His pink tongue licks softly at her fingers, and the pack moves in closer. Hungrier.

"Stop," I shout, my hands raised in surrender. "I'll get you the Kyanite if you leave immediately afterwards."

All heads turn toward me. "The Kyanite is spellbound and cannot be broken by anyone other than the Lord and Lady of the Keep. Do trust we have tried." Nashoba noses toward a smaller wolf to show its iron jaw melted clean off, a macabre sight to behold.

I take an emboldened step forward. "I'm Sondrine Renfrew, daughter of Queen Belisama Agni and Arún Andronicus. I have the power to take the Kyanite."

"Lies," the wolf spits.

He sees through my ruse, at least about taking the Kyanite. "I speak the truth. Ask Lord Kian and Lady Aniyu for confirmation of who I am."

Lord Kian's eyes flash with anger. "She's no more the queen's daughter than I or you, Nashoba." He gasps for air. "Leave at once, Sondrine, or witness the pending massacre."

"Why are you lying?" I demand of Lord Kian, my anger spilling over.

The wolf sniffs me with such force he nearly knocks me to the ground. "I smell the stone. Perhaps she speaks the truth."

"No, Sondrine," Lady Aniyu says in a thin voice. Her skin is so pale it nearly blends with the snow. She's dying, and so is Lord Kian. "The Kyanite must remain here or Winterhaven will be destroyed."

"I'll give you the stone on one condition," I say to Nashoba. "Call off your pack, make them leave Wintersgaard at once. Lord Kian and Lady Aniyu must survive for the Kyanite to be yours."

"There is no negotiation," the wolf snaps in a low voice. "Should they live, I'll not get far before an army is called to take me down. The lord and lady have alliances all their own."

"Force Lord Kian and Lady Aniyu to follow us, and without weaponry," I say. "With you nearby, they will remain in a weakened state, and I am no match for you given your size. If I fail to proffer the stone, you can kill us all. You have my word. As long as they survive, no one will come after you or the stone. It will be yours to keep."

The wolf paces. Without warning, he tears off one of Lady Aniyu's fingers. Her enfeebled scream causes one of my own. Lord Kian reaches for her, but it's futile—he can barely lift his hand.

"What are you doing?" I yell. "I've offered you the stone."

The wolf chews the finger, the sound of crunching gristle so sickening that nausea feathers the back of my throat. "My forewarning," he says, licking the blood from his chops. "Do not play me for a fool, girl."

I dash over to Lady Aniyu when Nashoba calls off his pack. As the wolves recede through the trees, the damning effect of their iron coats diminishes. Lord Kian is able to stand, and he manages his way to Lady Aniyu, promptly wrapping her bloody stump in a cloth.

Together we start for the crag with Nashoba looming at our heels. Lord Kian and I help Lady Aniyu through the forest, her footing slow and unsure. Undoubtedly she is in shock from the injury and loss of blood. Without once looking at Lord Kian, I can feel his outrage. At the situation. At me.

I'm thankful for our slowed gait because I need a plan. Even if I can decipher the inscription, I can't just hand over the stone. But Nashoba will make a feast of us if I refuse. I survey the forest branches in hopes of spotting the white raven. Or Shán. Or anyone at all. No one comes, and I shake away the thought. It is I who must do the saving, not someone else.

Too soon the sacred crag rises before us. Nashoba demands I remove two iron spikes from his coat to stake Lord Kian and Lady Aniyu to a nearby tree. With as much strength as I can summon, I drive the spikes though their robes and into the trunk. I have no choice but to do as he commands. Otherwise, Nashoba will call my bluff. For once I hope my strength will prove inadequate and somehow they will break free.

We cross the bridge, the wolf's gamey breath warming my neck. The Kyanite shines bright amidst the gentle swirl of falling snow. One portion of the orb is burnt, black liquid dripping to the ground where the wolf tried to take the stone.

"What are you waiting for?" Nashoba growls when I hesitate. "Make haste."

I point to the ceiling. "The spell needs to be broken first."

His hackles go up, revealing a metal box strapped to his neck,

230

presumably a home for the stone. "Get to it, then."

Nervously I read aloud: "*Through the stars I come. With me, I bring the treasure. Within me, I bring the Aether. The final gift to Winterhaven.*" Nashoba's head cocks to one side in wonder.

"The Cintamani Jewel?" I know my guess is wrong, but I reach for the stone anyway. The orb sparks and crackles with flame, and I pretend it burns my skin, sucking my fingers so the wolf can't see the lack of a mark. "Wrong guess."

"Try again," he snarls.

"These things take time. If you want the Kyanite, you must give me what I need."

A low growl from deep in his throat. He turns to leave.

"Where are you going?" I ask. "If you're checking on Lord Kian and Lady Aniyu, rest assured they are still pinned to the tree." I try to hide the desperation in my voice. The longer I can stall, the better their chance of escape.

"I shall return with Lady Aniyu's hand. Perhaps it will spur your thoughts. For each wrong guess, I will take a piece of her, until she is no more."

Blood drains from my face in a torrent because I know his word is true. As he turns to leave, I shout, "Stop! Bring me to the queen at once. It's me she ultimately wants."

"Your death does not spell eternal life, girl," he says without looking back.

"My death spells victory for the queen. She will rule Winterhaven, with plenty of time to find the stones thereafter." I

231

touch the orb and will the flames in his direction. Nashoba turns in surprise as they shoot past. "I'm no girl," I add through caged teeth. "I'm Sondrine Andronicus-Agni, and I command that you bring me to the queen." The air around the Kyanite crackles, and the orb's flames extinguish, the stone vulnerable for the taking. Although shocked, I'm quick to seize it.

The wolf approaches. His yellow eyes gleam bright as the Kyanite itself. "Your death shall come to pass in due course. My directive was to get the Kyanite. Now place the stone in the box."

I'm unsure of why the spell broke, but I can't just give him the stone. Yet he will eat me alive and carry the stone in his mouth if need be. With both distress and great reluctance, I set the Kyanite inside and secure the lock.

Steam exists his large nostrils as he sniffs the air. "I smell the stone."

"The scent is on my hands, and now it's on you."

His ruff shakes. "The Kyanite is fragrant, as though born of blooms. What I smell is salt and sea alike."

I shrug, honestly baffled by his claim. "You have the Kyanite, the one thing you came here for, and I kept my word. Now you must keep yours. You must leave in peace."

The wolf sniffs the space, nose to the ground. After one full roundabout, the sound of a blowing horn causes him to look up. Ears pricked, teeth bared, Nashoba is gone from the crag in three bounds.

Quick to follow, skidding over the icy bridge, I only stop when I see what Nashoba does: dozens of Mór circling above, a biblical sky filled with winged angels. At the forefront is Lord Kian with a curved horn in hand. Lady Aniyu is near the back, her face dangerously pale.

Nashoba shakes his coat with such force the Mór ease back, affected by the deadly iron. The wolf turns to me and backs me straight into a towering pine. His hot breath pours over my face, and I cower as I glance around the forest. The snow is still falling, but even if I could conjure a blizzard or a gale-force wind, it wouldn't affect him. His weight must be the same as that of the tree at my back.

"You have another stone," he growls.

He sniffs up my legs to my groin, then violently tears at my cloak. I scream reflexively, assuming part of me went with it. My flesh is not what drops to the ground. Before either of us can grab the Petard, more snow falls from the sky. Nashoba whimpers and backs away.

Not snow. One of the Mór is pouring sand in a circle around me. I snatch the Petard, the aquamarine stone shining bright in my palm.

"The Water stone," Nashoba says, his nose smelling the air. "Ione bestowed the Petard to you, and now you shall give it to me."

This is part of the Cintamani Jewel. I've been unknowingly carrying the gemstone since the Sanctuary of Caelum. Why would Ione not tell me? "You were promised the Kyanite, nothing else. Be gone with you."

233

Ears flattened in agitation, Nashoba prowls around the tree. Try as he might, he can't breach the sand.

"Do not move past the circle," Lord Kian instructs from above. "The brimstone will keep Nashoba at bay."

Brimstone. We'd sold jorums of 'brimstone and treacle' at Cimmerian's Curio Emporium. The sulfuric element is used medicinally to help children with various maladies.

Nashoba seems to laugh at Lord Kian in a sardonic sort of way. "My iron coat; the circle of brimstone. Both keep us at bay. You from me, me from the girl. We are at a standstill, Lord Kian. A peaceful transfer of the stone will cease any bloodletting. Otherwise you leave me no choice, and I shall call to my pack. The brimstone is sufficient in its restraint of me and perhaps half a dozen more. My pack is one hundred strong, however, and we shall breach the circle in mere seconds."

"He lies," Lady Aniyu implores weakly. The cloth around her hand is a blight of red as she perches in the tree's branches for support. Between the iron's effects and her grave wound, she will soon falter.

Nashoba skulks back and forth. "You can only stay aloft for so long, Lady Aniyu. Once my pack returns, you will be too weak to fly—all of you. Your kin will fall from the sky, and we shall eat you one by one, including the girl." He growls at me. "Surrender the Petard. If you do not, prepare to watch the Mór die a violent and painful death."

Nashoba leaps into the air and snags the wing of an

234

unsuspecting young man. The Mór recede farther into the sky, their screams matching those of their downed kindred. No match for Nashoba, the young man is nothing but blood and bone in mere seconds.

"Lord Kian," I beg through the wailing sounds of the Mór. "Take Lady Aniyu back to the Keep. All of you must go. Amass your army, your weapons. Anything."

"We vowed to protect you," Lady Aniyu proclaims. "We gave Shán our word."

"I can protect myself. Listen to me," I plead as they hang limply in the air.

Nose to the sky, Nashoba howls, long and mournful. He's calling to his pack.

"Stop," I cry out. "You can have the stone. Call them off at once, and I will give the Petard to you."

His bared teeth resemble a sinister grin. Panicked, I look to the Mór as the sound of a hundred wolves approach through the forest. And there they come over the hill, racing toward us, a sea of rolling iron.

The closer they move in, the stronger the iron's effect. Down goes one Mór, then another, dropping from the sky like fowl during the hunt. There are screams and howls and heckling, the snow a moving cloud as the wolf pack draws nearer.

There is no more time, no room left to negotiate. "Lord Kian," I yell in desperation, yanking out the pin of the spiraled conch shell. "Catch!"

I throw the Petard with all my might, well away from Lord Kian and straight into the path of the racing pack. Nashoba doesn't hesitate. He bounds through the snow, haunches bristling with muscle, and in a single leap, catches the Petard in his mouth. I turn to shield my eyes right as the sound of exploding metal punctures the air, akin to a hundred firing cannons.

I'm thrown down by the force. And where there was ear-splitting sound, now there is only silence and a high-pitched ringing in my ears. Dazed and in pain, I manage to lift my head and look about. Metal and innards strewn haphazardly, the snow wet with bloodshed. Nashoba and his pack are nothing but a carpet of iron shards laid out before the Keep. Those few remaining are gravely injured, and they limp or crawl away through the trees, whimpering in pain.

Amidst the debris there are feathers. Frantically I glance around for Lady Aniyu and Lord Kian. Both are perched in the tree above, and save for Lady Aniyu's finger, they are in one piece.

The silence and high-pitched ringing are replaced by the sound of horrible suffering.

"Zara, Bane, and Orfiel are dead," sobs one of the younger Mór, who points to three mangled bodies.

All eyes go to me, narrowed and disapproving and filled with a hatred so strong I must look away or be bowled over. The pin still gripped in my hand, I toss it aside and crawl over to the fallen Mór. Two are alive but tragically wounded. One has lost most of his right wing, the remaining bones like dangling, broken wind

236

chimes. The other, a young girl, flaps helplessly about, the snow beneath awash in blood. Her arms and wings are intact, but her torso is no longer a home to her legs. Their pained wailing haunts me to my core as I gently pull them away from the iron shards. Once we clear the battlefield, the remaining Mór move in to rescue their kin. They stagger on unsteady feet, unable to fly, the iron a deadly poison.

Lord Kian commands from above, "Aeshma and Elyon, get Cassiel and Mihr to the Keep so we may tend to their wounds. The rest of you, secure our borders. Should any intruder be found, bring them to me at once."

"Dead or alive, my lord?" one man asks.

"Dead."

The Sylphs head to the woodland in all directions. The iron's effects appear to lessen the farther they tread from the battleground; their slowed shuffles turn to quickened ambles, and soon they take to the sky in a brilliance of feathers and light.

An aquamarine glow rises in the distance amidst the heaps of carnage. The adrenaline within me is thinning. Pain shoots through my legs clear up my spine. Whatever progress had been made in the hot springs has been expunged, and possibly the damage has worsened. I limp over to retrieve the Petard. I'm still in disbelief, that two stones from the Cintamani Jewel are at the Keep. Or are they?

"The box with the Kyanite," I mutter. "Did it survive?"

A groan of pain accompanies each movement as I kick away

metal and snow and feathers. The conch shell protected the Petard; Ione was smart to build such a thing. But the metal box along with the Kyanite had likely been pulverized in the blast. I climb up the stone steps, closer to the Keep where Lady Aniyu and Lord Kian await. I know not what to say, because an apology of any sort, no matter how heartfelt and true, will fall short.

"Come with us," Lady Aniyu says kindly. "You are hurt and in need of care. Our medic will tend to your wounds before you leave."

"Forget Sondrine," Lord Kian says in a savage tone. "She is Duine, a plague thrust upon our very soil. Do you not see what she has done? The massacre she has brought forth? It is you who needs care. She can find aid elsewhere."

"We made a promise to Shán," Lady Aniyu reminds him. "We said we would provide safe passage to the Cloister."

"Shán is likely dead," he snaps. "Our promise died with him."

I stare at Lord Kian, stunned by his cruel remark. "I'll gather my things," I say with a heaviness I can't unburden.

The heady scent of smoke causes us to look to the woodland. In the distance, a dark plume hangs in the air.

Lady Aniyu brings her bloodied hand to her mouth. "The treehouse is on fire."

I trust her to see what I cannot. "My knapsack—I must save it."

Amidst Lady Aniyu's appeals to remain and Lord Kian's plea to let me go, I rush down the stone stairs and through the woods, only stopping when I see the treehouse fully engulfed in flame. The fire would not hurt me if I ran inside, but the knapsack and its contents are long gone, burned to a cinder. All that was part of my life from the Other World is forever erased.

Who set the fire? Who was in the treehouse?

Secretum Secretorum digs into my side, and I remove it with shaking hands. *Of course.* The book contains the secret—or one of many secrets—to eternal life. Zhang the Elder said as much. If Belisama can't retrieve all five stones, she will look for other things to keep her alive. Somehow I doubt the remaining Ferrum set the fire. No, Belisama was here in whatever form, looking for the book. The treehouse is yet another victim of her anger, not the first and certainly not the last.

CHAPTER THIRTEEN

I'd waited for the queen to show herself, demanded it aloud so we could do battle right there. So raw was my rage, I had every confidence I could kill her. And even if I lost, I'd be content with the effort.

Minutes turn to hours before I finally give up; she is long gone. After burying Kashmir, I take a long last look at the remains of the treehouse, the pristine birch gone to ash. Same as the memories of Shán and me. There one moment then gone forever.

By the time I return to the Keep, the sun is low in the sky and the news is dire. Mihr will never fly again, his wing so far gone it had been removed to insure his survival. Cassiel had bled out. I watch from the hallway as the Mór gather at her bedside in mourning. I don't dare enter.

Lady Aniyu is newly bandaged, the rose in her cheeks returned. She summons me to another chamber, where medicinal scents linger between the walls. The healer resembles Lady Aniyu, with her opalescent hair, although she is shorter, her face lined with age.

The healer gives me a phial of white willow bark for the pain in my legs along with a new knapsack filled with tinctures and medicines prepared for me at Lady Aniyu's behest. I stuff the Petard, the Taerou cards, and *Secretum Secretorum* inside. A new cloak is offered, but I decline. Though grossly tattered by Nashoba's teeth and the blistering explosion, the evergreen cloak has a strange sentimental value at this point, and I have no desire to give it up. However, I gladly take the proffered gloves and boots, both lined with rabbit fur for warmth. Heading into the mountains will prove a chilly prospect, and my guides sent these ahead for my use.

Lady Aniyu leads me to the tall, rounded doors that open into the bailey. Lord Kian joins us but says nothing. "We have something for you before you depart," Lady Aniyu says.

Lord Kian's face is mired in anger, and not until Lady Aniyu sets a hand to his shoulder does he remove an object from beneath his tunic and extend it for the taking.

Though it is wrapped in white cloth, the bleeding purple light is revealing. "You found the Kyanite?" So shocked am I, the words come out in a whisper.

Lady Aniyu replies, "We found it amongst the carnage, the metal box intact. Remember, each stone attracts its intended."

"If what you say is true then tell me, would the Kyanite have returned to you of its own accord, regardless of whether Nashoba had succeeded in taking it?"

"If the stones are stolen, they will return to their rightful owner. If they are given readily, the receiver shall be the new intended."

"But I was coerced into giving Nashoba the Kyanite. The stone was neither stolen nor given readily."

Lady Aniyu looks to Lord Kian for an answer, but he says nothing, so she continues with her thoughts. "An interesting point. Magic is pure, Sondrine. White or black. There is no grey area. If the intention is made with malintent, I must believe the stone would have returned to us. How quickly we cannot know, as the stone has always been in our possession."

"Why give the Kyanite to me?"

"The gemstone will prove nothing more than a temptation for the queen should it remain here. She will continue her attempts to steal it, and though a new spell could be cast, any spell can be broken given the right amount of time and the correct information. After all, you did so."

How I broke the spell is unclear, although something tells me Lady Aniyu knows, same for Lord Kian. At the moment it matters not, and from the look on Lord Kian's face, he is anxious for me to go.

Lady Aniyu finishes, "We decided the Kyanite would be of more use to you."

"You decided," Lord Kian says in a reproving tone.

Moonlight spills through the windows on all sides. I look from one to the other, discomfited by the charged hostility between them. Stuffing the Kyanite deep inside the new knapsack, I want to offer some kind of assurance, but Lord Kian excuses himself before I get the chance.

"How will you restore order to Wintersgaard?" I ask Lady Aniyu. "The fire was set by the queen herself, I'm near certain."

"You needn't worry," she says. "Our alliances are strong. Moreover, the iron will lose its potency now that the Ferrum have perished. Without the vitality of their blood, the iron will turn to rust with the continued snowfall."

I open the door to leave but stop short in the doorway. "Lady Aniyu, please accept my deepest apologies and extend them to Lord Kian. It was I who brought this death and destruction to Wintersgaard. Had I known this would happen, I would have told Shán to take me elsewhere."

The cool breeze ruffles her hair. "We knew danger could arise from your stay here. Shán asked to bring you to Wintersgaard, and after much contemplation, we complied with his wishes."

"I brought enmity. The Mór already hate Duine. I've deepened the divide."

Lady Aniyu remains silent, which I take as agreement. "You have a war to fight, I fear. And where there is war, there is loss. Never are there victors." She leads me across the bailey to the top of the stone staircase. "Your guides to the Cloister await below. Be well, Sondrine. And make haste, for although Nashoba is dead, his allies—the queen included—will attempt to hunt you and the stones."

With a heavy heart, I descend the steps leading into the woodland, a full moon cradled in the violet sky. *So much suffering, so much death.* I can't help but hear Lord Kian's dreaded words over and over again: *Shán is likely dead.*

Limping through the snow, I fight off the sting in my heart as I search among the icy trees for my guides. '*First impressions are lasting impressions,*' Aunt Henrietta used to snip. Viewing me as anything but adroit and strong-willed won't instill confidence, so I down some of the white willow bark with a scoopful of snow.

There is grunting ahead. A wild boar or perhaps more Ferrum. I use a copse of trees to hide behind, wishing I still possessed the ruby-hilted dagger. More grunting and now some loud chewing prompt me to peer around one of the trunks. A yak-like animal is feeding on a patch of sparse grass that willfully pokes through the snow. Black, wooly fur hangs down past the creature's belly, and large curving horns jut from its head. *Friend or foe?*

"Sondrine, meet Lulu," says a voice from behind. I jump in surprise at the sight of two men robed in red, both as bald as coots. "Be unafraid," he adds. "The maiwa are harmless."

So much for first impressions.

The shorter of the two has a face so heavily lined it's reminiscent of a parched desert floor. His frame is slight and stooped. An inverted triangle bisected by a horizontal line is stitched into his collar, no doubt the Cloister's sigil. The other man carries a definitive paunch but appears much younger and spryer. He smiles pleasantly, more than the occasion calls for. What is so amusing, I don't want to know, although I'm guessing it has something to do with me.

"My name is Yeshe," says the elder of the two. "And this is

244

Jinpa, a friend and guide alike. Our journey is long and treacherous, be forewarned. Now if you please." He indicates Lulu, and I assume he's going to help me mount the behemoth animal. But he lifts a leg and Jinpa steps in, motioning me to give a hand to help the old man into the saddle. Jinpa lights a lantern, hooks it onto Lulu's side pack, and they start through the trees.

Guess I'm walking. No coincidence we're traveling in the dark, the better to hide from our enemies. "How long will it take to reach our destination?" I ask, catching up and falling in line with them.

"Two days to the Cloister," Jinpa replies, his walking stick so tall it extends past his bald head.

"Which is where exactly?"

"The Cloister sits on dowsing lines, joined paths in the earth where the vibrational pull is strong."

Strange. Jeyna used the same terminology regarding the Taerou card. "Could you be a bit more specific?"

Yeshe points above. "We live our lives within the serenity of the clouds."

I've no clue what he means, only that it sounds ridiculously far. We walk from the upper forest to the lower, away from Wintersgaard and across wide open spaces, following the moon across the sky. Gone is the snow. The mountainous land is muddy and vast, filled with crags and carved in mirrored tarns.

Come daybreak, a small village lies at the bottom of a knoll, smoke bustling from its chimneys. For the sake of my aching legs, I hope we will stop for some rest and a hot meal. As we draw nearer, I see the smoke comes not from chimneys but the village itself, the buildings half-burned to the ground. The stench of burned flesh rises and falls with the wind.

Neither Yeshe nor Jinpa speak as we pass through. Fear grips my heart at the sight. I'd known the war had begun, but somehow, I'd figured it was closer to the capital of Isceald, not already spread to the midlands.

The Infernal must have done this, come out of nowhere, because the villagers were not in hiding. They were going about their day, pulling water from the well or farming with their wheeled ploughs. One villager, judging by the size of the corpse, was a child, a doll still grasped in skeletal hands.

Twice more we encounter such villages, all turned to ash and bone. We find no one alive. When the path begins to slope upward, I tilt my head to the sky. A mountain unlike those passed earlier stands before us, the top lost to a sea of fog. "Please tell me we are not climbing this thing," I say.

"We will tell you what you wish, but it will not be so," says Yeshe in earnest. "To reach the clouds, one must fly."

"With what?" I ask. "Do you have wings beneath your robes like the Mór? Or Lulu a pair hidden by her wooly coat?" Anything is possible. This is Winterhaven, after all.

Jinpa's smile suggests a hidden secret. "Wings are unneeded to fly. As long as the mind is clear, we will reach our destination."

My mind is far from clear. It's murky and burdened with exhaustion. And my gait is uneven, filled with pain. We start for the path and forge on, up and around the mountainside, my nausea growing with each passing step. At one point, Lulu leaves a steaming pile in her wake, and we stop while Jinpa molds it into the shape of a cake and covers it with thatch. Into the sack it goes, and then we resume our course. I'm sick beyond compare, with no understanding of why yak dung must be taken on our journey, only that the symbolism can't be ignored.

The higher we go, the chillier the gusts grow, and soon the sun is lost to the clouds. Sweat turns to ice crystals on the tendrils that peek from my hood, and with my head bowed to the wind, I'm grateful for the fur-lined boots and gloves. My nausea is unrelenting. I can't seem to catch my breath, and I use the mountainside to help me along. The white willow bark has long since worn off, and my body is officially in agony.

When it seems I cannot take one more step, Yeshe signals to stop. Jinpa helps the elder down and ties off Lulu, then they disappear through a small opening in the mountainside. Without invitation, I follow. The cave is small and dry, and I lie down, unable to lift my head from the dirt ground. Arnica or some version thereof might be within reach, but I'm too sick to dig around the knapsack.

Jinpa works expediently in getting Yeshe comfortable before digging a fire pit with his hands.

Weakly I say, "A spark can be created with two rocks. I can help build a fire and gather some wood if you'll only give me a moment."

"We are above the timber line," Jinpa says. He removes a few dung cakes from the sack and sets them into the pit. With a *click clack* of two rocks, a spark ignites the cakes. A pot of water is set directly on top, and a metal infuser filled with loose herbs is submerged once the water boils. The yak dung smells pungent but not so bad, more like fresh-cut grass than the expected. And soon the steeped herbs override the scent.

"This is sowhistle," Jinpa says, first serving Yeshe the infusion. "Clouded air is thin. The tea helps to chase away nausea and return balance to the body. Eventually the altitude will be friend not foe, but time is needed."

He prepares a second cup for me, and I gratefully sip the gingery tea. He's right; my nausea somewhat abates, and I sit on my knees, watching the elder nap while Jinpa cooks something in a second pot.

"Did you hunt for something before our journey?" I ask.

"Animals are sacred to us," Jinpa says. "They are our equals in every way. The Solitary diet consists of grains, beans, vegetables, and anything else not bearing a soul. Our pledge is to cause no harm."

With guilty eyes, I peer down at the emerald cloak. I know not what the pelt is made from, only that it is likely ermine. Killing the pheasant in the Petrified Forest is a story I won't soon be sharing. "These boots and gloves were given to me," I blurt as if accused of a crime I never committed. "Lady Aniyu said they came from you."

A smile rises across Jinpa's paunchy face. "We made those with our own hands from rabbits that naturally perished. We bury them proper and use their pelts if they will prove useful."

I take another sip of tea. "The Solitary sound quite compassionate. Will you be teaching me how to better my Elemental skills? Or will it be Yeshe?"

"The Solitary have a vast skill set. We are bakers, farmers, and much more. I for one am an alchemist."

My brow furrows. "There are Solitary who are Elementalists, am I correct? I'm to hone my skill set after all."

"You will be training with the Grand Scholari, head of the Solitary and the most skilled of all. I am no Elementalist, only a guide and friend, as Yeshe stated."

Grand Scholari. He sounds impressive enough. The ladled stew is savory much to my surprise, hearty and delicious as anything I've tasted. Perhaps more so. One more helping and I'm feeling better, at least physically. For the remainder of the meal and afterward, there is no conversation, and the silence allows me to lose myself in thought. I think of Shán, if he's truly gone from this world. And what of Guernsey? Is he still alive? I shudder at the thought. Even up here the danger feels palpable.

Moonlight shines into the cave and dances around the soft snores of my traveling companions. It lures me outside, and I'm left breathless by how far we've climbed, the valley below swathed in a layer of clouds. I pat Lulu on the nose, and she licks me with a warm, stinky tongue.

249

Stars blink and fall across the sky in every direction, reminiscent of the snow globe, and I wonder if it will ever be found. My thoughts turn to the stones in my knapsack. Perhaps Jinpa and Yeshe know of the Earth stone and its whereabouts. The Fire stone almost undoubtedly rests in Queen Belisama's hands. Aether, born from the heavens...does that stone even exist, or will it forever remain a mystery?

A ball of fire bursts across the horizon and lights up the evening sky. The crushing boom comes shortly thereafter, and everything begins to shake, the snow falling in a cascade around me. I try to pull Lulu into the cave, but she won't budge.

"Move, you daft thing!" I yell, but there is no fear behind those large brown eyes. With no other choice but to abandon her, I dive through the cave's opening as snow piles against the opening.

Remembering my travel companions, I look back to find Yeshe and Jinpa both propped against the wall. "There was an explosion," I stammer.

Yeshe nods, although his eyes remain closed. "Yes, we saw."

From their positions in the cave, there is no possible way they could have seen anything.

"Seeing is not only done with one's eyes," Jinpa elaborates. The two men appear tranquil and at peace.

"The queen is alive," Yeshe states in a thin, sage tone. "She wants her presence known."

How they can be so calm, I have no idea. "We're trapped. The snow is piling up. I tried to get Lulu inside, but she wouldn't

250

move." There's no need to point out the obvious. The poor creature is dead.

"Let sleep find you. For now, put your worries to bed," Jinpa says simply.

"We need to get out of here," I counter. "We've been buried alive. The air up here is already thin, and now there is nothing coming in." This hearkens back to our time on the Isle of Empyrean, when we were trapped with no way out. The queen has a knack for this, seemingly.

Yeshe is snoring, and I almost find it offensive. Jinpa says, "We are safe in here, with plenty of air to survive. If we leave now, and there is another disturbance, we will be carried straight over the mountainside. Please, do try to rest. Worry and fear are wasted emotions."

I look from him to the wall of snow. Sleep will be unkind tonight. I'll keep the fire going strong, with my worry and fear to keep me company.

***

No subsequent explosions last night. At some point I'd fallen asleep, and at an odd angle, because my neck aches with stiffness when I wake. Jinpa is steeping more herbs when I sit up and stretch.

"Once the elder awakens, we will continue our journey," Jinpa says, filling my cup with tea.

I look for Yeshe in the corner, but he's not there. And yet the barricading wall of snow is firmly in place. "Am I missing

251

something? Is Yeshe…invisible?"

Months ago, back in the Other World, this inquiry would have sent me straight to the nearest lunatic asylum. Light snoring from above answers my question, and my cup nearly falls from hands. Supine, Yeshe hovers near the ceiling, suspended in midair.

"The ground is cold and hard," Jinpa notes. "Bad for one's back. Heat rises, so Yeshe does the same. Far more comfortable above than below."

"How does he do that?" I ask in awe. "Can I do the same? Can he teach me?"

Jinpa points to his temple, nodding. "Remember we do not need wings to fly—none of us."

I nod in understanding. "Using my mind helps me with the elements."

My hands go into the cooking pit to scoop up some flames. With a little concentration, the fire weaves itself into a sparking ball. Jinpa watches with intrigue. Once the ball is large enough, I stand and hurl it at the top of the wall. Instead of bursting through to the other side, the fire sizzles and turns to ash the moment it hits, the same way my arrows had in the Petrified Forest. Disappointed, I say to Jinpa, "I was hoping we could get out of here with the aid of Fire. If we boil enough water, I can easily melt the snow."

Yeshe awakens and slowly sinks to the ground, his eyes bright and alert as he sits up and crosses his legs. "You are an Elementalist," he states. "How many of the elements can you use?"

"All four: Earth, Air, Water, and Fire. There is a fifth element,

Aether or Quintessence, but I have no idea how to find it, much less use it."

"Only four? Are you certain?"

Is this a trick question? "Well, as I mentioned there is a fifth, but—"

"I see eight, perhaps more," Yeshe says.

"Eight?" I laugh, for the thin air must be affecting his brain.

Yeshe takes some water from the pot and lightly douses the fire. Steam hisses and rises. Next he pours water onto a small patch of dirt on the earthen ground. With his finger, he mixes them together to make a small mud puddle. "Do you see?" he asks.

Dumbfounded, I stare at the Elder. "All these years I've been using the elements separately, not thinking to use them together to form something different and perhaps more potent." I look at the wall of snow, unsure of what combination could break it all down.

Jinpa walks over to the wall, and with his walking stick, he bores a hole at knee-level until light shines in from the outside. The wall, so thick, nearly consumes the stick. Six more times he does this in a linear sequence. One powerful kick to the top of the wall and the snow falls in a heap, no longer a barrier to the outside world. "Sometimes the simplest explanation is the best one," he remarks.

Cold air rolls in, and with it the scent of smoke. And there is Lulu, right where I left her, non-plussed by the whole event. "You're alive." I rush over and stroke her nose.

253

"The maiwa are hearty creatures," Jinpa says. "Often, they are buried in the avalanches of the mountains, but most manage their way back to the surface."

I'm thankful in more ways than one. First and foremost, that the poor creature didn't die at the expense of the queen's actions. Also, this means Yeshe can make it back to the Cloister. He seems too frail to continue by foot.

The sky is newborn, awash in pink and gold, a stark contrast to the black, roiling clouds below. Firebolts streak through them in a zigzag.

"Winterhaven is warming," I note. "Given the thundershowers below, Queen Belisama is winning the war."

"Firesmoke can produce rain," Jinpa says. "Salt can hurry it along. Did you know?" I shake my head. "There may well be a storm below," he says. "However, what you see is not cloud cover but smoke. Light can no longer pass through, which means there is only darkness below. Smoke rises. We must get to the Cloister at once or we will be entombed, choked of light, and of life."

***

The air continues to thin the farther we plod up the mountain. Every few steps has me checking the smoke below. For a time, the smolder had seemed to rise along with us, but for now it has leveled off, and above, clear skies shine down. Whatever Belisama caused to afford such an explosion, it was a corker.

Before we'd left the cave, Jinpa had filled a wineskin with the soothing tea, and now I sip the tepid liquid as we walk along.

Lucky for us, the avalanche affected only one part of the mountain and not the path we use for our climb. Otherwise I'm not sure how we would make it to the Cloister.

But make it we do, and a symphony of toiling bells calls out in greeting. The Cloister is a series of interconnected stone structures bookended by two towers, all set into the uppermost reaches of the mountain. As the clanging fades, voices rise up, a chanting of sorts, haunting and beautiful and mystical.

A hooded woman swathed in brown robes hurries over, her back hunched, her skin leathered. Time has been unkind. "Come with me," she says through her few remaining teeth.

Hubert Teasly would break out with a pox from her lack of dental care.

I barely get the chance to say goodbye to Lulu and my companions. With a steady grip at my elbow, the woman leads me through a string of connected arcades and into a barren room. One window, a lone chair, an unremarkable cot, and a deep wooden tub. Compared to the luxuriousness of the Keep, this chamber is bleak. A prison cell might offer more cheer.

The woman looks me over with a lazy eye. "Disrobe," she says in a clipped tone.

Caught off guard by her gruff demeanor, I say, "I'm quite tired and a bit nauseated from the thin air. I was hoping for some rest first. Then a tour. From what I've been told, there is a great library here, and I'm anxious to do some reading—"

"To stay with the Solitary, you must first be clean." She points

255

to a tub with a tremulous hand. "You cannot leave this space until it is so."

Each word feels like a lashing, and I'm ill at ease by her presence. But clearly neither of us is going anywhere until I remove my clothing. There is no screen to change behind; the room holds nothing of the sort.

"May I at least have some privacy?" I ask.

A colicky laugh. "You've got nothing I haven't seen before. Hurry now. Dinner awaits. Should you delay, the next meal won't be served until dawn."

She scoffs at my prudish behavior when I turn my back to her. Quickly I fling off my clothing and scurry into the wooden tub, so confining I must crouch to stay in place. I'm grateful my knees cover me.

The water is lukewarm at best. I reach for the bar of soap and folded cloth, but the woman gets to them first. She washes my back and then my neck a bit more harshly than I prefer. "What is your name?" I ask, recoiling from her touch.

"Eachna."

Eek is right. There is nothing pleasant about her.

"Please, Eachna." I edge away from her forceful hand. "While I appreciate your help, I can bathe myself and prefer to do so."

"Stand," she demands. "You are not allowed to wash away your own filth."

Slowly I do as I'm asked while keeping my back to her. This is no deterrent for Eachna. She comes about face and stares at the

256

Aeriscloque around my neck. "No ornamentation is allowed here."

She reaches to remove the timepiece, and I slap her hand away. "No," I growl. "If this goes, I go. There is no negotiation."

Eachna stares at me. Even her lazy eye is narrowed and unkind. When she takes my hand and begins washing beneath each fingernail, I know I've won this minor point. It feels surprisingly victorious. Under my arms the cloth goes in rough strokes, then across my breasts and between my legs, causing me to flinch.

"The goose has been plucked," she notes before continuing down to my feet.

How does she know? Then I understand. I'd pulled back, not because of where she was washing, but because of the sudsy water and robust strokes. I'm sore and tender to the touch, owed all to Shán, and I'm none the sorrier for it.

Still, this feels an invasion of the worst sort. Yet Eachna seems to be enjoying it less than I, if that's possible. She appears stoic, as though she's done this a thousand times to women and men alike. My guess is she has.

When the cloth is wrung dry, I step from the tub, and she wraps me in soft brown robes smelling of cloves and warmed sugar.

From her pocket she takes out a pair of scissors and a sharpened blade. "Sit." Eachna is a woman of few words. She toes the wooden chair in my direction.

Warily I take two steps back. "What do you plan to do with

those things?"

"Cut your hair."

My shoulders relax, and I offer my most arrogant smile. "My hair cannot be cut. It has a mind of its own and grows right back. Sorry." I'm not sorry one bit, and I hope she can read the sound in my voice.

Eachna parries with a conceit all her own. "Once you leave the Cloister, your hair will grow back to its former length. While here you will remain shaven."

"Shaven?" Cutting my hair is one thing. Shaving is quite another. "No," I say simply, thinking there is room for a second victory.

She raises a harried eyebrow. "If you do not let me shave you, you cannot remain at the Cloister. It is forbidden." She pulls off her hood to reveal a shiny pate all her own, covered in red marks as though she's been christened with wine.

Birthmarks. Or burns. Regardless of which, she looks downright frightening.

"We have no vanity at the Cloister." She pulls the hood back into place. "If you choose to remain here and learn amongst the Solitary, your ego must be shed."

So I have an ego. What's so horrible about that? I rather like my hair and prefer it on my head. I temper my petulant thoughts. I need to stay. Aside from honing my skills, I want access to the library here. Information about the Cintamani Jewel may well be within its confines.

Defeat is a bitter pill when swallowed, and I ease into the chair. The sound of the scissors is swift and wicked, and my inky curls fall to the wooden floor in a defeated cascade. With vigorous strokes, she lathers whatever hair remains, then slowly draws the blade across my scalp.

"So much blood," she mutters.

My eyes widen, and I swivel in the chair. "What did you say?"

Her tongue clicks against her gums. "Nicks, nothing more. The blade is sharp, to cut close."

A bony wave gestures me back around, and I do so but not before glimpsing my blood against the sharpened edge. Like an old, unwanted friend, nausea finds its way to my chest and rides through. My eyes close while the razor scrapes softly against my scalp.

"You are cleansed of all impurities and may walk among us in honor," she says at last and blots my head with a towel.

This I doubt. Since my arrival in Winterhaven, cursing and drinking and adulterated thoughts have added themselves to my repertoire. Murder, though unintended. And lovemaking—out of wedlock no less. I'm as impure as they come.

I pass a hand over my head. The smoothness feels foreign against my palm. Eachna spoke the truth—there is no regrowth. Evidently the Cloister has magic within its walls.

"Do you have a mirror?" I ask.

"Ego," she replies emphatically.

She's right, but I would very much like to see my bald head.

259

Then again, I may look horrid, and I would cry to my poor ego's content. She pulls up my hood and motions me to follow. The sun is no longer, and wind whips through the arcade as we hurry through to the other side of the Cloister. Garlic and ginger and burning yak dung greet us when we walk through the wooden doors of the fire-warmed hall.

Men sit at long wooden tables, their bald heads tipped to the bowls at their lips. I'm given some kind of lentil stew and then directed to an empty seat straight across from Jinpa. He nods without looking up from his meal. There are no utensils, so I sip directly from the vessel as everyone else does. No conversation takes place; the room is bloated with silence.

Apart from Eachna, do other women reside at the Cloister? Based on this sampling, the answer is no.

My bowl is filled a second time, and after I finish, Eachna escorts me back to my room. The tub is gone, and a dung fire burns in the hearth. "Tomorrow you will meet the most important of the Solitary, the Grand Scholari. Your training must begin at once. Tonight you must contemplate for two hours before bed."

There are no wishes of a good night's sleep, nothing other than the sound of the door closing behind her.

Contemplate what, exactly? I'm too exhausted to do much except read from *Secretum Secretorum*. The fire proves too low for the small script, so I set the book aside to add another dung cake to the flames. A shorn lock of hair swept into the shadows catches my eye. I pick it up and hold it to the firelight. The fuchsia is nowhere near the same as the queen's fiery hair. Yet there's no mistaking things. The two colors run in the same family, just different versions thereof.

CHAPTER FOURTEEN

The toiling of bells rattles my teeth and wakes me from a shallow slumber. Beneath me the flimsy cot shakes, and I cover my head with the pillow to block out the irksome noise. It's never-ending.

Are the bells a warning? Could the queen or the Infernal be here? I sit up and ponder the possibility, my eyes adjusting to the darkness of the space. Not much can be seen, although the stars that shine through my window tell me the smoke has not yet risen to the Cloister, and I breathe a little easier.

The door creaks open by Eachna's arthritic hand. "Time for learning," she says in a low voice.

My fingers fumble for the Aeriscloque, and I check the pearlescent face. Not even five o'clock. "This is an ungodly hour to be awake much less do anything else."

She steps inside and yanks off my covers. "This is when the Solitary rise, and the Grand Scholari awaits. Quick now," she snaps.

Unspeaking and guided by lamplight, we hurry through one arcade to the next, the cloak and knapsack at my back. The frigid air wakens me further, and I glance at each passing door, curious which might unmask the coveted library.

Eachna motions me into an empty chamber in the east façade. I only know the direction because the row of paneless windows allows a view of the mountains, the pale light awakening the horizon. The smell of smoke is ever-present, the land below burning to a cinder.

Shadows stalk the walls. The ceiling is vaulted, and the chilly space is lit only by kettled fires in the rafters. The door behind me closes. Eachna is gone. Panicked, I rush over and try the knob, certain I've been locked in. *Unlocked. This isn't Isceald Castle. I'm not a prisoner, I'm here of my own free will.*

No furniture occupies the space, so I assume we will need plenty of room to hone my Elemental skills. A mouse scurries across the floor, and I jump to clear its path. A light tap on my shoulder spins me on my heel. Eachna stands before me, and my hand goes to my heart. "You scared me, Eachna. I didn't hear you come back in."

"Never left."

"Yes you did. I saw you leave." When she says nothing, I further clarify. "I heard the door close."

"A closing door means not that one has left."

Irritated, I add, "True. However, this chamber is not so large you could disappear. You were gone."

"Did you not see? I moved right past."

I grapple for words but find none.

"Out with it," she scolds. "If you think something, say

263

something. No leader stands poised with confidence only to flounder like a common carp in need of air."

"The mouse...was you?"

Her head tilts at an odd angle. She points to the mouse traveling along the perimeter. I move closer and watch the mouse crawl through a small hole.

"Then I don't understand," I say. When there's no answer, I turn to see she's gone again. "Eachna," I call out in frustration. "What is your point? And what of the Grand Scholari? Is he here somewhere? Am I supposed to find him as some sort of task?"

A moth flutters before me. I hold out a hand, and it lands on my finger. Red markings dot white wings in the same shape as the markings on Eachna's head. When it flies away, I turn to follow its path and bump right into Eachna.

Lady Aniyu's words tumble back to me. *To grow, you must open your eyes. You must see.*"You? You're the Grand Scholari?"

"Preconceived notions," she chides. "You expected someone of great presence? Tall and full of intimidation? A man no doubt?"

My embarrassment comes with a flush to my cheeks. As evidenced by Guernsey, greatness comes in all sizes and shapes, even a hunched, toothless woman who can turn into a moth. I'm guessing she can change into far more impressive things.

"Lesson one?" I say to change the subject. "I've created fires and windstorms, tidal waves and even an ice ladder. Really, I've used the elements in so many ways. Back in the Other World, I created the first of many living creatures, and from there they grew in complexity." I tick off the iced butterfly, the fiery, two-headed phoenix, and Hoarus the ice dragon, my most remarkable creation to date.

Eachna scoffs, unimpressed. "A dragon of ice in a game of fire is of no use."

She's right, although it stings no less. I can hear her chiding me with *ego.*

"An army is needed," she concedes with a thoughtful nod. "Though you must kill the queen, you cannot do so alone. She has soldiers. You will need them as well."

"The Veneficum have created their own infantry along with a fleet. King Andronicus too has an army ten thousand strong."

She walks about the room, hands linked at her back. "People are born of blood and bone. Flesh cannot withstand fire."

I rub my arms to stave off the chill. "What are you saying? I will need an entire army born from the elements?"

"Embodied by is a more accurate term."

I think for a moment of the possibilities. "Fire begets fire. Air fuels it. Water could work, although what kind of army can be made from water?"

"Water kills fire; it is law. Water will prove useful. However, water will not help win this war, no."

Earth is the only remaining element. An image of a thousand stone soldiers come to mind, all marching through smoke and flame to defeat Belisama. The image sinks away as the realization rises. "Earth is my least favorite element, mainly because I am not well-versed in it. Recently I tried to escape a jail cell by manipulating the foundation. The only reason I got out was the hands of another, not by my own—"

"Your mind, not your hands, holds the answers." She spits at my feet before she heads to the door. "I'll return in two hours' time."

"What about the rest of my lesson?"

"Everything needed is here."

"I need you for the lesson, do I not?"

Her head shakes not in answer but in exasperation. "Clarity is what you need. Rid yourself of the fear, for fear will bring you down faster than a lion. The burning pyre is the perfect example."

I stare. "You're mistaken. I lost consciousness because—"

"Because you panicked. Did you contemplate last night?"

Her explanation startles me. But something tells me the Grand Scholari is rarely wrong. "Yes," I lie.

"Then you should know what to do. The answers should come."

"I saw nothing. I tried but nothing came to me, so I read instead."

Though her left eye is lazy, it is justifiably cynical. "Two hours."

"Some teacher you are," I blurt as she opens the door.

Slowly she turns back to me. "I'm no teacher. I'm but a guide, same as the rest of the Solitary."

When the door closes, I walk to the window and sigh with frustration. The stars burn cold, and up here they appear so large it seems as though I could pluck them from the sky. This reminds me of *World of Winterhaven*, and I pull the Taerou card from the knapsack. Four figures representing the elements; a woman; a wreath wrapped in the cosmos.

What does this mean? Jeyna said there was a strong vibrational pull. Of course, the images could just be reflective of me, for I am an Elementalist. Death should be the more concerning card.

Pale light breaks the horizon, but I'm uninspired by this space. Nothing new comes to me, how I should use the elements in a manner different from anywhere else. What I need is the library, to find information about the Cintamani Jewel. I've got nearly two hours. Easily I can do some reading and be back here by the time Eachna returns.

Where would they put a library? Two towers bookend the Cloister. One is the belfry, so my best guess tells me the other is the library. No one will know who I am with the hood draped over my head. I'll be yet another Solitary wandering the corridors of the Cloister.

All is quiet and cold, the wind sweeping through the courtyard as I hurry along. Predictably given my direction-challenged self, I'm completely turned around and have no clue where I am or where the tower is from here. When I round the corner, I'm met with a line of Solitary filing into a chamber, and I must wait before passing. I'm surprised to see so many up at this ridiculous hour.

The shuffle of feet comes to a halt. I peer from beneath my

hood, wondering why they have stopped. Jinpa is there, smiling and waving me into line. Eyes lowered, I adamantly shake my head, but he stands there and motions me in until I have no other choice.

Inside the chamber, the smell of seeped herbs wends through the air courtesy of the burning incense staked into clay pots. We sit on the floor; there are no stools or benches to be had. On a dais at the front, Yeshe sits on a wooden throne, frail and not long for this world.

Melodic chanting begins, the language unfamiliar, and the hairs on my arms stand tall from the haunting sound as it rises and falls along the walls. My eyes drift to a close to soak in the beauty. A second chant, then a third and fourth. Though eerily beautiful, this goes on for far too long. My window of time is closing.

Everyone finally stands, but instead of departing, they form a line to the dais. I'll risk exposure if I try to leave, so I can only follow suit. One by one, each of the Solitary approaches Yeshe and sits with him for a short while. The mood is not somber. To the contrary, there is laughter and love and compassion throughout. Many offer fruit or candles or flowers. Some have lengthy exchanges while others are brief. Adding to the revelry, one Solitary juggles oranges, only he does so without hands. Another rises into the air and performs a series of somersaults reminiscent of those done by Snap back at Isceald Castle.

The Solitary in line before me approaches Yeshe and takes a

white dove from the sleeve of his robe. The bird flaps its wings, each time releasing a sapphire feather into the Solitary's hand. I gasp inwardly not because of what the bird is doing, which is fascinating unto itself, but because I recognize Eachna's arthritic hand. She was next to me all along.

Fifteen times the bird flaps and releases a feather before it moves up Eachna's arm to perch there. She cups her hands together. Moments later, a beak pokes from her laced fingers, and a new bird feathered in sapphire emerges. The two birds fly about the room before resting on each of Yeshe's knees. "Fly, friend," is all Eachna says to the elder before she walks off the dais.

Her magic is in line with Snap's capabilities, and now I wonder what Eachna's story is and how she ended up at the Cloister.

My turn to approach Yeshe. Like the others, I sit before him, although I have no idea what to say. If I use the elements to create an offering, I'll risk exposure. More than anything, I want to ask about the Cintamani Jewel, but this seems neither the time nor the place. With nothing significant to offer, I take his hands in mine and say a silent prayer.

Though his eyes are closed, a smile rises from his thin lips. "It exists," he whispers.

Is he reading my mind? "What exists?" I ask in the lowest voice possible. "The Cintamani Jewel?"

He nods once. Something tells me Yeshe knows things about the universe, more than any book might reveal. "I possess two of the stones. Kyanite and Petard—Air and Water. Although I'm

269

unsure where the Earth stone might be, the fifth element is what eludes me, the stone born of the cosmos. Where might I find this gemstone? Do you know?"

His feeble forefinger points above then directly at me.

Is he senile or lucid? He seemed to have mental clarity on the way to the Cloister. Perhaps it's not so blatant. Before I can ask for further clarification, a tap on my shoulder tells me Jinpa awaits his turn. I chide myself for my stupidity. *Why didn't I ask about the Cintamani Jewel during our journey to the Cloister?* I thank Yeshe and wish him well. This will be our last encounter, I'm certain. If he's lucky, he's off to the Realm of Halcyon for a peaceful eternity.

The wind sweeps through the arcade when I sneak out the back way. Only a quarter hour remains before Eachna's return. The library will have to wait. When I miraculously find the chamber, Eachna is already inside, waiting. "Why do you defy me?" she snaps.

"I'm not defying you."

"Then why did you not follow my instruction? Winterhaven is burning down; do you not smell the air?"

My arms cross in defense. "Smoke is not something easily ignored."

"Time is of the essence. You will not remain here much longer. Should you not learn what needs to be learned, you will surely die. The Death Ceremony was not for you to partake in."

Blast it all. She knows I was there. Unsurprising, so I decide to make a clean breast of it. "Eachna, joining you was not my intent. Honestly, I was looking for the library. Jinpa waved me into line, and I could not forsake him."

Eachna moves toward me and stands too close for comfort. "Library? To what end?"

"The whole reason I came here. To train, yes. But also to read up on...something." I decide it might be unwise to tell her about the Cintamani Jewel. She'll mock me, tell me it's a crutch.

"The Cintamani Jewel is nothing without your training."

I'm stunned by her proclamation, but before my mouth can gape, I remember her previous instruction to say what I mean. "You're a Voyant and a shapeshifter."

"Do you not understand?" she says, ignoring my statement and the self-assured way in which it was said. "The power to destroy the queen must come from within."

"I'm an Elementalist, yes, but I don't know how to create an army from this." I gesture the room. "What is in here, exactly, that will help me create a thousand soldiers?" My voice is raised in frustration because the guesswork is too arduous.

Eachna shuffles over to one of the arched windows and stares outside. "You look in the wrong place."

I join her and watch as snow falls across the Cloister. "The king is keeping Belisama at bay by putting out the fires," I say more calmly. "Time is running dry, I do know. But at least he is inadvertently helping me by continuing to produce snow, no matter how little."

271

"This is not snow."

A stern sidelong glance prompts me to catch the flakes in my palm. Just like in the Petrified Forest, I rub them between my fingers. They don't melt, they dissolve to a gritty soot.

"This is ash," I relent in a whisper. *The queen is winning, after all, burning down the realm bit by bit.* "I can't imagine what Winterhaven must look like below, all of the wildfires, the land scorched to dust."

Eachna catches the flakes in her hands, brings them to her nose, and breathes in deep. "This ash is not born from the burning of land, but from the burning of souls."

***

Eachna demanded I spend the rest of the day alone contemplating. Meals to be had in my chamber. As if somehow my mind would be disturbed by eating amongst the wily silence of the Solitary. Their chanting threads the walls of the Cloister, and I find the sound strangely comforting as I stare into the fire and wonder how I'll create an army made from the elements. And once I confront the queen, then what?

The stones.

I've not had a moment to study them since the attack at Wintersgaard. I remove them from the knapsack and unwrap each one, their respective colors glowing in the low light. They vibrate in my hand, filled with lives of their own.

My hands tremble with excitement as I try to stack them. They won't fit together. In fact, they repel one another as if like poles to a set of magnets. Confused by this, I take out *Secretum Secretorum* to study the diagram of the five-tiered stele.

Now I understand. Fire rests between the two. I despair because finding the Fire stone seems as unlikely as finding the Aether, which seems downright impossible, regardless of what Yeshe thought.

I study the Fire stone, triangular in shape. *Was the stone part of the ivory chalice?* All at once, my heart falters. If so, then it is forever buried in the ashes of Mount Serius and the Cintamani Jewel is nevermore. How I wish the bejeweled chalice was pictured in the book, to see if any of the embedded stones were pyramid-shaped.

No. The queen sent Nashoba for the Kyanite. She of all people would know if the Fire stone was part of the ivory chalice.

I tuck the stones away and settle onto my cot with *Secretum Secretorum* in hand. If only I could decipher half of Aristotle's writings. Zhang the Elder could help me. If a Hereat was kept in the Cloister, I could find him and talk to him about the Cintamani Jewel. After all, he helped me decipher the Emerald Tablet. By turning the diagram upside down, the secret of eternal life was revealed. *So simple, so clever.*

Fondly I recall his nickname for me: Tiāntǐ. For the first time, I wonder what the word means and why I never thought to ask. Every name has a meaning behind it. Years ago, I'd learned Sondrine means 'Protector of Men.' Is my given name a coincidence or had my future been somehow foretold?

A gnarled hand grabs the book from my hands. Startled, I look up to see Eachna, who looks significantly scarier by firelight. "I should throw this thing into the fire," she hisses. "You are not here to read fabled tales."

I snatch the book back. "This holds countless secrets—answers to questions of the universe. The book speaks of the Cintamani Jewel; it may help in killing the queen."

"Myth," she says in her most reproving tone. "If the Cintamani Jewel could save us all, do you not think someone would have thought of this previous to now?"

Good point. I'm an idiot for not seeing the obvious. As a matter of fact, my idiocy seems to be my greatest trait these days. "The queen tried to get the Kyanite from the Mór. She believes the Cintamani Jewel exists."

"Myth," she hisses again, this time with verve. "If the queen believes the Cintamani Jewel will save her, she will be easy an easy conquest. She's desperate to stay alive for all eternity."

"If the jewel is a myth, then why do the stones exist in the first place? Why are they protected if they wield no true power? At the Death Ceremony, I asked Yeshe—he claimed the Cintamani Jewel was real." I open my knapsack and remove the Kyanite and Petard.

Eachna's lazy eye stares off in the distance. Her good eye appears unimpressed. She takes the stones and rolls them in her rough palm before returning them. "Contemplation will serve you better."

"What is contemplation?" I finally ask.

"Close your eyes and clear your mind. The fear will subside, and the answers will appear."

I sink onto the cot. "Don't the answers need to be within for them to come to the forefront? I have no idea how to build an army or how to kill the queen." The words are gutting.

"Your fear is besting you," she says in a harsh tone.

"Murder and death instill fear," I retort just as stringently. "Pardon me for being so dishonorable."

"Murder is the act of cowards. Destroying evil brings forth honor. As for death, why fear it?"

I groan inwardly. I always feel on the defensive with Eachna. "Because if Samsara truly exists, I don't want to die and come back as anyone else. I'm not done being me."

She almost offers a toothless smile. "Progress."

***

The following morning, I awaken on my own. Before my usual meeting with Eachna, I decide to look for the library. Regardless of what she thinks, the Cintamani Jewel exists. I hurry through the open colonnade, the endless smell of smoke a grisly reminder of the war raging below. The guilt is almost too much. People are dying as they fight off the Infernal and Tartarean and whatever other minions might be helping the queen. Meanwhile I am here, trying to figure out how to kill her. Those people do not have the luxury, so why should I?

Jinpa rounds the corner, startling me. "The library sits in the

275

tower at the far edge of the Cloister." He smiles, and I'm not sure if it's a knowing one or his usual demeanor. He hands me a tablet of parchment and a wooden box. "A sketching kit, an offering from Yeshe. Many moons ago it was given to him. He hopes it will prove useful."

I nod. "Please thank him. I'll treasure it."

"Remember, you have the answers: they lie within."

"Books provide answers too," I say in earnest.

He gestures down the colonnade. The smell of ink and yellowed pages surround us at once when we enter the library. Though nowhere near the size of the Great Tower of Annals, the sheer number of books shoved into every crook indicates the library is a treasure trove of answers. I'm enraptured by the sight.

"The Cintamani Jewel is what you're after," he states.

Are all Solitary Voyants? "I meant to ask Yeshe about it earlier, on our way to the Cloister. Do you believe the Cintamani Jewel is a myth? Eachna thinks so, but Yeshe told me otherwise."

"The stones themselves exist. Whether they were born from the Cintamani Jewel, no one truly knows." He pulls a leather-bound book from one of the topmost shelves. *Myths of Winterhaven* is tooled in the cover. "The story of how the Cintamani Jewel came to pass is referenced here. Remember, the Cintamani Jewel is cited in a book about myths, not a historical one."

I understand the insinuation. Still I press him for answers. "If the jewel were to exist, where do you believe it would have come from?"

"A higher being, perhaps. The cosmos are vast, so much so the jewel could be random. Many things fall from the sky. Yeshe knows more about the stones than any Solitary here, even the Grand Scholari, but he will soon take the knowledge with him." Jinpa hands me the book. "My laboratory is above. Pay me a visit should you tire of reading."

He climbs the wood ladder and disappears into the loft. Alone but with the company of a thousand books, I set aside the parchment and sketching kit and settle onto a bench, flipping through the book to the appropriate chapter.

In the Primary Age, the Immortal Faie ruled the heavenly skies. The Faie were born of the colliding of stars, and the two youngest were Josephina and her twin brother Fleuric. The siblings spent every hour of every day together, devoted to one another.

As talented as she was beautiful, Josephina could spin entire worlds and galaxies from her fingertips, expanding the cosmos one hundred-fold. Although Fleuric possessed no such talents, he admired and loved his sister more than a brother should.

By the time the Secondary Age came to pass, tens of centuries later, Fleuric could no longer hide his affections. One day while the twins played amongst the stars, Fleuric pulled Josephina into a deep kiss. Shocked and betrayed by her brother's actions, Josephina not only refused him, she admonished him.

The cosmos, though vast, suddenly felt confining, and Josephina fled to Winterhaven, a world created by her own hand during the end of the Primary Age. She needed time away from the Faie and most certainly from her brother. There among the frozen lands lived an honorable young man named Rhiseart. Rhiseart captured her heart, and soon they fell in love.

But Rhiseart was Duine and not Immortal. Decreed by Faie law, a choice was demanded of Josephina: become Duine and live out the rest of her years in Winterhaven or remain Immortal, renounce her love for Rhiseart, and return to the cosmos. Dissatisfied with the two choices, Josephina asked the Faie for a third: make Rhiseart Immortal to live among them, for she could not bear to watch him age and die while she remained forever young. Fleuric balked and at once reminded the Faie that his sister's request went against the laws of the universe. But the Faie overruled him and made a rare concession, granting Josephina her wish. Elated, she created the Cintamani Jewel, pearlescent in color and born from all five elements, to give her beloved eternal life.

Embittered and lonely, Fleuric grew increasingly jealous of Rhiseart. Upon learning of his sister's pending nuptials, he flew into a rage. To watch Josephina with another for all eternity was something he could not bear, so he stole the Cintamani Jewel and hid beneath Crann Bethadh, a massive tree in Winterhaven.

Josephina searched desperately for the stone, suspicious of her brother. When neither he nor the stone could be found, she asked permission to create a second jewel for her beloved. But the Faie chided her carelessness in losing the Cintamani Jewel and would not grant her request. Josephina grew despondent, but Fleuric was *gleeful his plan had worked.*

Yet Josephina chose to marry Rhiseart, forever relinquishing her Immortal station to become Duine. She bore him a daughter, Emmelyne, and they lived out the rest of their days in Winterhaven. Not long after his seventy-fifth name day, Rhiseart fell ill and died shortly thereafter. Two days after Rhiseart's passing, Fleuric visited his aging and grieving sister. Riddled with guilt, he admitted to stealing the Cintamani Jewel. He wanted her to have it, to regain her Immortality and once again live among the Faie in the cosmos.

Although outraged by her brother's actions, Josephina said nothing, for she planned to give the Cintamani Jewel to Emmelyne. Fleuric saw through her ruse, stating he had cursed the jewel. Should anyone but Josephina take possession, they would live eternally but in darkness and damnation. Josephina claimed the Cintamani Jewel could not be cursed as it was solely her creation, and spellbound. The Cintamani Jewel was the bringer of eternal life and of light. Darkness could not prevail.

Steadfast in their claims, the siblings battled fiercely over the jewel. Up though the treetops they rose, past the moon and stars, deep into the cosmos, until the jewel shattered into five individual gemstones. Fleuric, the stronger of the two, held Josephina back as the stones plummeted through the sky and disappeared from sight. Filled with a blinding rage, Josephina cut off her brother's hands so he could never again hold her back.

Banished by the Faie, Fleuric was forced to live eternally under

Crann Bethadh, watching Josephina and her daughter die while he remained forever alone. To this day, the star above the tree is rumored to be Quintessence, found by Fleuric and placed there in memory of his sister.

I close the book. Should the five stones be reunited, it seems unknown if the Cintamani Jewel will bestow light and smite the darkness or be a home to evil, one of death and damnation. *My luck, I would find all five stones, only to discover Fleuric's curse bested Josephina's spell.* Still, the one consistent thing remains: the jewel offers eternal life to the bearer. I must find it before Belisama does.

I start for Jinpa's laboratory when the bells begin to toil. I'm late for my lesson with Eachna. This does not bode well.

***

I practically fly into the chamber. Eachna sits in a lone chair, arms crossed. "You are late. Did you contemplate?"

"Of course," I say, fingers crossed behind my back.

"What did you see?"

"A meeting. With Zhang the Elder. Does the Cloister have a Hereat, perchance?" The old crone spits at my feet in answer. *Charming as always, Eachna.*

"No Hereat here," she says. "They are an invitation to the enemy or any unwanted visitor."

"Where is the closest, then?"

Her face turns redder than the marks on her scalp. "The Hereat, the Cintamani Jewel...These will not help you defeat the

280

queen. Stop looking—"

My hand goes up in defiance. "I know, I know, look from within. Well, guess what? Try as I might, I'm no further along. To be frank, I am failing."

She paces the empty chamber. "If the Cintamani Jewel did not exist for a fact, what would you look for right now?"

"Courage," I joke.

No laughter, not even a shadow of a smile. "Fear motivates our choices. You must see the world differently. Failure is learning, is it not? Each failure was born from courage."

I shake my head in disagreement. "My friend Bart was killed because of me. I failed him in the worst possible way."

Eachna tuts. "You were not his keeper. He fulfilled his destiny."

"He should never have come with me in the first place," I say with more force. "We were at the Ichor Samhain because I was seeking a Sablier, to see if the queen was my mother."

She stops her pacing. "And once you saw the evidence, did you return to the Other World?"

"No. Once I learned the truth, I knew I needed to stay in Winterhaven, to fulfill my destiny."

Eachna makes for her leave. "Lesson finished."

***

For the first time since my arrival at the Cloister, Eachna does not tell me to contemplate, so I return to the library to speak to Jinpa. The sketching kit and parchment had been left behind, and I take them with me up the ladder. A low, curved ceiling of stone; fore-edged books and maps soaking the ochery light of weeping candles; beakers coughing out colorful smoke. Like Zhang the Elder's laboratory, the space evokes an air of ancient mystery.

Jinpa pours powder into a bubbling beaker. "The Cintamani Jewel," he asks without looking up. "Did you find the answer you seek?"

"Have you read the story?"

"Many times."

I pull up a stool next to his. "Even if the lore was true, it's unclear if the reunited stones would smite the darkness or bring it to the fore. What are your thoughts?"

Jinpa ponders a moment then hands me a brown hard-boiled egg from a basket. "Make this stand upright."

"Eggs can't stand, given their shape. Besides, I'm an Elementalist, not a magician."

"They can. Go on, try."

Each attempt is a failed one, the egg miserably falling and rolling around the table. When Jinpa senses my frustration, he sets the egg aside and hands me a ball of heavily knotted rope. "Untie this."

One frayed end sticks out, and I tug and pick at the string using my nails, but it proves a thankless task. "The ball is wound too tight," I say, my agitation growing.

282

Jinpa shakes his bald head. "The knotted rope can be unraveled; the egg can stand."

"With magic," I say emphatically.

"No magic. Only your mind."

This I did not think of, so I close my eyes and concentrate hard, first visualizing the knotted ball unraveling and then the egg standing upright. Perhaps I don't need the elements to complete certain tasks. The possibility excites me, but when my eyes reopen, the knot and egg both lie there untouched, practically mocking me. "I give up."

"So soon?" he teases. "Think hard."

I can think to my heart's content. No way is the knot coming undone. No way is the egg standing. "Jinpa, you're making me feel stupid."

He wags a friendly finger. "No one can make you feel anything. You choose what to feel, others do not dictate. Now, have you heard of *Novacula Occami*, a principle of logic?"

"Truthfully I don't know much of Winterhaven's philosophies."

"*Novacula Occami* means the simplest explanation tends to be the best one." He'd said the same when he kicked down the wall of snow. Jinpa takes a small spoon and lightly taps on one end of the egg to form a flat base. Then he sets the egg on the table, where it stands upright.

"You didn't say I could fool with the egg in such a manner," I say in protest.

"I didn't say you could not." He takes a blade from a drawer, and with a swift movement, the knotted ball is cut in half. With a light tug on the frayed end, the knot completely unravels. "Alexander the Great proved this particular principle, known in both the Other World and Winterhaven as the Gordian Knot. A seemingly impossible task solved by creative means."

Alexander the Great once again. "What does all of this mean?" I ask.

"You tell me," Jinpa says.

I look from the egg to the unraveled ball of rope. "I need to expand my mind, to think of things in a different manner. The same way Yeshe said to use the elements together instead of separately. I'm not sure of the phrase in Winterhaven, but in the Other World there is an expression, 'think outside the square.'"

Jinpa nods. He points to the sketching kit and parchment. "You believe the queen has the stone of Fire."

"If the Cintamani Jewel is even real," I grumble. "Eachna told me to stop thinking about it."

"What does the stone of Fire look like? Show me."

Inside the wood box is a beautiful blue quill and cubed inkpot made of blue marble. Engraved on top of the stopper is the inverted triangle bisected by a horizontal line, the Cloister's sigil. I lift the corked stopper, dip the quill's tip into crimson ink, and sketch the pyramid representing the Fire stone.

The simplest explanation tends to be the best one. I stare at the sketch as though the answer should magically appear. *Think outside the square.* "Jinpa, I don't yet have the answer. However, I didn't come to the Cloister to hone my Elemental skills, did I? I came here to train my mind."

"Exactly so."

CHAPTER FIFTEEN

I watch from my window as the pyre below burns Yeshe's body against the dead of night. Bells toil, the Solitary chant, and though death is celebrated here, the mood feels distinctly somber. The glow from the flames spills into my chamber, commingles with the dung fire in my hearth, and breathes light onto the inked sketch propped against the wall.

If the answer is so simple, why is it so ridiculously hard to see?

An explosive sound booms outside, shakes the ground beneath me, and the sky briefly alights. For a moment, I believe the pyre is collapsing unto itself. But the horizon flickers not with lightning strikes but something far more sinister, a red cast against the dark of the clouds.

Eachna opens my door, a lit lantern in one hand, a pair of knee-high boots in the other. "Change into these and your street clothes, then gather your things. A raven came just now. The queen has been found."

My heart pounds in a fevered cadence. Five words I hoped not to hear, not so soon. The boots are similar to those donned by a soldier. My woolen trousers, cotton shirt—even the emerald cloak—feel foreign against my skin, especially the grey cap as I pull it over my bald head. I shove the inked drawing and sketch kit into the knapsack and follow Eachna through the Cloister. The sands in the hourglass are falling more rapidly now.

She leads me into the library, unfurls a scroll on a wooden table, and waves away the ensuing dust motes. A map of Winterhaven. Her arthritic finger points to a massive tree occupying a vast space in the upper eastern corner. The Dendrite Sea runs parallel.

"Crann Bethadh in the Desert of Katakum," Eachna says. "Where sea meets sand."

Crann Bethadh? The tree from the lore of the Cintamani Jewel. I say nothing. The story is myth, after all. "A desert. Perfect for Belisama."

"You must leave at once and traverse the mountains of Titan Dome, the ones you see from here. Katakum lies beyond, on the other side of the range."

She nods to the open window, and I follow her line of sight. A white raven sits on the ledge, looks on with aquamarine eyes.

"Guernsey," I say without thinking twice. The bird flies into the library and shifts into the old sorcerer. "How could I fail to see the white raven was you all this time? I suspected as much back at the Keep of Wintersgaard, when you led me to the Kyanite. Now it's so obvious."

Guernsey pats some ash from his shock of white hair. "Although your time at the Cloister has been brief and curtailed, it appears to have done some good."

Although I'm thrilled to see he's alive, my resentment has not abated, and I make it known by the tone of my voice. "The Sablier revealed all. Why lie to me where the queen was concerned?"

For the first time ever, a more kind-hearted look lives beyond the usual steel of his eyes. "My Foresight showed you would be requisite for this battle should it ever come to pass. My motives at the time were self-serving, admittedly. Winterhaven was not without enmity, not even in its beginnings. Yet I and the rest of the Veneficum did not want to see this world die. Your Elemental gifts inspired confidence to be sure. We hoped you would kill the queen without learning the truth. When that didn't come to pass, we agreed to tell you knowing it would cost us in both time and in lives lost, for you would not take the news lightly and without proof."

"You weren't wrong," I say without apology.

"Ah, but I was, you see. More often than not, a lie serves as nothing more than a betrayal. And this one was costly on all fronts. To lose faith in someone, to never again trust them, are the only things gained with a lie. I can offer an apology, and I do so with the understanding it will likely be denied. With all of my inherent power, this is the one broken thing I cannot fix."

My anger subsides, and my heart warms. "Self-serving or not, you saved my life when I was but an infant. And in the Other World, it was you who looked after me to make sure Henrietta kept her promise. That means something. An apology does as well."

Guernsey nods in appreciation. "You have exceeded every expectation, Sondrine. You will continue to do so, I trust." Another erratic boom upends the heartfelt moment, and books clatter from the shelves to the floor. "We must get you to Titan Dome," he says, his stern demeanor returning. "Carrig and his clan await. They will provide shelter and rest for a night, perhaps two, before escorting us to the desert's edge. From there, a contingent of the Veneficum's infantry will get us to Crann Bethadh."

"How do you know the queen is there? Did you finally find Eirene?"

"Eirene is dead." His voice is devoid of emotion, but the words themselves weaken my legs, make them feel cut off. Guernsey takes a seat at the table. "Belisama killed her."

"She was only a child," I cry as though somehow this should have saved Eirene.

Eachna shrugs, indifferent. "Such things are unimportant to Queen Belisama Agni."

"What happened?" I take the chair opposite Guernsey. "Do you know the particulars?"

"Eirene died in Mount Serius, I surmise. Remember, she was hiding in the shadows all along. When the queen drank the waters and perished, her soul lingered. The only viable way out of Mount Serius was through Eirene's body."

"What about me? Or Shán or even you or Snap for that matter? We were all there as well."

Eachna tuts. "Souls cannot jump into people's bodies at

289

random. They must ask, and the carrier must agree. Not any carrier, however. Like for like. Since the queen is vermin, so too must be the carrier."

Guernsey adds, "Mount Serius was imploding. The queen must have told Eirene she needed her help to escape and survive. Of course, Eirene agreed, not knowing she would die in the process. The queen knew Eirene was considered vermin, her heart and mind diseased beyond repair."

"It was the queen in the iron and bamboo cage?" I ask. Guernsey nods, and I remember Eirene's needled teeth and her threats. "Why come back to the Sanctuary at all?"

"To kill us both, I'm near certain," he says. "Little did she know I had spoken with Shán and Zhang the Elder prior to our heading into Mount Serius. We'd pieced things together, how Eirene was working for the queen. Per Lord Kian's instructions, I was to imprison Eirene while punishment was decided before taking her back to the Sacred Grove of Willeaux. The queen, posing as Eirene, did not know this, of course. The moment she found me, presumably to kill me, she was still in a weakened state. Her diminutive size only helped, for I easily trapped her in the iron-barred cage. At the time, I still believed the young sylph to be Eirene."

"When did you realize she was the queen?"

"Too late, I'm afraid. Do know her behavior toward you made her suspect. The *Chisana* Sylphs can be capricious, to be sure. Nevertheless her actions seemed extreme, uncharacteristic. The queen knew she must escape the iron cage for obvious reasons. However, no one at the Sanctuary was considered vermin. The Nereids have pure souls, as do the rest of us. She needed to make due with whatever came along."

The ominous way he states this sends a dire chill through me. "Dare I ask?" Guernsey pulls a molted snakeskin from the pouch of his robe. "The queen is serpentine?" I whisper.

Guernsey nods gravely.

"There were parasitic snakes on Ykuza," I say, recalling the battle in the ice cave. "Could one have been the queen herself?"

"Possibly. Each body is a host. Even in her enfeebled state of being, she managed to summon Ykuza and use his blood to strengthen her."

The memory of Captain Seybourne's quarters come back to me. "There were vipers aboard the ship I stowed away on. And Naedder," I gasp. "A man aboard the ship, he said he didn't believe in dying. '*Shed your skin, and you're on to the next life.*' He was a horrible man, vermin of the worst sort. I'd bet the queen started as one of those vipers and then invaded Naedder's body. But he was extremely ill, too ill to kill me. He was dying of dysentery, although she probably helped things along. She must have slithered back to the cage before we tossed his body overboard. I wondered how the Infernal found me in Taliin."

Guernsey and Eachna nod along, listening.

"Why didn't she kill me on the ship, I wonder?"

"She may have tried, unbeknownst to you," Guernsey says. "Or the opportunity may not have presented itself."

"I don't think she invaded Naedder's body until the end, because Naedder would have had ample time to kill me while I was locked away. But how did she get on the ship in the first place? We both started at the Sanctuary, so how did she climb aboard when I myself did not know a ship was going to pass through?"

"Spies are everywhere," Eachna crows as she pushes fallen books back into the shelves. "The queen has many allies. Any despicable vulture could have picked her up and dropped her on deck."

"The queen is exceedingly clever," Guernsey says, "and I surmise we may never learn the whole truth. The very fact she breached the sanctity of the Sanctuary, one of the safest places in all of Winterhaven, tells me much."

Macabre as it is, I finger the molted skin. "Did you hear what happened at the Keep of Wintersgaard?" I ask.

"Lord Kian informed me of both the Ferrum and the fire. No place is safe at this juncture."

I recall the forged path in the snow right below the treehouse, wide as an oak tree. "How big can she be?" I try to keep my voice from shaking. I fail stupendously.

"Sightings of the Infernal have lessened, from what I've heard," Eachna declares.

"What are you saying?" I ask. "She's one of them?"

"She's using their blood to gain strength," Eachna says. She looks to Guernsey, who nods in agreement.

I help straighten up the library, more out of nervousness than any virtue for order. "Why not become one of them? They are the vilest creatures in all of Winterhaven, are they not?"

Eachna rolls up the map and hands it to me for the taking. "The Infernal can only grow so big. A serpent can shed its skin, continue to grow. Ykuza is a prime example."

The thought of the queen in serpentine form and as big as Ykuza sets my heart racing. "I never figured out how to create an army. How will I do battle alone against something so monstrous, in heart and in size?"

"You are not alone," Guernsey assures me. "Our own infantry, though spare compared to the queen's, is ample. Camp has been made in the Desert of Katakum. Others will come by sea. Ione for one."

Before I can ask about Shán or King Andronicus and his infantry, the door opens, and Jinpa enters the library. "Yeshe has gone to the Realm of Halcyon," he announces. "I'm off to find some rest, but I wanted to bid you farewell and safe journey."

I hurry over and take his hands in mine. "Thank you, Jinpa. For everything." I whisper so Eachna can't hear. "I've yet to figure out the Fire stone, but I will continue to try."

"The answers lie within. Trust in yourself to see." He hands me the cracked brown egg and the unraveled knot. "Novacula Occami."

***

Eachna leads us out of the Cloister and through the back gate to the mountain range of Titan Dome. My farewell to the Grand Scholari is far less emotional than my farewell to Jinpa, and much more earnest. "While I haven't been the best student, I will take what was taught and do my best with it. Your efforts are appreciated and will not be forgotten."

"As Yeshe and Jinpa said, the answers lie here." She points to me. "Within, not without."

The earth rattles beneath us as Guernsey and I hurry out the gate and start down the mountain at a frenzied pace, the path so narrow we must track it in tandem. Moonlight is our only guide, reflected in the roiling smoke below.

"Can you apprise me of anything?" I ask while gasping for breath. I've grown accustomed to the thin air, but running makes it no easier to breathe.

"Shortly after you left the Sanctuary, I did the same, traveling to various locales in trying to locate the queen. Our good friend Zhang the Elder is the one who discovered her whereabouts. After sorting his affairs with Sold & Gilvers and renewing a pathway from there to the Isle of Empyrean, he reclaimed his seat with the Veneficum."

The news is encouraging. Zhang the Elder is a man of brilliance, his mind a much-needed presence in such matters. "Guernsey, do you know the meaning of Tiāntǐ, perchance?"

"Tiāntǐ means celestial. Heavenly body."

My surprise comes in the form of a sharp gasp. *What did Zhang*

294

the Elder know to give me such a name? For now, I shake the thought away, because more important matters lie at hand. "And what of King Andronicus? Is he still alive?"

Our pace slows as the path steepens. "My best guess tells me yes; however, it is but a guess, nothing more. His armies have been spotted in the desert and elsewhere, but the battles with the Infernal and Tartarean have been many and ongoing. Whether he has survived thus far is an unknown. His alliance with our infantry may have been renounced, unbeknownst to us. When his infantry was called upon due south of here in the town of Kirkwall, none showed. We lost many a soldier that day."

"No surprise," I scoff. "The king has his own agenda, as always."

We cross over a gorge by way of a precarious wood bridge that bounces with each step. The sound of water rushes from somewhere far below, but not until we're both on the other side do I attempt to look down.

"Has there been any snowfall?" I ask, my hand dragging the jagged mountain edge for better balance.

"Very little. As to whether the snow was conjured by the king or came naturally, we cannot know." Guernsey coughs from the smolder. "Fire and smoke prevail. Once you depart Titan Dome and head down to the desert, the smoke becomes all-consuming. Prepare yourself for what's to come. Below is chaos, the land a husk of its former self."

If the scorched villages we passed through on the way to the

Cloister were any indication, I know all too well.

We stop momentarily to catch our breath, and Guernsey pulls something from beneath his sapphire cloak. "Before I forget, I made a promise to young Snap to give you this maille."

Maille is the last thing that will save me, but still my heart warms. I fold the protective garment into my knapsack, and we continue on.

Two Infernal swoop down from the sky, screeching and scorching the mountain with their fiery breath and lighting up the night. My eyes go wide with fright. We slip and slide down the narrow, icy path, barely suitable for walking let alone running. The Infernal dive at us with their massive webbed wings in an attempt to knock us over the edge.

Guernsey stops so abruptly I nearly run into him. "Yonder," he pants. His clawed finger points to an alcove in the mountainside. "Crawl inside. Do not come out until the danger has passed."

"What about you?"

Guernsey looks at me grimly. "Once all is clear, keep going and follow the path. Titan Dome is straight below." He takes his sceptre in hand, white light bursting from the dendrites of the snowflake within, and jumps off the mountainside.

"Guernsey," I scream into the void, watching him fall through the sky.

White wings snap open as he shifts into an enormous raven, the same as in the Scissure of Lost Souls. The Infernal dive toward him, not quailing from the light, and amidst their screeches, they all disappear into the churning smoke below.

My whole body shakes as I glance at the alcove. *Hiding from the Infernal seems time-wasting. They'll return soon enough. I should continue to Titan Dome while the night persists. Come daylight, I'll be an easier target.*

A discerning eye the size of a boulder blinks at me through the darkness. Startled, I stumble backward, straight over the mountainside in Guernsey's wake. Before I can find the breath to scream, the ground rises up, sooner than expected. Five pillars of stone surround me.

Not pillars. Fingers. "Carrig?" I wheeze as the giant brings his cupped hand to his face. "You blended so perfectly with the mountainside...Did Guernsey know you were here?"

Never one to speak quickly, Carrig thinks long and hard before he answers. "Guernsey knows all, so I might say yes," he says in his booming voice. He sets me on his rocky shoulder, and I stand and hold on, the wind whistling around us as we climb down and around the mountain.

***

The Infernal have yet to return by the time we arrive at Titan Dome, and I fear they may have captured Guernsey. Or worse, killed him for the queen. I think of *War Cry,* sung by Eirene: *Through sleepless nights and days of peril, my heart awaits thy governance. For blood hath spilt, has strengthened thee, and darkness rises unto us. By fire's flame, by heat or cinder, death shall find the raven. The hour draws near, the time has come, farewell to Winterhaven.*

Guernsey is the raven. He needs to die; Eirene said so herself. Though he does not have the power to kill the queen, he can certainly lock her inside another piece of snowflake obsidian or do any other number of things until I can destroy her.

Carrig ducks through a massive opening in the mountainside as a spiked gate rises to provide entrance. A current of mulched dirt rivers through the cool air, and as we wade deeper into the cavern, lamplight bleeds through the darkness and grows brighter with each passing step. The revelation is extraordinary, a city in its own right. Perhaps as many as one hundred Regolith work throughout, hammering tools and mining the rock, giants inside a sea of stone. A bonfire the size of a small hut burns dead center while lanterns in the earthen walls resemble fire-lit houses set into a hillside.

All eyes go to us. Daunting whispers reverberate in the cave, the sound akin to the fierce winds of a storm. Something tells me the Regolith don't often encounter Duine or anyone else, considering the remote region of Titan Dome.

One Regolith approaches, the earth shaking with each massive footstep. Similar to Carrig's stone, the giant's rock is shiny black and blue and marbled in russet. He leans in close, sniffs me.

"This is the Elementalist?" he grunts with rancor. Rows of rotted teeth swim in a torrent of putrid breath. "Kill her now, and this nonsense will be done. The Duine can burn in hell; what should we care?"

Carrig holds a hand to the giant's chest to keep him back. "Meine, do remember our pact: we are part of the Veneficum. Our vote to aid in the queen's demise was a unanimous one. Should the girl lose, Belisama will strip away Titan Dome, and we will die."

Meine shoves away Carrig's arm, sending loose rocks every which way. He moves in so close their faces nearly touch. "Change my vote if I could."

Half a dozen Regolith set down their tools and form a ring around the two giants. *If this turns to a brawl, I'm as good as dead.*

"You say this now," Carrig charges in a rumbling tone. "But when the queen causes any one of these volcanoes to erupt, the lava will flow and take us down until we are no more. Belisama will do it, to rid the land of us. Months ago, you were confident this would be so."

Meine glares at me through the icy rock. "Let's say my confidence is broken." He spits on the ground before storming out of the cave.

Carrig sets me on the ground. One errant move, and I'll be pulverized. I've never felt so small, even as I stand tall and defiant. He looks around the cavern.

"Ruadh," he calls out, his voice a reverberation along the walls. Another Regolith breaks through the circle, a giant taller than Carrig, stone stained in red and veined in dense moss.

"We do not consume food," Ruadh says in a surprisingly kind tone. "Duine do, this we know. A meal was prepared especially for you."

Ruadh sets down a bowl made from woven roots, thimble-sized for them but much too large for me. Not wanting to appear ungracious, I thank them and peer inside the bowl on tiptoe. A mix of berries and leaves, possibly insects or worms. With my fingers, I scoop some up and taste the crude mixture. I choke it down, for it is positively the most awful thing I've ever eaten, worse than pickled whelk. Ruadh and Carrig and the rest look on with curious eyes as if I'm their Yorkshire Terrier and they're awaiting my reaction to the fresh kibble.

"Delicious," I cough out, my eyes tearing at the corners. "May I trouble you for some tea—no—water? Yes, water would do just fine."

With another rooted vessel, Ruadh catches water trickling down the cave's wall and sets it before me. The water is ice-cold and tastes of sulfur. One awful taste for another. Not what I'd envisioned for a last meal.

A commotion outside turns our eyes to the mouth of the cave. The earth shakes, and if I'm unmistaken, Meine is yelling obscenities amongst the screeching.

Infernal. They found us. Me.

Several Regolith storm from the cave to see what's happening, but Carrig warns me to remain inside. He doesn't need to ask twice. Moments later Meine approaches, a dead Infernal cradled in his rocky arms. Inky blood trails him, the creature's scaled body ripped in two. The stench is awful as he throws it into the bonfire.

"They know you're here," he sneers at me. "They'll do right not

300

to come back or we'll make a stew of them."

Carrig motions me to a makeshift bed of soft grasses perched on a ledge near the bonfire. From a bundle of trees on the ground, he grabs three whole pines and sets them over the burning Infernal. They are quick to catch fire, the heat beckoning the resinous sap to break free, and soon the cave smells more welcoming and the space warms considerably. He does this for me, I'm sure. Likely the Regolith don't require warmth, only keeping the bonfire as a means of light.

"Sleep now," Carrig says. "Once daylight comes and goes, I will give escort to the foot of Titan Dome. Walking in the darkness proves a safer prospect."

Safer. No such thing. It would not surprise me one bit if Meine 'accidentally' stepped on me during the night. I crawl beneath the soft blades of grass and watch the Infernal spark and burn, the dead white eyes staring into mine.

***

Lanterns blink the same as before, but the bonfire is lower, the Infernal burned to ash and bone by the time I wake. Wake is relative, for I never really slept. Between the sounds of the working Regolith and my own thoughts and fears, sleep was more foe to me than friend. The Aeriscloque reads half past two in the afternoon, and the lightning bolts point to sunny skies.

Carrig escorts me outside to guard me against the Infernal. I must use the daylight to contemplate, to clear my mind and prepare for the forthcoming battle. I drink in the light, knowing

301

this will be my last chance to see the sun again for a good long while—possibly forever.

My neck feels especially warm, and when I reach behind to wipe away the perspiration, my fingers tangle in strands of hair. Surprised, I pull off my cap, and inky curls tipped in fuchsia tumble out. Eachna had said my hair would regrow once I left the Cloister, and she was right.

Carrig leans against the mountainside, his body a near-perfect camouflage. Wild mustard covers the slopes in rolling swells of yellow, and I flop down and breathe in their honey-sweet fragrance. The idyllic setting is deceiving, the fulsome scent of smoke a reminder of the war below.

My eyes close, and I attempt to find clarity. *No Infernal, no queen, no Cintamani Jewel. Just the sound of my breath. Within, not without.* I try this for a time, but my mind wanders to all kinds of minutiae: how my clothes reek of firesmoke, how my armpits have a piquant scent endearing them to a hot bath. How worms taste worse than I ever dreamed possible.

Knowing Carrig is so close also lends to my inability to focus. I decide to momentarily suspend the contemplation, instead pulling out the map of Winterhaven to study the path through the desert. "How many days to Crann Bethadh?" I ask.

"Depends," Carrig says. "With no obstacles, two days perhaps. The battlefield is vast. Camps staked throughout the dunes with enemies at every turn."

A shiver runs through me despite the sun at my back. "Tell me about the Regolith. I've not been here long, but your clan works hard. Who do you work for?"

Carrig takes out a massive pipe carved in iron ore the length of my two arms. He presses some leaves inside and snaps his rocky fingers to create a spark. "We mine the ore and forge new tools and weapons for anyone in need."

"What do you do when you're not working?"

"The Regolith always work," he grunts.

I sit up, startled by his claim. "You can't be serious. No one works nonstop. There must be some kind of enjoyment to be had. What about family? Children?"

Pebbles run off his forehead when his head shakes. "We are but one clan, our children long since grown. When Titan Dome was active during the Primary Age, we were born from the lava within. The volcano here has been dormant for tens of centuries. Were it to awaken, it could well engender new kin once the lava cooled. The Regolith must be careful, for the molten rock which gave us life can kill us just the same."

"Surely you have friendships. Would you not say those in the Veneficum are close friends?"

"Aye." Carrig draws out the word as if he's never actually pondered such things and is discovering them for the first time. "The Veneficum are allies. The council has existed as long as the Regolith, nearly as long as Winterhaven itself."

Nearly as long as Winterhaven itself. This makes me think of the myth about the Cintamani Jewel. A thought niggles at me.

303

Lord Kian and Ione possessed the stones and are both are part of the Veneficum. *The stones attract their most powerful leaders.*

"Carrig, do you know of the Cintamani Jewel?" I can practically hear Eachna screaming at my audacity for asking. Carrig nods. "Do you believe in its power?" I prod. "Are you the keeper of the Earth stone, perchance?"

He looks at me, somehow unsurprised by my query. "The Cintamani Jewel may or may not be myth. To my knowledge, the Earth stone was never found."

I pluck petals of the flower near my foot, disappointed by his claim. "Thanks to Lord Kian and Ione, I have two of the stones. If I were I to find all five, I might be able to kill the queen."

He sucks hard on his pipe and exhales a long trail of smoke. "Two is a long way from five."

"True. But if you'd had the Earth stone, that would make three. And if the Fire stone is somehow obtainable, that only leaves one remaining stone."

"Those are many ifs."

I nod solemnly. "How I wish you and the rest of the Regolith could help me on the battlefield. The way Meine so easily destroyed the Infernal...That kind of strength would prove helpful. Though I need to kill the queen, I must get to her first and in one piece. Guernsey was supposed to accompany me, but he has yet to return, and now I fear the worst."

"Duine must fight their own battles."

"Why? If Guernsey was going to help me, and Ione too, then

304

why not the Regolith? Why is this the most you will do? If the queen wins the war, the Regolith lives are at stake, your destiny forsaken. You said so yourself. Would you not want the Veneficum's help if the queen succeeded in killing me?"

Eyes narrowed, he says with hardened defiance, "Help is something we would never ask."

The plucked flower gets tossed aside, and I scramble to my feet, hands on hips. "What is this nonsense? Lord Kian said the same of you and the others. What's the point of having friendships— alliances—if you can't help one another? You shouldn't need to ask, you should help without provocation. Hundreds, perhaps thousands, of Mór are stranded on the Rock of Morbid Bay because King Kartanesi imprisoned them in iron thousands of years ago. The iron will kill any Sylph who gets too close. Yes, the waters are treacherous, yet you and Guernsey—certainly Ione—could help free them." My voice is raised, and I'm unsure why. In the end, what does it matter what they can or cannot do for one another?

Carrig nods thoughtfully. "Your words hold many truths." I'm surprised by the concession, but the morose and depressing sound of screeching breaks up our conversation. "Infernal are circling close," Carrig says. "Get inside. Once the sun has set and darkness cloaks the earth, we will head to the battlefield."

***

As I crawl into my nest of grasses, the Regolith gather around the bonfire, sucking on pipes and talking amongst themselves in a tongue foreign to my ears. They do not whisper. To the contrary,

305

there is heat behind their words. Meine bellows something and then looks at me through the long flames with hatred in his eyes, as though I'm the source of their problems. It brings little solace to know I am not, that the threat of the queen is as real to them as to me.

Unnerved by the intense discussion, I open my knapsack and take the sketch in hand. The red-inked pyramid stares back revealing nothing new. How I wish I had someone to talk to. Jinpa or Yeshe or especially Zhang the Elder. He could help me find the stones to the Cintamani Jewel or at least better explain their whereabouts.

My heart pounds as I slowly turn the sketch upside down the same way Zhang the Elder did with the Emerald Tablet. Now the pyramid sits on its apex, more reminiscent of a gemstone. A ruby? Garnet? *No, a diamond.*

"The Dead Ringer," I exclaim, my voice lost to the Regolith's charged discussion. "That is the Fire stone. And Queen Belisama has it."

CHAPTER SIXTEEN

Ruadh fills my canteen with the sulfuric water as a goodwill gesture, but neither Meine nor any of the other Regolith offer me anything, not even a rote 'good luck.' I'm a lowly field mouse in their eyes, not enough to save Winterhaven or their very existence. If they'd offered me a slab of cheese, it would not have been surprising.

The view from Carrig's shoulder is far better than walking down the mountain on my own two feet and definitely safer. I bid a silent farewell to the starlit sky, to the snow drifts and greenery and blooms pricking the mountain, as we descend into the grey and doom.

Smoke hits all at once. Visibility is gone. Though I'm mostly immune to the lethal effects of smoke, it stings my eyes and irritates my throat. Farther into our descent, the smolder eases, more akin to a thready fog than the thick, opaque soup above. With it comes the desert heat and the wind, rising and snapping in wicked greeting. My grey cap is at once lost to it, my hair whipping in every direction. Hard to believe that in the frozen land of Winterhaven a desert exists at all.

We reach the foot of the mountain without incident. Standing in wait is the contingent, tiny figurines from this far up. One holds up a lantern. Another waves a flag of eggshell blue with a 'V' wrapped in an olive wreath, all stitched in silver.

Carrig cups a hand at his shoulder, and I step forward. "The future of Winterhaven lies in your hands," he says in his hard, booming voice. "May the realm preserve you, grant you favor, and bring forth a victory for one and all."

Forget the blasted blessings! What I need is your help! This is what I want to yell through the searing wind. But this is no time for a lecture, so instead I offer my profound gratitude and offer up false assurances of a swift defeat. His look reads of skepticism or concern or wholehearted disbelief. I'm unsure of which and don't dare ask. The giant sets me down, the ground shaking with each step as he vanishes into the smoke.

The contingent consists of two men and one woman, their heads and faces tightly wrapped in scarves, their bodies draped in a uniform of light blue muslin. Belts of leather harness both dagger and sword.

"Sondrine Renfrew?" says the taller of the two men, his voice raised to combat the howling wind. "Markus, here. This is Jaggen and Illonia."

Illonia cranes her neck, her green eyes squinting beneath the scarf. "Where is Guernsey? He was to accompany you here and all of us to Crann Bethadh."

I tell them of our encounter with the Infernal. "I'm unsure if he survived, to be honest," I finish. The words taste acrid, and the

308

look in the contingent's eyes seem reflective of my feelings. None of them appear particularly adept at protecting me, and my sense is they were, in large part, relying on Guernsey for my safety as well as theirs.

Markus says, "Guess we three will be escortin' you to Crann Bethadh. Per Sir Einfarí's orders."

"Shán is alive?" Hope lifts despite the whipping sand.

A wave of shrugging shoulders and raised eyebrows at my casual address. "No tellin'," Markus says. "The order was given near to a week ago, before we set sail from Lagos."

Shán made it to Lagos at least. This brings me solace.

Jaggen stakes the flagpole into the sand. "We best make haste. While moon is preferred to sun, it matters not to the enemy. First camp is far from here. Won't find it before sun-up. A good ten hours from now."

The desert air feels like a thousand burning fires even at this late hour. I remove the emerald cloak and mimic the contingent's headdresses with my own scarves, the sand like glass shards against my cheeks.

Our journey begins with the aid of Jaggen's compass and Illonia's lantern. Up one dune and down another we go, the blistering gales shrieking all around. My first foray through the Petrified Forest had been reminiscent of this, only now it is sand that nettles my neck and blazing heat in lieu of deathly cold.

No one speaks. Occasionally a canteen goes to parched lips. We four resemble saplings bowed by the wind, our progress slow yet steady. When we do rest, it's not for long, but as the hours tick by, the intervals stretch. The desert challenges our stamina. Cacti and salt flats dot the desert floor. Near to the six-hour mark, we stop at one of few rock outcroppings for a respite. My gait is uneven, worse than ever, my legs and feet numb with pain. I'm not alone: Illonia removes her boots and rubs the soles of her feet. She hands over a map to Markus.

"We'll make it to camp before dawn," he notes, his finger tracing through to our destination. "We're makin' decent time." The line between his eyes sharpens as he further studies the map. "Better than decent. Seems we've shaved off a good hour, perhaps two."

"I'll drink to that." Jaggen pulls down his scarf to take in some water. "The sun is one of many enemies. Perhaps our worst. Can't fight it off with weaponry, only endurance."

"Can you even see the sun through all the smoke?" I ask.

"In bits and pieces," Jaggen says. "You'll feel it, though. Hotter than a woman's cu—" He's about to say something untoward, but he looks to me and Illonia, sheepish, as though our female presence is cause to keep things clean.

"Hotter than the devil's scrote?" I say. Hard laughter all around, and the four of us clink our canteens together in kinship.

"Wish this were ale, not water," Markus says, licking his parched lips. "Soon enough, I suppose."

Jaggen nods. "A cold-water bath is what I'm thinking. Feels like the sand is permanently embedded in my face." He looks me

310

up and down. "Don't envy your position. You ready to face the queen?"

"Facing death is never an enviable position," I say, rueful. "I hope to taste victory. Or at least the ale Markus mentioned." More laughter and another round of toasting canteens.

The gut-wrenching sound of screeching kills the amiable moment.

"Infernal," Illonia whispers. She lifts the glass of the lantern and blows out the flame.

"We must hide," Markus says. He gestures to where two rocks meet at an angle, providing a low-lying shelter. "The darkness is on our side."

The Infernal sense me, because they circle not for minutes but for hours, the fiery gusts carrying their stink through the smoky fumes. We've lost the night and our lead, the sun creeping over the desert floor, bringing with it a crippling heat. I'm uncomfortable to be sure, but my companions are suffering far worse. They huddle against the shade of the rock and nurse their canteens. When the water runs dry, so too will their lives.

Think. The answers lie within. I wipe perspiration from my brow, my clothes soaked through to the skin. *Soaked...skin.*

"The Infernal will perish if wet," I mutter. No clouds can be seen through the smolder, but I recall Jinpa's claim: *'Firesmoke can produce rain.'*

For fear of raising their hopes only to fail, I say nothing to the contingent as I concentrate on the smoke-filled sky, surreptitiously using my wrist to help things along. The smoke funnels into a column, a literal smokestack growing taller and wider. Soon a thunderhead takes shape, so large it throws shade to the ground.

"You fool," Illonia hisses, slapping my hand away. "What do you think you're doing?"

"Saving your lives as well as mine." I explain how the rain will turn the Infernal to ash, thus creating safe passage to camp. "And," I add, "we can replenish our water supply."

"You don't understand what you've done," Markus says in a disparaging tone. "The wind is savage already. A pending rainstorm only makes things worse. They cause sandstorms with enough strength to take out a village."

The screeching has silenced, an ominous sign. Markus crawls out to chance a look. "Bloody wintry hell," he murmurs.

We scramble to his side to see what he does: a wall of sand the size and length of a mountain range barreling straight for us.

"Get back," he yells, and the four of us dive under the rock alcove, frantically digging with our bare hands to create a ditch.

We lie face down, and soon enough, the sandstorm moves in, fully engulfing us. I tighten the scarves around my mouth to avoid mouthfuls of grit as it pelts us mercilessly, the sound like a thousand steam locomotives. If I were to scream, it would never be heard.

'The answers lie within.' Rubbish! Look where that advice got us. A setback far worse than the Infernal. By the time the storm finishes, the heat will force us to wait until sundown before

312

resuming our journey. A twelve-hour delay before we make it to camp. If we make it.

I hand off my canteen to the others, for theirs have gone dry. So too will mine soon enough. Hours pass until the storm fully dissipates, and when the silence rises once again, so do we. It's deathly hot, and I can feel my companions' disdain toward me without an uttered word. Who can blame them?

The thunderhead remains, darker, more threatening. *Rain, you bloody thing.* I concentrate hard, but the air is too hot. If any moisture is letting loose, it's likely evaporating before it can reach us. We plod through the heat in silence. Like the faithful vermin they are, the Infernal return—four of them—their black webbed wings fanning the smoke and the sky. There is no means of escape, nowhere to run this time.

"We're done for," Markus states, his tone void of emotion. "Say a good prayer and hope we make it to the Realm of Halcyon."

"In how many pieces?" Jaggen asks.

Illonia and I dive to the sand to avoid the talons as the Infernal swoop down and land in a circle around us. Everyone draws their swords, laughable because the Infernal will wipe us out with a mere fiery cough.

Something white and shiny catches my eye: salt flats. '*Firesmoke can produce rain. Salt can hurry it along.*'

Jinpa's words compels every bit of concentration, and I send the salt swirling into the thundercloud above. One drop. A second and a third. The Infernal are unmoving as the rain patters down.

313

Ione said these superior Infernal were intolerant of water, same as their predecessors. Perhaps she was wrong, but something born of fire will die from water. *'It is law,'* Eachna said, an echo of my conviction.

I concentrate harder until the cloud unleashes a torrent of water. The Infernal attempt to fly off, their screams intensifying as the storm bears down. But the thundercloud is too vast. All four flounder in the air, the downpour a sky of arrows, pelting them to ash.

We do a victory dance, all four of us. Our canteens go to the sky to catch the water while the rain cools and sates us. The storm follows our path through the desert, and the mood of the contingent rises once more. Markus and Jaggen and I remove our scarves to embrace the wet. Illonia, more modest, keeps her scarf in place but takes off her doublet and ties it around her waist.

"How long will we remain in camp?" I ask Markus, my boots sinking into the muddied sand.

"Long enough for rest and a hot meal. The next battle is scheduled for sunrise on the morrow. Our army will do everything we can to get you safely to Crann Bethadh."

These good people have risked their lives for me, and I nod, grateful for their bravery. The storm begins to peter out, and the heat returns. But the cool weather helped us make better time. At the crest of a particularly large dune, a bevy of red tents dot the desert floor below, and I breathe a sigh of relief. We made it to camp.

314

Jaggen looks to the three of us, bewildered. "This is not—" A resonant thud. He gasps sharply and falls face-first to the sand, a knife in his back.

Terror-struck, we spin to find the offender, a bare-chested man with a shaven head, his body the size of a bare-knuckle fighter's. Another knife goes straight into Marcus's throat. Reflexively he pulls out the blade, the blood flowing endlessly as he collapses to the sand.

I start for them both, but Illonia pulls me back, stepping in front of me and unsheathing her sword. The man smiles broadly, as if he's saved the easiest for last. He even takes Jaggen's sword and tosses it to me, confident he can kill us both regardless of our weaponry.

"Run," Illonia whispers in my ear. "Go straight to the camp below."

I can't leave her here to die. Illonia is skilled with the sword by the way she wields the blade, but in no way is she a match for this man. Nor am I. I swing once, and he sends my sword through the air with a quick swipe. Illonia wards off his strikes, but it's a losing battle. He toys with her, makes her swing with every last bit of energy from within. His blade catches her cheek, and she screams in pain.

With both arms swinging, I send up a rushing tide of sand, somewhat feeble in strength but potent enough to stop him.

"My eyes," he roars, his feet stumbling over the other. "I can't see."

315

I start for my sword, to finish him off, but Illonia stops me. "Let's go," she says. "There's safety in numbers," and we run toward camp without looking back.

***

Cooking fires; uniformed women and men; decapitated heads of the enemy, spiked to makeshift walls. This is what greets us when we walk amongst the tents.

"You all right?" Illonia asks, panting. She sets a hand on my shoulder to guide me through the camp.

"Fine," I lie and try to take a proper breath. "What about Markus and Jaggen? We should go back for them. If not us then someone, to give them a proper burial. They'll rot otherwise, and the vultures will eat their innards."

"Too dangerous," she says. "That heathen could be back there awaiting our return."

My gut stirs with uncertainty. *Why would the man wait for us, especially with camp so close by? And why didn't Illonia kill him when she had the chance?* "At the very least, we need to let someone know what happened. That man could be here at any moment."

"Agreed," Illonia says in a careless tone.

As she leads me along, I notice a pendant tripped over her collar, previously tucked away. A bronze hammered skull with jade for hollowed eyes. *Where have I seen that before?*

"Pray, where might I find the privy?" I need a means of escape or at least a moment to ponder things alone. Something feels

316

horribly off. The predominant colors of the camp are red and gold, not the eggshell blue and silver of the Veneficum's infantry.

Illonia nods. "In here." She gestures the largest tent, located dead center of camp.

I'm doubtful of her claim. Any public privy, even in the Other World, is set at the outskirts, always smelled before seen. My instincts have not betrayed me when I step through the opening. The stink is there; however, it comes not from excrement but from the ruse of the man in the high-backed chair.

Illonia drops to a curtsey and tries to bring me along with her. I shake loose of her grip but not enough to flee.

"Sondrine, we meet again." King Andronicus sits behind a wood-carved desk. Two young men on either side cool him with fans of woven straw. His shoulders are stooped, his grey hair oily and unkempt. He looks frailer than last I saw him. Trying to create snowstorms of any magnitude has sapped him of his vitality. "Covered in filth, I see, the same as when I first laid eyes on you at Isceald Castle all those months ago. You do clean up quite nicely; this I remember well."

The grisly night of his attack comes back to me as though it happened only yesterday. Not just the sting on my cheek, courtesy of his knuckled backhand, or the way he forced himself on top of me, but the reek of his breath, a scent I will not soon forget. Knowing he is my uncle only adds insult to injury.

I bolster myself. *You drugged him and escaped. You ultimately won.*

317

"I was told this was the privy," I say with as much detachment as I can muster. "Seems about right. Reeks in here, worse than pigs in a barnyard."

I turn to Illonia and yank off her headscarf. "Adina," I spit. "I should have known, you spineless crone. We could have easily killed that man, given his incapacitated state. And Markus and Jaggen—they were part of the Veneficum's army. You switched the maps. Jaggen knew this camp belonged to the king and was about to say as much when he was met with the receiving end of a dagger."

"Bravo," Adina says with heavy sarcasm. "And you, Edgaar," she says to the bare-chested man as he enters the tent. "Got a bit close, pillock. This wasn't part of the plan." She cups her bloodied cheek.

Edgaar is a man of few words. He shrugs.

"The plan worked, all that matters," King Andronicus says. He signals Adina, who obediently hurries to his side. "Know you will be justly rewarded, both of you. This is quite the magnificent feat, for the capture of Ms. Renfrew has eluded so many." He studies Adina's cheek, takes a finger to the fresh blood. "A flesh wound, nothing to scar your pretty face."

His finger trails down to trace her nipple, then he squeezes. Disgusted by the lewd display, I look away. Adina moans, possibly aroused. More likely she's playing things up to get her greedy hands on the king's gold. "Clean up and wait in my bed," he says to her. "I have business to finish here."

318

"My king." Adina offers a swift curtsey and exits the tent.

King Andronicus nods to Edgaar. "Fetch the gift I had made especially for Miss Renfrew's homecoming."

When we're alone save for his servants, I look around for a means of escape. But every single person in this camp knows who I am, and no one will let me leave. Not so much for their allegiance to the king but to me, strangely. By now everyone must know it is by my hand the queen must die, and only then will their lives be spared. This is the irony of war. We must be willing to die to ensure our survival.

I'm about to question my capture when Edgaar returns with a man's severed head in hand. Black skin and wiry hair. A hand goes to my mouth.

"Captain Seybourne," I say, devastated by the sight.

The king clicks his tongue. "A good man to be sure. Yet he had you on his ship and let you go. Quite the betrayal, I must say." He shrugs, apathetic.

"I saved his life and those of his crew. Had I not done so, the ship would have been lost at sea along with the cargo. Delivered cargo, which got you paid. He spared my life as repayment but promised he would not do so again. Do you ever think before you go around lopping off people's heads? That perhaps there is more than one side—your side—to every story? Your allegiances would be far stronger were you known to be such a man, a king the masses looked up to. But no, you prefer people to live in fear. That's what a dictator does, thrives on."

319

The king drums his fingers in boredom, unaffected by my rant. "If you're quite finished, let us begin where we left off. Someone stripped me of my clothing. I was led to believe we had fucked on the night you spurned my marriage proposal. A blatant lie. You see, a man knows the scent of an unplucked flower, and none of your stink was left on me, nor was I raw on the day next."

He pushes the chair back and walks over to me. His face shines from the desert heat.

Chin raised in defiance, shoulders squared, I meet his steely gaze. "Quite the sleuthing on your part, Varius."

"Your Majesty," he hisses. "You drugged me. A criminal offense. Your head should be spiked to the Mourning Tree for committing such an atrocity."

A backhand to my cheek stings like the devil, but I refuse to flinch. In fact, I take one step closer. "You tried to rape me. If anything should be spiked to the Mourning Tree, it is *your* head, and I speak not of the one on your shoulders." I spit in his eye, not caring about the consequence.

Edgaar claps a hand to my shoulder in warning. The king waves him off, casually shaking out a handkerchief to wipe his face. A smile rises against his thin, peeling lips.

"You're quite a different girl from the one I met previous. Knowing death is so close frightens many. For others, it teases out courage, makes them bolder. For you it has done the latter, which renders you far more attractive, I must say. Once the war has been won, I will wed you then bed you, make you bleed until you bleed

320

no more, ripe with my seed. Our friend Adina is a magnificent lay. Yet a virgin is so much better, so much more...receptive. Wanting."

Nothing would please me more than to tell him my innocence was surrendered to Shán, his own flesh and blood. But the memory would be tainted, so I say nothing. The same goes for his insidious claims. No point in responding, because his twisted fantasy will never come to pass, not if I have a living breath left within me.

"What is your plan?" I ask, changing the subject. "Your infantry is supposed to be allied with the Veneficum. Are they not?"

"The goal is to get you to the queen. I need her dead as much as anyone. More so. If she dies, her threat will be no more, and I can rule Winterhaven in peace. However, there have been rumors that I am to follow the queen to her grave, and the killing will be of the Veneficum's doing. Therefore I have severed those ties."

Emboldened, I laugh. "You're decrepit, old man. You'll not survive this war."

He grabs my arm, his grip surprisingly tight. "This is not the first war I've fought nor will it be the last. I've killed many hundreds of soldiers in my lifetime, even children. I killed Lark; her head is staked to the Mourning Tree. Do not tempt me to do the same unto you."

He doesn't realize Lark is alive because of Snap's ingenious magic and quick-thinking. I feign shock. "Lark is dead?"

"'Tis so, I regret to say." There's no regret behind his voice, not a drop of remorse.

To keep the charade going, I could ask him why he killed the little girl, but it's unimportant. "You won't kill me; you need me."

He returns to his seat, takes a long drink from his cup, and clasps his hands. "The plan stands. I will get you to the queen and help you kill her. Once she is dead, you will be my bride, and we shall rule Winterhaven together. I'm a patient man, Sondrine, with many a woman to satisfy my needs until the main course. Now go wash up, for your stench rivals the lower reaches of Hell."

That night I don't sleep. Not because Edgaar stands guard outside my tent. Or the stifling desert heat or how I'm forced to listen to Adina please the king in the next tent over. No, it's direr. The collection of the Cintamani Jewel never came to pass; I'm the king's prisoner yet again; Shán may well be dead, same for Guernsey. The tears come unbidden, but they are not for me. They are for the lives lost. And for the many more who will die before the war is done.

CHAPTER SEVENTEEN

The early morning hours are spent in the privy. Fresh porridge with almonds and dried figs had been served to break our fast. Neither flies nor maggots had accented mine, but the scent alone had sent me running. Fear and food are mortal enemies; there is no room in one's gut for both.

Thoughts of the pending battle keep me sitting long after my lantern's oil has run dry, and my feet have gone numb with sleep. Having no choice but to wait outside the makeshift structure, Edgaar is none too pleased, either. When I return to my tent, I empty my knapsack onto the bedcovers to search for something to ease my sour stomach; it's twisted worse than the Gordian Knot.

This reminds me of Jinpa, and I pick up the ball of unraveled string. *Novacula Occami.* The inkpot has leaked, the string stained in red. With the bedsheet, I wipe the excess ink from the stopper and tighten it as the Cloister's sigil stares back. The maille too is stained, same for my clothes and the scarf wrapped around the Petard and the Kyanite. I unravel the stones, both untainted by the ink. Should my death come to pass, the stones will find their way back to Ione and Lord Kian respectively.

One of the many vials is marked 'sowhistle,' like the tea Jinpa made on the mountain. I mix the powder with some tepid water in a tin cup and swallow the whole thing down. My stomach growls belligerently.

Something catches the corner of my eye. The sight is so startling, I jump off the cot and stare in disbelief. The Petard is mounted on the blue marbled inkpot. Hovering over them both is the Kyanite, an empty space in between where the Dead Ringer should be. Hesitantly I take the stele in hand and try to pry the stones off one another. The magnetic pull is so strong it acts like a kind of glue. Unlike before, the Kyanite remains in place.

"Yeshe," I exclaim in a whisper. "The inkpot is the Earth stone." How he came to have it makes me wonder. Jinpa said the Cloister rested on dowsing lines, *'joined paths in the earth where the vibrational pull is strong.' Earth.*

My finger traces the inverted triangle bisected by the horizontal line on the inkpot's stopper. Not a sigil; a symbol. *For Earth?* The Solitary have been around for tens of thousands of years. Was Yeshe the intended? Or has the stone been passed down through the ages? For now, the answer will remain a mystery. What I do know: I now have three of the five stones.

Footfalls outside. I dump the stele into my knapsack and lie down, pretending to be asleep. Edgaar pokes me, brings me to the king's tent, where I'm forced to join him and Adina and his group of commanders—the King's Legion—as they sup while discussing the battle plan. I envy them all. They eat as though this is an ordinary meal and not potentially their last. The mindset—and stomach—of a true warrior.

Days ago, men and women were sent ahead to build trenches near the battle lines. Their army is five thousand strong, with the other half dead or scattered throughout Winterhaven. Infantry formation: deep columns, heavy in front, archers behind to protect them. Artillery and the King's Legion in the rear with me. It feels strange to listen to the King's Legion, as if I'm a valuable object, one in need of protection and care and delivery to the right place. Instead of a menial package, I've moved up in the ranks to a wooden crate of some import.

My trousers and shirt are traded for the military uniform of gold muslin, body armor, a sizeable sword forged of molten metal, and a shield made from cowhide. My swordsmanship is laughable. It matters not. The swing of a blade will not bring victory, although it may save me from an untimely death.

Something else might help, and I excuse myself for one last foray to the privy, this time to slip on the maille beneath my shirt. Though it's ironically stained red from the spilled ink, I'm glad to have the protection.

A horn sounds. The time has come. My given horse is a chestnut mare, and when I mount her, I look out to the thousands of soldiers before us. An infantry of men and women young and old with dogged determination beneath their metal helmets. How I mourn for them. They will risk their lives, die to get me to the queen.

The king and his legion join me on horseback. King Andronicus looks stately in uniform, a black cape at his back. So too does his legion, and even Adina has a striking presence about her. Quite the change from the corseted lass in the Barmy Goat.

Bringing up the rear are impressive catapults and battering rams hung on thick rope. I guide my horse around a set of unrecognizable contraptions: massive pulleys mounted onto wheeled carts. "What are these?" I ask the king, who follows at my side.

"Ballistae," he replies.

The arrows are atypical, much larger and far thicker than those used in regular archery. The three-feather fletchings too are huge.

"Arrows will bring down most, but not the Infernal," I say. "Certainly not the new fire-breathing breed. What do we have to safeguard us against the vile creatures?"

"These are carved of hollowed wood and filled with water, nock to arrowhead. Upon convergence with the intended target, they will burst open and turn the Infernal into ash."

"Impressive," I say, which brings a smug smile to the king's face.

"This is a game of fire, my dear Sondrine. And when one plays with fire, one always gets burned. Unless there is water. We shall claim victory, for water is a savior and always smites the flame."

His patronizing speech does not engender hope. Eachna had said, *'Water will not help in this war, no.'* I'll trust her insight any day over the king's. This kindles a thought, and I spur my horse forward to the front of the line. The king barks at me, but his voice is lost to the smoke and my blatant disregard of his commands.

I turn my horse to address the phalanx of women and men. Thousands of eyes peer from their helms. "The future of Winterhaven has been compromised," I choke out.

Boots shuffle in the sand; soldiers look to one another, uncomfortable and dubious. The smolder is stagnant and strangling, the wind not as fierce as the day previous, so my words don't come out as forceful as I'd hoped. *No. Those are excuses to serve my own ego. 'If you think something, say it. No leader stands poised with confidence and then flounders like a common carp in need of air.'*

I start again, this time with verve. "We live in a time of darkness and uncertainty, the future of Winterhaven compromised. Yet none of us were born missionaries. You owe nothing to anyone but yourselves. Go home now if it pleases you; you will be looked upon not with dishonor but with grace. War brings with it no heroes, no winners. Only suffering and death and sacrifice for a peace that may never come to pass. You must follow your will, your heart. This is not about courage. Only conviction can bring down the enemy, bring light to the darkness, and justice to the unjust. Oh, yes, we may defeat the queen, and in doing so, we shall taste victory. But it will be bitter, not sweet, at the expense of lost friends, of lost family, and at the loss of our very souls."

My message is depressing. Uninspiring. *Congratulations,*

327

Sondrine. You've managed to discourage an infantry of thousands.

"We fight for honor!" one woman shouts with a quiver of arrows at her back. "To the death!"

I nod along with the others. "And you will be justly awarded. Should you not survive this war, your loved ones will be your beneficiaries: gold, a lifetime's worth, paid out of respect for your service and sacrifice. Should you live to see Winterhaven free of tyranny, the bestowed gold will be twofold. You have this as my solemn promise to you."

Elated cheering as dejected eyes widen with hope. The king smiles uncomfortably, but my claims have been made clear. Should he not comply, should he survive and not I, this will be his downfall.

"I'm Sondrine Renfrew," I cry out. "I am but one woman, and I am nothing without you."

A roaring cry of solidarity. "Liberty for Winterhaven!" yells one man near the front. The army echoes in reply. Fists pound the sky, spears and sword drum the desert floor.

I turn my horse to lead the troops through the desert. The king and his legion gallop to my side. He nods his approval, but I could not care less. I'll happily use him to get me safely to the queen. With any luck, he'll perish soon thereafter.

Save for the wind, only the sounds of war accompany us. Armor clinking, horses' hooves against sand, wood wheels rolling across the desert floor. The heat is unforgiving, and when the sun rears over the horizon, it has teeth. Some begin to stagger. One young

328

girl goes down; next an older man.

I pull on the reins of my horse. "Is there a healer with us?" I say to the king and his legion.

King Andronicus signals to Adina, who reaches into her quiver and pulls out two arrows. With swift deftness, she spears the neck of each of the fallen. In seconds they bleed out.

"What are you doing?" I hiss.

The king takes a moment to drink from his canteen. "Putting them out of their misery. Would you prefer they suffer?"

"Water could have saved them. You offered no chance."

"The desert is an enemy, same as the queen. The infantry is well aware. We can linger here to finish this conversation or we can move forward and forge a path to Crann Bethadh, where my troops will have a better chance of survival. Standing still will do us no favors."

We continue on. Unlike my counterparts, I often slide off my horse to walk alongside and feed her water. I've secretly named her Enyo after the Greek goddess of war, because if we're going into battle together, she needs a brilliant name.

All at once, near the horizon, the queen's army spills over the dunes like a colony of ants against the largest hill. Tens of thousands to our comparative few. I squint, for the glare against the armored bodies is painful. Infernal prowl through the smoke-addled sky, although they do not breach the battle line. Dozens of them await the queen's command to scorch us to death.

"Hold up!" the king yells. On his command, the infantry stops marching. He pulls out the parchment from earlier and studies the battle lines with his legion.

"We're outnumbered," I say in the lowest of voices. "Any person here can see the same. I can create a thunderstorm. At the very least, the rain will kill the Infernal and give us a fighting chance."

"Your thunderstorm created a sandstorm of the worst sort," Adina says with contempt.

My eyes narrow. "Only the first. The second killed the Infernal and saved us."

"Do you have full control of your Elemental capabilities?" the king asks, piqued by the possibility. "And can you sustain them for a time? If so, both storms could prove advantageous. If not, they will only hurt our infantry as much as theirs."

"Full control, I'm unsure," I admit. My confidence takes a hit along with my pride.

Far ahead of the queen's army, a lone rider gallops toward us. The steed is a beast, the body charred and skeletal like those of the Infernal. But the rider is what's most concerning.

"The creature," I whisper. "What is—?"

"Tartarean," one of the King's Legion mutters.

The new race molded from flame and ash by Belisama herself. 'Only blades forged from molten metal can kill them.'

"Arm yourselves," King Andronicus commands. Arrows and swords are drawn, including his own. The king looks mostly unfazed, probably because a lone soldier is no true threat to our army. My sword feels heavy in my palm, but I hold it outright for the sake of the argument.

The rider stops before us, the stink the same as the Infernal. Mottled skin the color of ash and soulless eyes darker than the bowels of Hell. Reptilian hands grip an exceptionally long spear.

"I am Gristall, the queen's messenger," the Tartarean says through daggered teeth and a voiceful of gravel. "King Andronicus, if you give me the girl, let me kill her now, the battle will end before it's begun."

"I'm no girl," I say brazenly. "I'm Sondrine Renfrew. Tell the queen the battle will end once she's dead by my hand, no sooner."

Mocking laughter gurgles out of the Tartarean's throat. "Thousands of lives will be spared. One death to save so many?"

"What is in it for me to do such a thing?" King Andronicus asks.

I look to the king, miffed he is usurping my power and engaging in this ridiculous conversation.

A long, lizard-like tongue wets Gristall's lips. "The queen will give you the capital of Isceald and whatever cities you choose to rule. A dozen, perhaps more. Even the coveted Sanctuary of Caelum."

My heart drops into my chest. How I hope Lark and Snap are safe.

The king waves aside the stink with a gloved hand. "I'm the ruler of Winterhaven *now*. All of it. Why would I relinquish my power? Her death insures my sovereignty." He shakes his head, confounded by the proposition. "Something is amiss. Belisama is far cleverer than this."

331

Gristall stakes his spear in the sand and dismounts the horse. He releases the straps of the large pannier over the horse's skeletal back and out falls Guernsey, bound and gagged.

A chorus of gasps, including my own. When I start to dismount my horse, Guernsey looks at me with those unerring eyes and gives the slightest shake of his head. I stop myself, unsure of what to do.

"The queen thought you might reconsider her request," the Tartarean says. He steps on Guernsey's chest with one foot to keep him in place. "If so, he lives, and I shall personally escort you to the queen."

"And if I refuse?" the king says.

He removes the spear from the sand. "Death to him. And death to the many thousands in your infantry. You are greatly outnumbered. Likely you will die amongst your brethren, and the queen will have sovereign power over Winterhaven. This is a chance to survive and continue your rule."

King Andronicus looks to me, then back to the creature. "Regrets, Guernsey. And to the queen, I say: request denied."

"Death shall find the raven," the Tartarean grunts, and the spear plunges through Guernsey's torso.

I silently scream as blood rivers from the great sorcerer's body. My anger rises out of me, quickly surpassing the grief. Before I can launch my sword at the Tartarean, Adina and several others beat me to it, their arrows piercing the ashen neck and face. Then King Andronicus does what he does best: lops off the creature's head with a clean swipe. For once, I'm not sorry for it.

I slide off my horse and race over to Guernsey. He resembles an old man, his brilliant white hair matted with sweat, his mouth shriveled from dehydration. Despite the spear and the blood, his chest rises and falls steadily. Gently I remove the gag while a young soldier helps to untie his ankles.

"Don't try to speak," I say. "I can dress the wound. You'll be fine soon enough."

"And then what?" the king drawls in an annoyed tone from behind. "Strap him to the back of your horse?"

"Leave me be," Guernsey urges in a kind tone, one I've rarely heard. "This journey is but one. I'm on to another soon enough."

"You can't die," I whisper around the lump in my throat, and I take his clawed hand in mine. "I need you now more than ever."

Guernsey's eyes flutter to a close. The sun is unmerciful, and the infantry is fading from the heat. Sadly the king is right. We wouldn't be helping; we'd be taking a badly wounded man straight into battle.

"Yonder!" one of the king's command shouts.

The queen's army is at close range. Still, I can't let Guernsey die right here, and with the help of the young soldier, we carry him to the Ballistae and place him on the hind part of the platform. To the soldiers helming the machine, I say, "Guard him with your life; give him water as needed."

I study the long, protruding spear. "If you have the means to file this down, do so, but do not remove it, do you understand me?"

333

They offer nods of assurance more out of courtesy than anything else.

It's then I notice the maille, the mesh rings soaked in blood, peeking from beneath his shirt. My stomach drops. For whatever reason the magical armor didn't work, which means it won't work for me, either.

I start for my horse, more determined than ever to make it to the queen alive. Adina's whistle beckons. She and the King's Legion have moved to the rear, banded in a close-knit circle with Enyo in the middle. I'm a near-prisoner but say nothing as I grab my weapons and mount the mare.

I don't like this one bit, and I say so. "We should be leading these people into battle," I spit to the King's Legion. No response. "Out of my way," I say to the commander in front of me, tapping his shoulder with the flat of my blade. Nothing. No one heeds my claims. They have me blocked with nowhere to go.

King Andronicus gallops back and forth along the front line of the infantry. "Freedom or death!" he yells in a battle cry.

The infantry bellow and chant "Freedom or death!" over and over, and the first column runs straight for the queen's army. Chaos all at once. A sea of men and women colliding, sand kicking up, and the cries of death beating down.

"Shields to the sky!" yells the king, and we do so as a thunder of flaming arrows rain down. None strike my shield, but when I lower it and squint through the heat, a smattering of our soldiers are down. And then the Infernal come. A dozen or more. The first group of many, to be sure. They soar and dive and breathe fire onto on the masses.

"Mark!" the king yells, and the machines tilt up. "Pull! Fire!"

Dozens of water-filled arrows launch toward their intended targets. One by one, the Infernal are hit and burst into ash like a macabre fireworks display. The next column charges, but the queen's army is advancing, the sheer number so staggering we will be dead in an hour's time if things continue at this rate. I don't even bother using my mind; I fervently wave my arms to create a series of dust devils along enemy lines.

King Andronicus looks at me with disapproval in his eyes, but I care not. We need to disable the queen's army and take advantage of the moment. Sand whirls in every direction, the tornadic force consuming her soldiers.

"Mark your arrows," I yell to the infantry.

"Pull!" the king commands. "Fire!"

The sky fills with arrows. We repeat this tactic until the dust devils dissipate and scores of the enemy lie dead in the sand. But there is no room for victory as a new throng of Infernal bear down. Another round of water-filled arrows kills some while countless others escape. One in particular is undaunted. A carpet of fire blazes the battlefield, and with it comes the sickening scent of burnt flesh. Half of our infantry is nothing but charred remains in seconds.

"Freedom or death!" the king bellows, and our remaining columns and the King's Legion charge.

335

Sweat drips into my eyes as Enyo gallops at full speed. The commander to my fore is struck with a flaming arrow, the horse whinnying in fright as it stands on hind legs and dumps its rider to the sand. Enyo dodges right, barely avoiding a collision. Every which way, swords and arrows and daggers fly through the air. My shield is home to four arrows. Those left surrounding me have no choice but to disband to fight off the enemy.

Stealthily I slide down from Enyo and send her back to camp, as she will be killed soon enough if she carries me into the fray. I only hope she survives. Despite my uneven gait, I'm far better off on foot than on horseback. Crouching and wielding my sword, I stumble over bodies of the dead, charred beyond recognition. The scene is a mirror image of the waters in the Mourning Garden all those months ago.

To my left, one of ours is fighting a Tartarean. I plunge my sword into the skeletal body, killing the creature instantly. Another Tartarean, half-dead on the ground, grasps my ankle. I lop off its wrist and then sever the head with my steely blade.

Sand and smoke and death spin through the air. Panting and sweating, I stop to catch my breath as another Tartarean approaches over the dune, daggered teeth dripping with wrath and the intent to kill in its eye. I drop my shield; I'll need both hands if I want to have any chance of fending this thing off.

"Let's get to it, you ugly, despicable thing," I mutter.

The creature lunges, and our blades clash in a steely song. We dance across the dune, grunting with each arduous swipe. Luck is

336

on my side, because I duck and take off its weaponless arm. This doesn't slow the Tartarean. On the contrary, the creature backs me down the dune with brute force. I try to deflect as best as I can, but I'm no match; the Tartarean's one arm is stronger than my two.

The creature's blade catches my cheek and draws blood. As I cry out, my sword is knocked free, and I stumble, the sand beneath my boots too grooved for purchase. Down I go head over heel until bodies of the dead keep me from sliding further. The creature howls some sort of victory cry while raising its blade to the sky. I try to scramble to my feet, but the sword plunges straight for my heart.

A hatchet slices the Tartarean's head off clean, and the body crumples to the sand. Shocked, I look over to the perpetrator.

Adina. I thank her with a nod.

She extends a hand to help me up, and along with the king, we hurry to one of the ditches. We jump inside and crouch against the sandy walls, trying to catch our breath, joining a portion of our infantry along with the remaining few of the King's Legion. Above, flaming arrows sail past.

A string of obscenities from King Andronicus as he violently throws his gloves to the ground. "For months we've been wondering where the queen has been hiding and what she's been doing. Now we know. Along with more Infernal, she's created countless Tartarean. Soulless creatures unafraid to die."

"We're nearly out of weaponry," pants one of the King's Legion. "Two-thirds of our infantry are dead, by my guess."

Where is the Veneficum's infantry? They were supposed to help us. And Shán's fleet? The map showed Crann Bethadh at the border of the Dendrite Sea. How far are we from either?

"We can't stay here long," I say.

Adina peers over the trench's ledge using a scope.

"May I?" I ask, joining her. She concedes, and I set it to my eye. Reminiscent of a phoenix rising from ash, Crann Bethadh towers in the distance. My heart stops at the magnificent sight. The tree is like nothing I've ever seen, the size rivaling four Victoria Towers, with behemoth branches lost to the smoky sky. A strange sense of relief befalls me. Although farther than it appears, seeing the destination gives me purpose. *Too close to give up now.*

The desert is a graveyard, the bodies stacked, bloodied, and charred. Right when there's a lull in the fighting, a new contingent of the queen's army files over the hill, a good thousand if not more. More cursing and unrestrained panic from the infantry.

I offer Adina the scope, but she waves it off. "We're as good as dead," she says in resignation.

All at once the ground shifts and shakes beneath us. *The queen is creating another quake.* Sand fills the trenches. We will be buried alive unless we flee now. We start for the laddered ropes when a dead Infernal lands before us, as if plucked from the sky and thrown to the desert floor. A chanced look over my shoulder leaves me stunned. *Not a quake. Regolith.*

They come in from all sides, batting the Infernal from the sky and stepping on the queen's army. With renewed hope, we scramble from the trench and take advantage of our allied protection by shooting off arrows and whatever ammunition remains. The Tartarean howl and chitter like feral dogs in the screaming wind, unafraid to die.

"Carrig!" I wave my arms as he and Meine approach. Neither can see me. I'm one of many thousands on the ground, my voice lost to the wind and ravages of war.

A white raven flutters through the air zig-zag, gravely injured but managing to stay aloft. *Guernsey?* Past Carrig's face it goes before disappearing into the smoke. Meine points in my direction, and Carrig scoops me up.

"Are you wounded?" he asks, his gigantic eyes studying my bloodied cheek.

"What are the Regolith doing here?" I shout through the madness below. "You said this was our fight and you would never aid us in this war."

His brow of icy rock furrows, and he looks on long and hard in his usual way before offering an explanation. So Meine answers for him. "We lied."

CHAPTER EIGHTEEN

A full day of fighting is behind us, but the war is far from over. From the elevated view atop Carrig's shoulder, I watch Meine and the rest of the Regolith destroy the Infernal one by one as they yank them from the air and rip them in two. The queen's infantry has dwindled, a good many flattened by foot or by fist, the Tartarean no match for the giant Regolith.

Whether King Andronicus and his legion are dead or alive, I have no idea. No longer is there order on the battlefield, the scene devolved into chaos. Our own infantry has scattered, the killing happening in every direction.

We're nearing Crann Bethadh, resilient amongst the warfare. A falling red sun pokes through the smolder, the massive tree cast into eerie silhouette.

"For mercy's sake." I point straight ahead. "How many troops has she created?"

Another band of the queen's infantry marches over the sand. This time large machinery rolls out with them.

Carrig stops in his tracks. "All eyes to the fore," he shouts to his clan. "Slingers on the hill."

Before I can ask what a slinger might be and what it might do, boulders of molten lava launch through the air, too many to count. Carrig stoops to avoid being struck, others hurry out of the way, but the Regolith don't move swiftly. Many are hit in their various parts, wounding them, and one is completely obliterated into a pile of rubble, the lava melting the rock until the giant is no more.

Wild-eyed and filled with rage, Meine takes the carcass of an Infernal and bats the flaming boulders to whence they came. Wide swaths of Tartarean disintegrate wherever the boulders land. Yet still more come. Ruadh is hit in the leg and goes down right before us. Two Regolith pull their kin to the backside of a dune and out of the line of fire, but there's nowhere to safely hide.

"You must call off the Regolith," I yell to Carrig, clinging to the rock as he ducks every which way. "Belisama will kill you all if you don't retreat now. The Regolith will be no more."

"Not all of my clan are in the desert. Some were tasked with a different mission. For those of us here, we made a promise to get you to Crann Bethadh. And get you there we shall."

The burning sky tells us otherwise. The Regolith are too large, too easy a target. Close though we are, we will never reach Crann Bethadh at this rate.

A roaring sound surges through the war-torn battlefield. *What now?* From my pocket, I take out the scope from Adina and set it to my eye. Standing on the crest of a great dune is Ione, her trident raised high in the air. Head bent back to the sky, she appears to be chanting something.

The Dendrite Sea spills over the desert sand. Another bold

341

gesture with the trident, and a massive, white-capped wave rolls in, the whole of it devouring Belisama's army and sweeping it away.

Carrig and I look at one another in astonishment, stunned by the newly forming sea. He says with a nod, "To breach shore and desert alike takes tremendous power and control. The Mage does not disappoint."

A fleet rides the rising tide, blue sails sewn with the Veneficum's silver sigil. Hope blossoms within—Shán might be alive and helming one of the ships. Our troops are sparse, but those few survivors swim toward the ships to find rescue by their compatriots. Not to be outdone, the queen has a fleet of her own, the black sails sewn with a red-threaded serpent and manned by the Tartarean.

Carrig wades through the rising and churning sea as blazing boulders continue to charge past, the waves devouring them in a *coup de grace*. Cannons sound, punch the salty air with thunder. These come from the Veneficum, let loose in an effort to sink the queen's fleet. This offers a momentary respite, enough time to reach the tree relatively unscathed.

Crann Bethadh stands before us, compellingly exquisite and crowned in greenery. The trunk's lowermost half is underwater, and the sea skim's Carrig's midsection. How Crann Bethadh survived and thrived in the desert at all is a wonder. Enduring the salt of the sea and the frigid waters may be its downfall.

"I'm afraid this is all I can do," Carrig says in his gravelly voice.

He cups his hand so I can step on. "The enemy awaits."

"You saved my life, all of you. I will never forget it."

He sets me on the ledge of a door carved into the trunk. I look down to the turbulent waves and hope Ione gains control or we'll all drown before anything can come to pass. My legs feel unsteady, the dread in my gut heavy as I walk through the door and close it behind me.

Silence upends the cacophony of the desert and the sea outside. Lit torches stake the walls of the hollowed trunk, the only source of light in an otherwise darkened space. The air is as cool as that found in a cave, same for the patter of dripping water. Soft, soothing. *Ominous.*

Clutching the straps of my knapsack, knowing the stele is inside, I navigate the tunneled tree. Going down is not an option. The sea is rising, and my best guess tells me the queen knows this as well, so up I go, carefully stepping over stray roots, my body crouched to avoid the ones overhead. Adrenaline keeps a fine pace as it courses through my veins, helpful because the sheer exhaustion of today's events is enough to make me lie down and never wake up.

I trip over something, my feet completely ensnared. Panicking that I've been trapped, I attempt to disentangle myself quickly. I hold the culprit to the light. A massive molted snakeskin easily twice the length of me and thick as an oak. An icy fear shivers through me, but I toss it aside and continue on.

I've come to this fight without a true plan, not knowing how to kill the queen. *Within, not without.* The torches could aid in setting fire to the tree, and in turn killing the queen if I can trap her here, but damp wood doesn't make for promising tinder. Besides, the queen is well-versed in fire, and her ability to withstand flame and smoke likely mirrors my own.

Low hissing. My heart leaps into my throat as my hand goes to the hilt of my sword. The trunk walls twist and turn with each step, and when I round a sharp corner, Belisama is there, waiting for me.

I'm unprepared for the sight. From her belly up, she looks much the same, with her signature fiery strands and alabaster skin. Waist down, her legs are no more, replaced by a serpent's body of crimson scales that run down to a pointed tail. *Samsara.* The Veneficum had explained the concept, but this exceeds my every expectation.

"You've come to kill me," the queen says. Her soft, ethereal voice is the same as when we first met, but the jarring juxtaposition with her current appearance seems less fitting than that with her incorporeal one. "Of course, I'd had high hopes you would die on the battlefield at the hand of one of my minions. However, something told me you would survive the battle outright and fate would bring us here together."

"What are you?" I whisper, slowly unsheathing the sword.

A wicked smile pushes against sharpened cheekbones. "Do not let appearances fool you. I'm still Queen Belisama Agni. When Shán betrayed me in Mount Serius, I nearly died by his hand and

344

had no choice but to take the form of—"

"Shán never betrayed you. Oh, he fed you the fountain's waters, but they and the chalice were spellbound. Aristotle saw to it. Should they be used for the purposes of evil, death would result. You survived because of Eirene. You used her and then killed her for your own purposes. Have you no shame? She was but a child."

Emerald eyes glint in the low light. "For so long I'd lived in an altered state while locked inside of the snowflake obsidian. When I drank the fountain's waters, I tasted being whole again, and it was magnificent. Never again will I assume human form. But for all of the young Sylph's missteps, she made the ultimate sacrifice. For that I am grateful and told her as much."

"You lied to her, betrayed her in the worst way possible. She thought she was helping you escape Mount Serius. She had no idea you were killing her in the process." My anger surprises me, but I don't blame Eirene for her wrongdoings. She was a child, easily swayed by a cunning adult. "Do you truly think you can rule Winterhaven in this...form?"

"Vasuki is what I now am," she calmly replies. "Did you fail to witness my army on the battlefield? The Infernal, the Tartarean—ten thousand strong—all created by my own hand. An underground passage diverted lava flow from Mount Serius through to the desert. I was not yet strong enough to do so on my own, not in the form I assume now. Lucky for me, the Infernal are loyal beasts. Between the magma and the versatility of desert sand, a superior race was formed. If you believe my power has

345

weakened, you underestimate me."

The tree groans, and I wonder what is happening outside. Is the sea still rising? Something tells me time is running thin. "Why are you doing this? Causing so much death and destruction? I implore you to retreat, let the people of Winterhaven live as things stand now."

"Under the loathsome sovereignty of King Andronicus? The people need guidance, a true leader."

I scoff with contempt. "They do indeed but not from the likes of you. Last you were in power, you scorched the earth and enslaved the populace, the same way your mother did. Death and destruction and total dominion was the order of the realm. Tell me, how does this make you a true leader? You cannot. You only sowed enmity and discord and death, which is why people favored a maniacal dictator over you. Telling, wouldn't you agree?"

Queen Belisama hisses with contempt and lunges. With both hands, I swing the sword, and she has no choice but to heed the steely blade. Her serpentine body arches in defense. "Don't you dare tell me what my people need."

"I will tell you exactly what they need, *Mother.*"

Belisama's head tilts. Then raucous laughter erupts, hinting at a pair of ivory fangs, conduits for venom. Venom she will use to kill me. Belisama slithers to the corner opposite. "This is delicious and quite unexpected," she says. "I knew you were dim, but this is too much. Before we move on to more important matters, I shall leave you with this parting fact: I am no more your mother than you are my daughter."

The queen is clever. She lies. My hands shake around the sword's hilt. "I'm sure you remember trying to kill me at the Ichor Samhain." The queen smiles cruelly. "While there I found a Sablier. It took me to our home, where I saw you and Father shortly after I was born, and again at my Rite of Purification. The Sablier does not lie. Neither does Guernsey."

She looks at me with surprise. "Guernsey told you I was your mother?"

'Eternal death, where one can never return in any form, is only possible when flesh and blood commits the bloodletting.' I chew my lip. Guernsey had never said the queen was my mother—not in so many words. It had been implied. By him, by Shán. By me.

"Yes," I say firmly. "He said *'flesh and blood.'*"

"Oh, we are flesh and blood, that much I will give you. But Arún—your father—was never a husband to me." The queen's tone has turned soft, reminiscent. "How I loved your father from the day we first met and for so many years after. But my love went unrequited, for he loved another. Never one for losing, I fashioned an elixir so he would fall in love with me. It worked in the beginning, but lust is blinding, fleeting. True love is forever. And it was his true love for another—Gilleanne, my sister and your mother—that would render him never to be mine."

Gilleanne? My mother? I shake my head, not comprehending the insinuation. "In the Sablier…when the vicar asked who was to share in the responsibility, you said it was you and my father."

347

"*Share* in the responsibility. I was named spiritual mother, with no named spiritual father, as I was unmarried and King Andronicus was never asked."

The scene in the church replays in my head. My father had said "Aye" after Belisama agreed. '*Things aren't always as they seem.*' Guernsey had been quick to tell me this long ago. My father's affirmation could very well have meant he was conceding Belisama as the spiritual mother and not agreeing to the task himself.

The queen goes on, "For whatever reason, the Sablier brought you to the wrong moment in time. Had you watched the entirety of the ceremony play out, you would have seen the vicar ask, per protocol, who the parents were and what name they'd given to their child. You would have seen Gilleanne and Arún lay claim."

Silently I curse myself. The Sablier makes no mistakes. I'd been there but misread the situation. And the secret flirtation between the guardsman and the fair-haired woman had distracted me from hearing the rest.

"Where is Gilleanne, then?"

Belisama slithers back and forth, agitated by my questions. Why she's appeasing me at all makes me wonder. "Things got…complicated. You see, Varius was in love with Gilleanne, and when she chose Arún over him, it caused an even deeper rift between the brothers. Arún and Gilleanne wed in secret and moved to the town of Blythe to live out their lives. Soon after, you were born. But the king is much like me, I regret to say. Shortly following the Rite of Purification, he bludgeoned his brother with a near-fatal blow to the head and used the Dead Ringer to pose as Arún."

The Dead Ringer. I see it on the queen's finger, the Fire stone reflecting the firelight. Now the murderous scene in the Sablier makes sense. The king looked like Arún, so Belisama thought it was him when she kissed him. She'd tainted his drink with the elixir to try to woo him once more. But the elixir hadn't worked, not well enough. And after their kiss, she seemed to know it was not Arún.

"I was there when it happened," the queen continues. "Distraught, I fled, unable to tell my sister. But soon enough, she discovered what happened and told the king she would seek revenge. Enraged, the king kidnapped you, intent on taking your life as punishment.

"Gilleanne came to me and told me what had transpired. I never let on that I knew, but I wanted vengeance as much as she. However, Gilleanne was impetuous. Without my knowledge or even a plan, she went to Isceald Castle to get you back. How things played out is unknown, but the rumors intimate she traveled through the secret tunnels and became trapped. She died somewhere deep inside the bowels of the castle."

Zhang the Elder had gotten the story wrong. It had been Gilleanne, not Belisama, whom Varius had loved. He'd mentioned his memory did not serve him in the manner in which it used to. But I'd never questioned the story nor the specifics, and I should have. I should have questioned everything, even what I'd seen in the Sablier. When my father had seduced Belisama, he'd been under her spell. It makes me ill how she'd set me to her breast not to feed me but to tantalize my father. Poor Gilleanne. To think of her leaving them together as she hurried down the path in the emerald cloak—

The same emerald cloak as the dead woman in the secret passageway. The same woman who was my mother. My heart and head ache. It's all too much, too complicated. My only solace is that I now have a piece of her forever—the cloak tucked inside the knapsack.

"You need this, I presume?" Queen Belisama flutters her fingers to show off the Dead Ringer.

"How did you come to possess it? Did you steal it from the king?"

Her head shakes. "Varius stole the Dead Ringer from me. I'm the intended. That is why I knew he could not keep up his charade. I knew the stone would return to me soon enough."

The smell of salt carries through the damp air. Seawater has trickled in, wetting the tips of my boots. Time is running out. "You know about the stele, then?" I ask.

She removes the ruby from the ring's prongs and extends the stone for the taking.

Warily I eye her. "Why would you give me the Fire stone?"

"Tíne is the actual name. Because then the Cintamani Jewel will be only one stone short to be complete, am I correct?"

Now it's my turn to laugh. "If you know where the Aether stone might be, please do share, for I haven't a clue."

Belisama's red tail coils beneath her. "The stone is at the tree's head, right at the start of the heavens."

"The story is a myth. Josephina and Fleuric...It's all lore."

"Perhaps. But the stone is indeed there. Why do you think I chose Crann Bethadh of all places? You must climb the tree and retrieve the stone for me."

"Are you mad? I could never climb that far. Even if I could, I would never do so for you."

The queen lunges, knocking me to the ground and ripping off the knapsack with her fangs. "You have no choice. If you refuse, I will kill you now." She takes out the stele and slips the Tíne between the Petard and Kyanite. The hum, so loud, reverberates through the grooved trunk, through me. "So beautiful," the queen whispers. "Now go, make haste."

Shaken by her strength, by her wrath, I stumble to my feet. "If Aether is right above Crann Bethadh, then why have you not taken the stone?"

"Do trust I have tried."

No wonder she hasn't killed me. She needs me. Without losing eye contact, I pick up the sword. The fountain's water and the chalice could not be used for maligned purposes. Could the same principle hold true for Aether? Could Aristotle or someone else have had the foresight to cast a spell on the stone? Something tells me no. The queen knows something concerning the stone I do not.

"I'm not retrieving the Aether stone for you. I'd rather die than

351

give you eternal life." With a flick of my wrist, three of the four torches fall to the ground, the flames mixing with saltwater to create a potent wall of steam.

Belisama hisses, shrill and savage. I charge, but the steam is as much a deterrent for me; I can no longer see her.

"Predictable," she whispers from behind.

I jump from the sound of her voice and swing the blade blindly. When the steam dissipates, she's no longer there. More hissing from the next tunnel. Quickly I re-tie the knapsack straps, heave it over my shoulders, and follow the sound with conviction.

Belisama is studying the stele when I find her. Next to her is a torch. She fingers the flames, a message that fire is friend not foe; I should not even make an attempt. "You are much like your mother, Sondrine. Self-righteous to a fault." Coyly she sets a hand to her ear. "Do you hear something? A child, if I'm not mistaken."

Unsure of what Belisama is up to, I strain to listen. She slithers away, and I have no choice but to follow in her wake.

The sound grows louder. *Crying.* I trod faster through twists and turns, up the steepening slope of the tree trunk. My legs ache with pain, and when I finally discover the source, I gasp at the sight.

"Lark," I exclaim. She's on the ground, bound and gagged. The hollow of the tree ends here with only a door carved into the wall, yet Belisama is nowhere to be found.

Circumspect, I set down the sword and wriggle off the gag, her mouth cut and bleeding.

"Oh, Sondrine," she cries in a hoarse whisper. "Thank goodness you found me."

"I'm here." I hug the little girl so tight she yelps. Loosening my hold, I take her face in my hands. "Is Snap here as well?"

Lark whimpers. "We were flying atop Hoarus around the outermost parts of the Sanctuary when an Infernal swooped in and took me. Snap and Hoarus were knocked from the sky. How I do hope they both survived."

I study her face, then her hands and legs. "Are you hurt, Lark?"

"I'm thirsty is all."

She gratefully drinks the remaining water in my canteen. Careful not to cut her, I use my sword to free her of the ties when I'm knocked sideways with terrible force. My head hits a stray tree root. Lark's screams keep me conscious. Squinting through the pain, I see Belisama's tail coiling around Lark.

"Sondrine!" the little girl screams, her arms pinned to her sides. "Help me!"

"Let her go," I say, my voice shaking with rage as I find my footing.

Belisama smiles ruthlessly. "Of course. Once you deliver the stone, I will set her free."

Lark gasps for air, the tail constricting her every breath. I want to scream at the madness, but Belisama killed Eirene for her own purposes. She'll make good on her threat with Lark.

"How do I know you'll keep your promise? How do I know you won't hurt her?"

353

Belisama brushes the hair from Lark's eyes and then tugs the gag back around her mouth. "You don't." In a shot, she's out the door.

A balmy breeze hits as I follow, the smoke-addled sky surrendered to evenfall. I'm at the start of the crown. Seawater has crept up much of the tree's trunk. Ships sail through the newly formed sea, a strange sight to behold. One has cast its anchor into the tree's trunk. We are quite far up, farther than I expected. And yet the tree's upper crown along with the Aether stone is lost to the clouds. How I will retrieve it is beyond me.

Belisama and Lark are straight above. With no other choice, I start to climb. I also curse without remorse. The bough's branches are thick and clawing, helpful in maneuvering my way, yet each step brings the possibility of death. My injured and aching legs make things all the more precarious. Whenever I take a moment to gather my bearings, Belisama constricts her body around Lark. The little girl's cries keep me going.

Minutes turn to hours, and the once warm air has soured to a brutal chill as I climb through the tree's crown and head into the clouds. Taking advantage of the low visibility, I stop to slip the emerald cloak from the knapsack and pull it around my shoulders. Then I press on, trying to figure out how to kill Belisama without hurting Lark in the process. Thus far every possibility comes with it the same morbid answer: they will die together.

Novacula Occami—the simplest explanation tends to be the right one. Within, not without. Both Jinpa's and Eachna's voices call to me.

My hair is frosted, my breath crystalline when I breach the cloud cover. The pearlescent stone shines straight above, bright as the moon. But the Aether is far away, too far past the tree itself. My fingers throb with cold and fatigue, as does the rest of me. The stele in her hand, Belisama slithers up the tree with ease, even with the ice-coated branches and the little girl in her clutches. Lark looks unwell; her amber eyes are rolling.

"I need to rest," I shout, pausing to catch my breath.

"No stopping," the queen hisses. "I do not have to kill Lark outright. Constriction can cut off blood supply to her limbs, to her—"

"Enough of your threats," I chide. "I'm coming."

The queen offers a self-satisfied smirk. I reach for the next branch, but as I push off with my foot, my boot slips on the icy surface and down I go. The trunk is a slide beneath me, and I scream and claw, trying to grasp any wayward branch. A hollowed spot near the bough stoppers my fall, and the Aeriscloque flies over the collar of my cloak. Pain shoots through my spine and head, and I blink away starbursts behind my eyes. Belisama is far above, a shadow in the moon's light. I'm doubtful she'll descend the tree; she'll wait for me to catch up.

As I move to tuck the Aeriscloque back into the cloak's collar, the tiny hinged doors flutter open. The time matters not, nor does the impending weather, which oddly shows a storm of the worst sort: thunder and lightning and gale-force winds. Same as always,

355

the bronze and black dial show Polaris…

No. Aether. All at once, Guernsey's voice calls back to me. '*Tiāntǐ means celestial. Heavenly body.*'

"Within, not without," I murmur, the puzzle pieces easing together. "'*Through the stars I come. With me, I bring the treasure. Within me, I bring the Aether. The final gift to Winterhaven.*'"

Voices from below interrupt my thoughts. The cloud cover is thick, but if I'm unmistaken, it sounds like King Andronicus and his legion. He's stronger than I credited him for. *Does he want to help me?* The answer eludes me the same way killing the queen and getting the Aether stone elude me. He will only complicate matters, this is a certainty, so I tuck away the timepiece and start for the top once more.

Anger fuels my every step. If only Snap and Hoarus would show. A dragon born of ice would prove useful right about now. From what Lark shared earlier, I hope Snap is alive. Ice dragons can be reconstructed. Little boys cannot.

Lark screams. Belisama is waving her about like a simple stuffed toy. I can't go any faster. She won't kill Lark, not yet. But she will torture the little girl, bring her close to her dying breath.

"I'm coming," I say through angry tears. Despondent and exhausted, I have no faith that even if I retrieve the stone, Lark's life will be spared. My heart is dark, same as the night surrounding me.

Something catches my eye, a beacon of light due west, brighter than the moon and Aether stone combined. *Mór.* Hundreds—perhaps a thousand—flying through the sky. So beautiful, like a painted cathedral ceiling come to life. Lord Kian is in the lead, with Lady Aniyu at his side. Together they swoop in, each one taking an arm. With the rest of the Mór following, they carry me past the queen, past the crown of Crann Bethadh, deep into the heavens where the Aether stone awaits.

Pearlescent and flawless, the stone's beauty is beguiling. Confused, I look first to Lord Kian and then to Lady Aniyu, to ask why they'd come when Lord Kian had so adamantly sworn he would never help the Duine.

Lady Aniyu must read the questioning in my eyes. "The hows and whys shall be saved for another time. Do know the Regolith freed our imprisoned kin from the Rock of Morbid Bay. Carrig said it was due to your bidding. Consider this repayment. Now you shall have the Cintamani Jewel, and in turn light shall smite the darkness."

We bob in the frigid wind. "You don't understand. The stele is with the queen. She has taken Lark captive and will kill her if I don't surrender the Aether stone."

"Lark must be sacrificed," Lord Kian says. "The Cintamani Jewel in the queen's hands spells death for all Duine, and Winterhaven will perish."

My breath is clouded puffs. The Aether is white-hot when I take it in hand, the vibration nearly too much. "I can't ask you to understand, but Lark is like my child. Were she to die, I would

357

never forgive myself. Please, I beg of you to do as I ask and bring me to Queen Belisama now."

Lord Kian and the rest of the Mór look to one another, distressed. But Lady Aniyu bows her head accordingly. "As you wish, Sondrine."

They fly me to the bough of the same long branch where Belisama is coiled around the tip. The queen looks intoxicated by the emanating light through my fingers. Lark's lips are blue, her teeth chattering with cold.

"Sondrine! Do not give the queen the Aether, whatever you do."

The voice of the command touches something deep within me. Shán is giving the order. He's crouched on a branch below with King Andronicus at his side.

I'm thankful to see he's survived thus far, yet I remain fierce in my objectives. "Lark will die if I don't concede to the queen's wishes. I cannot allow that to happen."

The king appears stupefied when he sees Lark, for he believes he killed her months ago. His eyes narrow threateningly at me and at Shán; he understands he was deceived. But he shakes off the betrayal and hoists himself onto an offshoot of the branch that holds both the queen and me.

"Listen to Shán," he implores. "Pass me the stone, Sondrine. Lark's death will save the world of Winterhaven, do you understand? She will be a hero to all; I'll make sure of it."

Belisama slithers closer, her eyes fixed on the stone. "Give the Aether here, Sondrine."

"Let Lark go," I say to her. "Once you do so, the stone is yours."

"You play me for a fool?" she seethes. "I think not. Give me the stone first or I will kill Lark right now."

"No," I say calmly. I throw the stone in the air and catch it. The queen gasps in horror. "If you kill her, I will break this branch. We three will fall to our deaths, the stone forever lost to the sea below."

"She will follow through with her promise," Lady Aniyu says sagely, her magnificent wings moving in slow, measured movements to keep her aloft. Lord Kian nods once in agreement. Belisama looks to Shán to gauge his expression, but the grave look on his face tells her I speak the truth.

To reiterate my claim, I brace myself at the bough and jump on the branch. It moves up and down, destabilizing both the queen and the king. Quickly he regains his footing but not without cursing me. A portentous hiss from Belisama, but she relents, the ruby tail uncoiling and setting the little girl free.

Lady Aniyu dives in, takes Lark's hand in hers, and flies her out of striking distance of the queen. "Hang on tight," I yell to the little girl. "Lady Aniyu, take her to the ship below, to safety."

Once they've disappeared through the clouds, I hold out the stone for Belisama. "You kept your promise; now I must keep mine."

"Finally." She creeps closer, enraptured by the very sight, and reaches out to take the Aether. But the king snatches it from my palm.

359

"What are you doing?" I scream. "Give Belisama the stone."

He swings his blade in my direction, forcing me to step back, then does the same to the queen. "Hand over the stele," he demands of Belisama.

She hisses violently, baring her ivory fangs, readying herself to strike. The king is deft with his sword. With one quick swipe, he lops off her free hand with his blade. She screams in pain and slithers back to the branch's tip. "You will never get this from me," she shrieks, blood spewing madly from her stump.

"You have but one hand left," the king drawls. "The stele is ripe for the taking, if you ask me." As he inches closer, the stele flies from her hand into mine.

"Indeed it is," I say.

Dumbstruck, he whips around to face me. My whole body vibrates as the stele's power awakens. A gale sweeps in, so strong I must brace myself against the trunk. Branches break off, violently flying every which way. The Mór remain midair, but their wings pump harder to stay aloft. The king drops to one knee to keep his balance, and the queen tightly coils her body around the branch.

The wind stirs the water below and sweeps it into the air, where clouds form and mushroom to extraordinary heights. Thunder rumbles loud and low, and lightning streaks across the sky. A wayward bolt hits the trunk below, and fire alights.

The king crawls toward me. "We shall rule Winterhaven together," he yells through the wind and flying debris. "Hand over the stele now so we can be done with this." When he's mere yards from me, I climb to a smaller branch above. It won't hold me for long.

Crann Bethadh sways and groans in the raging wind. Branches break off, sharp and deadly, a sky filled with weaponry. King Andronicus stands and grabs my ankle.

"Do not defy—" A massive branch slices through the king's neck, pins him to the trunk. His eyes go white with surprise. "Me," he finishes, choking on his blood, his hand falling away.

"Aether," I say aloud, and the stone flies from the king's hand into mine.

Despite the fact he's bleeding out, the king swings his sword in a frenzy. Shán reaches up from the branch below, grabs the king by his boots, and pulls with all his might. The king's body is ripped free and falls to the sea below.

Fire crawls up the trunk, destroying Crann Bethadh. "Go back to the ship," I yell to Shán through the thunder. "Let the Mór take you."

Queen Belisama slithers closer. "You made a promise to me," she threatens. Her breathing is labored, and her pallor has gone from its perfect alabaster to a sickening grey. "Make good and surrender the stele and the Aether or I will kill you right now. Though my body betrays me, the venom within is potent."

"I'm not afraid to die," I say with purposeful resignation.

The queen lunges. But her fangs sink not into my neck but deep into the Aeriscloque's face. A white vapor seeps out, ethereal and hauntingly beautiful. The incorporeal figure grows in height and berth.

As if tasting poison, Belisama recoils. "Gilleanne?" she whispers aloud, her mouth dropping open in shock.

Gilleanne swirls through the Elemental storm. "Oh, dear sister," she says with vitriol. "How I've missed you and your wicked ways. To think of all the love and faith I bestowed upon you. And what did you give in return? Secrecy and deception."

The queen summons the flames from below and throws them at Gilleanne. They pass right through her and alight the branches above. "I loved Arún," the queen cries without apology. "He could have been mine, but you stole him away."

Gilleanne laughs acerbically. "Oh, Belisama. You never did see things as they stood. Your view of the world was always skewed. Arún never loved you, so you drugged my beloved and bedded him for your own greed."

"You want reparations? Look elsewhere. I will make no apologies, not ever." Mouth unhinged, fangs bared, she launches straight for me and knocks me onto my back. The stele flies from my hand and by the grace of the gods, Shán catches it.

Try as I might, with the stone curled in my fist, I can't push the queen off me. The bough cracks beneath us. Shán cannot climb up to help or we'll all tumble into the sea.

"Stand down," he yells at the queen, his sword swiping at her tail.

Belisama presses her mouth to my neck, and her fangs break through the skin. I scream in pain as Gilleanne dives between us

362

and knocks the queen away. But it's too late. The poison is quick to enter my bloodstream.

The queen attempts to strike again, but Gilleanne is an unbreakable barrier between us. Filled with hate and fury, Belisama rages, "If I cannot be ruler of Winterhaven, then neither shall another."

She calls for her minions, and in an instant, the Infernal approach. Breathing fire and smoke, they swoop through the clouds, while hundreds of Tartarean climb Crann Bethadh's burning trunk. The Mór do battle as lightning and thunder and roaring winds crash with malevolent force.

Queen Belisama laughs feverishly. "How fortunate your mother materialized to watch your death play out, Sondrine. True love if ever there was."

The tree is crumbling into the sea. "Sondrine, take the stele," Shán shouts from below. "Now, before it's too late."

My mind is liquid fog as he passes the stele to me. The venom is doing its job, my breath shallow and quick. Amidst the pandemonium, Gilleanne's soft voice swims through the maelstrom. "Be unafraid, be brave, my sweet Sondrine. Fight through the darkness, for hope is resilient. And where there is hope, there is eternal light."

With an unsteady hand, I place the Aether stone atop the stele. The five stones vibrate and converge to form a single, ornate sceptre. With the brightness of a thousand stars, brilliant light fireworks from the tip and impales the queen and her minions.

Belisama screams and writhes in bitter pain. Like the Infernal above and the Tartarean below, her whole body turns black as char.

"Make it stop," she groans savagely. Tiny holes puncture her body, white light pushing the black of her skin into the sky. Her face is incredulous, the picture of fear as it breaks apart piecemeal. "I don't want to die!" she cries out as the dark pieces rotate in the air.

Through the poisonous haze, I see they are locusts, a formidable swarm of tornadic force. When nothing remains of the queen but the echo of her screams, the locusts dive straight into the sceptre's tip, shattering the stones, producing a white-hot blast so loud and so strong the force hurtles me across the sky, straight into Death's arms to carry me home.

CHAPTER NINETEEN

"I should think this chamber perfect," says the voice of a young woman. "Windows to the east and west to enjoy the rise and fall of the sun each day. A balcony on the north side to watch the tides of the Dendrite Sea, and an enclosed solar facing south for drawing or whatever she might enjoy to pass the time."

"I am most pleased you like it, Your Grace," says a man's voice. "Might I be of further assistance today?"

"That is all. On the morrow, we shall discuss drapery and other décor. We must keep things cheery, would you not agree?"

"Indeed, Your Grace."

***

"Not so hard," chides the voice of an older woman, a nasality to her voice. "She's not dead."

"Might as well be," says another woman. "Why the queen makes us bathe her day in, day out, is beyond me."

"She believes one day she'll awaken. Can't blame her, really."

Sneering laughter. "The queen is delusional. This lump has as much chance of awakening as my dearly departed Jaren. A good husband lost to the ravages of the Stele War years back."

"Your loss I can appreciate, and you have my greatest sympathies. But show some respect. We would be in chains right now. Or worse, among the dead, were it not for her. You best not let the queen or king hear you speak in such a manner. You'll be released from your duties quick as a whip."

***

"Tiāntĭ." A familiar man's voice with a lilt of faraway places. Men and women conferring in whispers. *About me.*
Silence.

***

"Yes, good," says a man, his head to my chest. "Her heart sounds strong. All four humors are in balance—Fire, Air, Water, Earth. Reflexes are slow and still show damage, although they are responsive. Everything appears as it was the week prior." Clearing of phlegm from his voice.

"I've a different elixir for you to administer," says a young woman's voice—at once familiar—perhaps the same woman from a previous day. "As you well know, the leaders of the Veneficum were here yesterday to discuss a number of affairs regarding the realm. Zhang the Elder offered the newest of his many concoctions. Three drops beneath her tongue thrice daily. Perhaps this will be the one." A long pause. "I know what you're thinking, Healer Nairn. But we must keep trying and never give up."

"As it pleases you, Your Grace."

"Now if you'll excuse me, I must be off for an appointment."

Footsteps and a door closing. A deep sigh of resignation. The

366

shaking of a bottle. A hand to my mouth, opening it. *Liquid peppermint.*

"Before I depart," he says, "a few pricks to the feet to assure your legs are in working order. This should not hurt one bit." Light scrapings of a blade.

"Ouch!" I cry out.

My eyes push open to the sight of a man with a pointed beard and a red calotte on his grey tresses. At least I think so. My vision is hazy, and the light is low. He gasps loudly. He's here and then gone, his body hitting the floor with a loud thump.

***

People bustle to and from the chamber. The man with the pointed beard has an ice pack balanced on his head as he shines candlelight into my eyes. I wince from the pain.

"Sondrine, my name is Healer Nairn, personal medic to the queen and king. How do you feel, my lady?"

Like a slug drunk on laudanum. "Should I not ask the same of you?" I say, my voice reduced to an unintentional whisper.

Muffled snorts all around. "You gave me quite the start," he says with a self-deprecating smile. "Such an unexpected entrance."

My energy is sapped; taking a breath feels laborious. "Have I lost my sight? Everything is blurry and dim, and the light hurts my eyes."

"Typical given the situation, but I should think not, although time will be the better indicator."

Platters of food are brought forth, but the healer waves them away. "Chicken stock for now. As she grows stronger, solid foods may be eased into her repertoire." From a pipette, he squeezes a few drops of water into my mouth, my tongue like spun wool. I choke and cough but then beg for more. Each dropperful appeases my parched mouth.

"Must she remain bedridden?" a young woman to my left asks. Her voice is one of many heard as of late. My neck aches when I turn my head, though I can't see much anyway. "Fresh air would do some good, would you not agree?" she continues.

Healer Nairn dabs beeswax onto my lips. "Her legs are weak, her body unaccustomed to exertion of any sort, Your Grace. Should she desire a stroll, things must be kept to a minimum. My recommendation is a wheeled chair to start, progressing to a walking cane as time goes on."

Your Grace? This young girl is queen? I struggle to look at her, but the strain in my neck is too painful, so I surrender and let my eyes fall to half-mast.

"How do you feel, Sondrine?" she asks, her hand on my shoulder.

"Where am I?"

"Winterhaven," she replies. "The capital city of Isceald."

My pulse quickens, and a surge of adrenaline helps me to sit up. "Is this Isceald Castle?" Panicked, I look left to right, but only blurred faces stare back.

"Fortress of Síochánta," the queen states. "You must rest now. There will be time enough for answers later." She eases me back to the pillows with a gentle hand.

Fortress of Síochánta. My mind swims as it tries to remember such a place, but the effort causes fatigue beyond compare.

The healer calls for everyone's exit save for the queen's. Then he peels off the bedcovers and tugs the shift to my thighs. My fingers discover squares of gauze-like material. They cover my calves, both heels, and even my back, and I know this because he gently rolls me onto my side and lifts the material to inspect the skin beneath. "Be patient while I tend to your pressure ulcers," he mutters. "Now that you're awake, they should heal in due course."

"Pressure ulcers?" I croak. Though my memory is cloudy, I know of these ailments because they are common in the aged and the sickly. We sold elixirs for them at the emporium. "Something tells me I've been asleep a long while."

The queen sits in a chair beside me and takes my hand in hers. "A tick over four years, to be exact."

CHAPTER TWENTY

In the course of one week, I've managed to move on to solid food, albeit soft and repugnantly tasteless. Paperboard might be an improvement. My eyes too have improved, and I can now see the chamber, opulent but pleasant. Since my awakening, the queen has been absent, and there's been no mention of the king. Other than the fact that this is Fortress of Síochánta, no one has offered any details.

The Aeriscloque sits around my neck, the dents from Belisama's fangs gracing the front. My thumb traces them. Thinking about my mother's soul housed in the pendant all these years makes me wonder how.

Mairi bustles in, interrupts my thoughts. She has tended to my every need since I awoke. If I'm not mistaken, she's the elder who bathed me daily, as I recognize the nasality in her voice.

"Good morning, my lady," she says. "Time for a bath. Perhaps you might enjoy a true soak in a tub rather than the usual fare in bed. If it pleases you, I shall have the kitchen boil water and escort you to the bathing room."

"Thank you, Mairi, a bath sounds lovely. Perhaps while we wait for the tub to be filled, we could go outside for some fresh air? Is there a garden where I could stroll about?"

"You are not strong enough, my lady. And it's quite chilly out there. Winter is always here, but the true season is looming. Winds from the north and even a smattering of snow."

"The sun is out. And a rolling chair would suit me fine, as would a nice blanket across my lap."

Mairi bites her lip, clearly fretting my request. "The queen may not approve."

"The queen is not my warden. Or am I a prisoner here, unbeknownst to me?"

Her meaty hands wave off the query. "Goodness no. You are an honored guest. I will send for a guard to help usher you into the rolling chair."

***

Mairi pushes me through the gardens, past flowering trees and shrubbery, past a bubbling, three-tiered fountain made of marble. Thankfully it's not the blood-letting sort. After the stale air of my chamber, the fresh, salt-laden breeze is a welcome reprieve. While the city carries the familiarity of Isceald, something about it feels different, and I cannot put my finger on what.

"Mairi," I say. "As you might surmise, I have many a question after four long years."

"I'm sure you do, my lady. But I likely have no answers. I've been tending to you only for the last year or so. There are rumors, of course, about all kinds of things, but for me to parse what is true and what is not would be a disservice."

She huffs a little from the exertion of pushing me, so I gesture

371

toward a bench overlooking the city. "Please, call me Sondrine. And since my questions will go unanswered, do tell me your story. Did you fight in the Stele War?"

"Goodness, no. I'm far too old to be of any use on a battlefield. I was a nurse in a hospital near to here tending to the casualties of war, of which there were many. Still are all these years later. Much of Isceald burned to the ground, the hospital included. Whilst we were rebuilding, a call came from the queen. She needed nurses of her own to tend to you. You must know your awakening will only add to your legacy."

"My...legacy?"

"You're famous, my la—Sondrine. You killed Queen Belisama Agni. The whole of Winterhaven is indebted to you. When word catches fire you've awoken from a sleep meant to last eternal, you will be thought of as some kind of deity."

I snort. More like a demon. "Far from it."

Mairi clicks her tongue. "I've been a nurse for over half my life. Seen many a thing, strange happenings. Never has any patient awoken after so much time has passed. Usually they waste away to marrow and bone. You remained healthy, in part because the queen saw to it you got the best care."

"Yes, this queen. Who is—"

"Mairi?" Her name is being called from the far side of the garden. "Are you out here? I need you at once."

"Speaking of the queen," she mutters with a nervous glance. "Be sure to tell her this was your idea, not mine." She stands and smooths her apron. "Yes, Your Grace. I'm coming."

Though I try to steer the chair around, the wheels are too cumbersome. For now, it matters not, and my gaze returns to the rolling tide of the Dendrite Sea. So beautiful and yet a grave to so many.

"Sondrine," the queen says from the rear. "There's a terrible chill to the air. Are you comfortable out here?"

As she comes about face, I gasp audibly. Her hair is longer and braided, but the copper color and large amber eyes are unmistakable. "Lark? Is that you?"

She throws her arms around me, and I breathe in the familiar orange blossom. "Oh, Sondrine. How I wanted to tell you straight away. But I was unsure if you would remember me. Healer Nairn told me not to put any undue stress on you."

When she pulls back, I study her head to foot. Her cheeks bloom roses as they ever did, but she's taller, and her adolescence is marked by the décolletage in the low neckline of her blouse. I can't help but smile to see her in trousers. "Lark, I could never forget you. I don't understand, though. You are the reigning queen of Winterhaven? You sound so grownup, so please take no offense. You are still but a child."

Lark takes a seat on the bench as a large guard looms mere yards away. "Nearly thirteen years of age. A child to some, of a marrying age to others. I am the queen temporarily. Snap is king. We are ruling Winterhaven together." Tears gloss her amber eyes. "How I hoped you would come back to us."

373

She takes my hand in hers, and I squeeze it tenderly. "Lark, I need answers. I'm so confused. Four years—"

"I can't tell you everything in one sitting. Too many things have come to pass."

"Last thing I remember is destroying Queen Belisama atop Crann Bethadh. At least tell me how I got here. Please."

Lark concedes to my wishes. "Placing the Aether stone atop the stele created a blast so strong it was seen and heard in every corner of the realm. Had the Mór not been there, you would have fallen into the sea and assuredly drowned. They brought you to safety. With the queen and her minions dead, we declared a victory, and the war ended not long after. You were taken to the Sanctuary of Caelum to recover, although admittedly no one thought you would survive. Since King Andronicus was dead, the good people of Winterhaven called for a new monarch."

She wheels me across the garden to face north, where a hilltop sits barren. "Snap and I had Isceald Castle destroyed. The Mourning Garden is no more, and the heads of the dead have been buried and blessed. We've turned the grounds into a sanctuary to honor the fallen, those who died by King Andronicus's sword and in the Stele War as well. In turn we built this castle anew."

"Nothing pleases me more," I say. "But why bring me back here? Why not leave me at the Sanctuary of Caelum?"

Lark plucks a flower from a nearby rosebush and hands it to me. "Purely selfish reasons. I wanted you near, to tend to you along with the best healers in all of Winterhaven. The Sanctuary was too remote, and Snap and I could not rule from there. Isceald is the capital, and thus it was deemed we must reside here."

"You said 'temporarily' when referring to your reign. Who will rule in your stead?"

"Sondrine, you are an Agni and an Andronicus. Royal blood flows from both sides."

"Not so. My father was an Andronicus in name only, born to a commoner, although his mother—my grandmother—was certainly royal. Hence my father was only half royal, which leaves me a diluted quarter on his side."

"Even so, you are the truest royal alive. It's quite the long and sordid story; Snap and I—and Vinca—were sired by the king and one of his fair maidens. We may never know the lineage from whence our mother came, but all thoughts point to her being a commoner. Your 'diluted quarter' plus your mother's full royal blood puts you ahead of both Snap and me." She winks, self-confident in her statement.

The story of their paternity comes back to me; Shán had made mention of it at the Keep of Wintersgaard. *Shán.* His name comes so easily when so many things are a blur. Perhaps the mind forgets more readily than the heart. "Shán shared his suspicions with me. I'm comforted knowing he was your half-brother."

"Not was. Is. Shán survived, Sondrine. The Mór saved him, same as you."

Knowing Shán is alive brings tears of relief to my eyes, and I breathe in the rose's perfume. "Is he here in Isceald?"

375

Lark looks out to the sea, flustered by my inquiry. "No one knows. Last we saw him was two years past."

"Does he know I survived?"

"Oh, indeed. He was at your bedside every day for those first two years or so, at the Sanctuary of Caelum and here in Isceald as well. Then one day, he was not...."

The thorn pricks my finger, drawing blood, and the rose tumbles from my hand to the cold ground. "He thought I would never awaken. Shán has much to offer to the world, to any woman." I suck on my finger, the copper taste bitter on my tongue.

Lark picks up the rose and plucks a petal. "Along with my regiment, I've been searching for him this past week to no avail. Snap has relieved me of my quest."

"How is Snap? When I found you at Crann Bethadh, you said he and Hoarus had been knocked from the sky when the Infernal came for you."

"Snap slowed time. Had he not, he likely would have died. Still he broke his arm and leg and every single rib, but he's long since healed. Hoarus has a partly shattered right wing to this day and can no longer fly. Perhaps you could help repair it? Snap has tried with little luck."

The breeze rises off the sea, and I pull the blanket tighter. "You don't have to ask twice. Where is Hoarus? Is the weather cold enough for him in Isceald?"

"Hoarus is at the Keep of Wintersgaard, north of here and far chillier. Now that you are on the mend, Snap might ask for your help in creating a quarry here. Hoarus is lonely at the Keep. A mate for him might also prove advantageous, if you're so willing." She giggles into her hands, and I delight in the possibility.

"Lark," I say, returning to the previous topic. "Please call off Snap and your regiment. Shán deserves peace and whatever life he has created for himself. There's no need to let him know I've awakened."

"He's our half-brother, and while his wishes were made clear— that he has no desire to rule Winterhaven—he agreed to offer his consent on certain matters. With regard to the rebuilding of the realm, there are permits and financial matters too complicated for us."

I duck my eyes, embarrassed that I'd thought Shán's whereabouts concerned me. My yawn goes into my shoulder and is not unnoticed.

"As I mentioned, not every question can be answered right now," she says. "You need to rest."

"Fine, you may bring me back to my chamber. I do have one request. A meeting in the coming days with the Veneficum, attended by you and Snap as well."

Lark laughs. "Ambitious of you. Good to see. However, until you are officially Queen of Winterhaven, what I say goes. The Veneficum will meet here per your request but not until you are stronger. Sondrine, you've been asleep four years. After everything you've been through, another fortnight won't kill you."

This time it's my turn to laugh. And I do so heartily.

***

My reunion with the Veneficum happens after a third fortnight. My progress has been slower than expected, but I'm finally able to walk on my own with the aid of a cane. Offers of gratitude and warm handshakes happen as I receive Ione and Lord Kian and Carrig, but I hug Zhang the Elder tight when he tries to bow in greeting. While future meetings will be held at the Citadel, everyone has agreed to travel to the Fortress of Síochánta for my sake. Lark and Snap sit at the head of the long table with ledgers before them and quills in hand. Lucky for Carrig, the space is vast, with a vaulted ceiling. Guernsey's chair sits heartbreakingly vacant.

"Order, council members." Snap raps his knuckles on the table. His hair is still a brilliant white, but he's a young man now, with whiskers in need of shaving and more angles to his face. "Please be seated. We've come here today to discuss the future sovereignty of Winterhaven. Before we do so, I know each of you has updates. Our meetings since the war's end have been few and brief, as we have all been busy rebuilding the realm. Most of our gatherings have dealt with the state—and fate—of Sondrine. Now that she's come back to us, we must concentrate our efforts on Winterhaven's future. Additionally, for Sondrine to successfully rule this great land of ours, she needs to be apprised of the goings-on since the war ended. Ione, if you please."

Ione is dressed in her aqua silks, her dark hair entwined with shells and seaweed. "The Sanctuary of Caelum is safe once more.

Dozens of women and men were needed to secure our borders, as both Ykuza and the Infernal managed their way in." She nods knowingly to Lark and me. "In other matters, we must employ a cartographer. The Desert of Katakum's size has been halved, while the Dendrite Sea stretches farther to the west due to my influence during the Stele War. Every map in Winterhaven needs to be amended."

"Duly noted," Snap says and makes a record in one of the leather-bound books.

Ione continues. "On an interesting and somewhat peculiar note, Crann Bethadh burned down, we all know. Yet a new version has sprung up fully formed where sea meets sand on the new border."

Zhang the Elder nods. "Crann Bethadh was as old as Winterhaven itself, with deep running roots and a strange ability to filter saltwater while thriving in the desert air. A new tree is unsurprising and certainly feasible, scientifically speaking. Also, Crann Bethadh is unique to Winterhaven, a land born of magic. Either science or magic is a possibility."

Snap makes additional notes, then points his quill to Carrig. As usual, the giant takes a long moment to think. "The Regolith population is smaller due to the Stele War, but Titan Dome thrives. With the rebuilding of the realm, new tools are needed more than ever. Scarcely can we keep up with demand, and we will need to supplement our work with additional ironsmiths."

"Do you need funds to employ them?" Lark asks.

Carrig wags a rocky finger. "We have more gold than we need.

Our clan does not require much to live. We are content with what we have and find time to commune as well as work. A wise lady once taught me the importance of such things." He neither looks at me nor smiles, but it does my heart good to hear this.

"Lord Kian," Lark says. "Do you have anything to add?"

"How is Lady Aniyu?" I blurt.

Tight-lipped, he says, "Nine fingers are near as good as ten, she has come to find out."

My shoulders sag under the weight of his declaration. I'm saddened my presence at the Keep was so destructive to his people.

"Like the Regolith, we Mór are thriving," he continues. "With the help of Carrig's clan, our brethren are finally free of the Rock of Morbid Bay. Not all Duine have proven their loyalty, but some have earned our eternal trust." He offers a curt nod in my direction. For Lord Kian, this is a grand gesture.

"Word has spread throughout the realm you're alive," Lark says to me. "The good people of Winterhaven want to know if you'll assume the throne and when. What say you, Sondrine?"

All eyes go to me. "Before we get to such matters," I hedge, "I have questions. Lark, you and Snap assured me the Veneficum would offer answers once we convened here. Did the stele help me kill Queen Belisama Agni?"

Zhang the Elder takes out his dragonbone pipe and strikes flint to stone. "Tiāntǐ, that question is somewhat unanswerable. We know only one thing: flesh and blood were needed to kill the queen."

I nod. "Shán told me Aether can derive its power from the soul. Gilleanne's soul was freed from the Aeriscloque, and that makes me wonder if she played a part. By the by, it was Gilleanne whom the king loved, not Belisama."

Flame is drawn into the tobacco, and he exhales the smoke. "A coward's spine is curved," he says. "Valor stands tall. When I recounted the history of the queen, I confused the two sisters. The Battle of Crowns was waged by Belisama for love lost. Not that of the king's but of his brother's."

I wave off his apology. "The whole thing *is* confusing. Belisama was drugging Arún so he would love her. And the king, after using the Dead Ringer to pose as Arún, realized this. Anyway, knowing Belisama is not my mother grants a relief I cannot deny. Gilleanne was all good. Belisama started off the same, but she devolved into a nefarious and hateful woman."

"No one is comprised of all evil or all good," Zhang the Elder counters. "Both inhabit us; both seduce us. Hatred is easy, a spell not easily broken. In any given situation, there are always two paths to follow. Which one we choose ultimately defines who we are."

I nod. Knowing the Veneficum will not meet again for a time, I want to take advantage of the gathering. "With regard to your earlier statement, Guernsey admitted to lying about why I was brought to Winterhaven. At the Cloister, he apologized. But he lied yet again, for when he said, '*flesh and blood must commit the* *bloodletting*¹ he had me believe that Belisama was my mother, not Gilleanne. I cannot deny the betrayal."

No one says anything, and I suppose it's somewhat inappropriate to speak of Guernsey in such a bad light, especially because he's gone. But it hurts. "On another note, when the Sablier took me to the past, I saw Guernsey place the Aeriscloque around my neck. Does anyone know how my mother's soul was captured within its confines?"

"A question only I can answer." All eyes go to the entrance of the room. A smallish man walks in and takes a seat, grunting in pain as he tries to get comfortable. "Apologies for my tardiness. An errand ran longer than expected."

"Guernsey," I gasp. "I thought you were dead."

"For the time being, I'm among the living, thanks to young Snap here."

Other than me, no one looks surprised. "The Tartarean stabbed you," I say. "Though I saw the maille, your blood stained the desert floor. And me."

"Raven's blood," Snap says proudly in answer. "I made the maille for Guernsey, complete with pouches of blood in case he needed to deceive the enemy."

I nod along, remembering he'd done something similar for Lark back when the king thought he'd beheaded her. "I must admit I was surprised to see the maille. You said you wouldn't wear it, Guernsey. You said other things would kill you."

"I reconsidered. My Foresight is not infallible, and it turned out to be quite the prudent move. The maille was not perfect, however, and my body still aches to this day."

"Those aches are called age, my friend," Zhang the Elder says, and hard laughter fills the room. "Age is a wound that cannot be healed."

Guernsey gives a concessionary nod to the wise words. "As to your earlier statement and question, 'flesh and blood' was never meant to mean your mother. When Shan apprised me of the misunderstanding, I said nothing because my Foresight told me you would find the Sablier and discover the truth for yourself. It never occurred to me the events would be misconstrued. Moreover, at the Cloister, you stated the Sablier had revealed all. Therefore I believed you had learned about Gilleanne."

I sigh. "At the Sacred Grove of Willeaux, you told me things are often not what they seem in Winterhaven. But I think it holds true anywhere. Two people can see the same flower or hear the same song and offer two very different interpretations."

Zhang the Elder nods in my direction. "Too true, Tiāntǐ. We see what we want to see. Often we are blind to the truth that stands before us."

"About the Aeriscloque," Guernsey continues. "It was I who found Gilleanne in the tunnels of Isceald Castle. After King Andronicus kidnapped you, she used the secret tunnels so as not to be discovered. In doing so, she trapped herself, unable to solve the riddle etched into the wall. When I found her moments before her death—she had been down there far too long without water—I told

383

her what I knew of the future, how your destiny might play out. When I offered the chance to live on close to your heart, she agreed. Upon her last breath, her soul went into the Aeriscloque."

All is quiet for a moment. The story is incredible, and I revel in the knowledge that my mother had been so close to my heart. But my happiness sours. "In the Sablier, though I saw neither the beginning of the conversation nor the ensuing argument, my father indicated Gilleanne would no longer be drinking the fountain's waters. Had she been convinced otherwise, she'd still be alive."

Guernsey laces his clawed fingers. "Arún had no desire to be Immortal. And Gilleanne had no desire to watch Arún grow old without her."

Lark raises a hand. "My turn to ask a question of you, Sondrine. Right after the war ended, Lord Kian recounted how things played out between you, the king, and the queen. Why did you offer the Aether stone to Belisama?"

"I have a guess," Snap says, quick to answer. "By then Sondrine knew she was the intended of the Aether. If she willingly gave the stone to the queen, it would be hers to keep forever."

Lark nods, her eyes alight with understanding. "You knew the king would try to steal it. By doing this, the Aether stone would return to you."

"It was my hope," I say. "The king was a greedy man, we can all readily agree. Climbing Crann Bethadh, no easy feat at his age, told me he was there to win."

"How did you know you were the intended?" Lark asks.

"The Aeriscloque was my first hint, although in hindsight there were others. When I took the Aether in hand, I knew for certain. Belisama had tried and failed. And over the tens of centuries, many others must have made the same attempt. Had they been successful, the stone would have been elsewhere."

"Quite clever, Tiāntĭ," says Zhang the Elder with a knowing wink.

My legs are stiffening with pain, and the meeting has gone on long enough. "From what I can gather, Winterhaven is thriving under Lark and Snap's rule. I would be happy to serve as an adviser, but I have no desire to be Queen of Winterhaven."

Lark frowns. "What will you do, then? You're not going back to the Other World, are you?"

"Winterhaven is my home now," I assure her. "I should very much like to explore my lineage and learn more about my mother and father. Perhaps I'll even open an emporium of my own so I can make a decent wage and keep myself busy in the process."

"Your father made a modest wage as a carpenter," Snap says. "However, the Agni legacy was a wealthy one, and a fair amount of gold is yours to build whatever it is you choose."

"My father's small fortune, I'm happy to take. The Agni legacy will go elsewhere, and for the good."

"Isceald could use an emporium," Lark says happily. "Perfect timing, for the city is rebuilding as we speak. You would stay in the city at least?"

"I'm unsure of what the future holds, but for now I'll remain

385

here."

Snap sets the quill down. "Any other orders of business before we adjourn?" he asks.

"Aye," Guernsey says, his eyes tired, his breathing labored. "When I brought you to the Other World, Sondrine, I had no knowledge of the kind of person you would become. Oh, I knew you were special. And my Foresight offered glimpses. But time and experience can do strange and even horrible things to the best of people. Growing up without a parent is often devastating for a child. To be deprived of love is an abomination, the utmost failure of what life can offer." A ragged breath. "I'm honored to see how things played out. To see that you did indeed save Winterhaven, yes. But more so, to see that you turned into an extraordinary person despite all odds. My only regret is that I will not experience the future you. Before I arrived here today, I visited the Sacred Grove of Willeaux to say goodbye to the Chisana. And now I'm here to offer my farewell to you. To all of you. My journey here is complete. The Realm of Halcyon awaits."

Tears gather in my eyes, and the council sits steeped in a mournful silence. The words are heartfelt and sobering. And while I'm grateful Winterhaven will grow and prosper under Lark and Snap's rule, I don't feel joy in any measure. Perhaps I never will. People died for this triumph, and lost lives never feel like victory. Losing Guernsey feels like yet another battle scar, a wound that may never heal. Nor do I want it to.

***

There are few Hereats left in the world, and I'd had a hand—no matter how indirect—in the destruction of two of them. Since the Isle of Empyrean is far from Isceald and my recovery is still underway, Zhang the Elder had agreed to donate his to the Fortress of Síochánta.

Any Hereat can be a portal for unwanted visitors, so Lark and Snap have placed it in a secure vault at the top of one of the castle's turrets. Multiple keys are needed upon entry and exit, and Snap is busy working on magical elements placed in and around the chamber for safety precautions.

"You must tell me where you're going," Lark pleads as we climb a never-ending set of stairs. "Otherwise, how will I know where to find you should something go wrong?"

"Worry not," I assure her. "I'll be back soon enough. I promise this will not take long."

Lark scoffs. "Did you not say the same when you went back to the Other World last time? During your recovery, Shán told me what happened with your Aunt Henrietta at the emporium."

Though unamusing at the time, now I laugh aloud. "Too true. Well, I'm only going south of here. Not too far. If I'm still missing on the morrow, send in the cavalry."

"Not funny. And you're still unsteady on your feet." Lark takes the ring of keys from her pocket when we arrive at the vault. Nine separate keys are needed. The space inside is empty save for the Hereat in the center. Somehow it holds an air of grandeur here, unlike in Zhang the Elder's cluttered laboratory.

"I'm giving you an hour's time," Lark says.

I kiss her cheek. "Best make it two. See you soon." With the aid of my cane, I enter the Hereat one careful foot at a time.

Rolling hills on all sides rise before me. Snow crowns them all, but the land below is brown, and the road beneath my feet dusty and dry. A small village with a slack river running through nestles in the foothills, and I walk the main road with the wind at my back.

Much of the town is reduced to rubble, and what few stores remain are somewhat meager. The people look dour, their faces lined with peril, and even the children seem downcast as they loll in the streets.

After a time, I flag a hooded passerby, who walks with a wood leg, her embroidered cloak tattered and frayed at the hem. "Excuse me, miss," I say. "Could you please tell me where I might find the Dewar farm?"

She looks me up and down, much of her face in shadow. "You won't get nothing from old man Garvey. Used to have the best farm in the realm, and fed half the land. The war has been unkind to Birr. We're all but forgotten. We fought for Winterhaven, but those who survived got nothing in return. Families, cottages...everything gone."

I remember my promise to the infantry right then. The money from my birthright will be put to good use. "You were promised gold for fighting in the Stele War. You shall have payment within a fortnight, I'll personally see to it."

388

"Liar, Sondrine Renfrew. Or is it Queen Agni?" She pulls back her hood.

My eyes go wide. Gone are the soft features. Her hardened expression challenges the stone walk at my feet. "Sondrine will suffice," I say genuinely. "I'm glad to see you survived the war, Adina."

Her chin raises in defiance. "Barely. A Tartarean sliced my leg. Got infected, and you can guess the rest. Had to leave Taliin and come home. No one wants a gimp, not in my line of work. And with the king dead, my chance at riches has gone to the dogs."

Had King Andronicus survived, he may have kept her as a lover for a time, but never would he have given whatever he'd promised. In fact, the likelihood of surviving the king's temper would have had worse odds than surviving the war. Ending up in the Mourning Garden seems likelier.

"My recovery took longer than expected, and no one could have known of my promise except for those who stood witness that day and survived to pass on my words."

"That would be me and many others. We wrote to the queen and king and have yet to receive answer. Four years have passed. Something tells me our heroics will go into the history books, but the promised gold will remain a myth."

I shuffle on unsteady feet. "I'm unsure why your requests have gone unanswered. My word is sound, and you shall receive payment for your bravery. Should you need an honest job, please do come to Isceald. I would be happy to refer you to a great many people."

Adina bites her lip, discomfited by my gesture. "Garvey's farm is yonder, past the village. Follow the road down the hill—it will lead you straight there." She tugs the hood over her head and continues on to wherever it was she was going.

The barn is a stone structure streaked in soot, the thatched roof scant, with gaping holes. Roaming the penned yard are two cows, one donkey, and perhaps a dozen goats, all sporting more rib than girth. I wave to the farmer plowing the field. Through clouds of dust, he casts a glance my way but keeps working.

Does he not see me? Impossible given the emerald of my cloak against the stark backdrop. More waving from me brings more ignoring on his part, so I throw my cane over the low fence and awkwardly climb over. I say a silent apology to Miss Cornbaum. I'm officially more flapping chicken than graceful swan.

This gets his attention. The ghost of the ox looks confounded as the farmer sets down the plow and walks toward me.

"Good day," I say upon his approach. "Are you—"

He pulls a knife from his boot. "Get off my property or I'll skin you alive." A throng of hens squawk and cluck. "Tax collector, are you? Come to take my property away? I wrote the king and queen stating I've got nothing left to give."

My hands go up in surrender. "Please, I've come as a friend."

"I've got no friends. Now begone with ya." He reiterates his point by flashing the blade.

"She's Sondrine Renfrew, daughter of Gilleanne Agni and Arún

390

Andronicus, rightful Queen of Winterhaven and true heir to the throne."

I look behind to see Lark easily jump the fence. Though I shake my head at her for following me, I can't help but smile. "Good sir, likely you don't know me, but surely you know Lark Andronicus, the *reigning* Queen of Winterhaven?"

His mouth drops open. He sheathes his knife, drops to one knee, and brings his hat to his chest. "Please accept my deepest apology, Your Grace—Graces. Of course I recognize you both."

"No need to bend the knee," Lark says, abashed by his actions.

He looks up with pleading eyes. "I've no money to give, Your Grace. Truly, I wrote you and the king not long ago—"

"Kind sir, please," I say, offering a hand to help him to his feet. "I—we—come in friendship. Is there a place nearby where we might speak?"

Inside the meager two-room cottage, he boils water for tea at the hearth. The thatched roof is in the same state of disrepair as the barn. He offers bread and cheese, but I will only eat a little in deference to his hospitality, certain this is several meals for him.

He can't be much more than forty years of age, but hardship and the burdens of life have sown their seeds in the form of deep lines around his face. His hands rough with calluses, he pours the tea as he pulls up a small stool, joining us at the small table. "Your Graces, you must accept my apologies once again." His brow drips with nervous sweat. "Had I known who you were—both of you—I never would have greeted you in such a manner. To what do I owe

391

this great honor? And please, address me as Garvey and not sir. I'm not one for formalities."

I blow on my tea. "I feel the same, Garvey. Please, call me Sondrine. Your son Bart is what brings me here today."

Garvey's eyes widen, but his lip curls in anger. "Good for nothin' kid. Whatever he did—"

"He saved my life."

Garvey sets down his cup with defiance. "You must have the wrong Bart. My son was a good for nothin' coward. Sent him away to man up, and he came back to me in an urn."

"You have his eyes," I say gently. "Inquisitive and kind." His gruff demeanor softens. "You see, I met Bart when I stowed away on a ship sailing for Taliin." I delve into all the tales and spare no details. "He saved my life by taking the dagger intended for me," I finish. "Had he not been so courageous, my killing of Belisama at Crann Bethadh would never have come to pass. Winterhaven would be nothing more than fire and ash, and none of us would be having this conversation. Your son is a true hero. His tale will go down in the history books for centuries to come."

Tears swim in Garvey's timeworn eyes. "Bart's urn is in the barn amongst the pigs and goats, not in the grave out back next to his mother. Never said a proper prayer for him. No one knew how he died—no note came with the ashes—but rumor had it he'd met his demise at some traveling carnival. Sending on his body in an urn rather than a pine box...I found this peculiar but never cared to seek the truth. Figured he was murdered in some kind of foolhardy brawl." His voice cracks. "How can I ever atone for my wrongdoings?"

"By accepting these." I pull out a pouch of gold coins and a gilded medal brooch. On the obverse, Bart's full name is engraved; on the reverse, the head of a lion. "Please take these as a token of Bart's bravery."

"The medal I will take gladly," he says. "The coin I cannot accept."

"Why not?" Lark implores with a dash of reproach.

He cowers a little as if he'd misspoken. "A man has his pride, Your Grace."

"Pride can be a man's downfall," she states with an authoritative air. "Humility is a courage all its own. Your animals are starving. If they are well-fed, so too will be your village. The same goes for your land. The soil will thrive when nourished; your vegetables and grains will be so abundant they'll be primed to sell at the markets. In turn, Winterhaven will prosper." She smiles regally. "Besides, I am the Queen of Winterhaven. You must do as I say. Now if you please, take the bestowed gift."

Outside, Garvey digs a fresh grave next to his wife's plot. He scatters Bart's ashes inside, and each of us takes a shovelful of dirt to provide cover. Lark picks some wildflowers and sets them on top while Garvey recites a prayer. When he finishes, I take his rough hand in mine. "Although I can never repay Bart, I will do whatever I can to help you and your farm thrive. We shall see one another again, you and I. This I can promise."

The pulling sensation happens all at once, and Lark and I find ourselves stepping back through the Hereat and into the barren room at the fortress.

"Don't be angry with me," Lark says as if she's been waiting to say it from the start.

"I could never be angry with you. I'm glad you followed me."

Lark's cheeks bloom with color. "I was too frightened to lose sight of you. Unlike Snap, I don't possess any magic. I only hoped I could help in whatever it was you were doing."

"Your Grace," I say with the proudest of smiles, "you have kindness and compassion and an intellectual wit. You will be a great queen, and Winterhaven will thrive under your reign. That is a true gift, a magic all your own."

CHAPTER TWENTY-ONE

In many ways, the new emporium mirrors Cimmerian's, with its tinctures and medicinal herbs, the floor-to-ceiling shelves, and the oval glass cabinet. Unlike Cimmerian's, true magic lives within these walls. Cloaks made to withstand fire; daggers carved of ice; seeds that produce rain showers no matter where they are planted, even under someone's hat. Not by coincidence, many of the treasures use the elements in some capacity.

Quite a bit of time was needed to build the apothecary, longer than expected. During the construction period, I'd helped where I could, but building things was never my forte, so I did other things to pass the time. For one, I lent counsel to Snap and Lark whenever needed. Gold had been allocated to the soldiers of the Stele War, both to the survivors and the families of the deceased. Lark and Snap were happy to fulfill my promise. Also, they'd agreed to hire additional help, because an entire chamber filled with unread mail proved they could not handle things alone.

After creating an ample quarry for Hoarus, Snap and I traveled to the Keep of Wintersgaard to repair the ice dragon's wing. Lady Aniyu and Lord Kian and the rest of the Mór hosted a small feast upon our arrival. Being there reminded me of Shán, and had the treehouse not burned down, I would have been tempted to pay a visit.

Hoarus had grown threefold since last I saw him, his sheer size incredible and terrifying. The ice dragon recognized me at once, offering a soft growl through monstrous, daggered teeth when I approached him in the woodland. But it was Snap's appearance that caused the dragon to flap his good wing with excitement and roar with delight. To my great surprise, Hoarus breathed snow and ice rather than fire, and a snowstorm rained down on the Keep.

When it came to repairing the broken wing, many failed attempts ensued. But Snap's calming effect and my Elemental capabilities eventually won out. With meltwater and cool air blown straight from my lungs, a bevy of icy feathers were molded and attached to the broken section. Soon enough, Hoarus was successfully flying around the Keep of Wintersgaard. We'd journeyed home on the dragon's back, and wherever the land was barren and scorched beneath us, Hoarus dutifully brought snowfall to the realm.

According to the Aeriscloque, thirty minutes remain before my doors open to the public. A growing crowd outside anxiously awaits the town's new apothecary and emporium. The excitement is contagious, and I bustle about the shop as best as one can with a cane. I double-check the bottles of alkahest, a universal solvent, and decks of Taerou cards, with their moving imagery.

Behind the counter is a rolling latched ladder. The shelves

burst with natural remedies all from the forests and mountains of Winterhaven, many of them made by Zhang the Elder himself.

An urgent knock at the front door. "Twenty more minutes," I call out as I roll along to make sure the Lactarius Paralysis is fully stocked.

The door opens, allowing the street noise to bleed in before it's quickly closed and locked. A man approaches dressed in a hooded cloak of dark wool.

"Good morning, kind sir," I say. "The front door was supposed to be locked. I'm afraid you'll have to wait outside with the others. Won't be long."

"Lavender. Smells like Cimmerian's. And you."

My fingers grip the rungs tight. The voice sets fire to a kaleidoscope of memories. "How did you get in, Shán?"

He pulls back his hood and holds up a key. "Lark gave it to me for this one time only." He sets the key on the countertop and looks around the shop. "Impressive. I should think you'll do quite well here. 'Quint's Curiosities?'"

I climb down from the ladder and study his face, aged four years. A new scar through his right eyebrow. Perhaps a line or two around the eyes. "Renfrew was my past, and Henrietta and I were never related in the first place. In blood I am Agni and Andronicus, but both carry negative connotations. Though the elements are all part of me, the Aether is who I am. Quintessence. So I shortened the word to be my surname."

Shán nods agreeably. "Sondrine Quint. Suits you."

397

"What brings you to Isceald? I'm guessing not for the wormwood, although I do carry the medicinal remedy should you have stomach upset."

He smiles. "I'm thinking of putting down roots here."

His ring finger is bare, but this does not mean his betrothed is without one. "Do Lark and Snap know of your return? They valued your counsel before you disappeared."

"My counsel will no longer be needed. I've been wandering the realm for quite some time. In recent weeks, I found the one thing I've been seeking: a Sablier. You were lucky to have found one at the Ichor Samhain. This one was in a thief-infested ghetto due north of here. Took me quite a bit of time to earn the locals' trust, enough for them to let me make use of it. Far more time than I would have predicted."

Someone pounds on the window and points to their timepiece. Amiably I wave back. "Fifteen more minutes," I shout out. "Please be patient." My attention returns to Shán. "What were you searching for? Past or future?"

"Past. Whose paternal blood runs through my veins. Turns out King Andronicus was not my father."

"You'd suspected this?" My shock is evident by my whispered words.

"For many years. The Sablier showed that my mother Nalina had been in love with a man named Cassian Fairborne, a guardsman for the king. When she discovered she was with child, she had no choice but to lie and tell King Andronicus I was his

398

progeny."

I finger the key on the counter. "How did she know you were Cassian's if the king was also bedding her?"

"Many months had passed since my mother and the king had shared relations. She knew he was growing tired of her, and she feared she would end up in the Mourning Garden with the rest of his former mistresses. Her pregnancy was unplanned, but she and Cassian knew it would save her life. They fretted what I would look like, but by sheer luck, Cassian had the same color hair as the king."

"Why did he kill her, then?"

The sorrow in his eyes is palpable. "Six years into their affair, Cassian no longer wanted to share her with the king, and he was angry he could not be a father to his son. So they conspired to leave Isceald Castle for good. But the guardsmen were loyal to the king, not to my father, and certainly not to my mother. When the king confronted her about the rumor, he promised her freedom for the truth. She admitted I was Cassian's son and not the king's heir. He called her a liar, but it was he who had lied. He forced her to watch Cassian's beheading. Then he beheaded her. The king must have known deep in his marrow I was never his son. Never would he have admitted the truth, especially not when the realm knew me to be his heir. The truth would paint him a fool to his countrymen."

All at once, the scene in the church plays back to me. "Shán, I saw them. When I was in the Sablier, at my Rite of Purification ceremony. I sat between your mother and Cassian. I saw the initials NE on her purse. Nalina Einfarí."

Shán nods with interest. "Now I better understand your quest. Knowing the murderous King Andronicus was never my father has set me free. However, this means I share no relation to Snap and Lark. My duties will be relieved, but I have no ill feelings on the matter. I'll live my life as a commoner, content at knowing the truth."

"Shán," I say slowly. "Do you think Snap and Lark—Vinca too—were sired by the king?"

"We'll never know. For the good of the realm, this conversation should die right here, wouldn't you agree?"

I nod because I do. A Pandora's box that best remains closed. The din from outside seeps into the emporium.

"I'll leave you to your opening," he says, the smile returning to his eyes. "Before I go, I offer a small token of luck." From beneath his cloak, he opens the flap of a satchel and pulls out the snow globe.

"Where did you find this?" I exclaim.

"Guernsey gave it to me. My guess is he took it back from the emporium, but I suppose your question will forever remain unanswered."

Only the impressive stone base remains the same. No longer does the snow globe boast Isceald Castle. Instead, Fortress of Síochánta sits high on a hill. Below, the village of Isceald, hemmed by the Dendrite Sea. In the center, Crann Bethadh rises, the

Aether stone shining atop the crown of greenery.

"Thank you. It's magnificent." I shake the globe and watch the snow flurry. On closer inspection, my emporium is one of the village shops, and I marvel at the magic.

Shán takes my hand in his and leads me around the counter. The smell of firesmoke enters my senses, awakens them.

"Would you do me the honor of supping with me on the morrow?" he asks. "A new eatery has opened in town, and I should very much like to try it with you on my arm."

"I'll need your arm, for this is part of me, not only for now but possibly forever." I hold up the cane. "What will people think?"

"Why should I care?"

I laugh. "Ever the optimist."

Shán shrugs. "Due to the explosion at Crann Bethadh, my ears are no longer entirely in working order. I'll help you hobble along if you are kind enough to repeat yourself from time to time."

We walk to the front, and I turn the sign in the window. "The snow globe is a key," he reminds me as I unlock the door. "There are other worlds to explore should you be up for the next great adventure."

People flood in, stream past, and screams of delight come from adults and children alike. I watch Shán disappear into the crowded streets, and my gaze turns to the early morning sky, where Hoarus soars through the rosy clouds, breathing a storm of fresh snow onto Winterhaven.

"Not today," I say, maneuvering my way back through the crowded emporium. I tuck the snow globe safely inside the oval glass cabinet and lock it with a key. "Tomorrow is another story."

ACKNOWLEDGEMENTS

They say perseverance pays off, and I can't deny that cliché because this book took far longer to write than I could have ever imagined. As a matter of fact, I would like to thank my dear readers first and foremost. So many of you asked when the sequel to *THE SNOW GLOBE* was coming out, and I did not want to disappoint.

To Kelly and Tracey, thank you for your insight and your uncanny ability to cheerlead when this business has been a bear for us all. A literal Purgatory, I might add.

Heartfelt thanks to Sarah Kettles, editor extraordinaire. You've taught me that I should never be left to my own devices where comma placement and past participles are concerned.

Thank you to my family for your unwavering support. You've always been there for me, and I appreciate it.

And finally, my deepest gratitude to Don who makes me laugh even when I cry. I cannot imagine this journey without you at my side. And Clancy too, of course.

ABOUT THE AUTHOR

Jenna Nelson lives in Los Angeles with her husband and their saved-from-the-pound-pup, Clancy. For more about Jenna visit www.jenna-nelson.com.

If you have enjoyed this book, please consider posting a review on your favorite book-related site. This is the best way to show your support and to help other readers find THE CRYSTAL SKY. Thank you!